# Unison

## Eleni Papanou

Copyright © 2013 by Eleni Papanou
2nd edition, paperback - published 2013

PHILOPHROSYNE
PUBLISHING

ISBN-13: 978-0615889955
ISBN10: 0615889956

Book Cover design by Buzz Erlinger-Ford

*Unison* - 1st edition paperback © 2013 by Eleni Papanou

For updates, visit our website at:
http://philophrosyne-publishing.com

*For Antonis Ladopoulos,*
*Who had enough valor to hold the mirror in front of my face.*

# PART ONE

*"The real, natural man is just in open rebellion against the utterly inhuman form of life."*
*Carl Jung*

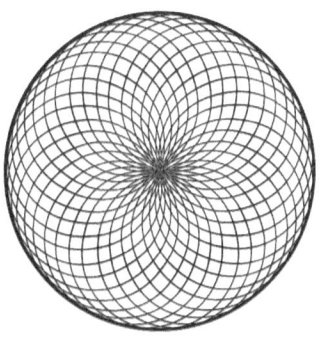

# ʀᴇꜱᴏɴᴀɴᴄᴇ

### First Incarnation

Time is relevant to sound. An infinite voice sings life into this universe, and I'm but one note resonating within this expanse of boundless potential. While that's an easy abstraction to grasp, my own potential remains elusive. After eight parallel lifetimes I've been adrift somewhere between struggle and mastery, both of which I now see as an illusion.

I first realized there was something unusual about me in my ninth year, shortly after winning the lottery to go on a camping expedition. My friend Wade and I had taken climbing classes to prepare for our hike up Emerald Mountain. Because of our age, we were restricted to the beginner wall which soon ceased to challenge us. When Headmaster refused to move us to the next level, we waited until the athletic center had closed for the night, then snuck inside to climb the advanced wall. The ropes and harnesses were locked away, and we ascended without them. Finding it difficult to handle grips positioned for longer limbs, I fell during my descent. After Wade yelled out my name, the outside world disappeared.

My awareness returned in the hospital, but my body remained unresponsive. I screamed and cried out in silence when I heard a doctor tell an Overmaiden I was in a coma and wouldn't last beyond the week. Seven days later my condition remained unchanged. To alleviate my increasing restlessness, I imagined myself exploring the deathlands. They had fascinated me ever since I learned about them at school, but the poison left over from the Great Cataclysm meant I could never visit them. The Earth I created had no limitations. There were no fumes to contaminate my lungs and no scourge to keep me from venturing too far beyond the dome. My arms morphed into metallic wings, and I flew over crumbling cityscapes that swayed like ghosts within the murky gray atmosphere. I searched for other life forms, but all I could see in every direction was a ceaseless expanse of decay and ruin.

Melancholia accompanied me on my lonely flight. I recalled Master Franklin's last lecture and how I expressed curiosity over the deathlands. He patiently reminded me that the mind of man has a flaw which makes us destroy ourselves. Without the curative implant to protect us from this flaw, we'd still be like the Outsiders, fighting each other. Envisioning the Ancients' graveyard gave me some comfort. If I were to die now, I'd die knowing the truth. Nothing existed outside Unity. Only in Unity could we resurrect a lasting peace. I was thankful to have the curative implant to spare me from the scourge. I was also thankful to the Overseer for selecting me to be born in Unity.

My sadness vanished as I flew over a massive seven-circuit labyrinth. I took a deep breath and blew away the haze to get a clearer view. The structure glistened like an opal under the sun. The elaborate output of my imagination inspired me to create my own reality to live in. I gave myself the powers of a god and returned the Earth to its pristine state before the arrival of humans. Trees grew, flowers bloomed, and rivers flowed freely again, begetting life to the deathlands.

After the Earth had healed from its injuries, my body transmuted into a spaceship. I glided through celestial seas, exploring distant galaxies and planets. The reality I created was more vibrant and exciting than the one I left behind, and I eventually forgot I was in a coma. Lifetimes of experiences went by, and I got older but never aged. I could've stayed here forever, but I was still tethered to a physical body, alive and waiting for me to come back.

The last world I visited had a crimson sky with black vegetation that sparkled under a red sun. When I landed to survey the terrain, a girl with the physiognomy of a cat approached me and said, "You don't belong here." She waved her hand in a circular motion and everything melted into blackness.

First came recognition, then dread as I remembered I was lying on a hospital bed, held captive by a body that imprisoned me. I heard female voices from the outside world talking about their lunch plans. *I want to die! Please, let me die!* If my thoughts were audible, they would've been loud enough to shatter the dome. I tried to revert to the paradise I'd created, but the darkness persisted. I begged, prayed, and pleaded until the tiniest speck of light materialized in front of me. It glimmered for several seconds before exploding and bathing me in a warm stream of light. I was ready to surrender my life to the light, when a low pitch began to drone, and the blackness resumed. "No, I don't want to stay! Please take me with you!"

I looked to see what was making the droning sound. It was an incubation tank with a baby floating in liquid white light reflecting the colors of the rainbow. I pressed the palms of my hands against the glass and felt a warm vibration. My whole body resonated with the tank like a tuning fork. More notes rang out, delivering the most brilliant chord I ever heard and still, to this day, haven't been able to identify.

A female voice called from behind me, "Six begin, Six alone, Six unite."

I turned to face a woman with light brown skin and large dark eyes. Her black hair cascaded down past her elbows, unbound by the regulation braids of Unitian women. "You cannot keep ignoring me," she said. "You must remember."

Such a beautiful creature didn't exist in Unity, and I couldn't help but stare at her with my mouth wide open. When I finally found the courage to respond, a baby's cries awakened me. In the hall, one of the holomonitors at the Overmaiden's station displayed a crying baby being removed from its incubation tank. I struggled to sit up, and when I attempted to stand, I collapsed. An Overmaiden hurried into the room and helped me back to my bed. I slept until a familiar voice jolted me from my slumber. I opened my eyes and faced the doctor who had told the Overmaiden I wouldn't last past the week. When I asked him about that, something in his expression kept me from revealing more because I shouldn't have heard anything; my brain showed barely any sign of neural activity. Not wanting anything to get in the way of my camping expedition, I lied and told the doctor I didn't remember anything else. He released me three days later and I returned to my ordinary life in my ordinary world. Because I had almost died, Headmaster waived my reprimand for breaking curfew and sneaking into the athletic center, but I was no longer permitted to contact Wade.

At the access, I found the children all neatly lined up in their camouflage jumpsuits.

Wade waved me to the front of the line. We were often confused for one another as we both had blond hair and were the same height. But upon closer inspection, he had a smaller frame and appeared emaciated. It worked in his favor as Headmaster doubled his meal portions, including dessert.

"Why didn't you call me?" he asked. "No one would tell me what happened to you."

"I'm not allowed to talk to you anymore."

"Why?"

"Headmaster thinks I'm a bad influence on you."

"Going to the center was my idea. I told him that."

"He doesn't care about the truth. Only rank matters to him and his army of purple zombies."

"Maybe Master Franklin forgot to tell Headmaster. I'll go ask —"

"After we get back. I don't want to give him a reason to leave me behind."

Wade nodded. "I hate all these rules."

"Me too." I glanced at Master Franklin, who was busy talking with the gate guard. "I better get in line before—"

Master Franklin spotted me and crossed his arms.

"That old purple zombie must have his eyes sewed on to the back of his head," I said with clenched teeth.

"Let me handle this," Wade said as Master Franklin approached us.

We bowed and gave him our best rehearsed smiles.

"Welcome back, Damon," he said. "I'm glad to see you're feeling better."

"Thank you, Master Franklin," I said.

The guard opened the access door, and the kids rhapsodized about all the activities Master Franklin had planned for them.

"I need you to step away from the line," he said to me.

"It's not his fault. I called him over," Wade said.

"I know, Apprentice Wade. You're not as clever as you think." Master Franklin looked at me. "I'm sorry, Damon, you won't be joining us on this trip out."

"Why? I'm all better."

"I know...but I wasn't told about your discharge. I gave your pass to Apprentice Simon."

"But I'm here now."

"So is Apprentice Simon, and he outranks you."

"Can I go on the next expedition?"

"You're free to sign up for the lottery again."

"What's the point in signing up again if winning doesn't mean I get to go?"

"Return to the dorm ... before you say something that will lead you to another reprimand."

7

"I don't care about rank!" My implant released an electrifying jolt of pain to my head, but my rage was stronger. "I won the lottery! I was supposed to go!"

The color emptied from Master Franklin's face. His eyes remained fixed and open.

"Master Franklin?"

He didn't respond, and I feared my outburst caused a heart attack that killed him right where he stood.

"Master Franklin!"

He clutched his forehead and then looked at me as though relieved. "You're okay."

"No, he's not." Wade said.

"How many times must I tell you not to speak without permission?" Master Franklin said.

"Damon told me he hasn't been feeling well all this week."

Master Franklin faced me. "Is that true?"

"Yes, Master Franklin," I replied.

"Why didn't you go to the hospital?"

While I was sweating over my response, Wade delivered it for me.

"He told me he had a lot of homework to catch up on and that he wanted to show you how he's now taking his schoolwork seriously." If there were a class for the art of manipulation, Wade would've easily scored above all Unitian children.

"That's very honorable," Master Franklin said to me. "But you also need to focus on your recovery. Without good health, you cannot move ahead."

Wade smirked at me as Master Franklin lifted his arm and stared into the optic of his hologue. "I'm leaving a message with Headmaster to confine you to the dorm grounds and relieve you of your cleanup duties for the rest of the week."

Wade took his place in line and gave me the thumbs up. Having a friend in the master's apprentice rank was beneficial, but I had to stay in my dorm for the rest of the week and do my homework. Summer was ruined. That seemed worse than a reprimand.

Knowing I'd be bored, I headed to an essential shop to buy some game privileges for my hologue. Arriving there, I peered into the display window and my eyes immediately focused on a violin. I was pulled into a vision where I was performing in a theater filled with purple sleeves. I made a mistake during a run of sixteenth notes and ran off stage crying. The vision was so real, when I came out of it I was in tears. I entered the store and spent all my remaining credits on the violin. I didn't like failing, even in a vision.

The violin became my constant companion. It kept me from missing Wade. When I first picked it up I instinctively knew how to hold the bow and position my chin on the rest. My bowing technique came with little effort, and within twelve weeks I had mastered all the major and minor scales. I was able to tune the strings without the aid of a tuner. Music wasn't my only area of improvement. Math and science, which I used to find difficult, now flowed as smoothly as my bow against the strings. Complex formulas were answered instantly in my visions and appeared as clear as projections in a holologue. When I began my next level in school, I tested ahead of everyone in my class. My grades even surpassed those in the highest level of the master's apprentice school.

Master Franklin believed I was cheating, and his inference was justified. From the moment we're placed in the tanks we're programmed to serve a specific purpose, and I had exceeded mine. I was meant to achieve no higher than the rank of green sleeve. I was admitted to the hospital to be studied by neurologists, genetic programmers, and psychological engineers. When all their tests failed to explain my fortuitous condition, I was considered an anomaly and released.

I thought my academic evolution would lead to an automatic transfer to the master's apprentice school. When no offer was made, I went to Headmaster's office and asked why.

"I want a bigger challenge, so I can show the Overseer how much more I can do."

"You're not challenged now?" Headmaster asked while twirling his thumbs on his desk. The rest of his body was stiff, and I almost laughed, envisioning him as a music stand. "Yes. But I can handle more."

"If that's true, you're not putting in your best effort. The Overseer chose your genetic profile to serve a specific purpose. Are you placing yourself above the Prime Wisdom?"

I addressed my response to his gyrating thumbs. "No, Headmaster."

He removed his hands from the desk and peered at me. "Do you understand why I must deny your request for transfer?"

I was about to tell Headmaster I lied and that I wasn't challenged, but his icy expression froze my tongue solid. "Yes, Headmaster."

"In the future, I'd appreciate if you take some time to think before launching a formal request. Complaining about your position shows a lack of gratitude. You must respect the Overseer and Prime Wisdom if you wish to earn the respect of your mentors."

I walked out of his office believing I'd never move beyond a green sleeve. To be given these talents and then be denied the freedom to use them seemed more like a punishment than gift. I entered my dorm, took the lift to the roof and hopped onto the ledge. Between the dome above and the ground below, I felt crushed and began to hyperventilate. There was only one way to escape my prison. I closed my eyes and revived the model world I created while in a coma. I spread out my metallic wings and was about to fly away, when I heard a female voice call out, "Six begin, Six alone, Six unite."

I turned and faced the woman from my vision. Startled by both the vision and what I was about to do, I ran back to my room. After the shock had worn off, I cried at my lack of courage to fly.

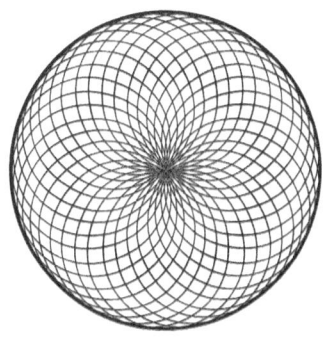

# thirty-two reprimands

Master Franklin called me to his office for a meeting. I entered and bowed to him, not caring why he had summoned me. If it was for a reprimand, I'd be stuck at my current level for another year. I didn't care about that either.

"How have you been feeling, Damon?"

The question, and the sincerity on his face, surprised me. I answered him by crying.

"Tell me what happened?"

Master Franklin listened to me, without interrupting, as I told him about my meeting with Headmaster and how my request for transfer was denied. He then asked me something I had not expected.

"Can you play me something on your violin?"

"When?"

He eyed my violin case, which I carried with me everywhere. "Now seems like a good time."

I played the Unitian Anthem, and after I'd finished Master Franklin became my greatest ally. Because of my musical ability he plotted to have Headmaster's decision overturned. He asked his colleague, Master Theodore, to privately instruct me on the violin. When he then refused to listen to me because of my genetic profile, Master Franklin concocted a cunning plan to have me heard. Before his weekly game of cribbage with Master Theodore, he hid me in a closet. After what seemed like a whole day had passed, Master Theodore finally won a hand and laughed triumphantly. I quickly rosined my bow.

"Congratulations," Master Franklin said to Master Theodore, as I positioned my trembling fingers on the fingerboard, pleading with them not to betray me. "It only took you eight hands to get one of your pegs further than mine. How about some music to celebrate?"

That was my cue. I closed my eyes and began to play one of Master Theodore's favorite pieces—a tender ballad with ample emotion I hoped to project onto him. A few measures after the bridge, the door flung open and a stream of cool air grazed my body, but I stayed focused and continued playing with my eyes closed. After I'd finished, Master Theodore glared at Master Franklin and then at me. "You begin this Firstday at sixteen-hundred sharp, and if you're one-sixteenth of a second late, don't bother knocking because music is all about perfect timing. Do you understand?"

I bowed. "Yes, Master Theodore."

"Any questions?"

"No, Master Theodore."

"Then you may go." He rubbed the palms of his hands and looked at Master Franklin. "I have to show someone he can't win all the time."

"Thank you, Master Theodore." I bowed again and ran out as quickly as possible. I didn't want to give him any excuse to change his mind.

The following year I entered a music contest and decided to play the song from my vision. I practiced in the morning and after school. My technique improved, but I kept fumbling through the same run of sixteenth notes. Master Theodore tried to persuade me to pick an easier song, but I refused. As the contest neared, I relented and chose something simpler but continued to practice the more challenging piece. After five days of no improvement, I was about to give up when my vision of performing in front of a room of purple sleeves returned. I was able to identify what went wrong: My fingers lost their positioning in the measure leading up to the coda. It was anticipating finishing the song without error that broke my concentration. When I ran off stage in tears, I came out of my vision and found myself in the middle of the difficult passage, still crying and playing my violin! My bow and hand were as one, gliding into the coda without the slightest hesitation.

I told none of this to Master Theodore and surprised him by flawlessly performing the music that had defeated me in my vision. I didn't win the contest, but second place made the purple sleeves take notice of me.

My high placing motivated Master Theodore to fight for my entrance into the master's apprentice school. He set up a meeting with me and the Chosen. The day before the meeting, Master Theodore called me to his office to perform a recital for Master Franklin. I played through all my original compositions and ended with the song that had at one time given me so much trouble.

Master Franklin stood and clapped. "Very nicely done! If you continue at that level, we'll soon be calling you Apprentice Damon."

All the praise made me momentarily forget I was in the presence of my mentors. "When I show the Chosen I'm the master of everything, they'll have to accept me."

Master Theodore and Master Franklin looked worriedly at each other.

Master Theodore then gazed harshly at me. "You're only to play them your violin."

"Why? They already know everything I can do."

"Not everything," Master Franklin said. "If we told them about your visions, they'd fear you."

"Why would they be afraid of me? I'm not as smart as a Chosen."

"The Chosen aren't smarter…just better connected," Master Franklin said.

I laid my violin in its case, trying not to appear disappointed.

"You must remain silent. If you flaunt all your abilities, the Chosen will see you as a threat to their positions."

I loosened my bow. "I'll tell them not to be afraid of me, and I'll prove to them that all I want to do is to be of service to them and Unity."

"A young man once thought as idealistically as you," Master Franklin said. "He also excelled beyond his genetic profile and wished to study physics. The Overseer assigned him as head janitor at the Science University. It was a warning to all of those in the service class who dared to challenge their positions."

"What happened to him?"

Master Theodore took my bow and inspected it. "He left Unity and tried to make a life for himself on the outside, but he didn't get far. A pack of wild dogs tore him apart. Unity Forces knew it was him only because of the ID marker in his implant."

"He couldn't have been that smart. I never would've run past the beacons."

"I know how bright you are, but you can be equally insolent." Master Theodore handed back my bow. "You must master your abilities before you can use them effectively. And then you must use them with prudence. You might one day be called upon to save Unity."

"Unity doesn't need saving. We have no enemies."

My mentors looked at each other again. It infuriated me that they thought their unspoken communication went unnoticed. "If you have something to say, tell me now!"

Master Franklin looked at me as he had done after I yelled at him for giving away my pass.

"Master Franklin, are you—"

"Our enemy can't be seen," he said. "It's no different from the enemy of the first generation of Unitians that came to live inside the dome."

"What are they? An army of ghosts?" I laughed.

"You're not that far off," he said.

I laughed again and stopped when Master Franklin glared at me. He knew just the right expression to get me to close my mouth and stand at complete attention.

"The Sacred Oath is the enemy of which I speak. Like a ghost, it can't be seen, but its presence is always felt. It rules us through our complacency and blind loyalty. It never gives up until we surrender to it, and most of us do. You must never surrender. Do you understand?"

"Yes, Master Franklin."

"This must be absolutely clear to you, Damon. Don't allow your impatience to govern your fate. If you tell the Chosen about your visions, we will no longer be able to protect you."

Master Franklin's warning scared me enough to make me cry. He placed his hand on my shoulder and softened his voice. "All this might seem unfair now, but when you grow up, you'll come to agree with me."

I left there not fully understanding what Master Franklin told me, but the potential for a janitorial assignment prepared me for censoring myself when I met with the Chosen. It was a wise decision; the ten highest-ranking purple sleeves unanimously ruled in my favor, and I was formally admitted to the master's apprentice school.

Master Franklin died in the middle of my third year at my new school. I lost more than a mentor. By welcoming my curiosity and encouraging me to ask questions, he made me feel I was more than the output of my genetic profile. His replacement, who looked like a rat with his narrow eyes and thin pointy nose, treated me as though I didn't belong in his class. He always made sure to remind me of my previous status whenever I didn't perform as demanded. I privately referred to him as the replacement. The replacement never earned a title or name because he lacked the honor of Master Franklin. I learned this when I raised my hand to ask a question, and he pretended not to see me. After being ignored through most of his proselytizing over the implant that saved us from ruin, I could take it no more and interrupted him. "How do we know the scourge still exists if the implants are always receiving the curative signal?"

"We don't speak out in class, Apprentice Damon. We wait until we're called on."

"You never call on me."

"If I answer your question, would you postpone your curiosity until you complete this level?"

"And until I get into University." I smiled and crossed my arms.

"Really?" He laughed. "Your future schoolmasters will be forever indebted to me." The replacement picked up a pointer and directed it towards a picture of the Overseer. "Who is that?"

"The Overseer."

"If the scourge no longer existed, He would have called for a meeting in Unity Hall to broadcast the great news Himself."

"But how does He know it still exists?"

"He knows because only He can channel the Prime Wisdom."

Everyone in the class looked at me, and the replacement twitched his eyes, daring me to continue.

"How can we know the Prime Wisdom is real if only the Overseer has access to Him?"

"Are you questioning the Overseer's honesty?"

"I only want to know why I'm smarter now than before I got sick."

"Why do you think you're smarter?"

"I don't know…maybe I found a way to channel the Prime Wisdom."

The room was so silent I could hear the replacement's heart beating from across the room. He slammed the tip of the pointer against the desk. "You will take back your profane assertion right now!" He dropped the pointer and rubbed his head. "Silent time begins now." He sat. "Let's all pray for Apprentice Damon to find his way back to Unity." The replacement closed his eyes, pressed the palms of his hands together and leaned his forehead against them.

Wade, whom I was now permitted to associate with since my upgrade in status, gestured to his head, indicating the replacement probably received a blast from his implant. Some of the other kids snickered, and the replacement shot open his eyes.

"Insulting our Overseer is not funny." He wagged his finger at me. "And you are not in the same genetic class as Him. For you to even suggest an equal position to the Overseer is blasphemous."

"I … I didn't mean any disrespect by my question, Master —"

"I warned Franklin not to encourage your rebellious outbursts, and I'm deeply disheartened to see my concern was merited. Report to Headmaster for a reprimand."

Headmaster had my reprimand ready when I entered his office. "Your schoolmaster was wise to suggest I have these ready to go for you." He handed it to me. "This one makes four. One more and—do you want to be transferred back to your old school?"

"No, Headmaster."

"Do you have anything to say in your defense?"

"No, Headmaster."

"I would add something to this discussion if I thought it would help." He waved me out of his office. I was even more determined to move past my genetic profile, just to prove him and the replacement wrong. But my schoolmasters didn't make it easy for me. By my final year at the master's apprentice school, I had thirty-two reprimands which I proudly displayed on the wall in my room. I joked to friends how I'd hang them up in my office after I had made purple sleeve.

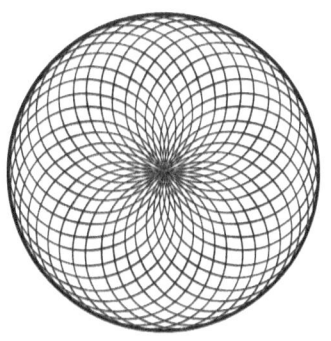

# among the chosen

I elected to study psychological engineering at the Science University, but the Overseer had the final say in what title I could attain. In special cases, a letter of recommendation from Headmaster can influence the Overseer's decision. I requested one and was refused because he didn't like the thesis I wrote in my final year of biology. He told me he'd reconsider if I recanted my theory. I refused, and Master Theodore got me another meeting with the Chosen so that I could argue my case.

When I entered the meeting room, the Chosen were seated around a table, ready to hear my defense. Sweat trickled down my back as I inspected ten faces bereft of any recognizable human expression.

I bowed in respect. "I'm honored to be called before the Chosen, even though the circumstances that bring me before you again have caused tension among the schoolmasters. I hope, after today, you'll see there is no cause for concern regarding my loyalty to Unity or to the Oath upon which it's founded. While writing my speech, I considered retracting my challenge—"

"A wise decision," Master Avery said. "It's dangerous to dispute psychological principles that have continued to serve us since their inception. Without the Prime Wisdom of our ascended first Overseer, our ancestors would have been destroyed along with the rest of the Ancients."

Most of the Chosen clapped, and Master Avery's smile betrayed the motivation behind his criticism: to prove himself worthy of his recent promotion into the Chosen.

Master Tyrus, the oldest and wisest purple sleeve in all of Unity, glanced at Master Kai who nodded his head and yelled out, "Immaterial!"

The Chosen quieted down, and the sweat that was limited to my back now surged like a waterfall down the length of my body.

"Your reactions show a disregard for progress," Master Kai said. "When current theories aren't routinely tested, they become dogma. We must move forward in Unity and not be afraid to listen to new ideas from the young among us." He looked at me. "You may continue, Apprentice Damon."

I bowed in respect to Master Kai and gave the Chosen my full attention. "All of you know when I first began my studies, I was of average intelligence. After my illness, my test scores were the highest among my peers. At first I thought what happened to me was by chance, but I now believe my abilities are intrinsic to all humans."

"How is that possible?" Master Kai asked. "All the tests you've been put through failed to explain how you surpassed your genetic profile."

"While I was in a coma I thought mostly in pictures, which I believe gave me direct access to a creative intelligence that lurks within the hidden mind. After I had been discharged from the hospital, I began to experience visions while awake. They happen while I'm performing tasks on an instinctual level—like when I'm playing the violin."

"Why is there no mention of visions in your discharge report?" Master Kai asked.

I was so excited that I spoke ahead of myself, but I didn't care. I had to disclose my advantage to effectively compete against all those with a more favorable genetic profile. "I didn't mention them because I thought they were only dreams."

Master Kai glanced over at Master Tyrus, who nodded.

"Proceed." Master Kai said.

"When my visions continued, I realized they were more than dreams, and I started to keep a visual record. I've uploaded some images. Feel free to look through them."

The Chosen all stared into their hololologue optics. Their interest in my sketches emboldened me to continue. "With the introduction of spoken language, we relied less on our intuition and more on our place in society. I'm convinced it was this contrived behavior that eventually unhinged us from our natural instincts that exist beyond the realm of words. When the scourge came, we were more susceptible because we weren't aware that anything was wrong until it infected the whole population. Apart from regressing back to primitive man, there must be a way to rejoin with this primal aspect and reclaim what was lost. A new man…a natural man would be born with the ability to function on both instinct and intelligence, integrating the two into total conscious awareness." I thrust my fist in the air. "A true Unity would emerge if we could all become fully alert of our actions. There would be no need for reintegration because there would be no more criminals or mental illness. The hidden mind would no longer be ravaged by the scourge."

"What is it you want to accomplish with your studies?" Master Tyrus asked.

"I request to study psychological engineering to help vanquish the scourge." I scrutinized the Chosen for a reaction, but they were unreadable. "Thank you for your consideration." I bowed in respect and turned to leave.

"Who do you think you are coming in here, challenging our greatest thinkers with no presentable evidence?" Master Avery yelled out.

I stopped and frowned at him. "I'm the evidence!" My implant released a shock. I kept from flinching and bowed to Master Avery, hoping no one noticed what happened. "I meant no disrespect, Master Avery." Whatever power came over me vanished, bringing back my fear. I wanted to recant everything I'd said, but the passion I felt electrified me more than the shock from my implant.

"That's a big presumption you just made," Master Kai said.

"And one that won't be easy to substantiate," I replied.

"Then why put your future at risk by challenging what has worked for us since our founding?"

"If the Unitian understanding of the brain was without flaw, I wouldn't be here to challenge that understanding."

"To be accepted in University, you must be willing to work with others," Master Avery said. "What you've demonstrated here today is an ignorance over the Corporate Hierarchy and—"

"We've heard enough for deliberation," Master Kai interrupted. He cupped his hands on the table and seemed agitated. "We'll have our decision in two weeks, Apprentice Damon."

"Thank you, Chosen." I bowed. "It will be an honor to serve, should I be accepted." I left the room and almost fainted from my show of insolence. I'd have to wait two weeks to find out whether my dissent would be rewarded or answered with a downgrade in status as Master Franklin predicted.

After four weeks of sweating, regrets, and trips to the pleasure room to forget the turmoil, the majority of the Chosen invited me to study psychological engineering. Only one voted against me, and I was surprised to discover it was Master Tyrus. I wasn't too concerned. It was Master Kai whom I most wanted to impress, and I had succeeded. When I completed my studies, I was handed four offers of assignment. I selected the research and development department of faith design and became the focus of every exploiter in the media. No Unitian ever received more than two offers of assignment. The future was mine, and purple sleeve didn't seem ambitious enough. I now wanted to be Overseer.

# beyond the beacons

The media attention had prompted me to soften my combative style. I began to compromise with those whom I disagreed with, including Master Avery. Why I acquiesced is unclear. Either the public's fascination with my celebrity made me transform into what they had imagined, or I wanted to be what they imagined. I didn't like either explanation. My slavishness reminded me of Master Avery's performance with the Chosen. Disgusted by what I was becoming, I took some time off to go sailing with Wade. The warm sea breeze failed to sooth my anxiety, and I spent most of the trip in a drunken haze.

Wade looked eastward with his binoculars. We no longer appeared similar; I was taller than him, and my hair darkened a few shades. Our skin was still the same pale white, but all

Unitians have a similar skin tone. I slapped on another layer of sunscreen to keep from burning.

"What do you think would happen if we pass the beacons?" he asked.

I glanced at Wade curiously because he knew the answer. "Isolation, followed by two weeks of reintegration."

"Two weeks? What if it's by accident?"

"Bad judgment doesn't change the outcome."

Wade stared at me as though trying to figure out a puzzle. Then he smiled. "That cute exploiter was correct. You really are amazing."

"And after the interview, I showed her how right she was...all night." I smiled back at him and took a sip of my drink.

"I disagree with her reason behind your genius." Wade shook his finger at me, one eye squinting. "You always find an answer that never challenges your opinions. *That* is what's amazing."

"They're not opinions." I looked down at the water, which was unusually calm for this early in the summer.

"Why don't you come to one of Master Tyrus's assemblies when we get back? If you listen to what he has to say, the rational brain you had before you succumbed to Master Kai's tired sermons will reawaken."

"The water looks inviting," I said.

"More proof that you've turned into a sleeve-worshipper. You'd rather change the topic than listen to contradicting opinion."

"Think I'll go for a swim."

When I placed one of my legs over the rail, Wade shot up from his chair. He pulled me off by the back of my shirt. I tried to free myself, but he wouldn't release me.

"You can let go now," I said. "My *rational* brain is functioning."

Wade flipped me around and shoved my back against the rail. "Right after you tell me what you were just thinking of doing!"

"Hard to say," I said without any hint of emotion.

"Try!"

"Remember Master Kai's lecture about cognitive assaults?"

"I make it a point to forget everything he says."

"I thought he was exaggerating…until today. It was like this massive bomb detonated inside my head. I wanted everything to stop."

Wade released his grip.

"I used to think being a psychological engineer was what I wanted, but now…I'm not as certain," I said.

"You have more than one offer of assignment."

"Once I made my selection, my other offers were voided."

"When did all this start? I thought you were eager to begin your assignment."

"I was." I clasped him by the back of his shirt and thrust his torso over the railing.

"Next time, we leave the berry ale home," he said.

"Now in this scenario, I'm angry at you for calling me a sleeve-worshipper and push you in. Whether you jump of your own volition or are pushed, the outcome is the same…you drown." I pulled Wade back up. "Reintegration won't be necessary if everyone is fully integrated. Neither scenario would occur, and all life would be preserved. It's only the outcome that matters."

Wade shook his head. "When did this happen? You used to laugh at the Corporate Hierarchy and their utopian rantings, and now you sound exactly like Master Kai." Wade looked at the shoreline. "You never answered my question. What would happen—if we passed the beacons?"

I went to check the navigation screen. We had sailed four kilometers past the beacons.

"Why did you do this?" I yelled.

"Master Tyrus believes the poison in the deathlands has dissipated. He's forming an expedition to explore beyond the tunnel, and I volunteered to go."

"Why didn't you tell me?"

"I was convinced once we were out this far, your sense of adventure would return and you'd volunteer with me."

"I'm not willing to die over a failed hypothesis!"

"How can you call it a failure? We haven't even gone out yet."

"The last team came back sick, and Nasia recently confirmed that with her life."

"That was over a hundred years ago, and Master Tyrus didn't believe Nasia's last testimony either." Wade gazed vacantly at the horizon. "We can do this. We can keep going and see for ourselves what's on the other side. Unity Forces will be too afraid to come after—"

"We're turning back now."

"It seems like they're not the only ones who are afraid."

I headed towards the helm.

"I can't believe this. You turned into the replacement."

I bolted at Wade and was about to punch him when my implant released a strong electrical stun, almost knocking me to the floor. He appeared surprised by my anger but not as surprised as I was. I massaged my temples to ease the pain.

"You even got his temper," he said.

"If I had his pointer, I would've flogged you with it."

"That assignment of yours has already drained the life out of you, and you haven't even started. Consider this my last rescue attempt."

"Why would I want to be rescued from a promising future? Why would you?"

Wade rested his elbows against the railing and stared out at sea. "Credit, power, and worship from the lower colors aren't enough for me."

"What else is there?" I asked.

"Nasia. I have to know what happened to her."

"You do. She bought the scourge back with her and died."

"I don't believe it, and we're about to discover her true fate very shortly."

I pulled Wade by the front of his shirt. "If you wanted to die to satisfy your curiosity, you should've left port without—" I was interrupted by a vision of him lying dead at the bottom of a ridge that looked like Emerald Mountain. The western side of the valley was a popular camping spot for Unitians and the last preserve not destroyed by the Great Cataclysm. I was trying to study the surrounding landscape when Wade grabbed me by my arms and turned me around.

"I'm here!" Wade yelled. "Right in front of you!"

"I know. Why are you yelling?"

"Think you took your own scenario a little too seriously. You kept looking down at the water, screaming out my name." Smiling, he crossed his arms. "Never really knew you cared so much about my well being."

"I had another one of my visions." I pushed him out of my way and ran to the helm.

"Must've been a frightening one. You looked more terrified than after you heard a dog howl for the first time."

"That's because it was just outside our tent."

"The implants can cause both visual and aural hallucinations after a stun."

"I'll run a diagnostic when we get…Slock!"

A Unity Coast Patrol vessel was on the approach, and I dropped anchor. Since we had passed the beacons, we had to wait to be escorted back to port.

"Astonishing," Wade said. "They never move that fast inside the dome."

"I hope all the trouble we're about to get into will be worth it."

"It will." He walked over to me. "What was your vision about?"

Several Unitians stood by the pier to watch us as we stepped off the boat. Wade made a show of it and waved to everyone.

"Loosen your sleeves, and forget about your vision. I already did," he said, beaming.

Had this happened the previous year, I would've been first off the boat, intoxicated by the shocked expressions and fingers aimed our way. Today, I feared dying of the scourge, or at the very least, losing my offers of assignment because of Wade's obsession over Nasia.

He leaned over to me and whispered, "Don't say a word. I'll handle this."

Border guards escorted us to the marina base station for in-processing. We turned in our plazers and met with two Unity

Guards who questioned us about our passing the beacons. Wade gained authority over the situation minutes after the questioning began. The two guards were completely absorbed with his dramatic version of our deep-sea adventure.

"This last year at University wore me down," Wade said. "A vacation seemed the ideal way to escape the drudgery of my routine, but all my fears and insecurities followed me out to sea. It was as though a massive bomb detonated inside my head. I wanted everything to stop."

He seemed on the verge of tears, and one of the guards helped him to a chair.

"After eight bottles of berry ale, my inhibitions were all gone." Wade's eyes narrowed, and he spoke almost in a whisper. "I climbed over the rail and was ready to surrender myself to the calm, inviting waters beneath me, but Damon stayed by my side and talked to me until my senses returned. Had he left me alone to check if we passed the beacons, I wouldn't be here answering your questions." Wade gestured toward me. "That man is a hero. He should be rewarded, not treated like a criminal."

The guards nodded in agreement, and it took a great effort for me to keep from laughing. They believed Wade's story, and after three days in isolation we showed no signs of the scourge. We were given back our plazers and released.

For most of our hike home, Wade was quiet until we caught sight of the dome. He stopped and gazed solemnly ahead.

"Did you find your answer?" I asked.

"We passed the beacons and didn't catch the scourge."

"We were lucky."

"Or we're being lied to. I have to know what Nasia really saw."

"A pile of rocks. She admitted it."

"If I see them for myself, I'll believe it."

"What if Master Tyrus's request for an expedition is denied?"

"I'll cross the old tunnel alone." Wade looked at me. "One way or another, I'm going to find out the truth."

During our trek back, Wade continued talking, and I listened. By the time we entered the dome, turned in our plazers and completed in-processing, he had talked himself out of his dark mood and even bet me a case of berry ale for our next paddleball match. With his competitive spirit in the forefront, I knew he'd be all right…for now. I was still concerned about my vision, and he tried to assuage me by blaming it on my implant or stress brought on by my last year at University. Both explanations were viable, but the image of him lying dead on the ground was difficult to forget.

Thanks to Wade's performance at the marina base station, I was rewarded with a larger loft, and my story was presented on every city screen. The attention led Master Kai to request that I work directly under him. I tried to thank Wade for his help, but he refused to accept my gratitude.

"After I beat you in our next match, the case of berry ale will be payment enough," he told me.

Wade didn't win the match but beat me in the following one, and that ended my obligation to him. He never brought up his role in my success, which made me feel less deserving of it. That didn't last for long. My ambition of making maroon sleeve before my thirtieth year made me forget what inspired me to begin my journey. By deception I moved up, and by deception I'd continue.

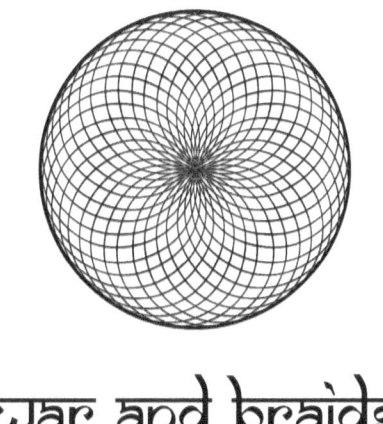

# war and braids

Master Tyrus's petition to explore the deathlands began after Nasia had returned to Unity with claims of having traveled beyond the old tunnel. She shocked all of Unity when she greeted the access guards with her hair cut shorter than my own, which was at shoulder length. Nasia's appearance sparked a passionate argument between the sexes, with women openly stating their desire to cut their braids. A sympathetic schoolmaster even orchestrated a time for women to toss the liberated strands from their windows in a show of solidarity. When over fifty of his students took his challenge, the schoolmaster was sent to reintegration for inciting a revolt. The farce continued when Master Avery gave a speech that was broadcast on every city screen. I bit my bottom lip to keep from laughing in front of the purple sleeves who were standing beside me.

"If we allow women to flaunt themselves with short tresses, we invite back the plight of the forgotten times when they nearly tempted men to destruction," Master Avery said with breathtaking certitude. "Our women are empowered by their designated positions in our society, but Ancient women fallaciously believed their sexuality empowered them. They used it in excess and ended up objectifying themselves, devaluing their own humanity. The temptation for unregulated sexual gratification was impossible to resist, and man lost his dominance over his primal nature. Revealing clothing, unbound hair, and face paint led man to detach from his morals, which opened the door to violence and greed. Unity between nations was severed and created the distrust that led to the wars of the forgotten times. If we let women tempt us back into submission, we'll repeat our violent past and eventually yield to self-destruction."

A video of an explosion followed and covered my laughter, which I could no longer contain. Although I agreed with the Sacred Oath, Master Avery's absurd argument successfully beclouded the real story: Nasia had pictures of a majestic city built beneath an Ancient temple. I was intrigued—and envious. Nasia had done what I had only dreamed about as a child, and I was eager to hear all about her adventures in the deathlands.

Four days after Nasia's return, Wade and I tried to visit her, but she was still in isolation. It was unusual to be detained more than three days. When we inquired if she had the scourge, we were sent away and told that if there was any news, it would be reported on the city screens. Wade feared something terrible had happened to her, and it was during this time he started to mistrust the Corporate Hierarchy.

"What do you think Nasia saw out there?" he asked me.

"I'm not making any judgments until we talk to her."

"What if they won't let us?"

"The only reason they wouldn't is if she has the scourge."

"No," Wade said. "Something's wrong. They wouldn't even let her give a statement to the exploiters when she first came back."

"There's no conspiracy here. The guards were following procedure. Isolation is mandatory for everyone who passes the beacons."

"Then why do I get the feeling they're hiding something?"

"You sound like a Striker." I laughed. "Sure you're not one of them?"

"I'm seriously considering membership. They've been making more sense than the Overseer lately."

"If Nasia has the scourge, she may be delusional—"

"I saw the pictures taken of her. She looked lucid in all of them."

"I hope you're right, but you have to prepare for the worst. A therapeutic dose of escape should alleviate your stress until—"

"Save the psychoanalysis for your internship. I *know* Nasia. If she said she saw something, I believe her. Any other explanation the purple sleeves throw at us will be a lie." Wade shook his head. "I should've gone with her."

"Then you'd also be in isolation."

"And with the woman I love." He peered at me. "But you have no idea what that means."

"I know how much Nasia means to you, but what you're saying isn't helping. You have to stay strong for the both of you."

"If anything happens to her, no amount of escape will help me. I'll never forgive myself for letting her leave alone."

I talked to Wade some more, but my counsel offered him no relief. Master Tyrus wasn't any more helpful as he also believed Nasia. His fascination with the Ancients led him to request that she appear for questioning before the Chosen. Before he had a chance to bring it up for a vote, Master Avery handed him a signed statement from Nasia. She now declared that what she saw was a hallucination brought on by the scourge. The image she captured was nothing more than a boulder formation.

Two weeks after her return to Unity, Nasia voluntarily ended her life, and her request for death was witnessed on every city screen. When she made her announcement, her hair was covered by a scarf so as not to offend the Overseer and Corporate Hierarchy. She appeared at peace and smiled during her delivery.

"I, Nasia 1306-111-3F put before you all a request for death. I don't wish to endure the late-stage symptoms of the scourge and have decided to end my suffering. Thanks for all the letters of support. I'm blessed to have lived and loved in Unity."

Wade raced to the hospital and tried to force his way in to see her. Unity Forces were called to restrain him while Nasia was given a lethal dose of escape. She died peacefully, and Wade was spared from reintegration because of his relationship with her. That would've been the end of the controversy had Master Tyrus not begun his own investigation. He examined reports and testimonies where several Unitians mentioned visiting a city beyond the old tunnel. Their testimonies were refuted after they were all diagnosed with the scourge, which ended up claiming their lives. Master Tyrus found it unlikely that people who never met each other would have the same hallucination. His doubts about Nasia's story prompted his decision to explore the deathlands, even if it meant his own death. Master Tyrus's conviction gained him a loyal following among the lower colors, many of whom volunteered for what his protégés referred to as the *courageous road to truth*. After a year of petitioning, Master Tyrus had enough support and presented to the Overseer a request for expedition.

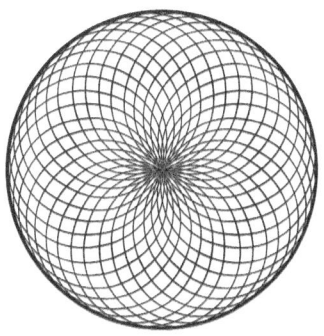

# stage rage

My vision of Wade's death became my biggest concern. Every diagnostic test I ran on my implant proved it wasn't malfunctioning. When I warned him against camping alone, he laughed and followed it up with his typical response that I needed to loosen my sleeves. I adopted a similar attitude when the vision failed to repeat itself and blamed it on the exhaustion and stress from my last year at University.

With Wade's impending death pushed to the back of my mind, I settled into my assignment, looking for opportunities to advance myself. One soon arrived when Master Kai called me to his office. This was my first official meeting with him, and I wanted to make my best impression. I tied my hair back and tucked it under my shirt collar. Most Unitians cut their hair if they make blue sleeve. Not going along with the unspoken custom was my way of rebelling without risking a demotion.

"You may sit," Master Kai said after I had bowed.

As I sat I glanced at all the commendations in the room.

"I have your first assignment. Handle this well, and you'll have one of your own to hang on the wall." He gestured at his commendations. "And after your five year apprenticeship, I'll take you on as my First, which means you'll be eligible to become a Chosen."

"I work for the good of Unity, Master Kai, not for an award."

"That's encouraging to hear in the midst of all the chaos. Earlier this morning a Striker attempted to disable one of the transmission towers."

"Does Unity Forces have any leads?"

"They have the Striker in custody. By sheer luck, the pulse bomb failed to detonate, and he returned to the location where he planted the device. A janitor, who'd just gotten off from work, contacted Unity Forces when she noticed him rummaging through the waste bin. That's where he hid the bomb." Master Kai opened his drawer and removed a remote controller. "They also found this on him." He handed it to me. "Do you know what it is?"

I inspected it. "It's a signal emitter used to test the transmission strength sent to the implants."

"However, this one can trigger auditory and visual hallucinations. It can also send hypnotic suggestions directly to the implants."

"How far away can this transmit?"

"All the way to the beacons. It can piggy back a signal off the towers."

I handed back the signal emitter, disappointed that it didn't explain my vision about Wade.

"During his interrogation, the Striker revealed they've been creating symptoms of the scourge for a group of purple sleeves who aren't happy with our current Overseer."

"To what end?" I asked.

"If Unitians *believe* they're infected, the treacherous purple sleeves would emerge with their own miracle cure. Everyone would naturally look to them as saviors."

"The curative signal would still be transmitting. How could they possibly explain that away?"

"By then the succeeding Overseer would already be in power, and he'd tell everyone they were mistaken. The symptoms came from a new disease, far deadlier than the scourge. Had it not been for Unity's heroic team of scientists, the killer disease would've infected everyone within the dome."

"Not everyone would believe such sensationalism."

"Most would, and reintegration would take care of the dissenters." Master Kai leaned back against his chair and clasped his hands together. "You have to appreciate the brilliance behind the plan. It would've worked had the Striker not been caught."

"Why wasn't any of this on the city screens?"

"We didn't want to start a panic, which is why we must stop this now. Unity must be restored."

"Permission to offer my opinion?" I asked.

"All my male protégés speak freely with me, Damon. I never cared for all the formalities of the Corporate Hierarchy. They stifle the natural flow of conversation." Master Kai picked up a glass of water on his desk and took a sip.

I nervously shifted my weight on the chair. "Why not send all those who support separation into reintegration?"

"Including Tyrus?"

I didn't answer. Master Tyrus still had his purple sleeve and to judge him would've led to a reprimand.

"Tyrus is very clever with his pronouncements," Master Kai said. "He knows when to stop. That's what makes him a threat to Unity."

"Is he with the Strikers?"

"I think he's the mastermind behind all of this, but I have no proof. The Striker in custody is only a middle man. He received his orders through letters and comnet messages that were successfully erased from the main database. Unity Forces tried to retrieve them and failed." Master Kai patted the desk with his hands. "And that's why I asked you here today. The Overseer must disprove Tyrus's erroneous views towards the outside. That's why you're here. I want you to write his next speech."

My heart beat in double-time. I wasn't ready for such a big undertaking. Failure at this juncture of my assignment could lead to demotion. "Master Kai, I appreciate your confidence in me, but I don't have Master Tyrus's years of service or his large base of supporters. Perhaps you should appoint someone with more experience."

Master Kai glanced into his holologue. "You were at the top of your class in faith design. The techniques you learned worked."

"I haven't tested them outside the classroom."

"I'm certain your friend Wade would disagree." He leaned forward and pressed both hands on his desk. "I was impressed by your quick thinking and ability to persuade him to seek help. I saw that same spark in you during your last speech to the Chosen." Master Kai sat erect and widened his eyes. "I'm the evidence!" Laughing, he slammed his hand on the desk. "I don't think I'll ever forget the look on Avery's face when you said that." Sitting back, he gazed at me reflectively. "Your talent will take you far, should you choose to use it."

I bowed. "I'll do my best to earn your respect."

"You'll earn more than that. If your speech helps the Overseer turn the purple sleeves against Tyrus, I'll personally hand you your first commendation."

"I'm humbled by your offer, but I must tell you, words alone won't stop the Strikers."

"I know. But we can at least stop Tyrus. This may bring the rebellious purple sleeves back to our side. No one likes to be on the losing team."

I left Master Kai's office doubting my ability to handle such an assignment. The only reason I got it was because of a lie. To trust in my own competence, I had to write a speech that would destroy Master Tyrus's support base. If I could do that, my success would be deserved.

With my first commendation in view, I spent hours orchestrating the right phrases and words into an inspiring message that would champion the Sacred Oath. The Overseer approved my speech. When he delivered it, I studied the crowd's reaction and was unexpectedly disconcerted when they hailed, cried, and laughed at all the right moments. My reservations vanished after Master Kai congratulated me. We couldn't be certain of the Overseer's success until Master Tyrus's next rally. When hardly anyone showed up, I knew a promotion was evident. The accomplishment reignited my passion, but I wanted to feel even greater fervor because I hadn't felt anything for so long.

Master Kai offered me my commendation following the Overseer's weekly assembly at Unity Hall. I got up and gave the usual acceptance speech. Near the closing, the woman from my vision entered the hall. Her presence took over the whole room, and I momentarily forgot where I was and what I was doing. When the spell seemed to pass, I looked out over the audience, slammed the side of my fist on the podium and shouted. "You're all primitives! No amount of promotions or privileges will elevate you. You're so intoxicated on self-praise, you believe your own lies. While the Outsiders move forward, you continue to devolve."

All the colors scoffed and hissed, but I didn't hear them. I pointed at the purple sleeves. "The Strikers will win! You'll eventually be outmaneuvered and defeated!"

In the midst of all the yelling and jeering, I focused on the woman from my vision. She spoke a phrase I hadn't heard since I almost jumped off the roof of my dorm. "Six begin, Six alone, Six unite."

I gasped at the sound of applause. It took me a few seconds to comprehend that I had just come out of a vision. A wave of vertigo overtook me. Master Kai had to help me off stage. He took me to the hospital for a full medical examination. Everything checked out normal, but I was far from the standard definition of normal. It just couldn't be confirmed by any medical diagnostic tool.

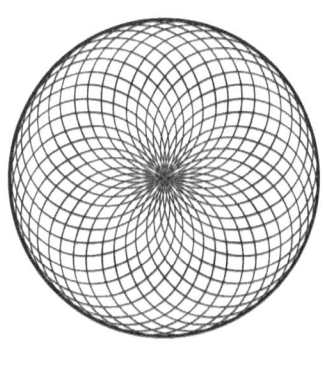

# harmony

As the longest-standing member of the Chosen, Master Tyrus was favored to become the 148th Overseer. After his request for expedition had been denied, Master Avery and Master Simon were the only two Chosen who stood by him. When the rest of them shifted their loyalty to Master Kai, he seemed relieved over his loss of popularity. I soon learned why Master Tyrus gave in so easily when Master Kai called me to his office. He wanted to go over the numbers of those I treated during the last phase of their reintegration. It was my responsibility to ensure they were psychologically fit to rejoin the general population. A recent increase of requests for death had me concerned over how it would affect my position as Master Kai's First, but I also took it as a personal failure that I couldn't help my patients.

"Everything I read in your report tells me you did nothing wrong," Master Kai said. "All the simulations you've written are exceptional. So exceptional that curates are calling you the new *Master* of faith design." He laughed. "I can see Avery cringe every time he hears that. You've been a thorn in his side since your meeting with the Chosen." Kai glanced at the report, and tapped his fingers on his desk. "Why do you have question marks after some of the patients' names?"

"There might be a new psychological disorder we've yet to encounter—one that would explain the increase in requests for death. The patients I singled out all had one thing in common: They claimed they felt as though the dome was closing in on them, and they all used a similar phrase. It sounds like a phobia of some kind—similar to claustrophobia but—"

"There's no new anything." Master Kai dismissively waved his hand. "The blame for the increase falls on Tyrus and the grandiose assumptions he made about life on the outside. During our last meeting he accepted the blame, and his admission was heartfelt. He had no idea his personal passion for exploration would be dangerous to impressionable young minds."

My thoughts immediately shifted to Wade. Since Master Tyrus's defeat, he'd spent most of his days drinking and sleeping. He only emerged from his loft to work and play paddleball with me every Seventhday. I had to start all the conversations; otherwise the sole topic of discussion would've been what we were wagering on. When I tried to offer him my help, he threatened to quit our matches if I didn't mind my business, so I complied. Alienating Wade would've made it difficult to keep watch over him, and I was afraid he'd be next in line to fill out a request for death.

"You look troubled," Master Kai said.

"My friend is one of those impressionable young minds."

"If you're speaking of Wade 1300-099-33M, he's lucky you were around to save him." Master Kai paused and looked at me reflectively. "I'm very proud of you, Damon. You've far exceeded my expectations—which is why you're going to ascend with me. As my First, you're privileged to be the *first* to hear my good news. Because I remained steadfast in my loyalty to the Unitian

Oath, Tyrus knew I'd be the better candidate to succeed the Overseer. He transferred leadership of the Chosen to me this morning."

"Congratulations, Master Kai." I bowed. "With you as Speaker of the Chosen, we should soon be seeing fewer requests for death."

"Not until those whose minds have been infected by Tyrus are emptied of his poisonous rhetoric. His rebellion caused a mistrust between the lower colors and Corporate Hierarchy. The Strikers are gaining more recruits, and the Chosen agree the only way to bring about a true Unity is to find a cure for the scourge."

Kai's declaration revealed the ideal opportunity. Being the Unitian who discovered the cure for the scourge would guarantee my ascent to purple sleeve. I went to work right away, reading everything I could about the disease. Little was known other than our brains were vulnerable to the infection since the Great Cataclysm. Those who retreated to the mountains brought the scourge with them when they returned to the lowlands. The dome protected our ancestors, but we were susceptible to the disease if we spent too much time outdoors.

What made the search for a cure elusive was that we still weren't sure if the scourge was bacterial or viral, but I didn't let that discourage me. I spent most of my apprenticeship searching for a remedy that would negate the need for the painful shock triggered by the implant. Using pain to keep the peace was barbaric and overlooked the thoughts and emotions that lead to aggressive behavior. Brain scans performed on Unitians about to begin reintegration revealed that their stored childhood memories entered their consciousness whenever they were agitated. In essence, they were reliving the same emotional responses through present day altercations that had nothing to do with the events that created the memory. Stored within the hidden mind, these regressive emotions confused Unitians when re-experienced during adult conflicts, creating internal discord between rational and emotional responses. I became convinced that these stored emotions were linked to the scourge. They served no purpose to the advancement of the human mind. If I could find a way to erase these destructive emotions, we would be fully conscious and have more control over our violent thoughts and actions.

I presented Master Kai with my proposal shortly after he promoted me to First. He placed me as head of a new project aptly named, Harmony. I devoted early mornings to brainstorming, my favorite phase of invention because everything seemed possible. When I had a worthwhile hypothesis, I'd work it out in my mind while playing the violin and later present it to my team. A half-year passed, along with a myriad of ideas, but none were viable. Master Kai came close to canceling Harmony until the solution filtered into my mind while I was playing my violin. I didn't need to look for a cause of the scourge; I only had to *erase* the offending emotions produced by it.

Master Kai granted me permission to study Unitians going through reintegration. Before they'd enter the chamber, I synced a brain frequency analyzer to their implant and searched for patterns in their emotional responses. As I expected, the study revealed that the frequencies of stored emotions were universally the same, and I spent nearly two years mapping out all their wavelengths. From my specifications, an electrical engineer designed an optical scanner with a built-in transmitter. I created a program that would scan through the distribution range of stored emotions and emit a remedial signal when one was detected. My quiescent neurogenic encoder effectively prevented violent behavior in all my test subjects. When an offending emotion arose, they entered a peaceful alpha brainwave state and ceased their abhorrent behavior.

After reading my results, Master Kai called me to his office.

"Your work is monumental," he said. "Can you make it work with the existing implant?"

"I designed Harmony to work in tandem with the curative signal. The frequency can be transmitted directly to the implant by targeting the neural-electrical resonance frequency of anyone who wants the upgrade. All they have to do is present their order at the nearest essential shop."

"This is promising." He glanced at the results again. "Why did you remove the stun?" he asked.

"The troublesome emotions are destroyed before they enter consciousness. But if you feel I should keep it in—"

"That won't be necessary." He continued reading.

To calm my anxiety, I viewed Master Kai's awards. When he was a blue sleeve, he received from his mentor the highest award of Most Honorable. I mused how one of those would make an excellent companion to my commendation.

"You're presenting this at the next Corporate. If this does as you promise, essential shops will need more workers to keep up with all the requests for service."

I bowed my head and fought hard to contain my excitement. "I won't disappoint you."

I demonstrated Harmony at the next Corporate meeting, and the Corporate Hierarchy aspired to start development right away. Six weeks later, it was ready for transmission. Unitians lined up in every essential shop to receive the upgrade that promised to erase all their childhood hurts.

Master Kai awarded me a commendation for my achievement and nominated me for maroon sleeve. If I won, I'd exceed my goal. I'd make it to maroon in my twenty-eighth year.

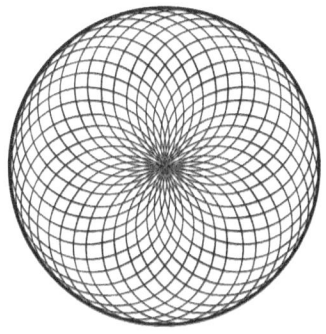

# the art of competition

Wade hadn't shown up for Harmony's launch, and I went to check on him to make sure he was all right. Normally, I wouldn't have been concerned, but he also failed to show up for our weekly paddleball match. When I got to his loft, he greeted me with a bottle of berry ale. He elevated it and said with a drunken slur, "Enter…if you dare."

Wade's living room was in disarray. Whatever had been attached to a wall or on a shelf lay broken on the floor. "You owe me two cases, plus an all-expense paid visit to the pleasure room." I hopped over a few piles of shattered glass and found a clean spot on the sofa. "This evening's mystery dates are going to be worth every credit. All the blues were talking about it at the satiation center today."

Wade finished the last of his drink and hurled the bottle at the wall. He walked over to an armchair filled with about four weeks of dirty laundry and rummaging through the pile, unearthed his hololouge. He stared into the optic.

"Explains why you didn't call to let me know you were forfeiting our game," I said.

"Just transferred over the fifty credits I owe you. The rest of my payment is in the kitchen. Don't drink it all in one night because I won't be betting again for a while."

"Is this about Nasia?" I asked.

He tossed his hands in the air. "It's always about Nasia." He fell onto the chair. "Did you know this past Seconday was exactly seven years after the day she died?"

"I did, and that's why I'm here. I found a way to help you get over her."

He waved me off. "I better not hear one slocking word about Harmony."

"This is something else I've been working on."

Wade eyed me suspiciously. He'd done that a lot lately.

The clean environment of my loft didn't seem to relax Wade. He sat on the couch, nervously tapping his foot on the floor. "This is a waste of time."

"If this works, many Unitians will benefit from it."

"You still don't know what you unleashed with Harmony."

"No one has to accept the upgrade."

"Given the choice between getting a stun or not getting one, I'd say Harmony will soon be transmitted to every Unitian's implant."

"That would be a move forward. The old way is savage."

"So is destroying our emotions."

"Only those from the past are affected."

"Past or present makes no difference to me. I'd like to keep all my emotions." Wade crossed his arms. "Even the ones you find offensive."

There was a knock at the door. I leaned back against the sofa cushion and crossed my legs.

Wade gave me a curious look." Aren't you going to answer that?"

"I'd like you to answer it."

"Why? Who is it?"

I waved my hand towards the door and smiled.

Wade walked to the door, hesitated, and then opened it. He stepped back when he saw it was Nasia.

"Aren't you going to invite me in?" she said.

He slammed the door. "Are you serious? Do you think a fabrication will help me get over a woman made of flesh and bone?"

I checked out Wade's brain scan on my hologlue. "Your neural activity is no different from real life."

"I don't care what that thing says." He looked at the door. "That was not Nasia. You have no idea what it means to connect with someone."

"I prefer rationality over giving up on life because of a woman."

"You were never with a woman long enough to make that judgment. Hand a girl a rose and throw her out of your life; that's all you know."

"I don't need to subject myself to a stifling relationship to see that you're suffering. The purpose of this simulation is to help hasten emotional detachment. If it helps you, we can use reintegration technology to help Unitians through the grieving process."

"Why bother? Most Unitians have signed on to Harmony."

"I intend to use this with patients who've recently lost someone in their lives. It can also help you uncover your stored emotions, but it won't work as quickly as Harmony. You've been reliving Nasia's death for the last six years. It'll take a few sessions to get to the root of your disturbance."

The doorbell rang again. "It's time to let go and move on with your life." I motioned for Wade to answer. "I'm sure that's what Nasia would want for you as well."

He glanced at the door, then back at me. "Mind your own emotions—if they still exist. I'm quitting this program."

The transmission chamber retracted from our beds, and Wade got up and walked out.

We arrived at the crail stop near Wade's loft. The door slid open, but he stayed seated. "I got the upgrade."

I shut the crail door and put it in wait mode. "When?"

"It's the oddest sensation. It's almost as if my body is in contradiction with myself."

"You're fighting the change. Allow Harmony to—"

"I don't want to be changed!"

"What do you want?"

"To be happy—for real."

"You will. Once you stop resisting the signal."

"Taking away my sadness doesn't make me happy. It makes me empty."

"Allow yourself to believe what you're feeling. Test subjects who did that had the best results."

"But I don't want to believe it. I want to feel it."

"They're both the same."

"They're not. Feelings happen from life experiences."

"Feelings are nothing more than nerve impulses. I compared them with events triggered in real life and those created in virtual simulations and found no difference."

"I don't care what your gauges, emitters, and scanners tell you. There is a difference. I scheduled the Harmony signal to be terminated. As of tomorrow morning, I'll be sufficiently depressed again."

Wade opened the door and stepped out. "This isn't natural. Harmony will end up destroying us." He walked away, but his words stayed with me.

When I returned to my loft, I worried over Wade's erratic behavior and what it meant about the effectiveness of Harmony. I played my violin until drowsiness shrouded my concerns, but sleep failed to offer me solace. Nightmares of Wade's death kept waking me up. I called him the next morning, and except for a hint of sadness in his voice, he sounded better.

The same dream continued for the next few nights, and I plugged myself into a brain frequency analyzer to check for abnormalities. When none was found, I created an uplink from my implant to my hologue. If any changes occurred, they'd be captured in real time.

Three weeks passed. I received no data. I hypothesized that anticipating the dream reappearing kept me from dreaming. I took a tranquilizer, thinking it would trick my brain into a relaxed state. It worked. I awoke after staring down at Wade's broken body at the bottom of the ridge. The test results depicted something shocking and unexplainable. There was an extra brainwave present, but it didn't show up in the readout. Beside it was a caption that read: *unable to identify, no compatible data.* I reran the test to ensure there wasn't a malfunction. As the results reappeared on the monitor, the wave that wasn't there came back. I searched through medical records for an explanation but found nothing.

I suspected the extra brainwave was the carrier of my consciously obtained reflections of future events. If my hypothesis was correct, COR, the name I'd given to the elusive brainwave, was the key to proving my precognition. I set the parameters in the brain frequency analyzer to capture COR and send out an alarm whenever it was detected. I decided to keep quiet until more data was gathered for analysis. My silence was prudent as I overheard Kai boasting to the Overseer about how he helped me develop Harmony. This was the lie that began to unravel my blind loyalty to Unity.

# infinite present

A flock of exploiters aimed their cameras at me as I made my way down the aisle of Unity Hall. I sought refuge in the preparation room to rehearse my induction speech. After delivering the introduction to my reflection in the mirror, I directed the rest of my oration to the chipped paint on the wall that reminded me of Master Avery's face. My recitation became more passionate as I envisioned him sitting in the audience, rubbing his hammer-shaped nose while pondering over how I surpassed his expectations.

Wade entered the room unannounced and stepped in front of me with his forehead creased. "Either you've finally lost your mind or—" he pointed at the chipped paint. "You've mesmerized the poor wall into silence with your hypnotic words and spellbinding gaze." Smiling, he handed me a bottle of our favorite alcoholic beverage.

"If I have the same effect with the Corporate Hierarchy, my career as a maroon will be off to a promising start." I inspected the label.

"It's not the cheap stuff," Wade said. "I know better than to insult an upper color."

"I'm technically a blue sleeve until my induction."

"Then I guess I'll give this to you after the ceremony."

Wade went to grab the bottle, and I pulled it back. "You were never good at keeping track of time." I removed the cap. "I see no reason for you to improve now."

"If that's professional advice, I'll gladly follow it." He lifted up his half-consumed bottle. "To your success."

We clanked our bottles together and drank.

"Enjoy it for as long as you can," Wade said. "When you finally acknowledge Harmony's destructive truth, it'll be too late to do anything about it."

"And once you experience its true potential, you'll be thanking me."

"For what? I can't get into a decent fight with anyone, and every woman I date is disgustingly happy all the time. I want a female to complain over how much I talk about sports. It's the natural order of things."

"That's a small charge to pay. Harmony will eventually bring an end to reintegration. You won't need to fill out another request for a new assignment because you'll be out of a job."

"Tempting…but I'd gladly continue to pay the higher price for a woman to lecture me over all the hours I spend in the pleasure room."

I was about to follow up with my own quip when I had another vision of peering over a cliff at Wade's dead body.

Wade waved his hand near my nose. "Still in there?"

I clenched his wrist. "We have to cancel our camping trip."

Wade pulled back his arm. "What are you trying to do, break my wrist?"

"I had another vision."

"I refuse to live out the rest of my life in fear of your visions. That would be far worse than your vision coming true."

I gulped down half my drink, trying to expunge the image of Wade's broken body from my mind.

"Loosen your sleeves. Now that I know about my possible death, all I have to do is be more careful when we get to the ridge." He laughed and finished off the contents of his bottle. "I'll even slow down so you can walk ahead of me."

The more I thought about it, the more plausible Wade's argument sounded. His foreknowledge could very well save him, but I still wouldn't be able to distinguish if my vision was a delusion or an altered destiny. For both my sake and his, I hoped it was the latter.

Kai started my induction ceremony with one of his parables. I can't recall which one because I was feeling anxious. Afterwards, he went on about how his department was responsible for Unity's reduction in reintegration sentences, with barely a mention of how Harmony made this possible. When he finally called my name to award me my maroon uniform, I stood up from my chair and almost toppled over. Everything around me appeared to be moving in slow motion, and my body swayed as though adrift on a boat. I walked to the podium and clutched the corners to anchor myself.

"You may begin now," Kai said slowly, stressing each syllable.

I leaned in towards the microphone and spoke. "Before I get started, I'd like to thank Master Kai for nominating me."

Everyone applauded, and I attributed my dislocation to stage fright. "I invented Harmony to help you find it within yourselves and each other. With three quarters of Unitians receiving Harmony's signal, I'm confident that one day everyone will enjoy a healthy mind, impervious to the scourge. I'm honored to move up within the Corporate Hierarchy and promise to serve for as long as I'm alive and of sensible mind."

A female voice called out, "Can you predict the future and promise us Harmony won't be misused by a future Overseer?"

My COR alarm sounded and everything seemed more familiar than the earlier moment. Flashing lights on my face and Kai directing his guards seemed more like memories occurring in present reality. Suddenly overcome by vertigo I collapsed to my knees. The floor drew me to it like a magnet, and I fell forward, landing on the palms of my hands. As I attempted to get up, my elbows buckled, and my chest pressed into the floor. All the surrounding voices blended and softened to a barely audible level.

"Six begin, Six alone, Six unite," said a lone female voice.

It took all my effort to lift my head and look towards the door where the female from my vision stood. Her long hair poured down like streams of glistening black water, and I was surprised no one noticed. She extended her hand to me, and as I stretched my arm to her, all the sounds were again at full volume. My body lightened, and I sprang to my feet. "Who is she?" I got up and pointed towards the mysterious woman.

Kai assisted me off stage. "Don't you see her? She's there—by the entranceway. Her hair is unbound!"

Kai squinted his eyes. "Where? Every woman I see has her hair braided according to regulation."

I looked back at the entrance. The woman from my vision had vanished.

"I'm sorry your induction was ruined," Kai said as he entered my loft.

"When I heard her voice…everything seemed so familiar," I said more to myself.

Kai sat on the couch and rested his feet on the coffee table. I cringed at the action which never disturbed me before.

"We'll find her."

"She's in her thirties, her hair was out of regulation and—"

"I meant the female who interrupted your speech."

"I don't care about her. The woman—I think she—" I stopped myself to run a COR scan on my hologue.

"The long hours you spent on Harmony are beginning to affect your mental health. Don't allow it to deflect you from the value you've added to the Corporate Hierarchy. I can see you moving far beyond even your own expectations."

I didn't acknowledge Kai because I was more interested in making sense of the test results. I had to know what happened because I'd almost completely lost myself, and I had to know why before I lost myself again. If the woman from my vision hadn't shown up, I don't think I would've found my way back.

"I'll cut off your access to the lab if you don't take some time off to heal yourself," Kai said.

My attention returned to my mentor, who I was now starting to loathe. Except for Master Avery, I never felt such a strong dislike for anyone. "You're right." I bowed my head to Kai, wanting to get him out of my loft so I could analyze my COR readings. "It's been a long day, Master Kai. Forgive my insubordination."

Kai bowed in return. The reciprocal gesture reminded me I had just been promoted.

"You've been through a lot," he said. "I strongly urge you to take your vacation early."

"I have a lot of work that needs to be done by the end of next—"

"Consider this your first day. I'll see you back in three weeks."

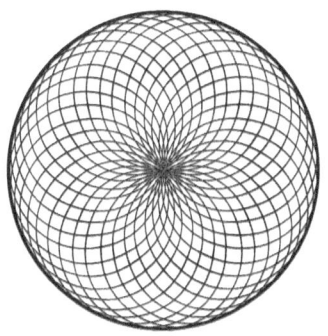

# outsider

I departed for Emerald Mountain a day ahead of Wade. Between my visions and growing hatred for Kai, the time alone worked better at easing my anxiety than Harmony. I pitched my tent at the base of the western side of the peak. After the canopy of juniper and pine had concealed the last traces of sunlight, I went to sleep. Dreams of Wade's death taunted me until the motion alarm I set went off and I heard footsteps outside.

"Who's out there?" I cautiously separated the tent flap and aimed both my plazer and flashlight towards the mouth of the trail. The woman from my vision stepped into the light beam's path.

"Who are you?" I edged closer to her, and a name came to my mind. "Sutara?"

Smiling, she entered the thicket.

I tracked her along the dark narrowing path, but soon lost sight of her. On my way back to my campsite, I was surprised by a wild dog. Sitting on his haunches, he was eerily still. I clutched the grip of my plazer, stepped back, and took aim. The dog growled and leapt at me. I fired my plazer and woke up to the sound of my COR alarm and a splash of water on my face.

Wade hovered over me with his overturned canteen. "Wake up, my Lord. Today, we're climbing to the top of the high ridge. Master Tyrus showed me all the blind paths of the motion sensors. Unity Forces will never see us leaving…or returning."

I may have been half-asleep, but I still recalled our sailing adventure that ended with a Unity Force interrogation followed by three days of isolation. I shut off the alarm. "I'm not risking it. I'm stopping at the beacons this time."

Wade yawned. "Had a rough time at work. Could use some time alone." He walked out of the tent.

"You slocking reckless—" I slid out of my sleeping bag and followed him. "You know I can't leave you alone!"

"Grab your things. I'm leaving now."

I stormed back into my tent and rolled up my sleeping bag.

Wade pushed apart the tent flap. "What are you so worried about?"

I stuffed my lantern and the rest of my gear into my backpack.

"You're a Unitian hero. They'll tolerate more from you," he said.

"Your death is starting to sound preferable to a reprimand from Kai."

"Does that mean you're coming along?"

"We'll camp in the valley tonight and watch the meteor shower." I zipped up my backpack. "If we must risk reintegration, let's make this trip the envy of all Unitians."

Reaching the top of the high ridge, we had a breathtaking view of Unity. The dome glistened like a diamond but seemed small in comparison to the bordering land.

"This is why I break the rules." Wade was staring at the outer-patrol station. "What gives them the authority to deny us a view like this?" He tugged his climbing cable, which he'd secured around a large tree trunk.

"I'm going first." I tossed my already secured cable over the precipice.

Navigating beyond the beacons was hazardous. We had to climb down a treacherous escarpment to maneuver around the eroded rock that separated the two faces of the mountain. When we finally touched ground on the eastern side of the ridge, Wade's enthusiasm was washed away by another mountain looming on the eastern side of the valley. Whatever lay beyond the peak was invisible to us. Wade picked up a stone and pelted it over the edge.

"Master Franklin once told me that life is a perpetual test," I said. "When one obstacle ends, another one presents itself."

"Everything has an—"

A wild boar charged ahead of us with an Outsider in pursuit. "I claim that boar!"

The Outsider took aim with his longbow and shot the boar on its side. Laughing, he ran over to his catch. "She's a real beauty, isn't she?" He clumped the boar's legs together and tied them.

Wade smiled and approached the Outsider. "She's attractive —for a boar."

"Can't wait to take her home and skin her." The Outsider swept his tongue across his top lip.

I looked from the boar to the Outsider in disgust.

"Makes me feel like God peeking into His creation." The Outsider stood and gazed at the carcass. "It's the purest gift of all —to witness your next meal in its rawest and most unspoiled form."

I was repulsed by his blasphemous words and rotting teeth that even a purple sleeve dentist couldn't hope to salvage.

"You boys from Dome Dungeon?" he asked.

Wade laughed. "I've called it similar names."

I slapped the side of Wade's arm.

He whispered, "Loosen your sleeves. We never met an Outsider before. This could be a lot of fun."

The Outsider flung the carcass over his shoulder. "Got nothing to say to you then," he remarked and started to walk away.

"Why not?" Wade asked.

The Outsider turned and probed us top to bottom. "You all talk weird."

"In what way?" Wade inquired.

"Let him go," I said.

"You all sound the same. It's creepy," said the Outsider.

"Creepy? What does that mean?" Wade asked.

The Outsider shook his head. "Exactly what I mean. Normal folk don't get confused so easy." He was moving off again.

"I'm not confused!" shouted Wade. "Just curious."

The Outsider hesitated for a moment, then whirled around and delivered a stare as deadly as the arrow that pierced the boar. He dropped the carcass, retrieved his bow and snatched an arrow from his quiver. "Curious, huh?" He pulled back the cable and aimed the arrow at Wade. "Your…curiosity is rare to your kind. You don't even know how things out here work."

"I'm willing to learn." Wade crept closer to him.

"Don't go any further!" I whispered loudly. "He's got the scourge!"

Wade continued walking, and the Outsider kept his aim. Wade stopped inches away from the arrow's tip. The Outsider further retracted the drawstring. I feared that Wade was about to meet the same fate as the wild boar. After a few tense moments, the Outsider relaxed his aim and eased his bow. Laughing, he said, "None of you ever came this close." He picked up the boar and tossed it over his shoulder. "You're either brave or out of your mind. Either way's okay with me."

"What now?" Wade said.

The Outsider crinkled his forehead.

"What do I do next?" asked Wade.

The Outsider cleared his throat and spit. "Get it?" He smiled.

Wade cleared his throat, spit and squinted his eyes. "I'm not getting anything."

The Outsider chuckled and shook his head. "Leave Dome Dungeon. Being scared and curious is a hell of a lot more fun." Finally, he walked off.

If Wade yearned to die, I refused to watch him live out my vision. I started back towards Unity.

"Everything okay?" Wade asked when he caught up with me.

"That diseased Outsider had his arrow aimed at you, and you were talking to him as if you were one of his protégés."

"He was harmless."

"How can you be sure?"

"Don't see an arrow in your chest." Wade laughed.

Still agitated from our encounter with the Outsider, I threw a punch at Wade. He jerked sideways, scarcely escaping my fist.

"You're slocking crazy!" I yelled. "We could've gotten killed!" A blast of pain ripped through my head, and I winced.

"Thought they were going to remove the stun alarm," Wade said.

"They kept it in for newly formed emotions." It was another lie. Kai told me the stun would be disabled with the upgrade, but on the first day of transmission, the Overseer announced it wouldn't be removed until every Unitian received Harmony's signal.

Wade shook his head. "I didn't notice it while we were out on the bay, but it's all so obvious now. You can't see beyond the dome." He walked off in the opposite direction.

"I can see way beyond your limited imagination!" I ran towards him. "And my vision of your death will become reality if you continue these crazy stunts."

"That Outsider was friendly."

"He's got the scourge."

"How do you know?"

"He thinks he's God. Delusional thinking shows up in the late stage."

"He said he felt like God."

"Same difference." I can't recall why I was so angry. Maybe Wade was right and the Outsider wasn't a threat, but I had never witnessed anyone take such pleasure in killing.

Our debate continued while we set up camp, and it carried on throughout dinner. When the sky darkened, we extinguished the campfire to get a clear view of the meteor shower.

"It's good to be out of Dome Dungeon and connected to a true intelligence," Wade said.

I opened a bottle of berry ale. "Are you referring to the trees, wild boars, or the psychotic Outsider with the rotting teeth?"

"Don't you ever wonder what's up there?" Wade motioned to the heavens.

"I sometimes have these vivid dreams about traveling in space. It's so real that when I wake up, I'm disappointed that I'm still on Earth." I sipped my drink.

"And confining. We're stuck here, and there's no escape. It's as though we're trapped inside a room even though the door is open."

"Is this about Nasia?"

While I waited for Wade's typical response, he picked up his portable telescope and aimed it at the sky. "I want to forget about life on Earth for a while."

"Me too." I lay with my hands crossed behind my head and gazed at the night sky, wishing I could be a part of it, as I was in my dreams.

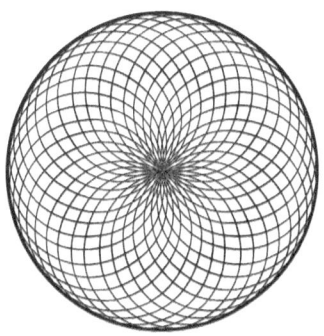

# old woman

Wade and I hiked along the bank to the top of the high ridge where we came upon a waterfall that spilled into a river. On the eastern side was a small cabin with solar panels on the roof.

"I had no idea Outsiders had access to modern technology," I said.

"I'm heading down," Wade said.

"What if the Outsider who lives there is dangerous?"

"After facing that boar hunter's arrow, I'm feeling brave."

"Better rethink your assertion. Stupidity can sometimes be confused for bravery."

"Loosen your sleeves. Once we make it down, there won't be a ridge for me to fall off of." Wade smiled and walked ahead.

We made it to the valley two hours later. Wade knocked on the door, and an old woman answered with the barrel of her plazer trained on us. "Passenger or loyalist?" she asked. She had long gray hair held back by a scarf wrapped around her forehead.

I clasped the grip of my plazer, and Old Woman shifted her aim towards me.

"Answer the question or go back. I want no trouble."

"We mean you no harm," Wade said. He lifted his hands up slowly. "Put down your plazer," he said to me.

"Are you out of your—"

"We'll be here all day because I'm not leaving."

Old Woman smiled at Wade and sneered at me.

I clutched the grip of my plazer and eased it out of my holster.

"Slowly," said Old Woman.

I placed my plazer on the ground and kicked it aside.

Old Woman inspected us for a few moments before holstering her weapon. "You sound like a reasonable Unitian," she said to Wade and laughed. "Don't think I ever said that before." She pointed at me. "Don't confuse my good cheer for camaraderie. If either of you start preaching the Sacred Oath, you won't be welcome any longer."

A large dog with long golden hair ran out, almost knocking us over.

"Don't be afraid. My Shisa wouldn't hurt even the tiniest ant," Old Woman said.

Wade followed her into the cabin. I wanted to leave, but my vision kept me its prisoner.

Old Woman and Wade went through their introductions. I was more interested in the living space. On the eastern side of the main room was a large open panoramic window with a stunning view of the mountain we first spotted on the forbidden side of the ridge. As I admired the scenery, the shutter closed.

"Impressive," Wade said.

I turned around, and Old Woman had a remote control in her hands. "A good way to get attention." She reopened the shutter.

I nodded in the direction of a large opening in the back wall. "What is that for?"

"It's a fireplace. I use it when I don't have enough power stored to run the electric." She looked at it solemnly. "That happened only once—and it was so many years ago."

The wall opposite the window had shelves filled with sculptures of strange creatures. I picked up a figure of a human with an elephant head. The body had four arms and a prominent belly.

Old Woman touched the trunk with her wrinkled index finger. "Ganesha."

"What does that mean?"

"The Ancients that worshipped him believed all the universes of past, present, and future existed in him."

"At the same time?" I asked, intrigued over how that would affect my precognition.

Old Woman seemed confused by my comment.

"Did they believe past, present, and future happened all at once—within the same space?"

"The builder of this cabin would've laughed at your question," she said. "I inherited all that you see here from him."

Old Woman surveyed the room as though admiring a palace. She fixed her gaze on a picture of an older man and young woman, standing in front of the cabin. "Torrin was a brilliant engineer. He never concerned himself with unearthly conjectures." She laughed. "Typical scientist."

Torrin seemed familiar; I'd seen him before but had trouble discerning where.

"A trip to New Athenia might hold the answers you seek," Old Woman said.

"Where is New Athenia?" Wade asked.

"Across the old tunnel. The journey is long but well worth the effort." Old Woman opened a drawer in her desk, removed a folded sheet of paper and handed it to Wade. "I can transport you over, if you'd like."

Wade unfolded the sheet. "It's a map!" He held it out to me. "I knew Nasia wasn't hallucinating."

I examined the map. It showed territories on the eastern side of the tunnel.

"Before the Great Cataclysm, people lived in different parts of the world and had their own languages and customs," Old Woman said.

Wade noted a highlighted spot on the map that read, New Athenia. "What would I see here?"

"The heart of New Athenia is the Alexandrian Repository. It preserves the histories of all known Ancient races. My first visit profoundly affected me. It expressed a reality greater than Unity."

"I want to go," Wade said. "When can you take me?"

"Go there, and you'll end up dead like Nasia." I tried to seize the map, but Wade pulled it away.

"You'll be fine," Old Woman said. "The scourge is a lie."

"Master Tyrus was right," Wade said.

"How can you trust an Outsider over—"

"I'm not going back." He examined the map. "Made the decision before I left Unity."

My vertigo returned and I observed the room in a state of disarray. All the trinkets and statuettes were scattered and broken on the floor. Underneath one of the shelves lay Ganesha with a broken trunk. I picked up both pieces and placed the trunk over the chipped face.

Wade shoved me, forcing me out of my vision.

"Shut that thing off," he said.

I turned off the COR alarm and surveyed the surroundings, trying to reconnect with everything.

"It wasn't another vision about me, was it?" Wade asked.

"There are more to my visions than you."

"Come with me, Damon. This New Athenia sounds like the most amazing place on Earth."

"If that were true, Outsiders wouldn't be lining up at all the accesses to become Unitians."

"Hah!" Old Woman said. "The Sacred Oath might as well be tattooed onto your brain." She pushed her palm towards me and looked at Wade. "Let your friend remain in his fantasy, and join me outside where the beauty of reality is more dynamic than you've ever imagined."

The exterior of the cabin was well constructed and impressive. It took Torrin several years to complete the construction as every piece had to be smuggled out by the Strikers. Whatever he couldn't get from them, he managed to pick up in New Athenia.

"The solar panels were the most difficult to acquire," Old Woman said. "Torrin had to pay a rider with a wagon to bring them back from New Athenia. It took him almost half a year to find an electric trap. A Striker finally managed to sneak one out for him. It can store weeks' worth of energy."

"How come no one ever discovered this place?" I asked. "All your electronics should've been picked up by the outer-patrol station."

"There's a covertly placed transceiver on the western side of the eroded ridge. It's masked by deception jamming that communicates with a wireless signal interface inside this cabin."

"You have access to the comnet out here?" Wade asked, surprised.

"Along with live feeds of the middle ridge delivered by motion sensor cameras. I saw you both coming. Until today, this cabin was undetectable. All the walls are lined with steel mesh. It makes the whole cabin invisible to radar, but now that you know I'm here, it's useless." She grabbed the handle of her plazer. "Maybe I should've shot you."

Wade laughed. I reached for my plazer.

"You'd be dead already if that's what I wanted," she said.

Ignoring the continuing banter between Wade and Old Woman, I admired the impressive vegetable garden. Each line of crop had an irrigation ditch connected to a canal that linked to the river on the western side of the cabin. A sluice-gate controlled the inflow of water. There was also a small pond beyond the garden where Old Woman said she went when she needed time to reflect.

"Potatoes, cucumbers, onions, and carrots." Old Woman surveyed the rows of crops. "Tomatoes, cabbage, spinach—and there's plenty of fish in the river. I have everything I want here." She looked reflectively at one of the chairs on the porch. "Almost everything."

Wade was gazing at the mountains. "I could live here. It's peaceful."

"I'm glad we have growers in Unity to do this tiresome work," I said.

Wade ignored me and continued his worship of Old Woman. "What made you leave Unity?"

"The decision wasn't easy—I was a purple sleeve."

"She lies," I said. "No purple sleeve ever leaves Unity."

"They do when they're in love with an orange sleeve."

"No tenets exist that restrict relationships by color," I said.

"What color are you?"

"I'm a maroon sleeve."

"When you—if you make purple sleeve—you'll adjust your opinion." Old Woman went back inside.

I nudged Wade's arm. "Old Woman is in the late stages of the scourge. We should leave now."

"Maybe you're the one who's sick, and we're part of the cure."

He left me alone. The isolation of my faith and opinion forced me to question whether my devotion was misplaced, but I didn't carry the thought long enough to commit to an answer.

I examined the picture of Torrin with the young woman.

Old Woman explained, "That's me—when I first arrived here over twenty years ago. My orange sleeve never met up with me at the city border, so I went without him."

"A foolish decision," I said. "You gave up your honored life as master to live like an Outsider."

"Left more for myself. Uncertainty is liberating."

"Being scared and curious is a hell of a lot more fun." Wade smiled at me.

Old Woman glanced up at the picture of Torrin. "Sounds like something Torrin would've said. At first I thought he had the scourge." She twirled her pointer finger next to her ear and smiled. "I was surprised to find him here because they told us he died. He was a Chosen."

"Why did he leave?" Wade asked.

"He never talked about it and requested I never ask, so I didn't. Torrin believed in and taught the ways of the Ancients. This cabin was his classroom, and I was his willing student. Through the years, other Unitians and local Outsiders came to hear about his travels."

"Where is the master of the Outsiders now?" I asked.

"He left me a little over a year ago, during our last trek to New Athenia." She looked up at the picture again. "He died in the old tunnel."

"Don't you get lonely?" Wade asked.

"I tried returning, but all my years on the outside made me too independent to restrict my existence to a small dome. The collective folly of Unitian dogma felt suffocating, so I came back here."

"Your loneliness has obviously affected your judgment," I said. "Wade is a curate. I'm sure he can help you."

"How are you so sure your judgment is better than mine? All your understanding comes from Unity. That hardly sounds objective to me."

"Your selfishness clearly demonstrates why 'mine,' and other words related to the false nature of self should be stricken from our language. Only with Unity can we rid the world of the destructive influence we've inherited from the Ancients."

Old Woman applauded. "They programmed you well. Keep that up, and you'll make a fine purple sleeve." She turned to Wade. "How about you? Are you alive, or is your head plugged into that Unitian insane asylum as well?"

"As a curate, I help Unitians through reintegration, but it seems more like I'm harming them."

"How can you harm them by helping them?" I asked.

"Unity's idea of help is no different from the violence of the past," Old Woman said.

"You're nearing a visit from Unity Forces, Old Woman."

"I've known they were coming since I opened my door to you. I knew when I looked into your eyes still filled with sleep."

I glanced at my hololgue. Wade pushed down my arm.

"Damon, let her speak."

"This is what leads to violence. We can't allow this Outsider a platform from which to spew her vile delusions."

"I'm sure you'd like to throw her—along with that woman who interrupted your induction—into reintegration for daring to disagree with you. If you shut your slocking mouth long enough to listen, you'd realize other viewpoints exist besides your own."

This intense anger rose within me, followed by another blast of pain to my head. A part of me wanted my vision to come true. A part of me wanted Wade to die because he was a threat, although not in the way I'd imagined. He forced to the surface things I didn't want to face: my own doubts over the Unitian Oath that began when Kai claimed credit for my work.

Wade looked at Old Woman. "I lost someone close to me. She was sent for reintegration, and they told us she died of the scourge."

"But you don't believe that," Old Woman said.

"Nasia viewed the world as I did and wasn't afraid to question common knowledge. Whenever we were together I could be myself, without all the pretenses."

Old Woman smiled. "In Unity we can be enslaved, and in Unity we can also come together as individuals. This contradiction confused me at first."

"I could tell her anything because I knew she'd understand." Wade wiped his eyes with his sleeve. "Now I have no one to confide in. It's unbearable—the loneliness I feel."

"Nasia was passionate about her beliefs," I said, "but I never thought she'd go to such an extreme to prove them. Introducing you to her was a mistake."

"It was the smartest thing you ever did. Before Nasia, I didn't know what it meant to feel alive."

"Then why have you been a walking dead man for the past seven years?"

"I never found anything else to live for."

"You have to live for yourself." Old Woman unclasped her hologue and handed it to Wade. "And you can only do that after you free yourself. Make the effort to see ahead, or you'll remain as you are."

I grabbed Wade's arm. He pulled away and took the hologue.

"It's anti-Unitian!" I yelled. "Read that poison, and you'll probably succumb to the scourge, like her."

I tried to grab the hologue from Wade, and he gave me a violent push.

"Are you sure you don't have the scourge?" I asked. "You haven't even read what's in that thing, and see how irrational you're already acting."

"I have the…the…" Wade rubbed his head. "I can't even think of a word to describe what I'm feeling."

"Right," Old Woman said.

Wade scowled at me. "I have the right to do as I choose."

"If you listen to her, you'll end up living in the middle of the woods communing with wild dogs and boars."

"Sounds like paradise compared to Unity." Wade walked away from me.

I glared at Old Woman. "This will be the last day you'll speak your seditious words."

Her gaze remained relaxed. "What have I said that you find threatening?"

I gripped my plazer.

"Killing me won't silence your doubts. It'll make them scream louder." She stared at my hand on the plazer and then at me. "I'm old and tired," she said. "This was Torrin's crusade, not mine. Do it, if you must."

Old Woman walked to the counter and calmly poured herself a glass of water. "I'm usually not this candid with visitors." She sipped some water.

"What do you want from us?" I asked.

"Nothing."

I looked from Wade to Old Woman.

"I can only hear the truth when I make the choice to listen," she said. "It took me over fourteen weeks of watching Torrin's interactions with Unitians to understand. If I ask you to think or live as I do, I'd be worse than the Overseer." She glanced directly into my eyes. "You'll learn this in your own time."

"For that blasphemous remark, you'll be brought up on charges of treason." I peered into the optic of my holologue. A sudden blow to the back of my head threw me to the floor, rendering me unconscious.

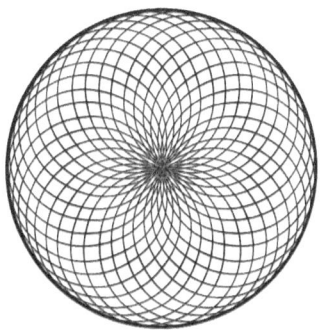

# hiking past the crossroad

Wade sat motionless on the chair by the window. He didn't even flinch when I regained consciousness, groaning from the throbbing pain at the back of my head. Fearing Old Woman had killed him, I tried to call for help, but my holologue was missing. I took a deep breath and sat up.

"In case you're looking." Wade raised an arm in the air. Three holologues were strapped to his wrist. He extended his other hand and waved my plazer. "You gave me no choice. I didn't want you to turn her in."

"Your regret is touching. Where is the old woman now?"

"I told her to leave."

I grabbed the edge of the counter and slowly lifted myself to my feet.

"I can't feel anything, except for the stun from the implant," Wade said. "Harmony stole everything else." Wade stood and faced me. His eyes were vacant. "The most gloomy revelation came to me while you were unconscious."

"If I had my hololugue I would've recorded it to honor the day my best friend attacked me to save an Outsider."

Wade placed his forearm in front of his mouth. "PC 1328-256—in triplicate. A day of confusion, admission, betrayal, and remorse. Anything else you'd like to add?"

"Think you covered everything." I pulled out one of the dining chairs and sat.

"I'll begin with my confusion as I'm sure that's the most glaringly obvious. This world is alien to me. I have no clue how anything works here. The Corporate Hierarchy is turning us into machines, and almost every Unitian is accepting it with a smile on their face."

"If you kept Harmony's signal, you wouldn't feel that way. You'd see how it's making us better than we were before."

"I feel worse."

"I thought you had the signal terminated."

"My desire and longing for Nasia never returned—until we got out of the range of the transmission towers." Wade came over to me. "Take a reading of my implant. I'll bet it's searching for Harmony's signal."

"Return with me to Unity, and I'll run a complete diagnostic."

He pounded his fist on the table. "Next comes my admission. I'd rather die than go back to Dome Dungeon. The Overseer is tracking us like a herd of animals. By the time he's done nothing will be ours, including our own thoughts."

"It'll never come to that."

"How can you be so sure?"

When I couldn't think up an answer, I recalled the woman who had interrupted my induction with a similar question. I had no answer for her either.

Wade took a deep breath and softened his voice. "If the scourge is a lie, that means they killed Nasia."

"You have to stop this, Wade. You're highly respected and have a favorable future ahead of you. Don't throw it away on an unproven theory."

"Credit, power, and worship from the lower colors still isn't enough for me."

"What else is there?"

The COR alarm sounded, and a chill surged within me.

"Something I can never have." Wade turned off the alarm, unclasped my hololegue from his wrist, and handed it to me along with my plazer. He moved towards the door. "There's no escape when everyone wants to live in a prison."

Wade ran out of the cabin. I contacted Unity Forces. Moments after I'd disconnected, Old Woman came in with her plazer aimed at me. Shisa ran in behind her, growling when she saw me.

"Sit, girl. It's okay," Old Woman said in a gentle voice.

To my surprise, the beast listened. I grabbed my backpack and edged toward the door.

"Go now," Old Woman said. "I won't give up my cabin to you or any Unity Guard."

"Unity Forces will soon be here to arrest you, and you'll answer for your crimes before a confessor." I staggered out of the cabin and fell down the porch steps. My motivation resumed when I caught sight of Wade making his way to the top of the ridge.

I found Wade pacing along the edge of the ridge, mumbling to himself. I slowly crept towards him.

"Stay where you are. I'm not finished yet." Wade nodded at the hololegues strapped to his forearm. "These two are still recording."

"You can stop this. You don't have to—"

"I'm finished with confusion and admission, so I'll move on to my betrayal." He raised three fingers.

"This is about Nasia?"

"It's always about Nasia." He laughed and then stopped. "No. That's not true. It's about me being a coward. Nasia is dead because of me."

"Unless you gave her the scourge, I don't see how that's possible."

Wade stopped pacing and clenched his fists at his side. "There's something I never told you. Nasia planned on crossing the old tunnel and I was supposed to go with her. The night before we were to leave, I changed my mind. I didn't want to risk my assignment placement. Nasia was so angry with me that she left by herself. Apart from her request for death, that was the last time I saw her alive."

"If you went along, you would've also filled out a request for death."

"Or we might've made a life for ourselves in New Athenia."

I continued to move closer to Wade.

"Stay back!" he yelled.

I stopped. "It wasn't your fault. You didn't give Nasia the scourge."

"You're not getting any of this, are you? They lied! Nasia didn't die of the scourge. They killed her because they wanted to silence her. I'd bet my life that what Nasia saw on the other side of the old tunnel was New Athenia."

"If they wanted it kept secret, they never would've let Nasia speak after she submitted her request for death." The sureness of my response vanished when I recalled the frivolous debate over Nasia's hair and how Wade was never permitted to meet with her. "Don't do this, Wade. If you don't want to go back, I won't stop you."

"I'm always going back, and I can't stop. Every night, I remember Nasia's last words to me. Do you know what they were? Sleeve-worshipper. I was so angry I let her go." Wade's eyes filled with tears. "I let her go! I abandoned her!" Softening his voice he extended four fingers. "Remorse. I should've been by Nasia's side."

My hologue beeped and I quickly glanced into the optic. Unity Forces responding that they were on their way.

"Now I know why I got so mad at her," Wade said. "She was right—and you're about to be as well."

"I'd prefer to be wrong."

"Why fight destiny when it's deserved?" Wade smiled and extended his arms to his side. "We both know how this must end."

I ran to him as he let himself fall backwards. Just as in my vision, I stared down at my friend, lying dead on the ground. I screamed until my lungs ran out of air. A scan on my holologue revealed COR was still present. It had been since it showed up in Old Woman's cabin. I caught myself deliberating over a comparative data report and was disgusted with myself for focusing on my work when Wade had just died. How had the human brain evolved into something so dysfunctional and self-serving? Wade and Old Woman were wrong; the scourge was real. There existed inside the brain an unyielding sickness that triggered an unquenchable addiction. The more I tried to stop myself from wanting, fantasizing, and desiring, the more intense those feelings became. I vowed never to rest until the scourge was confined to an entry in the Unitian Medical Encyclopedia.

I made my way down the ridge, clinging to my last few strands of faith that Wade's accusation was wrong. I tried not to look down at his body while I ran a diagnostic on his implant. My heart sped as the results splashed across the screen. Wade was correct; Harmony's receiver was active.

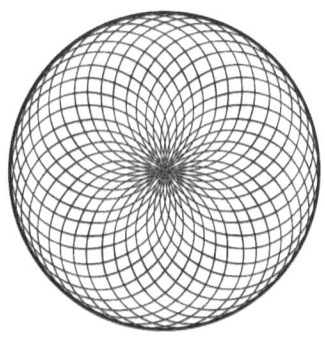

# dangerous knowledge

By the time Unity Forces had stormed Old Woman's cabin, she was long gone. I suspected she escaped to the other side of the old tunnel. After I'd returned home, I read through the incident report and found no mention of either her or Torrin. I conducted a search in the citizen database. There weren't many Torrins on file, but I discovered his designation when I found an image of him standing beside the 146th Overseer.

Torrin was Master of Reintegration Technology. He was almost killed after his office had been blown up by Strikers who opposed his invention of the implant. They never found who caused the explosion, but things settled down once all the Unitians were chipped. After the last Overseer had died, Torrin was elected among the Chosen to become the next Overseer. The night before his induction, he was accused of stealing credits from the treasury. He disappeared before his reintegration hearing. Looking for Old Woman was futile as I didn't know her emergence year. I inspected over three thousand images of female purple sleeves born between sixty to seventy years ago. None were a match, and I gave up the search.

The feeling of having met Torrin before followed me to the crail stop where I was struck by another vision. Torrin lay on the floor, and Old Woman was kneeling beside him, weeping. They were in a narrow room lined with long benches. All the windows were dark, and a row of handles hung from the ceiling. Two doors, similar to those on a crail, slid open. Sutara entered and said, "Return to the cabin."

The COR alarm rang, jolting me out of my vision. A woman who arrived at the stop while I was consciously unavailable, watched a two-seater crail that was pulling up.

"Are you waiting?" she asked.

The vertigo I experienced during my induction was back. Everything around me swirled in a nebulous stream of colors.

"Are you okay?" The woman inquired. She appeared like a splotch, barely distinguishable from the background. "Should I call a medic?"

I heard her, but my brain wouldn't give me the words to respond.

"I'm late for my shift," the glob said. Would you mind if I—"

"You can take it if you shut your slocking mouth," I said.

The glob conceded to my request, floated into a larger glob and drifted away.

"Six begin, Six alone, Six unite," Sutara's voice called out.

I stood and lost sense of where I was. The spinning sensation in my head worsened. I must have passed out because I awoke in the hospital with no idea how I got there. My assigned doctor kept me overnight for observation after a brain scan detected my pineal gland was enlarged. He suggested I get some sleep, but my concern over the extra brainwave kept me up all night.

The next morning, I received a visit from Kai who knew more about my condition than I did.

"You've mystified all the doctors in this wing," he said. "The second scan revealed nothing out of the ordinary. Your doctor says you're in perfect health and will be discharged today." He handed me a complimentary credit card for the pleasure room. "You'll get at least a dozen rounds of mystery date with this. If you'd like, you could take the rest of the week off."

"Thanks, but I'm ready to come back."

"As you wish. I'll see you tomorrow morning." Kai made it as far as the door, but I stopped him with my next question.

"Why was Harmony still transmitting to Wade's implant after he requested it shut off?"

Kai tapped the door frame with his hand and turned to face me. "This is difficult for me to tell you." He pulled one of the chairs near to my bed and sat. "Master Lyle had him under suicide watch. He thought it made sense to keep the signal active."

I knew Wade had suffered from depression since Nasia's death, but I doubted Kai's explanation.

"Considering what happened, that was a wise decision," he said. "As a psychological engineer, I'm sure you agree with his diagnosis."

"I do. Master Lyle is an exceptional doctor." What I really wanted to say was, "I don't believe a slocking word you said," but I had to pretend to be a sleeve-worshipper for a while longer. Purple sleeves expect their protégés to demonstrate complete faith in them. Knowing I didn't mean what I said gave me the strength to continue my charade.

"Concerning the beacons—"

"I couldn't leave Wade. I had to go along to make sure he didn't hurt himself."

"No further explanation is necessary. I read the report and see no need for a reprimand. In fact, this may lead to another promotion. You helped us stop a threat to Unity."

"What threat was that?"

"The woman in the cabin helped the Strikers by leading Unitians across the old tunnel. We found her contact, and he's now being reintegrated."

"Who is the woman?"

"Her identity is not permitted to be disclosed."

"Why?"

"No one cares about some old eccentric woman in a cabin. If we reveal her name, the Strikers will use her as a martyr."

"Explains why I couldn't find her file in the citizen database."

"Her name is unimportant, but yours is now respected among the Chosen. Continue your hard work, and you'll soon earn the title, Master."

My desire to advance my utopian Unitian model gave me the purpose I'd been looking for, and it helped get my mind off Wade's death. I continued my work on the scourge, believing a cure lay within COR. If the elusive brainwave allowed me to predict future events in my life, outside the realm of time, I could record how the brain reacted to events before they occurred, making negative behavior avoidable. This would be more effective than Harmony. The pain and suffering we inherited from the Ancients would no longer exist, and Unity would be ours.

I had to find a method to identify the frequency of COR, which I believed was linked up to one unified field that contained all the matter of the universe. I called this field the Progenitor. After almost four years of research, I wrote a proposal demonstrating how my work would benefit Unity and submitted it to Kai. I never mentioned I'd located COR. That was my advantage over him and the rest of the Chosen. I had knowledge, dangerous knowledge that guaranteed my ascendancy. Only after my induction to Overseer would I reveal my secret: I had identified COR's frequency.

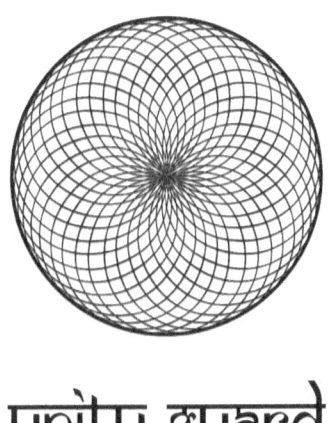

# unity guard

Kai threw a party to celebrate his fifty-fifth year. The night felt more like a board meeting than celebration, and the only thing I found amusing was a garish fountain sculpted in the image of the Overseer. His hands pressed together as if he were praying, and from between his fingertips spouted a steady stream of wine, the only alcoholic beverage in Unity besides berry ale. There weren't too many visits to the fountain. Most of the purple sleeves spent their time complimenting each other while censoring their true opinions. To say anything that countered the herd meant a collective snub and a misplaced invitation to the next Chosen event.

I drank until I was drowsy enough to tolerate the tedious, well-guarded conversations. While conjuring up creative ways to get myself uninvited to the next function—without getting a demotion—I realized how much I missed Wade's companionship, especially our trips to the pleasure room. We'd start off at the number wheel and end the night with mystery date. Whenever I won the call, wagering Unitians who knew my reputation mobbed around the presenter to place their bets. I'd enter the guessing room, and when the lights shut off, the anticipation of my date's arrival never failed to arouse me. Once she'd arrive, I'd listen to the rhythm of her breath, feel her every curve, and slowly unravel her braids. I never left the room without my fantasy playing out, and oftentimes I indulged beyond what I had imagined. When it was time to place my bet, I'd carefully scrutinize the expressions of the three women during the revealing phase and usually guessed correctly. The last time I played mystery date with Wade, we both bet one-hundred credits. After I'd announced my guess, opened the envelope, and called out the name of the winning girl, the room filled with cheers.

Thinking about Wade made me want to visit the pleasure room. On my way out, Kai approached me with Tyrus, wearing his black wide-brimmed hat. The only time I saw him without it was during my last meeting with the Chosen. At sixty-three, he was an avid outdoorsman and spent most of his vacation time mountain climbing or sailing. I always thought he'd be dead by now. Only twenty percent of Unitians live past fifty and out of those twenty percent, only three percent make it to sixty. The exception to this was the Overseer and the Chosen, who sometimes lived decades longer.

Tyrus bowed his head. "Congratulations, Damon. It's about time you progressed to maroon sleeve. Things here have been far too agreeable. If my old age doesn't claim me, boredom soon will."

After I had bowed, Tyrus shook my hand. The gesture was considered unusual between a maroon sleeve and purple sleeve. Even Kai was never this casual with me.

"Kai tells me you've come up with something that will make Harmony obsolete," Tyrus said.

"We're still in the development phase."

"How far along?"

"Far enough to know we still have a long way to go."

"I'd like to get together and discuss—"

"Get your hoofs off me, you slocking swine!" a woman's voice yelled out, and the COR alarm went off.

I switched it off, and the three of us ran into the foyer where a female Unity Guard had just slapped a maroon sleeve across the face.

Lidian was a growing embarrassment to Tyrus. Many of the purple sleeves voted against his induction, but Tyrus fought for him without disclosing why. Whatever the reason, Tyrus got enough support, and Lidian was inducted.

"I'm not a crailer!" the female guard said. "You can't just grab me like—"

"I o-o-only wanted an explanation." Lidian pulled out a handkerchief and wiped sweat off his face. "I ne-ne-never meant a-a-ny harm. I—"

"Flora, please calm yourself, so you can tell me what happened," Kai said.

"He grabbed my arm because I refused to meet him later." Flora rubbed her head, probably from the stun she received from her implant. "When I tried to pull away, he wouldn't let me go."

Kai smiled at all the purple sleeves in the room and then, with no change of expression, struck Flora in the face. "Why do you tarnish my emergence day by not addressing Lidian by his formal title?"

"Master Kai, forgive me, I—"

Kai placed his hand gently over her lips. "Apologize to the one you offended first."

Flora bowed to Lidian. "Protégé Lidian, forgive my insubordination."

Lidian stared at Flora, seemingly horrified by her comment. "I-I-I was wrong. Yo-yo-you're no different from them. You're a —"

"Our protocols make us more civilized than the Outsiders," Kai said to Flora. "Try to remember that before disrespecting a higher color."

Flora bowed. "Your Wisdom is always welcomed, Master Kai."

"Confrontation is best handled with gentle kindness. Remember that next time." Kai kissed Flora's forehead and then turned to Lidian. "You'll report to reintegration tomorrow morning."

"Yes, Ma-Master Kai," Lidian said.

"Get out of my home."

Lidian bowed and hurried out the door.

"I may have just been proven wrong," Tyrus said to Kai.

"Let's see how reintegration works before formulating a conclusion," Kai said with a hint of sarcasm that didn't escape me.

I sensed a strong familiarity to Flora and volunteered to take her home. We caught a two-seater crail for privacy. I could smell sandalwood on her hair and already imagined myself unraveling her dark auburn braids.

Flora lived in the Security Parish, and I only had a few minutes with her before she'd get off to pick up a connecting route.

"That was either a foolish or courageous stunt you pulled at Kai's," I said.

Flora's face filled with anger.

"I still haven't made up my mind between the two. Can you help me out a little and tell me what happened?"

"He—I meant, Protégé Lidian—made me mad."

"To hell with Lidian. No one likes him, and I imagine half of everyone at Kai's had to hold themselves back from cheering you on." I took a break to enjoy Flora's surprised expression. "You must watch yourself. The Corporate Hierarchy doesn't tolerate disrespect. They forgot how the real world operates." I laughed to myself when I realized I had almost directly quoted the boar hunter. "They're creepy."

"They're what?" Flora asked.

"Something an Outsider once told me. I'm still not sure what it means, but it seems to fit."

Flora stared ahead, avoiding me.

"You should've hit him harder—or put him down with your plazer."

She turned to me and hesitated for a moment. "I almost did."

"What held you back?"

Flora quickly looked forward. "You can get off at the next stop. I'm okay now."

"Don't be so guarded with me. I don't care what you say about anyone."

She examined me as though trying to figure out if I was serious and then stared ahead again.

The crail stopped, and the door slid open. "Happy journey, Unity Guard." I saluted her and got up to leave.

"I'm heading over to the observatory," Flora said.

I turned to look at her.

"Do you like stargazing?" she asked.

"Are you inviting me?"

"If you want to come along…I'll consider."

"I'll *consider* going if you're asking."

Flora crossed her hands on her lap, and I whistled one of my compositions. Four-and-a-half measures later the door slid shut, sealing me into my destiny.

The twelve telescopes that lined the circumference of the observatory sat unused. Flora appeared uncomfortable with our isolation. She escaped my gaze by staring into a nearby finderscope.

"I come here whenever I need to relax," Flora said.

"What about this do you find calming?" I peered into the telescope near Flora's.

"I picture myself as one of the stars, distant, unnoticed, and beyond capture."

A sadness overtook me as I thought about Wade during our last night out, and my own desire to get lost within the stars. "I dreamed that I could fly among them." I felt Flora's gaze on me and turned to face her.

"I had similar dreams."

Flora's eyes conveyed a sincerity I hadn't seen in many Unitians. I immediately knew I could trust her, even though we had just met.

Flora looked back into the finderscope, and I fixated on a small, heart-shaped beauty mark below her ear. I envisioned her raven hair unbound and flowing below her elbows in long curls.

"Why do you want to escape?" I asked, hoping her answer would help me understand why Wade had taken his life.

"I don't like to be restrained," Flora said. "The freedom of open space—I want to have that, always." She smiled at me.

I went to embrace her, and midway pulled back. My hesitation surprised me as I wasn't shy around women.

"I wouldn't have minded," she said, her arms encircling my neck. "Something about you seems—spacious."

I needed no further motivation. I pulled Flora against me, my whole body vibrating. It was almost as though I was resonating to her. She kissed me, and I gladly responded. From that day onward, we were inseparable.

Flora moved into my loft three weeks later. She cleared out one of my drawers and left a few changes of clothing. Normally such forward behavior from a woman would have bothered me, but we had a lot in common. We hiked, camped, went horseback riding and spent many nights at the observatory, gazing at the stars. Flora filled the void left by Wade's death. On the mornings I woke up alone, I missed her and found my weakness disturbing. Worried I'd succumb to the pitiful state Wade found himself in with Nasia, I entered an essential shop to pick out a farewell rose. As I held it in my hand, I recalled a conversation I had with Wade. "I prefer rationality over giving up on life because of a woman," I had told him.

"You were never with a woman long enough to make that judgment. Hand a girl a rose and throw her out of your life—that's all you know."

When the florist asked me to look into the scanner, I tossed the rose on the counter and returned home. Flora showed up later that night, and I felt closer to her than ever. Even the idea of parting with her seemed to make me want her more.

Wade and Flora had similar temperaments. They both had a mistrust of authority, which is why Flora was handed the assignment of Unity Guard. The Overseer believed rebellious personalities had instincts that made them ideal for security. They could easily spot a Striker or anyone else with abnormal behavior because they exhibited similar characteristics. An ingenious idea, although risky as quite a few Unity Guards were discovered to be Strikers.

Flora constantly questioned my loyalty to Unity, and I started to wonder if I was attracted to her because I missed my arguments with Wade. Unlike Wade though, Flora was a good cook. I deemed her the master of my kitchen for her marinara sauce; it was the best I'd ever tasted. Food typically brought an end to our disagreements. Once the serving trays and dishes met the table, eating surpassed my desire to win whatever it was we were arguing about. There was only one occasion where I lost my appetite. It happened shortly after Flora had served me roasted chicken for my thirty-second emergence day.

"You like it?" she asked after I'd taken my first bite.

I bowed my head to her. "Kai should have you cook at his next party." I picked up a napkin and wiped my mouth.

"Why don't you call him by his title?" Flora pulled out her chair and sat.

"There's no need for ceremony when we're at home." I poured some wine into our glasses.

"Did I hear you correctly? When *we're* at home?"

"You know what I meant." I tossed a napkin at Flora and she caught it.

"Explain yourself."

"Do you have all night?"

"Start talking," she pulled the plate away from me, "or you'll lose your dining privileges."

"Yes, Ma'am." I saluted her and smiled. "Should I drop down and give you twenty, first?"

"*Fifty*, if you can handle it." She placed her elbows on the table and leaned her chin between her hands. "Or you can tell me what you meant. Should I have my loft reassigned to someone else?"

"I'll do the fifty," I pulled back the plate, "after I eat. I'm hungry." I swirled some pasta onto a fork and took a bite.

"You can barely make it to twenty, *coward*." Flora playfully threw a napkin at me.

As I caught the napkin, my COR alarm went off and a vision came to me. Flora lying dead on the floor with a plazer blast to her head.

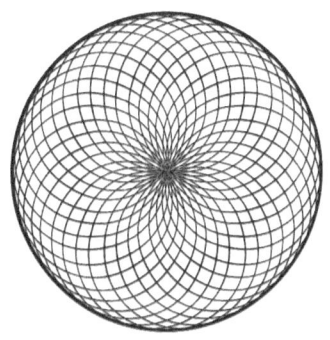

# strikers

Kai entered my office, but I was preoccupied with predicting the time of Flora's death and failed to notice his arrival. He cleared his throat to get my attention.

I stood and bowed. "My apologies, Master Kai. I didn't hear you enter."

"I take no offense. Your ability to hyper-focus has been known ever since you failed to report outside your dorm during one of the monthly fire drills."

"Master Franklin didn't take that too well."

"Don't worry. I won't be sending you to the hospital for a hearing test." Kai laughed and handed me a folder. "It took almost half of a year of waiting, but as of this morning our patience has been rewarded. The Overseer approved our project."

I raged inside when he said, *our*. "Please tell the Overseer that I'm honored to serve him again."

"I will." Kai picked up a picture of Flora. "How is our spirited green?"

"Still a mystery to be solved." I clenched my teeth behind a smile. "Must explain why we've lasted this long."

Kai looked at the picture. "A fox enters a henhouse with the intent of leaving with a hen between his teeth. But he's swayed by their easy life and carefree nature. Food is brought to them daily, allowing them plenty of leisure time." He put the picture back on the desk. "The fox is seduced by their easy existence and forgets he's a fox. Eventually the hens start calling him Hox. When another fox enters the henhouse, he selects Hox for his dinner. Before Hox can say a word, the fox snatches him up in his jaws and carries him away." Kai looked at my commendation on the wall and then at me. "We have a responsibility to first serve the Corporate Hierarchy. Once you lose sight of your purpose, you'll lose your identity and become easy prey to those who know their proper place."

"Why does it make a difference now?" I asked. "We've been together for over—"

He handed me an envelope. "Your purple sleeves are being sewn as we speak. But don't tell anyone I tipped you off. You're not supposed to know the results until after the official announcements go out."

I tore open the envelope and removed my nomination notice. This was what I'd worked for all these years. As I read through it, my ambivalence returned. I stood a good chance of rising high within the Corporate Hierarchy, but it would mean leaving Flora behind—at least until I got to a high enough level where I could get away with breaking a few rules.

"Harmony's success, along with your recent proposal, inspired the Overseer to make the nomination Himself. He believes locating the Progenitor will be a great benefit to Unity."

"My proposal never mentioned locating the Progenitor. We can't measure such a force because it exists beyond time." I was relieved I had kept COR's frequency a secret, and after what I'd just heard, I considered taking the secret to my grave.

"Once we find a way to study it, we'll move beyond controlling our emotions," Kai said. "The Overseer believes we can delete undesirable behavior in the gestation vessels. Every emergence day will produce healthy babies, free from the scourge."

"When humanity grasps the knowledge that we're all connected to a seemingly infinite power source—and that our actions are already recorded somewhere beyond time—we'll make better choices because it will be conducive to our survival."

"Your passion never fails to sway me, but this time history proves the impossibility of your idealism. Greed is a destructive counter-force to our Unity, and we must do everything in our power to ensure it doesn't destroy us."

"It won't, if we don't allow it to."

"From our position, that would be possible. However, not everyone shares our determination. Only when we hone in on the Progenitor can we hope to create our own Unity. Once we're all cured of the scourge, there will be no need for integration or reintegration. And with a little *modification* to COR, we can release it as a dissonant signal and rid ourselves of the Outsider menace. All the land within the beacons will be ours. If we're successful, we can build more towers and spread our Unity beyond the western side of the Emerald—"

"COR cannot be contained— or manipulated. We'll destroy ourselves as well."

"We can stay in the old bunkers until completion."

An intense rage swelled inside me followed by a sharp pain in my head. I seized my plazer from the drawer and shot Kai. It all happened so quickly that he didn't have time to react.

Kai tapped the desk. "Are you all right, Damon?"

"I'm fine." I went to sit down and realized I was already seated.

"For a moment, I thought you died. Your pupils were dilated, and your eyes stopped blinking." He eyed his holologue. "I'm setting up an appointment for you at the hospital. You can have the rest of the day—"

"That won't be necessary." I wanted to massage the area of my scalp still throbbing from the stun, but Kai would've noticed. "I was up all night working and didn't get enough sleep."

To avoid suspicion, I'd set the COR alarm to vibrate. The problem was it made getting out of a vision more difficult. I tried to focus on Kai, but everything in the room was still spinning.

"If you need personal time, I can have someone else examine the data you've acquired," Kai said.

I wanted more than personal time; I wanted off the project, but I wrote the proposal that turned my ideal of a true Unity into the genocidal fantasy of a madman. One thing became clear on that day: The Overseer was no man of God, and the only Prime Wisdom he ever received was from his disturbed mind. Unity was being ruled by a psychopath. My goal of succeeding the Overseer now became a matter between life and a destruction that would be linked back to me if permitted to happen.

"I'd rather be the one to continue," I said. "Getting someone else to take over will slow our progress."

Kai smiled. "I appreciate your devotion. The Overseer will be pleased to hear you're with him."

I stood and bowed, relieved there wasn't a plazer in my desk because I would've used it.

"Starting this Firstday, I'll be away for the week. You're in charge until my return."

Kai left the office and I pondered over my vision, comparing it to the one I had of Flora. Apart from Unity Guards, no one below purple sleeve is permitted to carry a weapon inside the dome. *Did I murder Flora and then use her plazer to shoot Kai?* It seemed likely because my vision placed Flora at my loft. Getting her plazer would be easy; she kept it in the nightstand drawer. I reasoned if Flora wasn't around me, whatever circumstances led to her murder wouldn't happen. And if I stole the plazer from her, that meant I wouldn't kill Kai either. I convinced myself that my theory was sound and stopped at an essential shop on my way back home. A rose in my hand complimented my ego. Better to be the man who saved the girl than the man who gave up his ideals to get a promotion.

The aroma of Flora's tomato sauce cooking on the stove overpowered the smell of the rose I was holding. I hid it behind my back and ventured into the kitchen where she was chopping lettuce.

"I didn't expect you so early. Dinner won't be ready for another hour," she said.

I stood behind Flora and placed my free hand on her hip. "Smells great." The scent of sandalwood on her hair and touching her made me momentarily forget my conversation with Kai. Flora was opinionated, argumentative and stubborn, yet I cared for her more than any other woman I've been with. I again thought back to my discussion with Wade when he said, "Hand a girl a rose and throw her out of your life—that's all you know." I now knew more, and while I still preferred rational over emotional relationships, I found myself hesitating at what I was about to do. *Is this what it feels like to connect with someone?*

"Hard day?" Flora snapped her fingers in front of my face. "You seem preoccupied."

"Actually, I have good news." I twirled the stem of the rose between my thumb and forefinger.

"I'm listening," she said.

"You're looking at a future purple sleeve."

Flora's excited expression vanished. "Congratulations. I know how much you wanted—" She narrowed her eyes. "I smell roses."

I showed her the rose, whereupon she pushed the cutting board off the counter and stormed off.

I followed her into the bedroom. "Slow down a minute, and give me a chance to explain. After the conversation I had with Kai today, I have to make some sacrifices. As a purple sleeve, I'll be able to help keep Unitians safe."

Flora took her suitcase from the closet, staring at me as she placed it on the bed. "You'd take your own life if he so demanded." She opened the lid.

"This can be temporary. After my induction, we can be together again."

"No thanks. I'm not attracted to sleeve-worshippers."

I shut the suitcase. "I worship no one, including the Overseer."

Flora picked up the rose. "Then why this?" She tossed the rose at me, the stem grazing the side of my face. "The other women you were with may have found your departing gift sentimental, but when I look back on this day, I'll remember you as a coward." Flora grabbed some clothes from the closet, opened the suitcase and tossed them inside.

"We don't have to part this way. I still care for you." I went to touch her face, but she pushed away my hand.

"Don't you see how stored emotions arise from negative past experiences?" I asked. "They're counterproductive because they lead to hostile actions."

"Spare me the sermon. I'd rather hear one of Kai's dull stories."

I slapped Flora's face. "You'll address him only as Master Kai!"

She put her hand over her cheek. "Not me." Smiling, she said, "Kai's been after me since he appointed me Unity Guard. I could've had servants and whatever else I desired."

"You should've been honored that a Chosen considered you in that way." The rage I felt towards Kai came close to breaking through Harmony's defenses.

Flora started to cry. "You're as dead as the rest of the high colors."

"We'll continue this after Harmony calms you down."

"I never got the upgrade," Flora said. "I didn't want to turn into a heartless machine like you."

A wave of vertigo came on swiftly, almost knocking me off my feet. It was followed by a vision of Flora lying on the floor with a plazer blast to her forehead.

"Doesn't seem natural—to ignore my feelings." Flora threw more clothes into her suitcase. "I like facing everything in my life —even betrayal."

"The purpose of Harmony is to make us better than the Outsiders."

"Can you predict the future and promise Harmony won't be misused by a future Overseer?"

I looked at Flora with a combination of anger and confusion.

"Yes. It was me. I was the one who spoiled your induction ceremony." She picked up her suitcase and stormed off.

I followed her to the foyer. "Did you ever care about us, or were you sent by the Strikers to spy on me?"

Flora turned around. "I care about Unitians. They're being programmed like robots, and it scares me." She broke down and wept.

I glanced at my hologue.

"Who are you calling?" she asked.

"Reintegration is the best cure for a Striker."

"If there's a cure for wanting to be free, I don't want it."

"We *are* free—even more so now with Harmony." I took her suitcase. "The reason you can't recognize it is because your childhood emotions come out whenever you feel threatened. They get confused with present situations and that's happening to you right now. If you were receiving Harmony's signal, you'd know there's nothing to feel threatened about."

Flora placed her hands on her hips. "I don't *feel* the least bit threatened by you. You're nothing but Kai's puppet—"

I was about to strike her again, but she managed to land one against my gut first. I slammed her against the wall. A sharp pain shot through my head as I got my hands around her neck and squeezed. "How dare you raise your hand to a color higher than your own! I'll see to it personally that you're demoted to orange sleeve and that you spend the rest of your life riding laps all over Unity in a crail!"

Flora's eyes were unfocused. Worried I'd be the cause of her death, I quickly let go.

"Come on," I said, out of breath. "I'll take you to reintegration. A few treatments, and you'll be all better. And if you give me the names of whatever Strikers you know, I promise not to tell anyone that you were the one who interrupted my induction."

Her eyes widened as though she had just seen something that terrified her. "It's too late, it's too late, it's too late," she said in a rhythmic whisper.

"You say that now because you can't see beyond your fears, but there is a beyond." I clutched my forehead, still aching from the stun. "Once you let go of your inhibitions, you'll see Harmony is the only path to happi—"

"It's too late, it's too late, it's too late." She continued to repeat the phrase, her voice growing louder and more frantic with each pass.

"Take slow, deep breaths," I said.

She pushed at me and walked away, now yelling the words.

I connected to the hospital and requested emergency services. Those few seconds seemed like forever until a human voice finally greeted me.

"I need a medic team sent to—"

*Remember,* my own voice rang out loudly in my mind. A familiar terror jolted my attention back to Flora, who now stood near the balcony with her plazer aimed at her head. I ran to her, and she shot herself. She slumped to the floor and appeared exactly as she had in my vision. I never considered that Flora would take her own life.

Having foreknowledge offered no advantage, no extra insight, no added intelligence. I wept because I should've learned this after Wade jumped off the ridge. I wept because Kai was right; my ideal of saving humanity was a fantasy—as was my proposal. For that recognition I was grateful. I also wept because my impossible idealism had to be proved false by the death of a woman, whom I only now realized I loved.

I pulled Flora onto my lap and rocked her. "Why did you do this?"

With her still in my arms, I connected to Unity Forces. They arrived within ten minutes of my call. During the questioning, I did not reveal her confession about interrupting my induction. My role of sleeve-worshipper was officially over.

Flora encrypted her files, but I had no problem gaining access. My decryption program cracked her password, giving me access to all of them. The one that first caught my interest was Freedomline. Strikers had formed a network that helped dissidents leave Unity. Those who wished to flee were referred to as passengers. They were shuttled to a secret location outside the border where the conductor would guide them to the other side of the old tunnel. Freedomline hadn't been operational in four years because the conductor failed to show up for the last transport. With no one else to lead them, the frightened passengers returned to Unity and were reintegrated.

There was no other information about the Strikers. Flora rigged her hologue to delete the incriminating files after her vital signs had ceased. My retrieval program was able to save only one file. It was a list of Unitians she delivered to the access for transport out of the dome. I paused when I came to Holly 1307-242-W. This was no routine transport. Holly was a recently nominated Overmaiden. During the Overseer's marriage ceremony, she attempted to escape, but Flora apprehended her. On their way to reintegration, Strikers attacked Flora and left with Holly. Flora suffered a concussion and spent two days in the hospital. She had put her life in danger to free someone. That kind of conviction I never understood, and I hoped Flora's holojournal would help me gain some extra insight. I hesitated for a moment and then opened the file. There were many mentions of Tyrus, and the entries about me revealed Flora had doubts about us since the night we met. One phrase, in particular, lingered in my mind for the rest of the day.

*Damon is like a child. He believes the Corporate Hierarchy is in service to help Unitians. His privileged childhood made him an idealist of an impossible reality.*

Impossible reality? Is that what I believed in? Or was it an impossible idealism like Kai said? That Kai and Flora could make a similar assessment of me was disturbing because it meant there had to be some truth in what they said. The puzzling characteristic about truth is you don't always have to listen to it, but when it screams you have no choice but to hear.

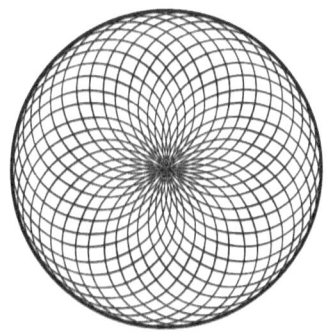

# a late night confession

The Crystal Tower Cafe was the premiere restaurant in Unity. With my impending promotion, I was allowed admittance every Sixthday, during lunch hours. Normally, I would've been eager to partake in the privilege, but I wasn't there for the relaxed environment where every dress code edict was dismissed. The purple sleeves were served by undermaidens who wore skirts so short, you could almost see the full length of their thighs. Their unbound hair fell loosely past their shoulders, and the neckline of their uniform plunged low enough to reveal the secret narrow passageway between their breasts. Should a purple sleeve become enamored by one—or more of the undermaidens, he could retire to a relaxation room for personal servicing.

An overzealous orange sleeve greeted me at the reception stand and scanned my nomination card. He led me to my table, talking about the previous week's football match between the yellows and oranges. His narrative continued as an undermaiden served me my drink. They moved on, the orange sleeve extending his discussion to the undermaiden, who escaped to serve a purple sleeve.

I was aroused by all the emancipated hair and exposed skin until the undermaiden who served me was recruited by a purple sleeve. She smiled as she walked off with him, but as they neared the relaxation room, the undermaiden nervously twirled a strand of her hair between her fingers. As they neared the door, she hesitated, trying to engage the purple sleeve in conversation. He wasn't in the mood to talk, and he pushed her inside the room. I had a strong urge to rescue her and had to remind myself no crime was being committed. Undermaidens are born to service men. That's what genetics dictate for this class. Nevertheless, biological engineering can yield unforeseen results, and I'm proof of that. The myth that supported the dome was unraveling, yet I still believed Unity was the most beautiful city in existence. I admired the skyline that reflected against the dome at night, and the golden lights that shone on Unity Hall, yet my urge to depart from them forever was strengthening. Deciding which way to turn wasn't as simple as hating the Corporate Hierarchy for their hypocrisy. This was the only life I knew, the only life I understood.

After consuming baked chicken with mashed potatoes, two slices of apple pie, a dish of bread pudding, two cups of coffee, and three glasses of wine, I'd witnessed enough to know that most of the undermaidens weren't happy with their assignment. With that acknowledgement, a visit to the relaxation room lost its appeal. I was about to leave when Tyrus showed up, attracting the usual stares over his refusal to dress to code. When he saw me, I waved him over. I apprised him of my progress with COR and filled his glass with wine. With a few more drinks in him, I was sure I could get him to talk about Flora.

After his sixth drink, Tyrus said, "I've tried to make sense of what happened, and I can't." "Flora had a strong spirit—one of the strongest in all of Unity."

"And one of the most headstrong."

"Which is why I find her death suspicious. Flora was the last Unitian I'd expect to take her life. She was a rare gem shining alone in a world of pyre."

I had read that same phrase in Flora's journal. It was in reaction to her questioning why she couldn't choose her own assignment, how she thought it wasn't fair she couldn't study astronomy. Tyrus appreciated Flora's inquisitiveness and made himself available to all her questions and doubts about Unity. Just as Master Franklin was my protector, Master Tyrus was hers.

"She told me she admired you," I said. "Your name came up in practically all our discussions."

"It's typical for a protégé to view their master as a divine authority. Most of the Corporate Hierarchy expect that kind of devotion."

"Do you?"

"I did—for a while," Tyrus poured some more wine into his glass, "but I soon grew tired. The role is impossible to live up to."

"Think I'd enjoy that kind of worship."

"Evaluate your wish with prudence because you're close to attaining it." He sipped his drink, and we drifted back to discussing COR. "The Overseer couldn't stop talking about you in his last assembly. He insisted you were nearing a breakthrough."

"It's too early for such declarations; COR is still only a hypothesis."

Tyrus seemed assuaged by my statement, so I decided to push further. "If it's authenticated, the Overseer believes we'll be able to cure fetuses of the scourge before they're transferred out of their gestation vessels."

"Would that be possible?" he asked.

"Depends on my success in locating COR."

"How far along are you?"

"Far enough to know we still have a long way to go." I laughed, recalling the last time I said that to him.

"Maybe it's for the best. I warned Kai that man isn't meant to rule over nature, but he thinks it's our destiny to do so. Do you agree?"

Tyrus's seventh glass of wine led to greater insights about Flora. Right then I knew Tyrus viewed me similarly: the inventor who cares more for his invention than the people whom he claims he wants to help. I told him, "I agree with your first impression of me."

"Why? You're serving Unity well."

I stood. "You'll change your true opinion of me very soon." Walking away, I knew what I had to do—the only thing that would make things right.

In my lab, I pretended to do some extra work on COR. With Kai's higher clearance, I could access the main database through his computer. I snuck into the office after his temporary replacement went on his lunch break and was relieved that he hadn't signed out. It's not unusual as Unitians at my level don't achieve purple sleeve unless they display complete devotion to their mentor. When I opened up my personnel file, I discovered how they made certain I was the right candidate to consider for purple sleeve.

After I'd passed out by the crail stop, I was taken to a reintegration center and placed inside a simulation. While I was walking with the Overseer, Kai stepped out of a crowd and was about to shoot him. I threw myself in front of the plazer beam's path, saving the Overseer's life. When they'd finished testing me, they put me in the hospital where I awoke with no memory of what had transpired.

I opened a file called *Harmony for All*. It was a private memo the Overseer sent to the Chosen. He approved their edict to transmit Harmony to every Unitian, without their consent.

The image of Wade lying dead at the bottom of the ridge affected me more now than when it happened. *You warned me, and I didn't listen. I hear you now, my friend—and so will the Overseer and his purple herd. They'll all pay for what they've done to you.*

I uploaded a security camera network map into my hologue and a file on the last Striker attack, complete with the schematics of the pulse bomb that failed to detonate; then proceeded to the lab where I obtained a vial of escape and three

106

syringes. Arriving at my loft, I made three darts using the needles from the syringes fusing them into cotton buds. I never would've considered that something used to clean my ears could be turned into a deadly delivery system. For that I could thank the Striker who set the pulse bomb. A box of these lethal darts was found in his loft, which he intended to use to assassinate the Overseer during his next assembly. No wonder Kai was desperate for the Overseer's speech to sway public opinion.

I tested the darts, and satisfied my scheme would work, I coated the tips with toothpaste, patting on enough escape powder to knock someone out without killing them.

My weapon was lethal, but not as practical as a plazer, which I'd need after leaving Unity. It would've been easier if I kept Flora's, but I had to turn it in to avoid further questioning.

If everything went according to plan, the escape wouldn't be as easy as being handed a plazer at out-processing and hearing a cheery access guard say, "While our border guards keep our sector safe for your enjoyment, please remain vigilant over possible contact with Outsiders. Should one approach you, immediately report to the outer-patrol station for assistance. Fire your weapon if that's your only option. Thank you for your cooperation and enjoy your vacation."

According to the security camera network map, there was a blind spot between one to three meters away from each crail stop. I headed to the service parish where there was less traffic due to the lack of essential shops and satiation centers. I scuffed the floor with the bottom of my shoe to mark the area and hid behind the corner of a building where I waited, growing more nervous with each passing moment. If I missed my target and was discovered, they'd put me through so many reintegration treatments I wouldn't be recognizable to my present self, which I no longer recognized anyway. *Who am I?* Everything that defined me had died along with Flora.

To pass the time, I read one of her stories on my holol’gue. They were written while she was still in school. I was surprised at having discovered them since Flora never told me she wrote. The story was about a space adventurer who lived on a planet ruled by women. *How very Flora,* I thought to myself. The captain—

who, of course, was female—visited Earth and plotted to liberate Unity with the aid of the Strikers. I became deeply engrossed when I got to the part where the captain, who is never named, was about to take down the Overseer with a weapon that was only lethal to those who killed innocent people. My reading was interrupted when a Unity Guard came on patrol. No one else was around, and I readied my weapon.

When the guard stepped between the markers, I blew into the straw and nailed him on the arm. He collapsed, and I ran over to check his pulse. Satisfied he'd be okay, I grabbed his plazer and left. This was the easy part. I spent the next four nights orchestrating my farewell gift to Unity.

The night before Kai was due back, I had received notice that I won the nomination to purple sleeve. All the nonsensical and misguided dreams I wished to accomplish at this level were brought to the surface. I tried to drown them in liquor and when that failed, I headed to the pleasure room where I emptied out Kai's gift card with several rounds of mystery date.

When the announcer called my name, a group of eager Unitians crowded around me.

"Please..." I pushed my palms forward to stop the crowd from gathering around me. "Save your credits. I'm not functioning at optimum tonight."

The wisest among the group announced he wasn't betting on a drunk man and headed, with a few others, to the cribbage table. For those who placed their bets on me, I kept silent and took comfort in knowing I wouldn't be the only loser tonight.

As I sat in the dark waiting for my date, I finally understood what Master Franklin told me when I wanted to tell the Chosen about my visions.

*The Sacred Oath is the enemy. Like a ghost, it can't be seen, but its presence is always felt. It rules us through our complacency and blind loyalty. People like you are a threat to its continuance. It never gives up until we surrender to it, and we always do. You must never surrender, Damon.*

I surrendered, and had only just noticed. Master Franklin's words continued to loop in my mind until the door opened.

"Have a seat," I said.

The fragrance of musk floated in with my mystery date.

"Hope you didn't bet too much tonight because I just found out I'm a loser." I rolled up my promotion notice that I'd carried around with me all day.

The cushion lowered when my date sat beside me. I wanted to tell her to leave, but I didn't want to be alone.

"A few promotions and the accolades that followed kept it hidden from me for a while." I crumpled up the notice and tossed it into the darkness. "I'm too tired to fight the truth because it's screaming loudly, and it hurts. It hurts so much I want to go deaf, but the screaming isn't coming from outside. It's inside my head." I laughed. "There's no escaping."

I felt a burning in my eyes, and my mystery date took hold of my hand. This small act of compassion surprised me.

"You're more effective than a curate." I laughed quietly. "Nothing slocking makes sense here, and we purple sleeves—I include myself because I was just nominated—make the least sense in all of Unity. Existing in our own individually created realities, we think we're smart enough, superior enough to know what's best for you and everyone else."

I placed my hand around the back of my date's head, gently pulled her towards me and whispered in her ear. "Want to hear a secret?"

She squeezed my hand tighter, and her breath quickened.

"We don't know a damned thing more than you, and we sure as hell don't know more than an Outsider." I leaned my head back against the wall and wept, knowing Flora's death led me to this enlightening moment. "We don't know anything."

My date embraced me in her arms like an Overmaiden would an infant, and she stroked my hair. We sat like this for the rest of the round, and I immediately recognized her when it was time to make my selection. She was the only one with an empathetic sadness in her eyes. I won the round, and everyone cheered, especially my date who bet half her pay on this win. She earned every credit. I hadn't felt such peace in days.

# end transmission

I lured Kai to my loft by telling him I was close to discovering COR's frequency. Less than an hour later he was on my couch. When he put his feet on the coffee table, he knocked over my violin bow and made no attempt to pick it up. I was unfazed. His brazenness would make the presentation of my gift more memorable and satisfying. By the time our meeting adjourned, Kai would know exactly what I thought about him.

"Before we get down to business, how are you feeling, *Master* Damon?" Kai grinned. "Have you prepared your induction speech yet?"

I gathered my bow and placed it on the coffee table. "Thanks to Harmony, I feel as calm as I did before Flora killed herself." I sat beside Kai, threw my feet on the coffee table, and crossed my hands behind my head. "I needed some external stimulation last night, so I went to the pleasure room and had the most arousing and healing encounter with a yellow sleeve." I smiled recounting the memory. "When we got back here *Danielle* continued her unique therapy—all night."

Kai cleared his throat. "I would also like to offer my counsel, although it won't be as unique as your friend from last night." He laughed and then cleared his throat again when I didn't laugh with him. "I, along with all the Corporate Hierarchy, acknowledge your pain. We're here to support you during the healing process. Should you need any—"

I clapped my hands. "That was one of the most pathetic performances I've ever witnessed. You would've been more believable if your eyes didn't shift slightly to the right whenever you lie."

Kai removed his feet from the coffee table. "Flora's death is obviously having an adverse effect on your emotional health. I recommend a visit to a curate for—"

"I've made some interesting observations over the last few days. Many of them brought me to realize I've wasted a lot of time doing a lot of nothing."

"The confusion you're feeling is—"

"A part of who I am," I sat up. "All my emotions define who I am. As do all my doubts and opinions." Leaning towards Kai I positioned my face in front of his. "I'm not a machine. I'm Damon." I tapped my finger on my chest. "Damon. Is that easy enough for you to understand, or should I write it down for you?"

Kai narrowed his eyes. "You don't have COR's frequency... do you?"

His question made me smile. "Even if I did, I'd never reveal it to you, *Kai*."

"Why did you call me here?"

"Did you want Flora for yourself? Is that why you wanted me to leave her?"

"Ah, I see what this is about..."

"Do you really? I find it hard to believe that you can figure out anything on your own. Every good idea you've had lately came from me."

Kai kept calm, but failed to mask the anger in his eyes. "Emotional responses are a reaction to our misinterpreting the boundaries of our relationships. Once we attach ourselves too seriously to a relationship, our judgment becomes impaired, and we display inappropriate behavior as you're doing now."

"Is there anything you haven't plagiarized? I read that in the medical encyclopedia filed under B for *brainless* disease." I picked up my violin bow. "We're in a symphony conducted by a psychopath and performed by blind idealists."

Kai's voice grew louder. "The only thing that's keeping me from demoting you to green sleeve is that you're my First. Anyone else would've been handed a reprimand followed by a visit to reintegration for speaking to me with such disrespect."

"What makes me different?" I asked sincerely. To my knowledge, no one had ever talked to Kai as I had and gotten away with it.

"I made you my First because I saw the potential for greatness in you, and I still feel the same. However, with that potential comes the risk of deluding yourself into thinking your vision of Unity is more righteous than ours. It's not. You're confusing your personal passion with what's already been proven to benefit Unity. Tyrus did the same thing, and—"

"Lost his chance to become Overseer. I get it, except I think Tyrus is better off. Ascending to a position that leads to a permanent psychosis isn't something most sane men would willingly aspire to."

"Stop creating conflict where there is none, or I'll have to—"

"Throw me out of this collective band of lunatics and sleeve-worshippers? Don't bother. As of today, this former blind loyalist can see clearly." I pointed the bow at Kai. "Tell the head psychopath he's going to have to find someone else to continue playing his discordant orchestrations because I quit."

"You're the blind one. I've seen it happen before. You've placed yourself so high above your assignment you can no longer see Unity—"

"I see clearer in this moment than I ever had in my entire life."

"What you *had* was everything. You were denied nothing …"

I stood and looked down at Kai who took a step back.

"You're correct—*Hox*." I glanced at my hologlue and set the holoscreen to public display. Live feeds of the four transmission towers appeared alongside a status bar nearing completion.

"What is that counting down to?" he asked, not masking his fear very well.

I walked over to my desk. "Life in the henhouse was amusing for a while...until a fox entered and reminded me of what I wasn't." Pulling out the stolen plazer from the drawer I aimed it at Kai.

He slowly raised both his hands. "You're experiencing a symptom of the scourge. You need to get your implant checked right now."

I laughed. "If that's true, you're in big trouble because I don't want to be cured. I'm enjoying this—*symptom*."

"Killing me will hurt us all," he said. "Violence is a virus. If it's not stopped, it would move from Unitian to Unitian until all we've worked for is left in ruins."

"If you understood what you were a part of, you'd welcome Unity's destruction." The status bar was near completion, and I counted along. "3, 2, 1..."

The four live feeds turned to snow. "As you can clearly see, where the last Striker failed, I succeeded. You'll find my data on the Progenitor have also gone extinct."

"I'll see to it that you are demoted to orange sleeve for this!"

"Where I'll spend the rest of my life crawling in the sewers." I approached Kai, glaring down at him. "Your threats don't scare me, Kai. The Overseer won't enslave the Unitians with my help."

"How dare you make this about you! You don't own this project!"

"Without me, there would be no project!"

"We'll locate it without—"

I smacked the side of Kai's head with my plazer, and he fell to the floor.

"You'll lose all you worked for." He slowly got up to his knees.

"I already have."

Kai grabbed me from behind my knees, and pulled me down. As I fell I shot him, and he collapsed onto his back. There was no need to call a medic; Kai was dead. I secured my backpack, turned around for one last glance at my home and was gone.

# PART TWO

*"To hope means to be ready at every moment for that which is not yet born, and yet not become desperate if there is no such birth in our lifetime."*
*Emily Dickinson*

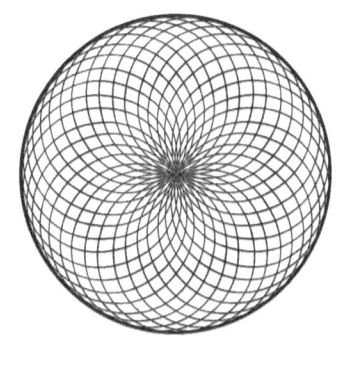

# hell and nature

No matter where you go in Unity, your location is monitored in the main security station. The Chosen guard the secret well because they're exempt from being tracked. Although I'd destroyed the towers, I moved as if I were on the run. I wanted to put as much distance between me and the menace I had let loose upon every Unitian. While I was free, Harmony would go live again after the towers had been repaired. That was my legacy, which would now be credited to Kai. He could have it because it was a legacy I didn't want attached to my name, though it would forever be linked back to the mind that invented it. I believed in the Unitian Oath. Before the Overseer desecrated my proposal with his vision of a greater Unity, I even believed he was our father who wanted Unity for all. But somewhere, underneath all these beliefs, something felt slightly off. Had I dwelled a little deeper, I would've discovered that I believed in a fantasy.

I swiftly maneuvered past the eastern side of the eroded ridge and continued my pace until I caught view of Old Woman's cabin. It appeared exactly as when I first saw it years before. Thinking she might've returned, I decided to visit. I knocked several times at the door and when no one answered, I entered. Everything inside was demolished. Electronic equipment, and all the sculptures from the shelves lay broken on the floor. I picked up the Ganesha and positioned the trunk in its proper place, just as I had done in my vision. The only thing undamaged was the picture of Old Woman and Torrin, which still hung on the wall. It was in eerie contrast with Old Woman who sat on the chair facing the window with her skeletal hand gripping the armrest. I could've sworn she was smiling up to the moment of her death. Her jaw was the only recognizable feature on her face. The rest of it had been blown off by a plazer blast. I was now responsible for three deaths.

Out of respect, I performed the sacred burning ceremony for Old Woman. Reciting the Sacred Oath, I felt a connection to the words, but not out of any residual loyalty for Unity. Old Woman was the only person who would have understood my transition, but she was dead, as was her once prized vegetable garden. Thick black smoke from the pyre spread over years of weed overgrowth, and the irrigation ditches were filled with soot and pebbles. Everything here emitted death. I had to get out of there before I allowed myself to succumb to the same fate that claimed Flora and Wade.

As I walked alone in the woods, the world seemed alien and undefined. I could no longer trust my own perceptions because everything I'd learned came from Unity. Master Franklin and Master Theodore were the only two purple sleeves I trusted, and even they didn't know much about the outside. Here, in the woods, the quieting sounds of nature soothed my aching soul. Taking it all in, I got lost in each moment gliding into the next. I let nature pull me into her realm until I couldn't differentiate myself from her. A rock was no longer just a rock, and a branch no longer just a branch. Each touch from my fingers shot a message to my brain and forced me to question my judgment of what I held in my hand. From the smallest grain of sand to the largest mountain, I joined with the output of a living Earth's evolution: breathing, shifting, changing, and rearranging into wondrous displays of sentient artwork. This was where I belonged.

My transcendental wandering was interrupted by a pack of wild dogs. As I gripped the handle of my plazer an arrow flew past me, piercing the leader of the pack. He yelped, fell to the ground, and the other dogs ran off.

A female Outsider emerged from out of a tuft of bushes with an arrow pointed at me. "Don't move, or the next one will pierce your heart."

"He's all yours," I said.

"Put down your weapon."

"Since we have nothing to argue over, why don't we both lower our arms?"

"I cannot honor your request. Your people kill everyone that doesn't live in Dome Dungeon."

"They're *not* my people."

"How come you're dressed like them?"

"It's too long a story to explain with an arrow aimed at my heart."

She pulled back the drawstring of her longbow. "It's ready to slice right through it if you give me any trouble."

"I know this may be hard for you to believe, but I trust you more than them."

"Why would you trust me? Trust comes from a shared history, and we only just met."

"Where I come from everyone acts neighborly, but that's all it is—an act. Most of my peers would've shot me in the back for a promotion if they thought they could get away with it. At least you have the honor to show me your intention."

"Got no intention here." She slowly lowered her longbow. "Your words sound sincere, but your face betrays their truth."

I holstered my plazer and offered her my hand. "I'm Damon."

"Signy." She shook my hand.

I tried to examine my first female Outsider without being too obvious. (I didn't consider Old Woman a true Outsider as she originally came from Unity.) Signy's hair was bound—but not braided, and her clothing appeared to be made from the hide of an animal. Her most shocking feature was her dark brown skin color.

"What are you going to do with the dog?" I asked.

"I'm skinning and cooking it when I get home. Come along if you like. All enemies of Dome Dungeon are welcomed in my village."

My stomach writhed at the thought of eating a dog. "Thanks for the invitation, but I'm heading off to the old tunnel."

"You won't reach it until nightfall, and you'll be greeted by more dogs—and bounty hunters. They like to hit people from where you come from. The reward would be high for your capture."

"Where's your village?"

"On the way to the tunnel." She smiled and threw the carcass over her shoulder.

The term "Outsider" took on a counter meaning after I'd visited Signy's village. The villagers dwelled in small straw huts with umbrella-shaped roofs. A man who lived with a woman and children was part of a unit known as a family. Females with unbound hair walked freely and gave birth to their own offspring. I'd heard this before from Wade. Several women, who returned to Unity following a long absence, brought back tales of females giving birth like wild dogs. They denounced their stories after reintegration, so I never took the assertion seriously.

All the villagers had different skin tones, ranging from the pale color of Unitians to Signy's dark brown. She was shocked to hear I had never met anyone with dark skin. I didn't mention Sutara because I still wasn't certain she was real.

Signy's interaction with her son, Shawn, made me sense something was missing in my own life. He entered the hut while Signy and I were peeling potatoes for dinner.

"Can I have a cookie?" he asked.

"It's almost time for supper."

"Just one, Mother...please. I promise I'll eat all my food."

"What will happen if you don't eat all your food?" I smiled at the boy.

"I won't have another cookie for the next ten days."

Signy opened a jar, and Shawn removed a cookie.

"You're as cunning as your absent father," Signy said.

"Thanks!"

Shawn ran outside, and Signy continued peeling a potato.

"What is mother and father?" I asked. "I'm unfamiliar with these words."

She stopped peeling and stared at me in disbelief. "Shawn is *born* from me, so he calls me, 'mother.' My husband—the man to whom I was married—he's Shawn's father."

"Where is he now?"

"The coughing fever eternally silenced him last year." Signy eyed me strangely. "Don't you have parents where you come from?" She noticed my confusion again. "Your mother and father are your *parents*. How were you born without them?"

"We never meet our parents; we're...*born* in incubation tanks." I laughed. "I never imagined using that word in relation to humans."

"Why not?"

"In Unity, 'born' is a term used for animals only."

We continued peeling potatoes, and I pondered over the many Unitian deceptions I'd uncovered since I left Unity. I was certain there were more, and that became apparent during dinner while observing the loving interaction between Signy and Shawn. It made me realize the full extent of what had been stolen from us and left me feeling angry—not just for myself, but for all of Unity's children.

Shawn waved a serving tray in front of me. The roasted dog looked appetizing, but my stomach strongly disagreed.

"No thanks."

"Your loss." He put down the tray and picked up a piece of meat with his hand. "My mother makes the best dog in all of our village."

"I'm sure she does." I picked up the salad bowl and spooned my third portion onto a plate. "I can't get enough of these tomatoes. Never knew they could be this sweet."

"What do they taste like in your village?" Shawn asked.

"Nothing. There's absolutely no flavor to them."

"Why do you want to cross the old tunnel?"

"To see what's on the other side, of course." I smiled and patted Shawn's head.

Signy passed me a bowl of herbed potatoes. "Now that we're acquainted, I must warn you not to go to the tunnel."

"Did any of your people ever travel across?"

"Only once. Now none of us dare to even enter."

"Why?"

"Hell lies beyond its confining walls."

I laughed, and Signy angrily walked over to the wash bin.

"Please...come back. I'm not laughing at you."

She rinsed a plate, refusing to look my way.

"I used to believe in hell, but I don't anymore," I said.

"Why not?" Shawn asked.

"The explanation sounds too crazy to be real."

Signy turned and faced me as she dried the plate. "What did you believe?"

"After death, those of us with a diseased brain emit garbled frequencies. The diseased essence can't integrate with the Prime Wisdom and is lost in an eternal nothingness. Those who ascend are joined with God for an eternity and add to the knowledge that is channeled by the Overseer."

"I'm too confused by that explanation to be scared."

"Me too," Shawn said.

"Fear has been the most effective tool used to control my people. Most Unitians never leave the dome out of fear of catching a disease that would damn them to hell."

Signy sat back down. "Sounds a little like us."

124

"Perhaps one day, you'll find the courage to explore beyond the tunnel."

"I always dreamed of exploring the world, and even flying on a giant bird through the heavens, but this is my home. I'm content here with Shawn." She smiled and lifted the plate of potatoes. "Have more. Your journey will be a long one."

Signy set up a cot for me, and I ended up staying for two days. I got to know the villagers, some of whom had lived past seventy years. Each aged face I greeted proved the scourge was a lie, which meant something else was shortening our lifespans. Every possible reason I imagined disturbed my sleep, but as I awoke to a people who appreciated everything they had, I felt uplifted and ready to continue my journey.

On the morning of my departure, Signy prepared a large breakfast for me. With my stomach filled with food, I continued my journey. On my own again, I thought about Old Woman, Wade, and Flora. Internal arguments, self-condemnations, and rants accompanied me down narrow paths and spacious fields of tall grass. Some thoughts brought me to my knees and made me want to give up, others made me want to get up and keep going. This went on until I caught a glimpse of the old tunnel. I paused to admire the mysterious structure I had fantasized about since childhood. And like a child I laughed as I ran to the opening.

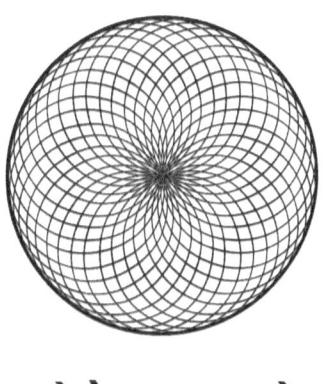

# old tunnel

Beyond the archway of the old tunnel the light had slowly faded. My lantern was the only thing that kept me from disappearing within a seemingly infinite blackness. Signy had told me it would take ten to twelve hours to cross to the other side of the old tunnel. With my lantern fully charged and a spare battery in my pack, I wasn't concerned about being left in the dark.

I had read an entry about the tunnel in Old Woman's hololgue before I surrendered it to Unity Forces. The structure was near collapse shortly before the Great Cataclysm, and an indestructible synthetic material was developed to reinforce the frame. I thought it was hyperbole until I glided my hands over the smooth surface. The light from my lantern revealed neither a scratch nor a chip, and I realized how far we'd regressed technologically.

Approximately two hours into my trek I met a Unitian couple going in the opposite direction. The female was pregnant.

"Where are you headed?" I asked.

"Back to our village," the woman replied.

"Near the valley or sea?"

The woman eyed her male companion who shined his lantern in my face.

"All the way up north—beyond both mountains," he said. "When did you leave Unity?"

"Three weeks ago. I'm heading to New Athenia. Have you been there?"

"We just came from there. My wife wanted to visit before giving birth."

"How much further do I have until the exit-way?"

"About another seven hours. If you want to stop for a rest, there are some trainlets about halfway in. They used to carry the Ancients from one side of the tunnel to the other. There are many of them in here, but only the first one you'll come across is safe. If you stay, make sure to leave some form of payment for the careman." He removed a map from his pocket and handed it to me.

"Already have a map," I said.

"With the trade routes?"

I examined his map. "Anything else I should be aware of?"

"Only that you made the right decision to leave. There's a lot to see on the other side. Safe journey."

I made it to the trainlets three hours later and found one that was vacant. The only thing I could afford to part with was my multipurpose knife. I opened the payment box and a lame man with tangled hair, unsuccessfully held in place by a bandana, hobbled over. He tapped his cane on the ground in several short bursts.

"Hello, Hello, Hello there, Chap." The tone of his greeting sounded as though he knew me. "Name's Sephroy. I'm the careman of these 'lets."

"Damon." I shook his hand, hoping he wasn't the carrier of a fatal disease.

"Damon, Damon, Damon. Interesting name, Damon." He stretched his head towards me, squinted his eyes and then widened them. "Suits you, Chap." He snickered and positioned his cane in front of him for support. "Back's been acting up more so than usual today. I'll let you stay free of charge if you clean up my 'lets."

I accepted Sephroy's offer, relieved I wouldn't have to part with my knife. He motioned to a nearby cart with his cane. "All the cleaning supplies are in there. All the waste goes into the vat behind the last 'let."

As I entered the first trainlet, every joint in my body locked. Behind several rows of seats two long benches faced each other. Overhead, a line of handles dangled from the ceiling. This was the room from my vision of Torrin and Old Woman. After my shock had dissipated, I carried the waste bucket outside. As I opened the lid to empty the contents into the vat, the stench made me reconsider my deal with Sephroy. I ran to his cabin to relinquish my knife.

"I was counting on your help today." Sephroy grabbed his lower back. "Don't know what your word is worth in that dome dungeon of yours, but out here, it's all we got."

I handed Sephroy my knife. He looked at it and then at me. "You've forgotten the meaning of honor." He reached to take the knife, but I placed it back in my pocket.

I resumed the cleaning, which wasn't anything more than throwing away rubbish, replacing the two supplied sleeping bags, and pulling up the shade to let travelers know the trainlet was vacant. The worst of it was the waste buckets. I gagged several times before my nose got used to the stench. The vat where I dumped the waste was filled with compost, which didn't help mask the odor. A network of helpers showed up in intervals to remove the waste, in exchange for tradable items that Sephroy acquired through payment or from procurements made outside the tunnel.

After I'd finished cleaning, Sephroy invited me to his trainlet for a meal and some advice on how to successfully live on the outside, which I needed. I still had no idea how I was going to earn a living. So far, most of the skills out here seemed more suited for orange sleeves.

"How did you know where I came from?" I asked, talking to avoid eating whatever was on the plate in front of me.

Sephroy reached across the table and clasped my hand. "You have the hands of a girl. Only men from the dome have hands like a girl." He laughed.

I stared at my plate, trying to think of an excuse to get out of there.

"Dog." Sephroy shoved a piece of meat into his mouth. "Too many of those four-legged demons running around." He chewed with his mouth open. "I never can seem to kill enough of them." He waved his fork at my plate. "Are you going to eat that or make it your pet?" He laughed again.

As I examined the contents of my plate, I couldn't get my mind off my last visit to the waste vat. The smell still lingered in my nostrils.

Sephroy was grinning as he picked up the cooked dog from my plate. "The squeamish type, aye Chap?" He took another bite. "Better learn to take what you can get if you want to survive out here. If that truth is too harsh for your pretty hands to hold on to, you might as well go home and paint your fingernails like the ladies from your dome do." He laughed and then swallowed more food.

I snatched a piece of meat from the serving tray and took a bite. My gag reflex immediately went into effect and I ran outside to vomit. Phantom smells of human waste, cooked dog, and vomit followed me to my trainlet. Once inside, the lantern light and drawn shades isolated me in my own world and inspired me to play a soft melody on my violin. With my senses drained of the offending smells and flavors, I fell asleep still holding my violin.

The first hint of light that beamed into the tunnel made me quicken my pace. I emerged from the darkness, and the fresh salt air washed away the revolting odors from the previous night. I gazed up at the clear blue sky. *I'm here. I'm really here.* I bolted toward a cluster of seagulls, laughing and screaming like a child once again. I cooled off in the water, then walked along the beach, heading east. After ten kilometers, I spotted a small village with stone bungalows built in a circle formation. The village was long abandoned, but beyond the dilapidated gate was a functioning well. I searched through the bungalows looking for items to trade but found nothing of value. I filled my canteen and continued my walk, along the way meeting different tribes that spoke in their own dialects. I managed to earn tradable goods and meals by plowing fields, cleaning stables, and doing any menial task I could find. On the outside, there was no color to ascend to. Everyone did everything. It was a humbling experience.

I took hundreds of pictures and traveled many days, but refused to keep track of how many during this incarnation. Not following a schedule was liberating.

I passed through many parishes and cities, exploring ruins from the forgotten times. Fractured buildings and crumbling walls filled a landscape of overgrown weeds and cracked cement, reminiscent of my visions during my coma. Ancient roads still in existence were filled with vehicles that didn't require tracks. These haunting locations of the forgotten times told the desperate tale of civilization coming to an abrupt halt as people went about their daily activities. Time's passage turned their remains to dust, but each vehicle told its own unique story. The ghosts within these rusted metallic shrines shared the same ending. It disturbed me to think about what went on in the minds of the population in their final moments, but witnessing the truth freed me from the Unitian lies.

Each day passed into the next, and I had no idea when I'd arrive until I saw New Athenia in the far distance, recognizable by the Ancients' marble palace on top of the Acropolis. At the sight of the large edifice beneath it I fell to my knees. It was the seven-circuit labyrinth I'd envisioned while in a coma.

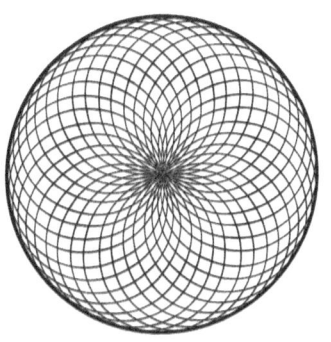

# new athenia

    Small villages lined the outskirts of New Athenia, and new neighborhoods were still being constructed. Nevertheless, most immigrants first tried to gain residence within the labyrinth. According to historical record, an eccentric Ancient, Callias Zane, built the impressive structure shortly before the final war of the forgotten times. The enemy was formidable and came from a planet of demons that were a cross between feline and human. God freed Callias, who had been held captive in a dark dungeon. He instructed Callias to collect all of humankind's knowledge and then journey to New Athenia with his family. At the foot of the Acropolis, he was to spill a bottle of God's blood onto this sacred ground and wait for a miracle to happen. Callias did as instructed, and New Athenia miraculously arose from the puddle of blood. When the felineoid demons arrived for their final assault, God transmitted his golden shield from the heavens, and New Athenia was saved. I don't believe the historical record, but it doesn't make the story any less fascinating to hear, especially when it's acted out on Foundation Day.

The labyrinth is twelve kilometers in diameter with four well-guarded entranceways. The material used in its construction makes it sparkle like an opal on a sunny day. I ran my hand across the surface; it was so smooth, it felt almost as though I was touching air. Like the tunnel, the material was indestructible. Many first-time travelers to the city conduct their own experiments, either out of disbelief or to keep up with the New Athenian tradition of testing the claim out for themselves. Not long before my arrival, a man started a fire near the south gate. All it managed to do was scare a few people who were waiting to enter the city. The Athenian authorities didn't appreciate his curious behavior and denied him entry.

To be allowed inside the city, I had to relinquish my plazer, but I was free to reclaim it upon leaving. Two guards escorted me to a room where they found a translator who spoke my language. I was granted a visitation pass for three days after answering some questions about where I was from and what brought me to New Athenia.

When I first entered the gate, I felt as though I could experience the whole world within New Athenia's borders. The people who lived and visited here were of different races, some of which I had never seen before. Their skin color was a mix of various shades of brown, tan, gold, and red—even their eyes varied in shape.

Athenians live within the wall of the labyrinth and speak Knosian, a robust language invented by Callias Zane. He wanted a neutral language to unite the myriad cultures that came here. A rooftop multi-passenger crailway system circumnavigates the city. Gardens and parks decorate the winding paths that lead to restaurants and cafes on the western side of the labyrinth. In the center sits the Alexandrian Repository that houses the history and art of the Ancients. It was modeled after a library that originated in an Ancient land called Egypt. The colonnade in front of the entrance serves as a stage for weekly concerts and plays. A large amphitheater arcs around the repository and is typically filled for every performance. On the top floor is an observatory that's open to the public on weekends.

On my first night, I made the ascent to the Acropolis and marveled at the Parthenon, a temple built to honor the gods of the Ancient Greeks. As I hadn't yet learned Knosian, I observed and listened to the rhythm and cadence of New Athenian life. By my third night, I decided to stay longer and applied for a residence pass. I had to offer a service with a vacancy as there was only a limited number of passes available. Wanting nothing more to do with psychological engineering, I tried out for the New Athenian Orchestra.

I auditioned for Maestro Manolis, a flamboyant man who used dramatic hand gestures while he spoke. I had to take a step back a few times when his fingertips got a little too close to my eyes. The maestro was indifferent to me until I played him one of my favorite original pieces of music. It so impressed him that he sat at the piano and accompanied me as though we had played together before.

Maestro Manolis awarded me a chair in his orchestra and assigned me to work in the music library, which was located within the Alexandrian Repository. I spent most of my free time downloading Ancient music and books into my holologue. I passed many hours listening to the symphonic music of the Ancients and I connected to Wolfgang Amadeus Mozart. Like him, I played the violin and was considered a prodigy in my youth. Listening to one of his sonatas, I understood why Manolis played so well with me. My original composition sounded almost exactly like the first movement of Mozart's *Violin Sonata No. 22 in A Major*. Was any of the music I wrote my own? I had no way of knowing for sure. If COR allowed me to see into the future, did it also allow me to peek into the past? Everything I'd accomplished in my life would have to be questioned. I could never again assume my work was authentic. I could never again assume anything.

I played my first performance twelve weeks following my arrival, and Manolis personally sponsored me for a residence pass. I enjoyed all the benefits of an Athenian, and I had the option of becoming a citizen. Having been a Unitian for so long, I was reluctant to commit to another oath. New Athenia was impressive, but it was still structured, with its own set of rules and regulations. I had one year to decide whether to stay on. If I opted out, I'd have to relinquish my residence pass since space was limited in the city. When the deadline neared, I wanted to explore the Ancient territories further east, so I chose to go.

Shortly before my departure, I encountered Holly at a crail shop. She walked over and sat down next to me. Her curly red hair, milky skin, and freckles made her stand out in Unity and also here in New Athenia. Recognizing me, she got up to leave.

"You can reconnect your body to the bench now. I'm no longer a Unitian."

She sat back down. "I know you." She pointed at me. "You're Damon, Flora's friend."

"She talked about me?"

"All the slocking time." She rolled her eyes.

"Hope she didn't reveal any of my less-flattering qualities."

"Several, but I forgot most of them."

I raised one of my brows. "What brought you to New Athenia?"

"A new life."

"This is the place to find one. When did you arrive?"

"Been here four weeks." She smiled. "I don't like staying in one place for too long."

"Unity will do that to you," I said.

"Boredom and me don't mix well either."

"I'm playing my final performance tonight with the New Athenian Orchestra. Come as my guest, and I promise you won't be bored."

"My ex-boyfriend told me the same thing when he took me to see them. I fell asleep."

"Are you sure he wasn't the one who put you to sleep?"

"Maybe." Holly smiled. "I'll have to go tonight to be sure. If I doze off, I'll have my answer."

"If you manage to stay awake, the Maestro is throwing me a going-away party afterwards. You can come to that as well, but I can't guarantee you won't fall asleep there. He isn't famous for his parties."

"Why are you leaving?"

"Boredom."

We both laughed, and Holly took a crail with me to the amphitheater. When we got out, I clasped her hand and we ran inside.

"What's the hurry?" Holly asked.

"I'm a little late."

"Not because of me, I hope."

"It is, but don't worry. The Maestro and I are like brothers."

I led Holly to a seat in the first row. "I feel privileged."

"If you don't mind, choose a different word."

She smiled. "Unlearning old habits is difficult."

"I haven't unlearned mine yet either."

I headed over to the stage. Manolis was agitated at my showing up only moments before they were to begin. "Just because this is your last day doesn't give you the right to demonstrate such unprofessionalism."

"I'm going to miss you." I embraced Manolis and he patted my back.

"Me too." He pushed me away. "Now get to your chair before I throw it at you."

He thrust his hand at me, and I jumped back almost falling onto the lap of a flute player. A couple of my friends were snickering as I sat down. I shot them a friendly little Athenian gesture with my middle finger and quickly rosined my bow. Manolis crossed his arms, waiting for me to finish.

I played my best that night. Maybe because it was my last performance, or because Holly was watching. It was probably a little of both. Manolis and I ended the night with Mozart's *Violin Sonata No. 22*.

The ballroom was filled with friends and fans waiting to say goodbye to me. As I was talking to three female admirers,

Manolis arrived with two glasses filled with champagne. He handed one to me, and we shared a toast.

"I'll miss our duets. Very few people can keep up with me," I said.

"Yes, it's hard to keep up with your self-glorification." He sipped his champagne, and the three women giggled. Manolis raised his glass to them. "Damon seems to think he's the Maestro."

"There's only one Maestro, and you're looking at him right here, ladies." I raised my glass to Manolis as Holly entered the ballroom.

"Are you sure you won't reconsider?" Manolis eyed Holly and then me.

"I'm never sure about anything anymore." I excused myself and walked over to her.

Holly and I talked all night, and I stayed for an extra day to hear about how, with Flora's help, she escaped Unity. She couldn't tell me the identity of the Striker who led her out of Unity because she had also been knocked unconscious. Once they were out of the city, the Striker wore a mask to not compromise his or her identity.

Holly talked about her travels to the Ancient cities of Rome and Cairo, and I filled her in about Flora. Being with Holly made me feel less lonely. I stayed another week, which turned into still another week, and I finally ended up accepting citizenship so that I could live with her. We soon got married and things were never boring again. In less than a year, Holly became pregnant with twins. The news came as a great surprise to us both, and reawakened my anger over how the women in Unity were deprived of motherhood. The towers transmit a special frequency to the implant that prevents conception. In the early spring the transmission is halted, so that females can conceive. When pregnant women start experiencing symptoms, they believe they're suffering from female blight and obediently report to the hospital to be cured. The fertilized eggs are removed from their wombs and placed into gestation vessels. After ten weeks, the fetuses are moved to the standard incubation tanks.

I've studied many cultures throughout history and never before has such cruelty been demonstrated against a people. The founding Corporate Hierarchy demanded they be the only ones looked upon for guidance. Along with their quest for dominance, to achieve their selfish ends, they obliterated the natural development of families. Eventually, everyone forgot the truth, including those who distorted it.

This discovery reignited my anger towards the Corporate Hierarchy. Many women I had been with came down with the female blight, including Flora. A short relapse into drinking forced me to admit I was mostly angry at myself because I had believed the lies. I decided to focus on what I had rather than what I'd lost. The birth of my boys melted away my fury, replacing it with fatherly pride. As the twins grew older, I spent most of my days teaching them math and science. I taught Aaron how to play the violin. My other son, James, preferred sports. Aaron became an astronomer and James a playwright. Holly died shortly after my seventy-fifth birthday, and I played in the orchestra for another five years before retiring.

Several days after my final performance with the orchestra, I took my granddaughter to the duck pond in the central park. There was something relaxing and contemplative about the ducks. It took so little to satisfy them. All I had to do to make their day was toss them a few bread crumbs.

Our visit was cut short when I felt a sharp pain in my chest. I didn't want to panic my granddaughter, so I told her I needed to go home and rest. While waiting for a crail, I fainted and woke up later on a hospital bed. Aaron told me I'd had a heart attack. Being confined to a bed made me restless, and I took out my frustrations on the nurses. They started arguing over who would come to me when I called.

I kept busy by looking at pictures and movies from New Athenia and Unity. I stopped to admire a picture I took of Flora while she was in the middle of braiding her wet hair. It was one of my happiest memories from Unity, and remembering Flora made my heart ache, more from losing her than from my illness.

I reflected on her image for two days and then erased it. That was the only way for me to let her go. I felt guilty for missing another woman besides Holly, who saved me from my loneliness, gave me my two sons, and made my life complete. I found an image of her holding our boys and smiled over the memory of that day.

A nurse with large dark eyes entered my room.

I sat up and told her, "I want to leave. They can't make me stay here any longer."

The nurse sat down next to me. "You'll be leaving soon." She touched my forearm. "Be patient."

I lay back down. "I have nowhere else to go. I'm all alone now."

"Obviously you're not alone because I'm here."

"I don't know you."

She looked at me crossly. "You do, but you always choose to forget."

"Sutara!"

She smiled. "Six begin, Six alone, Six unite."

"Two of us now remember. You came to me when I was a boy. You saved me."

"I didn't save you."

"You were there. I saw you. Can you wake me up again?"

"I cannot."

"Why not?"

"Remember. You have to be the one to remember."

"Why won't you tell me?"

"You don't want to know. That's why you can't remember."

My eyes widened. "I see now. I must stop myself."

"Will you?"

"Yes."

"Do you promise to remember?"

"I promise."

Sutara cried and hugged me. "For the first time, I believe you."

I opened my eyes and found myself in the cabin with the Ganesha figurine in my hand. "Ganesha, keeper of past, present and future, I promise not to run away next time. I promise to

make things right." And those were the final words I spoke at the
end of my first incarnation.

# beyond capture

## Second Incarnation

The COR alarm rang as I stared down at Wade's lifeless body. In my last incarnation my intuition had told me to run, but I successfully cajoled myself into believing I could help build the Unitian ideal. In this incarnation, I listened to my intuition. I still can't explain why I chose to act on it since I wasn't yet aware I'd done this all before.

I set up camp within the cover of the forest while Unity Forces stormed through Old Woman's cabin. The next morning, I returned to scavenge for supplies and found the interior in the exact state of disarray as in my previous incarnation, except Old Woman had just been killed. Shisa made an appearance while I was performing the sacred burning ceremony. She spotted me and growled. Recalling her obedient behavior with Old Woman, I kept very still and tried to mimic the tone of her voice. "Good girl. I'm not going to hurt you."

Shisa's snarling intensified and I thought she was about to attack. Then her attention shifted to the blaze and I slowly backed away. She circled the flames whimpering, and I ran inside the cabin to get my plazer. Shisa charged at me when I came out, and I shot her. She made the most disturbing sound before falling to the ground. Her breathing was shallow and labored, but it was the sadness in her eyes that compelled me to get my med kit. I tore one of my shirts to tie her mouth shut. "It's okay, girl. This is so you won't bite me." I poured some alcohol onto a gauze. "This is going to hurt, but it'll make you all better."

Shisa raised her head slightly, whimpered, and then lowered it again. I took that as her granting me permission to continue, and I gently pressed the gauze onto her wound. She yelped, and I stroked the top of her head. "It's all over now. Good girl." I dressed her wound and as I finished, I petted her cheek. The act felt natural, which surprised me. I hadn't known dogs could be domesticated.

She looked at me as though she understood I wanted to help. I slowly unraveled the muzzle and she licked my hand. I carried her inside, laid her on the couch, and gave her some water and nourishment. Then I tidied up the cabin. Over the next two weeks, I absorbed the silent calm of nature and reawakened my passion for adventure. An entry about New Athenia in Old Woman's holologue made me eager to go exploring.

When Shisa was fully healed, we left for the old tunnel. As dusk neared, I set up camp near the river and headed out to fish. It took me an hour to hook my first one, but Shisa had no problem catching her dinner. She dropped a trout in front of me and barked at it thrashing around on the dirt.

"Are you trying to make me look incompetent?"

Shisa ran back into the water, and two catches later my question was answered.

As I roasted one of the fish on the fire, she walked over and sat beside me, patiently waiting for her dinner.

"You're smarter than the Corporate Hierarchy." I petted her. "While you're free to roam this beautiful forest, they're locked inside a dome, following a deranged old man who claims God is talking to him. Who believes such crazy things?"

I waved Shisa's dinner in front of her. She wasted no time appreciating the honor of being first served and chomped down on the fish.

"The truth is, I believed—for a while." I jabbed a fish with a skewer and positioned it near the flames. "I stopped believing in the Sacred Oath a long time ago, but I still wanted to be accepted by the purple sleeves and Overseer. Eventually, I got what I wanted, but the price I had to—" I stopped to smile as Shisa lifted her head and licked her lips. "You handle tragedy a lot better than me. Think I'll follow your example; it's undignified for a psychological engineer to complain." I kept my word and slept calmly that night.

The COR alarm sounded when I spotted the trainlets. Sephroy approached me pushing a cleaning cart.

"Hello, Hello, Hello, there, Chap. Name's Sephroy. I'm the careman of these 'lets. Looking for a stay?"

"Could use a rest." I shut off the alarm.

"Third one from the back is free. If you got nothing for trade, you can help me out and rest later. I could use a break." He rubbed his lower back.

I pulled out a pen given to me by Kai at the start of my assignment. As Sephroy inspected it, I examined his wrinkled face hoping to trigger a vision.

"Got no one to write to."

"It's gold."

"So."

"Real gold."

"Can't buy or trade anything with a pen, even a gold one."

"You can melt it down—"

He handed it back to me.

I took off my backpack and opened the flap.

"I'll take that." Sephroy swiped my utility knife from my belt clip. "Could use one of these."

"That's my only knife." I snatched it back.

Sephroy crossed his arms. "You'll have to clean out the 'lets if you want to stay."

I rummaged through my pack and pulled out a tin cup and dish. "How about these?"

He took them from me and tapped the cup with his finger. "Payment accepted." Sephroy walked me to my trainlet and thumped his knuckles on a slotted box attached to the door. "If you're staying tomorrow night and I'm not around, drop your payment in here." He looked at Shisa. "You can give me your dog. That'll cover you for three days."

"Shisa is not for sale."

"If you change your mind, I'll be in my 'let." Sephroy unlocked the padlock on the door. "Pull down the shades when you get inside—that'll remind me this one's taken." He tapped his head. "Memory's not as crisp as it used to be." He pulled out a folded sheet from his pocket. "Got maps for sale, if you're interested."

"I have my own."

"Well, well, well. A prepared dome dweller. May be hope for your kind after all."

"How can you tell where I come from?"

"The confused look on your face," He said laughing. "All of you look that way when you first get out." He grabbed my hand. "And you got the hands of a girl."

I pulled my hands away and had the strongest feeling I'd had this conversation before.

Sephroy squinted at me. "I was only pulling your chain, Chap."

I stared down at my hands and then at Sephroy.

"With some time out here, they'll both be broken in." He extended his wrinkled hands and wiggled his fingers. "Sooner than never, they'll be looking a lot like these little workers." Snickering, he walked away.

I entered my trainlet and Shisa hopped in behind me. Once I'd gotten settled, I read through Wade's hologlogue looking for anything that would explain his state of mind. Only one entry stood out. It was dated almost four weeks before we left for our hike. Wade test-ran a new reintegration simulation, and began to experience side effects he couldn't explain. Images of Nasia's request for death began to haunt his dreams, and after three sleepless nights, he went through another session to see if he could discover what triggered it. Finding no answers, he fell into a depression and contemplated filling out his own request for death. The rates of requests for death didn't drop when Kai replaced Tyrus as Speaker of The Chosen. One of my patients posted her request on the city screens and Wade announced, "Either the Corporate Hierarchy altered reintegration technology, or you're not a very good psychological engineer."

"Or maybe both," I joked, but wasn't laughing.

I recalled the signal emitter that Kai showed me. The Strikers used it to induce hallucinations, but if the Corporate Hierarchy somehow managed to modify reintegration using the same technology, it could be used to induce dreams. If Wade was the victim of such technology, it would explain his volatile behavior. I had no way to prove my theory, and even if I could, I was still partially responsible for his death. While my hands didn't push Wade over the precipice, my words and actions failed to keep him anchored to the ground.

I was roused from sleep by a rapping at the door. Picking up my lantern, I shined it on Shisa. She was still asleep on the floor. I slid open the door and was met by Sutara, who appeared terrified.

"You must go back to the cabin now," she said.

"And do what?"

"If I tell you, it begins all over again. I'm getting tired." She cried. "I don't want to do this anymore."

"I'll go, after I see New Athenia."

"Stop wasting time! You've already seen it before!"

"When? I never even set foot in the old tunnel."

She stomped her foot on the ground and threw her hands in the air. "You're so infuriating!" She ran away.

I chased after her, but she disappeared into the blackness of the tunnel. Shisa's barking woke me up. I had run about a kilometer while asleep.

"Thanks." I leaned down to pet Shisa. "I might have run all the way to the other side of the tunnel if you didn't wake me."

We met up with Sephroy on the way back to the trainlets. He tapped his cane on the ground in three short bursts as he said, "Easy, easy, easy, Chap. The way you were running—thought a fire broke out in your 'let."

"I was out for a walk."

"Looked more like a run." He turned his lantern light on Shisa. "Change your mind about the dog?"

"How many times do I have to tell you she's *not* for sale!" I walked away, annoyed and shaken. A starlit sky always comforted me, so I left the old tunnel and set up camp on the beach. I fell asleep under a clear and spacious sky and dreamed about a beautiful woman with raven hair who accurately verbalized my mood for the evening.

"I picture myself as one of the stars, distant, unnoticed, and beyond capture."

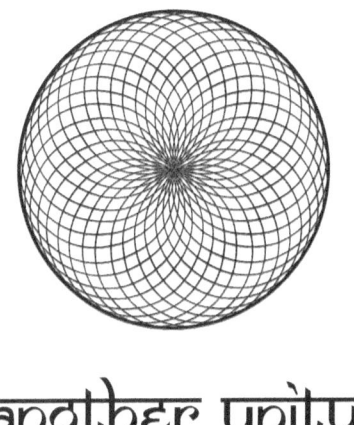

# another unity

New Athenia was in the middle of a summer festival that began on Foundation Day. For thirty days, the repository was the polestar of music, art, and theatre. Concerts and plays took place almost daily, and the downtown arena sponsored weekly sporting events.

I had to learn a new piece of music for a performance, but too much was going on for me to remain inside. Wandering the crowded streets, I listened to music, admired artwork, and watched dancers, mimes, and actors performing in the central park. When the concert was two days away, I locked myself in my flat to practice. After I'd learned the music, I rejoined the festivities and ended up at my favorite cafe where I drank wine and watched pedestrians pass by. While listening to some patrons discuss the latest play at the amphitheater, a familiar voice called out my name.

I looked up at the last person I'd expected to run into outside of Unity. "Lidian?" I stood and shook his hand. "When did you arrive?"

"Two d-d-days ago. And you?"

"I've been here for almost one year."

"Why did you l-l-leave?"

"Too many reasons to state over dinner." I extended my hand to a vacant chair.

"Thought you'd never ask." Lidian sat. "I ha-haven't eaten all day."

"What brings you to New Athenia?"

He surveyed the diners in the restaurant as though he didn't want anyone to hear him. "Master Tyrus di-did something awful, and I got blamed."

"Doesn't sound like the Tyrus I remember."

Sweat was starting to form on Lidian's face. "He's very good at hiding wh-who he, wh-who he is." Lidian spoke softly. "He ki-ki-killed a crailer, and ne-next morning it was m-m-my face on all the city screens instead of his. I thought about turning myself in, but they never would've believed me. The Corporate Hierarchy ne-never turn against each together."

"How do you know it was him?"

"I was with him the night the girl disappeared. He took me to a satiation center to celebrate my in-in-du-ction to maroon sleeve. After we h-had enough to drink, we decided to hire a couple of crailers for the evening. A four-seater pulled up with two women, and we left with them. Master Tyrus got off with his date—two stops be-before I got off with mine." Lidian reached for a napkin and blotted the sweat off his face. "Th-they found the woman, wi-with her throat slashed, ho-holding the medal of merit Tyrus gave me fo-following my induction. I still don't know how he managed to steal it wi-without me noticing."

I thought it was peculiar how Lidian had stopped using Tyrus's formal title, but I had done the same thing with Kai. And with no memory of what he did to Flora, I didn't suspect anything unusual. Lidian always stuttered when he was nervous.

A server came by and Lidian asked for berry ale.

"They don't have that here," I said.

The server gave Lidian a menu and left.

"Berry ale is the only thing about Unity I miss—along with mystery date." I lifted my carafe and poured some wine into Lidian's glass. "How did you hear about this place?"

"A weird Outsider in the old tunnel s-sold me a map." Picking up the napkin, he wiped his face again.

"Are you thinking of staying?"

"What kind of work is available here?" he asked.

"I'm with the Orchestra. Do you still play?"

"Brought my trumpet with me."

"I can set up an audition, if you like."

"I still have to learn Knosian. I can't become a resident until I pass the written exam."

"I got in without speaking a word of it. I'll see what I can do for you."

"I'd appreciate that. Got nowhere else to go."

I ended up sponsoring Lidian so that he could remain until his audition, and I helped familiarize him with the orchestra's repertoire. He had some trouble mastering the baroque pieces and I didn't think he'd pass his audition. I recommended he use his musical skills to instruct children and got him a job at the conservatory.

Lidian and I regularly visited the Rock Room, a bar that played loud Ancient music called rock-n-roll. Manolis hated it, saying it probably brought on the Great Cataclysm. I enjoyed the loud and raunchy style enough to buy my own electric guitar, which was the main instrument of that genre. Impromptu night was the best time to visit the Rock Room. Every musician had a chance to go on stage and show off. I'd usually perform something from my favorite Ancient rock band, Tearing Nations.

After I'd finished playing a set, I returned to the bar and found Lidian standing beside two women. He came over and whispered in my ear, "The blonde woman said she wa-wa-wants to go home with me. Wha-what should I do?"

I inspected the woman. "Have fun."

"I wa-want to, bu-but, I'm not a good talker like you."

"Don't try so hard, and you'll be fine."

He nodded his head and returned to his date.

I ended up talking with the blonde's friend. Dina was an artist and had an exhibit at the repository. We discussed her work and I took her to my flat to get a critique of a few of my own paintings. I had started taking art classes, and I wanted some constructive advice. Dina fixated on a portrait of the woman with auburn hair, whom I dreamed about the night I slept on the beach.

"What do you think?" I asked.

"You paint like a man with abundant passion."

Her critique led us to the bedroom where I freely expressed more of my abundant passion. Dina and I fell asleep in each other's arms, and the rest of the night would've been peaceful had it not been for the pounding fists on my door. As I opened it, a police-guard pushed himself in, shoved me against the wall and restrained my hands behind my back.

"Damon 1300-333-1M, you're under arrest for murder." I hated hearing my Unitian identification number, but I had to use it on my entrance form since I had no formal surname.

"This is a mistake. I didn't murder any—"

"You'll remain silent until you have legal representation."

Dina entered the foyer, half asleep. "What's going on?" She yawned.

Security took Dina and me to headquarters. After a few hours of questioning, they realized I was innocent. Luckily, Dina had been with me all night, or I would've been charged with murder. The victim was Lidian's date. I reported him as the last person to be seen with her. He was arrested, and the presiding judge revoked my residence pass because I was his sponsor. Manolis told me I could appeal, but I'd reached my threshold of inequity. The similarities between New Athenia and Unity were greater than the differences. Everything seemed to be about conforming to prejudicial laws. It seemed that the only way I could truly live free was in isolation, so I decided to go back to the cabin.

The murder troubled me during my journey west. Unfortunately for the victim, I had failed to detect Lidian's mental instability. My psychological engineering skills were proving to be inadequate outside the dome. I doubted whether they were any more effective within.

Arriving at the cabin, I was relieved to find it uninhabited, although I wasn't surprised. An entry in Old Woman's journal revealed that Torrin chose this portion of the valley to build his cabin because of its desolation. Most Outsiders relied on being in close proximity to each other for trade relationships. Torrin had to hike long distances to procure the items Strikers couldn't get to him. After he'd died, Old Woman preferred to make do with less.

I cleared away the cobwebs, and restarted the solar trap. It was sunny outside and I didn't have to wait long for power. Tending to the garden took longer. I had to pull out the weed growth and dig out the irrigation ditches that were almost completely refilled with dirt. I brought back some seeds to plant new crops, including barley, which I had come to appreciate in New Athenia. I settled into my hermetic life and started taking long walks with Shisa, to familiarize myself with the neighboring paths, and introduce myself to the local Outsiders. I traded my own crops for apples, pumpkins, and pears.

Before the snows came, a Striker named Roth found me fishing by the river bank. In exchange for supplies, he asked for my help leading Unitians across the old tunnel. Still remorseful over Harmony, I thought it was an effective way to absolve my conscience. Every four weeks, on Fifthday, I'd meet up with Roth who had Unitians for me to transport through the old tunnel. He'd also bring me a fresh pack of supplies for the cabin. The most unexpected transport was Tyrus. It took him a few moments to identify me and then another few moments to get over the shock.

"I almost didn't recognize you with all that hair on your face and head," he said. "You look like a cross between a wolf and a bear."

"No one to impress out here but wolves and bears."

"And an old Unitian purple sleeve who's too tired to laugh—but I'm near hysterics on the inside." Tyrus marched ahead.

Rubbing my beard, I followed him. "Think the women back in Unity would be horrified or impressed by my new look?"

"They'd probably prefer you over most Unitian men."

"Why did you leave?" I asked.

Tyrus didn't respond and was silent during most of our walk back to the cabin. I no longer believed Lidian's story, but I kept my hand on my plazer.

"My conscience wore me down," Tyrus finally said as we started our descent towards the middle ridge. "I was too exhausted to fight it any longer."

"Would you like to stop and rest?"

"I would like to forget."

Tyrus continued walking, and when we got to the ridge overlooking my cabin, he stopped and seemed confused. "I haven't been well lately." He rubbed his forehead.

"Are you sure you don't want to stop and—"

"I'll be okay." He continued ahead.

Inside the cabin, Tyrus set down his backpack and was immediately drawn to the panoramic window as were most Unitians who'd visited.

"We'll leave first thing in the morning," I said.

"No rush. I'm interested to hear about your travels."

"Haven't traveled much lately."

"Oh? Why is that?"

"Unity exists everywhere. This is the only place where I can live freely."

"I wish you had kept that to yourself."

"I got thrown out of New Athenia because of Lidian 1299."

"201-11?" Tyrus appeared worried.

"He said you murdered a crailer."

"Lidian is the murderer. He left before Unity Forces could get to him."

"He also killed an Athenian female."

"Not everyone can be reintegrated. Some people are too damaged. I warned the Overseer about such a thing, but he believes he can solve all of Unity's problems because of his Prime Wisdom."

"The Overseer is insane. I don't even want to contemplate what his *Prime Wisdom* will tell him to do next."

"Transmit Harmony to fetuses."

"Why haven't I heard anything about—"

"I couldn't risk telling anyone until I cleared the beacons."

I slumped onto a chair. "When that woman interrupted my induction, I thought she was a threat to Unity, but I was the threat. I condemned a whole population to slavery."

"Don't blame yourself, Damon. We all believed in the Overseer. He gave us what we all wanted—to be part of something larger than ourselves."

"I spent the last year asking myself why I blindly followed the Sacred Oath, and I haven't come up with an acceptable answer."

"The Overseer must be stopped. He's now telling everyone that he's god." Tyrus lost his bearing, and I helped him to sit down. "He had miraculous graphics made in his image, and he projects them into the minds of the public each morning and evening."

"The Chosen agreed to this?"

"They're all spineless. They don't want to lose their color or privileges. That's why I resigned my Chosen seat. I was no different from—" Tyrus gazed at the pictures on the wall and froze when he noticed the one with Torrin and Old Woman.

"Did you know them?" I asked.

"I knew Torrin. He was a well-respected Chosen." Tyrus looked curiously at me. "Is he here?"

"He died a little more than two years ago. Do you know why he was accused of treason?" I asked.

"The charge was a fabrication. He had something on the Overseer but wouldn't disclose anything until I committed to testifying on his behalf. I had too much to lose, so I turned him down. Torrin was soon removed from the Chosen and stripped of his purple sleeves—supposedly for stealing credits, but those loyal to him refused to believe he was guilty."

"What did you believe?"

"Torrin was headstrong, domineering, and argumentative. He'd always speak the last words at a Corporate meeting. After he'd been demoted, the Corporate Hierarchy mistakenly believed he was forever silenced." Tyrus appeared to reflect upon the picture of Torrin. "He blew up the towers and left Unity in a blaze of fire." Tyrus laughed. "Good thing he left when he did. I don't think he would've been able to top himself after that one."

He glanced at a picture of Wade and me standing at the top of the ridge. "I told Wade the game was fixed. You're forced to submit to someone's ideology when you don't have power, and you force your ideology on others when you have power. If he'd heeded my advice, he would have been okay."

"With advice like that, what did you expect him to do?"

"Get the slock out of Unity." He leaned back into the chair and closed his eyes. "I must rest now for a while."

Tyrus and I had nothing more to say for the rest of the day. The only thing we had in common was Unity, something we both wanted to forget.

In the morning Shisa and I walked him to the old tunnel. We had to spend several hours in a trainlet so that he could rest. When we got to the other side, I handed him a map. "Be safe on your journey, Master Tyrus."

"Please, don't call me that anymore." He placed the map in his coat pocket.

"You're the only man who deserves that title." I bowed to him.

"Thank you, Damon. Your sincerity almost makes me believe it."

"Believe it. You were the only one who voted against my entry into University. You were the only one who saw through me."

"I did, but not for the reason you think." Tyrus smiled and was on his way.

# off the canvas

I'd been sketching by the river's edge when Shisa arrived with a pine cone in her mouth and dropped it near my feet.

"Not now, Shisa."

She nudged it over my foot.

"You win." I tossed the pinecone, and she ran after it until a rabbit made itself a more interesting target.

"That should keep you busy for a while."

I continued with my sketching, concentrating on the shading and blending, the most difficult technique for me to master. As with playing the violin, when I sketched, time disappeared. However, on this morning, it moved slower than the snail that had been inching in my direction since my arrival. I scrutinized my work and wasn't satisfied with how I'd portrayed the light reflecting off the water. Frustrated, I closed my sketch pad. *There's always tomorrow.*

Shisa hadn't returned, and I whistled for her. When she failed to appear, I headed home expecting to find her along the path. About halfway down, she emerged from the brush and barked.

"It's about time."

Shisa kept barking and pacing back and forth along the width of the path.

"*I'm* the one who should be barking." I waved a thumb at myself. "I've been looking for you for the past hour."

I walked ahead, and Shisa strutted beside me, still barking.

I stopped and crossed my arms. "I'm sorry, but I'm not in the mood to play now. I'm hungry." I rubbed my belly.

She whimpered and I smiled at her. "Wait till you see what I'm planning for breakfast, you'll—"

Shisa ran to the cabin and I sauntered along behind her. She waited for me, her barks now sounding more desperate.

"All right. You win, again."

Shisa led me down to the middle ridge. Reaching the side that overlooked my cabin, she stopped and circled around an unconscious female Unity Guard. I glanced up at the steep crag from where she had fallen; almost a four-meter drop. As I looked down at the injured guard, the COR alarm went off. Struck by a wave of vertigo I struggled to keep on my feet.

The guard moaned, and I shut off the alarm. "Stay still. Your back may be broken." I kneeled beside her. "Can you move your legs?"

She slowly moved her heels from side to side.

"I'm going to call—" I gasped when I noticed a heart-shaped beauty mark on her neck. The guard lifted her head, and I immediately recognized her. It was the woman I painted and hung on my wall in New Athenia. "Flora?" I grasped my forehead as memories from my first incarnation jetted into my consciousness. I clearly remembered our first night at the observatory, how Flora's hair looked unbound, and the blast from the plazer that ended her life. I recalled it all as clearly as my first hiking trip with Wade.

Shisa sat next to me. I petted her and said, "You keep watch over her. I'll be back." I ran down to my cabin to retrieve my med kit while memories of my past incarnation kept streaming. *You don't actually believe you're reliving your life? It's obvious you're being reintegrated or suffering from the scourge.* The rebuttal came on my way back up the ridge. *The scourge isn't real. I've already proved that to myself. This can't be reintegration; everything looks too real, and my knowledge of being tested would be enough to wake me up—unless some new technology was developed since my departure.*

Shisa met me halfway up the ridge. "I thought I told you to stay with the guard."

She followed me back up and when we arrived at the clearing, Flora was waiting with her plazer aimed at me.

"You're safe here." I showed her my med kit. "I can help you." All the feelings I had for Flora in my first incarnation returned, which confused my interpretation of the present situation.

"Don't move." Flora walked slowly towards me. "Raise both your hands where I can see them."

Shisa growled.

"It's okay, Shisa."

Shisa didn't seem to agree with my assessment and continued to growl.

Smiling at Flora, I lifted my hands in surrender. "You're Flora, right?"

"How do you know my name?"

"If I tell you, you wouldn't believe me." I laughed. "I don't believe me either." I approached her. "My cabin is nearby. We can continue this—"

Flora fired a warning shot that pulled me back into the present reality.

"Stay where you are!" she yelled.

Shisa growled and bolted towards Flora.

"Shisa, no!"

She on her hind legs and Flora shot her. Shisa fell to the ground, blood pouring out from beneath her.

Flora stared at me with a coldness that made me question if she was human. "Damon 1300-333-1M, you'll submit to the Corporate Hierarchy of Unity and refrain from speech until a confessor is present."

"She wouldn't have hurt you."

"All words and actions will be used against you in the court of ideals."

I kneeled down and stroked Shisa's head. "She wouldn't hurt even the tiniest ant."

"Didn't look that way to me."

I glared at Flora. "Shisa doesn't like plazers."

Shisa whimpered softly as I stroked her behind her ears. "Sorry I couldn't protect you."

After one last cry, she closed her eyes. I clutched the grip of my plazer, ready and willing to exact justice.

"Cease your action!" Flora said.

"What if I don't? Will you put me down like her?" I pointed at my dog.

"Unity Forces are on their way. There's nowhere else for you to go. You must return to Unity and answer to the charges."

"What are the charges?"

"Only your confessor can reveal that information."

"I'm not going there. I'd rather die than return to Dome Dungeon." I reached for my plazer and Flora fired. A stinging sensation radiated across my chest and I fell onto my back.

Flora pressed her boot against my hips and secured my weapon. "Don't move, and you'll be safe." She stepped back, her plazer still aimed at me. "When you begin reintegration, clarity will be restored to your diseased mind."

With painstaking effort, I managed to roll on to my abdomen. "Is that where I am now? Reintegration?"

"Stay still. You need medical attention."

I got up on all fours and crawled to the precipice. I wasn't going to wait for Unity Forces to take me to reintegration, and if I was already in reintegration, none of this would make a difference anyway.

"Stay where you are!"

From a kneeling position I admired the cabin. A wave of peace carried me to an acceptance of what I had to do.

"Don't move any further!" Flora shouted.

I dove forward but didn't feel myself hit the ground.

When I opened my eyes, Sutara was looking down at me. "You must remember sooner."

"Is this reintegration?" I asked.

Flora peered at me from over the edge and then disappeared from view.

Sutara knelt beside me. "What you were isn't who you are anymore. You must believe that, Damon."

"I can't."

Sutara cried, and I placed my hand on the side of her face. "Not until I stop myself from inventing Harmony."

"There will always be something you'll want to change. You must stop your self-recriminations and remember."

I had another excuse to follow my own course. Flora came flying over the cliff and landed beside me. A thick stream of blood flowed from out of a plazer blast wound on her chest. I surveyed the top of the ridge. Someone was staring down at us, but from that height I couldn't see who it was.

Flora turned her head towards me.

"Who shot you?" I asked.

Her mouth opened, but no words came. Her eyes remained fixed with no hint of recognition in them. I meant nothing to her, but I had loved her—and still did. From my perspective, love traveled beyond emotions and even beyond the realm of time. It transcended both, but I wouldn't comprehend the depth of that realization until many incarnations later. The sun beat down on me as I took hold of Flora's hand. Believing I'd see her again I smiled while tears burned a trail down my face, bringing my second incarnation to a close.

# the careman

### Third Incarnation

My first night in the cabin ushered in a series of dreams that dislocated me from my present reality. I encountered people whom I had never met from lands I never visited. Unfamiliar mountain paths led me to outdoor cities with tents. Exotic animals with humps on their backs carried people across a barren ocean of sand, and I spoke in a language I'd never heard.

The dream that disturbed me most repeated itself almost nightly. I lay dying on a dirt path. Thick roots emerged from the ground, wrapped themselves around my whole body and pulled me into the earth. Dirt surged into my mouth and nostrils, and I'd wake up gagging and coughing. Shisa stayed by my side during these times, as though she knew I needed comforting.

I thought once I got to New Athenia I'd recover, but during my stay in the trainlets I had the most horrible nightmare. I was staring at Wade's dead body lying at the bottom of the ridge, and he suddenly stood up and pointed at me.

"You did this. It should be you."

I then died in his place and was sucked into the ground by the large roots from my previous dreams. I awoke to find Wade sitting on one of the benches, his arms crossed.

"You know why you're here, don't you?" he asked.

"Damnation."

"Glad to see you're not the same pretentious slock I left behind."

The door slid open and Old Woman entered. "That's where you're wrong. He's still pretentious, and a slock." She sat down beside me. "You would've done anything to impress the Corporate Hierarchy."

"Everything I did was for the Unitians. I wanted to make a better life for them."

"By controlling their emotions? Didn't you trust your flock, *Lord* Damon?"

"It was never about trust."

"It's always about trust," Wade said, now sitting on the opposite side of me. "That's why they're transmitting Harmony to fetuses now. They're not out of the tanks yet, and the purple sleeves are already treating them like criminals."

I laughed. "Now I know none of this is real. They're not transmitting to fetuses."

"Oh yes they are," Old Woman said. "You and the rest of the Corporate Hierarchy don't trust each other; that's why you want to control everything and everyone around you."

"It was never about control."

Wade asked, "Then what did you mean when you said, 'If we lose control, we lose everything?'"

"I *never* said that."

"You did," Old woman said. "And the time has come for you to confess—"

"I have nothing to confess to!" I stood and frowned at her. "You have no right to judge me! Had I known Unity Forces were

164

going to kill you, I never would've called them. And as far as Unity is concerned, I have nothing to do with what's going on there anymore!"

"They're using your technology," Wade said.

Old Woman came to me and cupped my face with her hands. "I understand your pain," she said softly, "but justifying your actions doesn't exempt you from their outcomes."

I looked into Old Woman's eyes. "I didn't know." I placed my hands over hers. "I never meant for you to get hurt."

"I didn't get hurt, Damon," she said softly, "I died."

I dropped my hands to my side. "I'm sorry," I sniveled, "I'm so sorry."

Wade chuckled. "There's no hope for you. Even out of Unity you grovel like a sleeve-worshipper."

Old Woman chortled along. "And he cries like a baby as it's first pulled out of an incubation tank."

I pushed Old Woman away and clutched my head with both hands, trying to block out the voices.

"Covering your ears won't keep you from remembering what you've done to us," Wade said. "We died because you and the Corporate Hierarchy are afraid of losing control, which would mean a loss of your power and your precious privileges."

Old Woman stood in front of me. "We're all a threat to you. Our independence forces you to see a truth that most of us already know."

"What truth is that?"

Wade came over and whispered in my ear. "I don't need to tell you because you already know it."

"He does, but he refuses to acknowledge it," Old Woman said. "He's a coward like all the purple sleeves."

I moved towards the door.

"I'm going to tell you, whether you want to hear it or not," Old Woman said. "You were never really in control, and you never will be because control is nothing but a fantasy created to subjugate others—and yourself."

"That's where you're wrong! I'm in control now! I can walk away from here because neither of you are here."

I headed to the door, and Wade blocked my path.

"I'm here, and I'm not going anywhere." He waved his finger in my face. "As long as Harmony exists, I'll never leave you alone."

I saw Wade's dead body on the ground and woke up. I leapt out of bed and sprinted outside until my breath was depleted. Exhaustion cancelled out my anxiety, and I returned to my trainlet, drained of emotions. My late-night run became a daily ritual; it was the only way I could get to sleep. The dialogues with Old Woman and Wade continued for the next three days, until I couldn't tell if I was awake or dreaming.

Someone rapped on my door right after I'd yelled at Wade for blaming his death on me.

"If you didn't call Unity Forces, we'd both be on our way to New Athenia!"

"I'm not going there," I said. "Only sickness and ruin exists on the other side."

"You know that's not true. You've been there before."

"I never set foot beyond this tun—"

"No pay, no stay, Chap," Sephroy shouted from outside.

I slid open the door. "I don't have anything else I'm willing to give away."

"How about you work for me? Could use some help around here." He spied Shisa, asleep on the floor. "Or you can give me the dog."

I agreed to work for him, and in a few days my senses adjusted to the wretched smell of the waste buckets. Sephroy paid me with chick peas and lentils he got from his network of traders. Most of my business was with a local who came by with wine, dried fruits, nuts, and seeds. I avoided most of the other visitors except for a gypsy woman on her way to rejoin her caravan.

She read my fortune by holding both my hands. "You're going to travel the world, find riches, and rule over a tribe who will worship you like a god."

I didn't believe her, but she was the most entertaining visitor to the trainlets. We played gin rummy, exchanged anecdotes, and traded a few items. I collected candles, a deck of cards, and two woven blankets. One became Shisa's bed, and the other I saved for a future trade.

I began to worry about Shisa not getting enough sunlight, and I persuaded Sephroy to take her with him on his next trip out of the old tunnel. When I brought Shisa to him, she didn't seem pleased with her new companion. "If she doesn't return with you—" I flipped my plazer around in my hand and aimed the barrel at Sephroy. "This is what will be waiting for you on your return."

"Think the tunnel is getting to you, Chap. When I get back, you should go outside for some sunlight."

"Light is pain. Light forces me to see things, and I hate being forced to see things."

"Hmm. You sound a little weird, even for a dome dweller. I hear you talking to yourself a lot, lately. That's what happens when you stay on the inside for too long."

"I'm not talking to myself. My friends are staying with me."

"Sounds like you got a lot of them." He looked at Shisa. "Come on you."

The dog didn't move.

"Go." I petted Shisa and gestured towards Sephroy. "And remember what I told you."

"We're on the same team here, Chap. Try to remember that next time you talk to your *friends*. I haven't gotten a good night's sleep since they showed up." He shook his head and walked off with Shisa.

My conversations with Old Woman and Wade continued every day. They'd show up before I turned in for the night, when I got up in the morning, and while I cleaned the trainlets. Lost in my delusions, Sephroy started to avoid me after he'd returned.

Following another tiresome exchange with Wade and Old Woman, I went for a run. When I returned, I was surprised by a figure wearing a wide-brimmed hat. I shined my lantern on him.

"Master Tyrus?"

Tyrus shifted his lantern towards me. "Damon?" He eyed me from top to bottom. "What the slock happened to you?"

He approached me, and I ran to my trainlet. "I'm not going back! Never! Do you hear me? Never!" I shut my door and pulled down the shades.

Tyrus knocked.

I called out, "I'm not going back!"

"I'm not here to hurt you. I left as well. I'm here with two other passengers."

"How do I know they didn't send you to get me?"

"Have you ever heard of a purple sleeve entering the old tunnel to chase after a defector? Even Unity Forces don't wander this far."

I opened the shade and surveyed the visible area. "No one ever accused them of being brave." I slid open the door and Tyrus entered.

"How long have you been here?" he asked.

"Why do you want to know?"

"You look as though you could've been born here."

"I sometimes feel that way." I sat down on the bench.

"Did you go to New Athenia? On my way over I met some Outsiders who suggested I visit."

"Never made it past here."

"When are you leaving?"

"I'm not. There's nothing beyond here for me."

"It's not your fault, Damon."

"It's all my fault."

"Then I should condemn myself to this prison because I'm guilty of the same thing."

"Did you kill someone too?"

"No. Did you?"

"Everyone who receives Harmony's signal. They're always around here to remind me."

Tyrus examined an altar I had made in remembrance of Wade. A small tea light flickered in front of Wade's picture along with a few of his personal belongings. The gypsy woman who gave me the candles told me about altars and how her people used them to honor their highest-regarded teachers.

"Their ghosts talk to me," I said.

"As long as you listen, they'll continue."

"I'll listen for as long as they want."

"You sound like a tragic hero from one of those dreary Unitian operas." He sat down next to me and removed his hat. "Do you want to end up like one of them—stuck in reintegration, reciting the Sacred Oath for an eternity?"

"I can write better than most of those composers."

"Wouldn't take much effort."

I glared at him. "Am I in reintegration now?"

"This is all real. Too real." Tyrus fanned himself with his hand. "You smell as if you haven't bathed since you left Unity." He probed me for a moment and then eyed his hologue. "You need to leave this place."

"Why? I like it here."

"The conductor who took care of the transports hasn't been heard from for almost twelve weeks."

"How unfortunate."

"The Strikers wanted me to take over, but my health is faltering. I'm volunteering you."

"No thanks. I already have an assignment."

"It's the least you could do, since you're responsible for the conductor's death."

"Tell them you made a mistake. I never met the conductor."

"You turned her in to Unity Forces."

"Old Woman was the conductor?" I closed my eyes, only now remembering Kai's comment about her helping Unitians cross the tunnel.

"And now so are you. To keep Freedomline secure, the Strikers will never know your identity, except for your contact who will bring the passengers to you."

"I won't be there to receive them."

"I never go back on my word."

I got up and batted one of the overhead handles. "How self-righteous of you, *Master Tyrus*. Should I bow and thank you for imparting your wisdom on my lost soul?"

Tyrus shot up and rammed me against the door. "The time has come to wake up and leave this asylum. If you're serious about penance, you'll help."

"I'm in no condition to help anyone." I laughed. "I'm out of my slocking mind, and I have no desire to reenter."

"You're going to help. Even if I have to drag your slocking ass out of this tunnel myself. Talking to ghosts will only destroy you."

He threw me to the ground and stared at his hololopue. "Your first transport is in two weeks. If you don't show up, you'll be responsible for the three Unitians who will be sent to reintegration." He positioned his hololopue in front of my face. "These are the logistics of the meet. I suggest you download them to your—"

"You slocking purple—" I rose to my knees. "You no longer have authority over me."

Tyrus pulled me up by my shirt. "Stop with the self-condemnation and act like the man you used to be."

"I was never a man. Unity doesn't breed men."

"Then transform yourself into one because we need you."

"I'm staying here." I crossed my arms. "You're going to have to find someone else to help ease your conscience."

"How about your conscience? Does it let you sleep at night?"

"I abandoned mine long ago. Must explain why I sleep like a baby."

Tyrus punched me in the jaw. "I don't believe you. I'll beat you all day until I do."

"No need." I slumped down on the bench. My head ached. Everything ached because I knew I had no other way out. "I'll be there."

Tyrus bowed his head. "Thank you, Damon. You made the right decision." He flopped onto the bench and rubbed his temples. "I hope New Athenia's doctors are as skilled as Unity's."

"What's wrong?"

"I'm not sure yet."

I helped him to his trainlet and met the other passengers who turned out to be Lidian and Holly. I had a brief reunion with them, then went back to my room and packed.

When the first light from outside shone in the tunnel, Shisa ran on ahead. I had kept her in the dark for so long, I thought she'd never want to see me again. I later caught up with her near a small brook and was surprised she waited for me. Shisa was more than my companion, she had become my strongest ally.

I returned to the cabin and was horrified by my reflection in the mirror. I could've passed for Sephroy. My hair was a long, tangled mess, and I appeared grossly underweight.

With sufficient rest and a daily dose of high-protein meals, I regained my strength and weight in time to lead my first passengers across the old tunnel. I traveled with them all the way to New Athenia where I spent hours downloading Ancient books, music, and movies at the Alexandrian Repository. Watching the New Athenian Orchestra perform, I was tempted to audition. In the end, my commitment to Tyrus won out, and I returned to the cabin. I got lost in my daily routine of chores, nature walks, sketching, and playing my violin. Life was peaceful until Shisa's barks led me down the path to where Flora lay unconscious. When she became lucid, and I had gotten over the shock of remembering my previous two incarnations, I knocked her out. I didn't want a duplicate performance of our deaths.

## PC 1309-119-24F

I inspected Flora's Unity Forces Badge. The date at the bottom read: PC 1309-119-24F. Something about the date seemed important, but I had more immediate concerns. In my last incarnation, Flora was followed by someone who wanted her dead. I examined the three public holoscreens that displayed live feeds of the upper and middle ridge. All were quiet, except for a deer running for the cover of the woods.

Flora grunted, and I picked up a plazer from the desk.

"Where am I?" she asked.

I sprang up from my chair and waved the plazer Flora noticed was missing from her holster.

"Damon 1300-333-1M, you'll submit to the Corporate Hierarchy of Unity and refrain from speech until a confessor is present. All words and actions will be used against you in the court of ideals."

"How do you plan on taking me in without this?" I spun the plazer around in my hand. "Learned this trick from you."

"How did I get here?"

"That question is what's keeping me from shooting you."

Flora crinkled her forehead and swiftly reverted back to her well-rehearsed act of a Unity Guard in complete control of her emotions. She played the part well, but I wasn't fooled.

"Your ignorance is the only thing that's keeping you alive," I said.

"Threatening me will only make things worse for you. You can't escape what you did."

"What *I* did? You were injured, and my dog led me to you. When I came back with my med kit, you thanked me by killing her and shooting me."

"I never met you before."

"Which is why I have the advantage now. I can change events before they occur." I looked up at the picture of me and Wade. "But the one thing I most want to change, I can't because my memory was restored four years too late."

Flora's dumbfounded expression demonstrated my biggest fear. *Am I in reintegration?* I couldn't immediately commit to an answer and that terrified me. In the midst of my momentary lapse of awareness, Flora vaulted off the couch and ran to the door. I caught up with her and pinned her against the wall. I studied every inch of her face, her eyes, her high cheekbones, her raven hair: She was exactly as I remembered her. *This is really happening; I'm reliving my life.*

Flora sat tied to the chair while I played my violin. The rocking of my body as my bow glided across the strings calmed me, and I needed calming. I played a slow melody that brought back my conversations with Old Woman and Wade during the twelve weeks I spent in the trainlets.

"Ghost Tears." I placed my bow on the table and put my violin in its case. "I wrote it when I believed I could talk to them."

"Sounds beautiful." Flora appeared to be holding back tears.

"I'm sure you've been told I was once a well-respected psychological engineer. Unity Forces' mind-pacification tricks won't work with me."

"Why did you leave?"

I picked up Old Woman's holologue. "My friend and I ended up here and met Old Woman. She told us her name, but I didn't think it worth remembering. I searched through all her files, and there isn't even a mention of it." I turned to a passage in her holojournal and read aloud.

*"Away from Unity I have no one to please but myself. I initially resisted indulging in the pleasures I found in this cabin and beyond the old tunnel. I always regarded myself in relation to Unitians, and I believed succumbing to my own interests and desires was blasphemous. However, once I distanced myself from the Sacred Oath and listened to my own voice, the truth of who I am emerged from within me and took over. Torrin was right. I'm more than a Unitian, a scientist and a woman. When the realization first struck me, I unraveled my braids and ran outside in the rain without my clothes on. I cried, laughed, and sensed so much, I didn't think I'd be able to contain myself from this immense outpouring of joy and happiness."*

"What do you think?" I asked.

"Sounds like the ranting of someone in the late stages of the scourge." Flora glanced at a small replica of the Parthenon displayed on one of the shelves.

"That's the Parthenon. It overlooks New Athenia—a city far more impressive than Unity and not only because of its architecture; the Alexandrian Repository houses the history of the Ancients. Athenian Scientists and scholars continue to learn about them as Outsiders still bring items they've salvaged from the ruins of past civilizations."

"Why do they do that?"

"To keep their histories alive." I looked up a passage about New Athenia in the holol
ogue and handed it to her, but she refused to take it.

"I also thought Old Woman suffered from the scourge, but not my friend." I pointed to the picture of me and Wade. "He believed Old Woman's tales of peoples who spoke with different words. I didn't—until I went and saw for myself. Almost everything on the shelves came from my travels to New Athenia." I picked up the Ganesha. "Except for this piece." I held it up for Flora to see. "It was the only thing that survived after Unity Forces showed up and destroyed everything. I replaced as much as I could—" I glanced up at the picture of Old Woman and Torrin.

Flora looked at it. "What happened to her?"

"Unity Forces executed her." I put Ganesha back on the shelf. "And your fate will be the same unless we figure out who wants you dead."

Flora struggled to free herself again. "Your confusion will only get worse if you don't return to Unity. Only reintegration can restore your clarity of mind."

"Reintegration is used to control Unitians."

"You can't think clearly when you're in the late stage of the scourge."

"And who's going to cure me of this disease? You?" I walked over and knelt in front of her. "Why don't you travel with me beyond the old tunnel and confirm if what you believe about the Outsiders is true?"

"Return to Unity with me before it's too late to save yourself."

"Unity is the disease. Leaving is the only cure."

"When you're separated from Unity, you can't recognize the calm because you're lost in chaos."

"You're a robot repeating the words of those who programmed you," I said, trying to keep my frustration from surfacing.

"Without Unity you'll always be alone."

"Can you speak for yourself and explain what any of that means?"

"You're sick, and reintegration is the only cure."

I closed my eyes and tried to calm myself. "This is going nowhere." I untied her. "Go." I went back to my desk. "What you've evolved into is too painful to observe." Flora's reflection in the window revealed she hadn't moved from the chair. "You've turned into everything you fought against."

"I'm not here to fight. I'm here to help." Flora got up and walked towards me.

I slammed my hand on my desk. "Get out of my cabin! I don't know you."

Flora extended her hand to me. "I'm not going to leave you alone because you *do* want to return with me. You *want* to be in a safe place with people who care about you."

Unity Guards are trained in the art of hypnosis, and Flora was attempting it on me. Even though I was aware of what she was doing, her calm and quiet voice soothed me and made me again question whether I was being reintegrated. "I also want you to be in a safe place. That's why I won't go with you. I won't be responsible for your death."

"I can't leave here," Flora said. "Not without you."

The cuckoo clock on the wall chimed and Flora glanced at it.

"Charming, isn't it?" I said after the tenth chime.

"If you say so," she said, trying to hold back a smile.

"You could get one for yourself if you come with me to New Athenia."

"The only place we're going is back to Unity."

I crossed my arms. "If you love it there so much, why did you interrupt my induction to question me about Harmony?"

"I wasn't even near Unity Hall that day."

"You told me it was you."

"I never told you anything. We only just met."

"Are you a Striker?"

"I'm loyal to the Sacred Oath. I'd never join up with those terrorists."

I shook my head. "You look like Flora, but you sound nothing like her."

"Where did we meet?"

177

"You're not asking because you want to know."

"I'm trying to help you see that what you're saying is impossible."

"Twice at the bottom of the ridge and once at Kai's emergence party. In my first incarnation we were together, and you hated everything Unity stood for. You tried to get me to see the truth, but I refused to listen. Now everything seems to be in reverse, and you're the one not listening." I laughed. "Maybe you shot me to get even for the rose I gave you."

I slowly maneuvered myself towards her and she took a step back.

"If you're that woman I described, the one who thinks for herself and hates being told what to do, then you know we're on the same side."

"Come back with me then," Flora said in a shaky voice.

"If I'm right, whoever shot you and pushed you over the ridge followed you here."

"I came alone."

"Are you certain?"

"Certain that you need to return to Unity and soon. I've never witnessed anyone in such a late stage of the scourge."

"I'm *not* sick!" I threw my hands in the air. "Everything I told you happened."

"It seems that way because you can't tell between fantasy and reality."

"I'm here, you're here, and someone wants to kill you. Death will soon be your reality if you don't listen to me."

"If we never met before today, that makes everything you're telling me false," Flora said.

"Play along a while longer. If I'm wrong, I'll agree with your diagnosis."

"You'll come back to Unity?"

"I said I'd agree. I'd rather plummet to my death again than go back to Dome Dungeon."

She looked at me strangely and then shook her head.

"Are you remembering something?"

"What you just said—it sounded familiar to me."

I snapped my finger. "I think I said something similar to you in my last incarnation."

"Feeling as if you've had the same conversation before isn't unusual," Flora said.

"It is when two people are recalling the same one."

I heard Shisa barking and let her in. I left the door open for Flora. "You're free to leave if you still think I'm delusional."

Flora placed her hand on her hip. "You're delusional, but I'll play along."

"Why?"

"Because I want to hear you admit you're wrong," she said.

"This is starting to sound like one of our old arguments."

"Did we have many?"

"Not enough."

I locked Flora's plazer inside my desk drawer, along with mine.

"Is that smart? If someone is coming to kill me, we'll need those."

"It'll be easier for us to talk without a plazer between us." I nodded at the holoscreens. "When the intruder arrives at the middle ridge, her face will be on one of these three screens."

"Her?"

"Keep watching. When *whoever* arrives, it will prove you were tracked by your implant. The towers don't transmit this far out, and the whole cabin is impervious to scanners."

"The implant isn't a tracking device."

"Go on believing that if it makes you feel better." I got my backpack and started throwing in some supplies.

Flora stared at the holoscreens. "If what you say is true, then why are you packing?"

"In case I'm wrong about all of this."

"Paranoia is another symptom of the—"

I waved my hand in the air. "If you insist on staying, kindly censor out all references relating to the scourge."

Flora shrugged her shoulders and examined the Ganesha statue.

"You never told me about the accusation against me?" I said.

"How did you know there was an accusation? I never mentioned it."

"The same way I knew you interrupted my induction." I slapped my head. "My mistake. I forgot everything I said was *false*. Maybe you have a better explanation?"

Flora rolled her eyes and put the Ganesha back on the shelf. "They say you assassinated the Overseer."

"I haven't been to Unity since I left four years ago." I went into the kitchenette and opened two overhead cabinets.

Flora followed me in. "You were identified."

"By whom?" I removed two lanterns and a spare battery pack.

"Only a confessor has that information."

I attached the lanterns to my backpack. "What did they tell you about me?"

"You've allied yourself with the Outsiders and want to overthrow the Overseer, so you can take his place."

"That's not all together a lie. I had aspirations to be Overseer two incarnations ago, and I stood a good chance because of my success with Harm——"

A plazer blast forced open the door. I positioned myself in front of Flora to shield her.

"Your motion sensors don't seem to be working very well," she said.

Kai entered the cabin, his plazer pointed at me. "Impressive. Even with your Outsider appearance, the ladies still can't seem to resist you."

Flora pushed past me and walked over to Kai. "What are you doing here? Did you follow——"

Kai slapped her across the face. "Address me by my title when you speak to me."

"Why are you here, Kai?" I asked. "Purple sleeves don't usually go on security assignments."

"A herd of cows graze in a pasture and two wander away. The farmer approaches and the cows fear he's going to pick one of them for slaughter. One of the cows that had ventured away returns to the herd. The farmer chooses the one who stands alone." Kai pushed Flora to the floor.

I charged him and he shot me in the stomach. Grabbing my abdomen I fell to the floor.

"You were never good at blending in with your environment." He took aim at me again.

Flora got to her knees and cried, "I'm loyal only to you, Master Kai. I was close to his capture."

"You never showed me any respect since you began your assignment. Why should I believe you now?"

Kai leveled his plazer at Flora and smiled.

I glared at him and said, "During the time of the Ancients, there was a mythological beast known as a vampire. Sleeping in a coffin by day, he waited until night to come out and feed on the blood of the frightened villagers."

"With stories like that, no wonder the Ancients were so violent."

"Vampires are real, and I'm looking at one now. You drain the life out of your victims by feeding off their continual suffering."

Kai relaxed his aim and Flora sighed in relief. "Suffering leads to rebellion and revolution. It's loyalty that nourishes us and keeps us in power." He looked down at Flora. "Would you go with me to Damon's bedroom and show me how loyal you are?"

Flora glanced at me, then back at Kai. "You're my mentor. If that's what you wish, I must comply."

Kai smiled at me. "I think I've proven my point." He trained his plazer on Flora. "Only you were always above submission, which is why it hurts to see you sink so low to save yourself." Her eyes widened in terror as Kai brought the barrel close to her head. "Your brand of loyalty is unappetizing. I'd rather go hungry." He shot Flora and she fell backwards, dying instantly.

Shisa nudged the door open from inside my bedroom.

"Since when did you turn into an executioner?" I asked.

Kai turned his plazer on me. "A green is a nonessential, and your return isn't advantageous to—"

Shisa growled. Kai turned around in alarm and I seized him by the legs and pulled him down. We struggled for control of the weapon. Shisa bit Kai's arm, forcing him to release the plazer. I seized it, forced Kai onto his back and shot him. As I rolled away, Shisa came to my side. "Next time, try to wake up *before* we get shot." Shisa lay beside me, and I petted her until I lost awareness of my third incarnation.

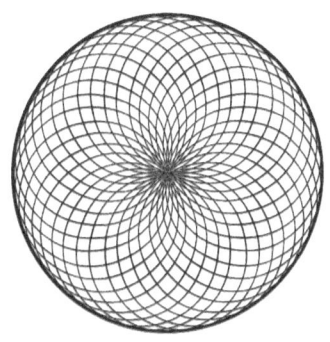

# howls in the tunnel

## Fourth Incarnation

A dense fog engulfed the path to the old tunnel. I had to keep calling out to Shisa to ensure she hadn't ventured too far ahead. The fog cleared and we stopped near a brook and caught some fish for lunch. As Shisa finished her portion, I removed my trout from the fire and placed it on a dish to cool. I sliced off a piece of flesh and Shisa licked her lips. "If you want more, you'll have to catch another one yourself."

She rested her head on her paws and whimpered softly.

I cut a small piece and tossed it to her. "Only because you reminded me I'm human." I pointed at her. "I doubted it until you showed up."

Shisa finished eating, looked at my plate and barked.

"I couldn't leave you all alone. That's when I knew a heart still beat inside me." I cut another sliver of meat, took a bite and spoke with my mouth full, something I hadn't done since childhood. "Wade and Old Woman almost had me convinced I lost my humanity, until I realized they believed in an illusion." I sighed. "Idealism is the scourge, but they couldn't see it because they were in the late stages." I tossed Shisa another piece. "They tried to infect me, but I was immune to their influence. That's why I'm still alive, and I plan on staying that way for a long time." I bit into another piece of warm flesh. "From today onward, I'm going to live only for myself." I spit out some bone that got caught between my teeth, then stood up and yelled. "I'm free!" I howled loudly. "If I want to act like a wild dog, no one can stop me!"

Shisa stood and cocked her head to the side.

I tilted my head in response. "Are you with me?" I howled again to motivate her and she barked.

"Glad you agree. You wouldn't have wanted to be around me when I was loyal to the Sacred Oath; it made me boring and predictable."

She barked again.

"Not sure of what I am now, but acting like a dog is a lot more fun." I howled and Shisa joined in. After several more howls and barks, I felt less anxious and thought I had stumbled upon an innovative style of therapy. That made me laugh. *You left Unity, you deranged slock. From now on, the only patient you'll be treating is yourself, and what you have is incurable. So get used to mocking yourself because you're nothing but a joke.* I laughed again because I felt like one.

We made it to the old tunnel before nightfall and stopped at the trainlets. Sephroy's body odor nauseated me, and I wanted nothing to do with him, even after the COR alarm had gone off. I wanted to forget everything that reminded me of Unity, especially my work. I paid Sephroy, entered my room, and liberated myself from the weight of my backpack. The fish I cooked for Shisa and myself was digested hours ago. I had some nuts and dried fruit that I gave to her. She ate the meager portion in one bite and looked at me, expecting more. "That's the last of it. We'll need to find some more food when we get out of the tunnel. My humanity won't do us any good if we starve to death."

I uncapped my spare canteen, which now belonged to Shisa, and gave her some water. I then got out Old Woman's hologue and started reading her journal. One of the entries familiarized me with Torrin. He had studied at the New Athenia University and traveled further east visiting Ancient territories that once had exotic names like China and India. They were called "countries," and many more existed during the forgotten times. Such colossal territories were unheard of after the Great Cataclysm due to dwindling fuel resources. I continued reading Torrin's words.

*We're more like the Ancients than the Corporate Hierarchy dares to admit. Shortly before the Great Cataclysm, countries shared a common bond of greed, power, and dominance. Most citizens blamed their leaders, but they all played a part in the eventual downfall of civilization. The more everyone had, the more they wanted. Even as their cities crumbled, they couldn't stop from gorging on every commodity they could steal or go to war over. When resources were depleted, they fed off each other. The inertia of greed made turning back impossible. What's most disquieting to me is they were in the midst of collapse before the Great Cataclysm. There existed within them a self-destructive mechanism. On their ascent towards their greatest accomplishments, they were destined to fall to their deaths before reaching the apex of their successes. This was repeated through every age, and no leader seemed to learn from his or her predecessor. This same destructive mechanism still exists in us today, and I look upon it as a good omen. Unity will fall. I hope to live long enough to witness the dome crack and see all my Unitian brothers and sisters free from oppression.*

*Unity will fall.* Torrin's words echoed in my mind. *Unity will fall!* For the first time I believed it was possible. The purple sleeves and Overseer were as vulnerable as the rest of us. I wept and laughed, desperately wanting to tell someone the news. I slid open the door, stepped outside, and shouted toward the western end of the tunnel. "Unity will fall! You purple slocks don't have authority over anything but your own delusions, and they'll eventually destroy you!"

Shisa came outside barking. I mimicked her, then howled until people emerged from their trainlets.

"None of us know what the slock we're doing!" Laughing like a raving lunatic, I pointed at the crowd. "Not any of you." I slapped my chest loud enough for it to echo against the walls of the tunnel. "Not me." I glanced at Shisa, who barked. "But I think *you* know." I laughed and howled again.

The travelers shouted at me and Sephroy hobbled out, tapping his cane on the ground until we all were silenced.

"Quiet, quiet, quiet!" he yelled. "If you want to stay here, you have to keep quiet. People are trying to rest."

"That's a great idea. I'll be doing that for the rest of my life —resting." I smiled.

"See that you do, Chap. All that mouth flapping of yours is getting old, and I'd like to rest as well."

Sephroy looked at me wearily, and I watched him as he walked off. Something about his words haunted me the rest of that night, but by the next morning I was more eager to explore New Athenia. To maintain civility, I tried to find Sephroy to apologize for the disturbance. I couldn't find him, so I went on my way.

Once I had settled into my flat I joined the New Athenian Orchestra. I learned the musical compositions quickly and a quarter of a year later, I was having full conversations in Knosian. Stories started to show up in print and on screen about what a quick study I was. My favorite headline was "Wolfgang Amadeus Mozart is reborn in New Athenia!" For laughs, I decided to play the part and showed up for a performance dressed as I'd seen Mozart in a portrait. The audience loved it, as did Manolis. He insisted I repeat the act for future concerts, and he soon started dressing like Frédéric Chopin, another Ancient composer. We staged composer feuds with both scripted and improvised dialogue. We threw a few insults at each other, then played our instruments and argued over who was the best musician. Neither of us would concede, and we'd leave it up to the audience to make the deciding vote by waving either a red or blue flag. More often, the blue flags dominated, which meant my victory.

With my new success, I started to forget my Unitian past. Alcohol and women filled most of my evenings, and I indulged in both as often as I could. I once made the mistake of showing up drunk to one of my rehearsals, and Manolis almost removed me from my seat. He banned me from the performance and told me if I ever showed up drunk again, I'd be ejected from the orchestra. I took him at his word and drank only on days I didn't have to perform or rehearse.

After our Foundation Day performance, I went to a cafe I often frequented for dinner. Halfway through my carafe of wine, the COR alarm rang. I looked up at who'd just arrived and shut it off.

"If I were paranoid, I'd th-think, I'd think you had that set to go off at my arrival," Lidian said.

"Maybe I did." It took Lidian a moment to get that I was joking. I got up and shook his hand. "Good to see you. When did you arrive?"

"I-i-in time to enjoy the summer festival." He examined my costume. "What are you wearing?"

"They tell me I'm Mozart—reincarnated."

"Who's Mozart?"

"To answer that question here would be impossible."

He looked quizzically at me.

"He's one of the Ancients' most revered composers, but that's an oversimplification. Only upon hearing his music can you begin to comprehend his artistry."

"I planned o-on going to the music library tomorrow. Th-th-thanks. Mozart Reincarnated—I'll definitely look him up."

I laughed and motioned to the chair. "Have a seat. I'm sure you'll have a lot more questions about life in New Athenia."

Lidian joined me for dinner and went through his own carafe of wine, recounting his story about how Tyrus tried to frame him for attacking a crailer. In my drunken state, he sounded convincing.

"That old man tried to ruin my life too," I said. "He was the only Chosen to turn me down for admittance to University. Before the decision, I thought it was Avery who was going to deny me."

"He ha-has them all fooled." Lidian poured more wine into his glass. "Your success with Harmony mu-mu-must have made him furious."

"Wouldn't know. We never met to discuss it."

After dinner, we staggered to the crail stop, and Lidian, clutching a bottle of wine, continued his diatribe against Tyrus. I tried hard not to think about my Unitian past, which until today I'd successfully put out of my mind. As we sat and waited for a crail to arrive, a bouzouki player standing outside a late-night cafe plucked out an Ancient Greek folk song while Lidian grumbled about how miserable things had gotten since I left.

"Eh-eh-everywhere you go, there's a camera watching you," Lidian said. "I asked my confessor to locate a feed that could prove I left the crail alone, and he told me they're a-all reco-co-recorded over the next day. Wh-what's the point in having them i-i-if they're, if they're going to erase them?" He sipped his wine. "That's just more proof that they don't want to know the truth."

"You mean that they're dumber than your average Unitian?"

Lidian laughed. "G-g-g-glad someone else sees it besides me. I never believed they were better than the rest of us."

"If only I were that smart. I never would've invented Harmony."

"Is that why you left?" Lidian asked.

"One of many reasons."

Lidian complained about everything, from feeling like an outcast his whole life to how the purple sleeves lived above everyone else. It made me think of Wade, who I wished was here to see New Athenia. He would have admired the labyrinth, and the eclectic crowds within its walls. I'd never appreciated his unique way of turning a bad situation into something advantageous until meeting Lidian, who was starting to depress me. Catching a glimpse of two of my favorite ladies, Lyra and Gale, I began plotting my escape.

"See those girls?" I said. "I know them very well."

Lidian looked at them. "Th-they're beautiful."

"Do me a favor and get me another bottle of red wine." I handed him a few credit chips. "Meet me back here, and I'll introduce you."

"Sweet or dry?"

"I'll let you decide."

Lidian hurried off, staring at the girls as they approached.

Lyra sat on my lap and draped her arms around me. "Don't tell me you're going home so early."

"Could use some company." I pulled Gale onto the bench.

"Will your friend be coming back?" she asked.

"What friend?" I kissed Gale and did the same with Lyra.

A crail stopped, and the three of us got in and left. I told myself I'd call Lidian the next day and apologize. I was sure he'd understand.

I woke up the next morning lying between Gale and Lyra. My head ached, and I had to be at rehearsal in an hour. I stumbled into my clothes and headed for the rehearsal hall. As I walked to the crail stop, I noticed that everyone was staring at me. I got into a crail and heard someone yell, "Go back to where you came from, you savage!" I looked outside and someone smashed an egg against the window.

I got off at the repository and as I arrived at ground level, a large mob approached with Manolis in the lead.

"Leave now, and don't ever show yourself here again," he said. "You brought shame upon my stage!"

I tried to push myself free of the crowd.

"What did I—?"

A tall police-guard grabbed my arm and pulled me away. "You're to accompany me to the enforcement house."

"What are the charges?"

"They'll be announced by the judge."

We took the lift up to the crail stop. When the door opened, I was met by more angry faces.

"You have no soul," an old gypsy woman shouted at me. "The dead aren't welcomed in New Athenia."

We boarded the crail and the door shut. People banged on the window until the crail took off. Arriving at the enforcement house, we entered the judge's chamber, where I was reunited with Holly.

"What happened? Are you all right?"

"How could you just leave him alone?"

"Leave who?"

"Lidian." Holly cried. "It was awful."

"What did he do to—?"

"My first impression of you was right; I knew you were a heartless monster."

The police-guard wouldn't let me continue the discussion. He led me to a large table and directed me to a chair. Holly sat at the opposite end of the table. Through most of the hearing, she wouldn't look at me.

The judge entered and sat at the head of the table. He lifted a bell and rang it. "Damon 1300-333-1M, you're charged with moral dereliction."

"What does that mean?"

"You will not speak until I grant you permission."

"Yes, your Honor."

He faced Holly. "I viewed your recorded testimony, but you must give a live account for the judgment."

"Yes, your Honor." Holly bowed her head. "I just got off work and was on my way to the crail stop, near the third tier of the amphitheater, and I saw a man pacing up and down and crying. I walked over to see if he was okay. That's when I recognized Lidian."

"Did you meet him here?" the judge asked.

"No. We're both from Unity."

"So noted."

"I asked him if he needed help. He told me the world is hollow." Holly glared at me. "Everyone's greedy—only out for themselves, and he was tired of living in a world without meaning." She looked back at the judge. "I told him I wanted to help him. He laughed at me and said I'd probably be as helpful as Damon. 'All you Unitians are the same,' he said. I asked him what he meant, and he told me Damon sent him off to buy some wine, promising to introduce him to his lady friends. When he returned, they were gone. He said he'd felt lonely his whole life and hoped things would be different here, but he had trouble making friends. I told him I'd be his friend, and I reached out my hand to him, but he wouldn't take it." Holly broke down and cried.

"What happened next?" the judge asked.

"He ran to the ladder and climbed the arch. I yelled at him to stop." Holly looked at me again. "He said he'd stop when he hit the ground and that his blood spilled on the stage would be owned by Damon and the rest of the Corporate Hierarchy." She cried harder. "He jumped. That's when I called security."

The judge crossed his hands on the table. "Your story sounds consistent." He faced me. "Do you have anything to add?"

"I had no idea Lidian was suicidal."

"Did you leave him alone last night?" the judge asked.

"Yes, but how was I to—"

"I'm not familiar with Unity's fellowship laws, but in New Athenia, we pride ourselves on our compassion for each other and for those who visit us. By leaving the victim alone with alcoholic beverages, you helped create the state of mind that led to his suicide."

I slammed my hand on the table. "That charge has no basis in reality!"

The judge clutched the handle of his bell.

I quieted my voice. "Lidian's state of mind isn't something I nor anyone else could've created."

"Were you drinking last night?"

"I had some wine with dinner, but—"

"Could your judgment have been impaired?"

"I only had one glass."

"Your server at the restaurant claims you finished a whole carafe."

"That still doesn't make me negligent. The only one who could've stopped Lidian from killing himself was Lidian."

"Is that your defense?"

I leered at the judge as I contemplated an answer. "It's the truth."

The judge glowered at me and rang the bell. "Damon 1300-333-1M, as the indirect cause of Lidian 1303-201-111's death, you're hereby charged with moral dereliction. As of today, your residence pass is revoked, and you're to leave the city. Two police-guards will accompany you to your flat so that you can gather your belongings."

"Can I return for a visit?"

"You forfeited that right when you walked away from a human in need. Why don't you ask yourself why a man with your training failed to recognize someone who was obviously suffering." He rang his bell. "Dismissed." He stood up and left the room.

I set up camp a few kilometers outside New Athenia to plan my next move. My decision came after Sutara visited me in a dream. We were both in Old Woman's cabin.

"You must come back."

"Why?"

"To remember."

"If I go back, I'll remember?"

"You will, but not everything."

"Then why go back at all?"

Sutara rolled her eyes. "Honestly, Damon, your questions sound childish, and you're the older one."

"You don't look that much younger than me." I smiled and Sutara raised her eyebrows, obviously not amused.

"You're going to have to give me more," I said. "Manual labor and encountering Outsiders with bad teeth doesn't entice me to return."

"I'm not here to make decisions for you. But if you stay here, you'll lose yourself." Sutara walked to the door and opened it. "And you may not find your way back again."

"Why do I always see you?"

"When you remember, you'll know," she said and left the cabin.

I was still unsure whether Sutara was real, but I decided to listen to her anyway. My taste for civilization had soured again, and the isolation of the cabin seemed like the ideal place to sort through all that had happened. On the journey back, I thought about Lidian and the judgment against me. I was too caught up in my own life to notice his pain. Was that a justifiable excuse or was Holly right about me? *Am I a monster?*

# the next fifthday

Sitting beside the river sketching the cabin, I heard Shisa barking as she often did chasing a rabbit or some other small animal. I continued my work until a young Unity Guard took me by surprise.

"Damon 1300-333-1M?"

I showed him the barrel of my plazer.

The guard took a step back. "I'm not here to take you in." He offered his hand to help me up. "I'm Roth."

I stood on my own and kept my plazer trained on him. "What's a Unity Guard doing this far beyond the beacons?"

"Relax your aim, and I'll tell you."

Shisa ran to my side and growled, and Roth took several steps back.

"Either say what you came to say or leave," I said. "And whatever you decide, make it quick. Shisa isn't very patient."

"I've been watching you for the last thirty days."

"You're brave." I rubbed my scruffy beard. "Last time I looked in the mirror, I almost frightened myself away."

"I'm a Striker."

"And I'm bored." I indicated Shisa. "Talking to her is more exciting."

Roth stared at Shisa, then back at me. "Are you familiar with the old tunnel?"

"I've been through it."

He smiled. "I'd like to recruit you as our conductor."

"Why would you need a conductor? There's not much demand for an orchestra out here."

Roth shook his head and laughed. "Now that's what I'm looking for. Someone with your sense of humor would be perfect to lead Unitians through the old tunnel."

"I don't do charity work."

"We can pay you for each transport."

"Credits aren't worth anything out here."

"I could bring you supplies."

"And anything else I request?"

"As long as it can be carried out."

"A case of berry ale would be a great start."

"I'll pay you on the day of your first transport."

"When do we start? I'm thirsty."

Roth looked at my plazer. "Why don't you put that away first. It's hard for me to concentrate on business with that aimed at me."

I secured my weapon. "Who did you use as a conductor before?"

"That old lady you turned in. I was one of the guards who arrived after you placed the call about her and the cabin, but I didn't know who she was at the time. On the next Fifthday, the conductor didn't show for a transport. The Strikers sent a coded message through the comnet and told us the woman in the cabin was the conductor, and that you alerted Unity Forces about her. Why did you turn her in if you planned on running?"

"I didn't *plan* anything. I had no idea that the old woman was the conductor. Must be why Unity Forces killed her."

"The incident report states that 1300-099-33M murdered her and killed you before diving off the ridge."

"Wade didn't kill anyone. He was halfway up the ridge when the old woman was already back in the cabin. I told Unity Forces that when they questioned me."

Roth squinted his eyes. "Unity Forces never questioned you."

"I gave my statement before——" I suddenly recalled leaving before Unity Forces arrived. What I couldn't fathom was why I was about to tell Roth I'd returned to Unity. "Think I've been away too long."

"The logistics of how the conductor died isn't important to us."

"It is to me," I said. "Everyone in Unity thinks Wade is a murderer."

"If Unitians don't care enough to question the actions of Unity Forces, why do you even care what they think?"

"I don't. I'm only concerned about Wade's honor, a word most of you Unitians don't understand."

"You can let me know what really happened, and I'll get it out on the comnet."

"I will, when you tell me how you knew I was out here."

"The last Striker who worked with the conductor was given a new post after she was killed. I was recruited to search for an Outsider willing to transport for us, but I found only one, and he greeted me with his longbow. I almost gave up the search until I spotted you on the ridge. It looked like you were sketching a picture of Unity."

Roth spoke the truth. I remembered the day well. I was lonely and decided to hike up the ridge and sketch the dome. As much as I hated Unity, I still appreciated its beauty.

Roth peered into the optic of his holologue. "On the next Fifthday, I'll be here with your first passengers."

"What about my cabin? Unity Forces already know about its location."

"With the old lady gone, they have no interest in a deserted cabin in the woods. You're all set to go. I'll bring you a wireless signal interface with the next transport. Luckily, the guards never found the transceiver. They're a lot harder to acquire."

"Do you know the old woman's name?"

"Only her recruiter has that information, and he was sworn to keep her identity secret to protect her and maintain the security of the Strikers' network. We'll continue with the same protocol. I'll be the only Striker you'll ever meet and the only one aware of your identity." Roth showed me a map on his hololgue. "We'll rendezvous at the top of the ridge, on the western side. You'll have to help the passengers navigate around the eroded portion of the mountain. If you ever show up for a transport, and I'm not there, you'll wait another eight weeks before returning."

Roth arrived that following Fifthday with the passengers and all the supplies he'd promised. I presented myself with a clean shave so as not to frighten anyone with my Outsider appearance. I spent the next few years transporting passengers across the old tunnel, presuming inspiration would find me again. It never did. All the hopes, dreams and desires passengers expressed to me sounded childish and unrealistic. I held back the temptation to blurt out that the paradise they sought was a phantom. I kept my opinions to myself. My life as an Outsider clearly demonstrated one person's idea of Shangri-La was another person's deathland.

My indifference came to an abrupt end when I was reacquainted with Flora, who lay unconscious at the bottom of the ridge. Regaining my memory was as unsettling as it had been the last two times. Rather than bore the reader of this testimony with all the denials, hysterics, and expletives that accompanied my returning memories, I'll move on to the first thought that zapped across my mind after I'd knocked Flora out by striking her with my plazer: *Is this love or hate?*

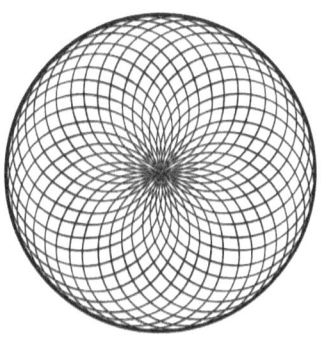

# killing flora

Flora's emergence date still held my attention. Using the security clearance ID I had gotten from the purple sleeve in my first incarnation, I tried to pull up the headlines for that day, but I couldn't get through to the comnet. I went to check the wireless signal interface Roth replaced for me, and found it to be working. The problem had to be with the transceiver, but there was no time to hike to the western side of the ridge to run a diagnostic.

"Where am I?" Flora asked as she struggled to free herself from the chair I'd tied her to again.

I glanced up at the holoscreens; there was no sign of suspicious activity.

"Where am I?" Flora screamed.

"Heard you the first time." I swung around to face my feisty guest. "I just chose to ignore you." I stared at Flora with unveiled contempt as I recalled our last meeting with Kai. "Tell me why you'd bow to Kai, who treats you no better than a crailer, and I'll answer your question."

"Damon 1300-333-1M, you'll submit to the Corporate Hierarchy of Unity and refrain from speech until a confessor is present. All words and actions will be used against you in the court of ideals."

I leapt out of my chair and walked over to her. "Your delivery isn't as amusing this time around."

Flora glared at me, and I struck her face with my fist. Blood trickled from her nose, and her eyes filled with rage. I went to the counter to get a towel. When I tried to clean her face, she turned her head away.

"I'm about to lose the life I've made for myself because of you and Kai. This time, I'm not going to make it easy for either of you."

"Kai isn't here. I came alone to help you find your way back."

"You did not come alone, and you won't find your own way back if you don't do exactly as I tell you."

Flora thrashed her shoulder forward and snarled. "If you plan on having your way with me, I'll make sure you experience plenty of pain."

"As enticing as you make it sound, we won't have time for that."

"What do you want?"

"Take a step outside the small circle you've drawn around yourself and look at the complete picture. If I wanted to harm you, I would've already done so."

"That's a good sign. If you can restrain your primal instincts, you can be cured."

"Then on the other hand, you did shoot me and kill my dog. It only seems fair I return the favor."

"I don't see a plazer blast."

"You'll see one soon if we don't leave now."

"No one wants to harm you, only help you find yourself again."

"I'm not lost."

"You've been out here so long that you forgot who you are."

"I'm certain of who I am and of what I'm saying."

"You want to go back to Unity with me. It's the scourge that's not allowing you to think clearly."

I placed my hands on both arm rests and leaned into Flora until the tips of our noses touched. "The scourge is a lie. Unity is the disease, and leaving is the only cure. You knew that at one time." I stood. "You need to relearn it now."

Flora spoke softly. "We are one in Unity. You're lost because you forgot the meaning behind the Sacred Oath."

I retreated from her seemingly incurable devotion. She'd have to succumb to her misguided loyalty on her own. With my foreknowledge, I had the advantage. I wasn't going to waste another second waiting for Kai to kill me. Unity Forces would eventually give up their search for me, and I'd be able to return to the cabin. A fact not known beyond the Corporate Hierarchy is that if a fugitive isn't captured within a year, the case is closed. Unity doesn't have the resources to continue a longer search.

I contacted Roth to inform him of what happened. The transports would have to be postponed until my return. Since the comnet was down, I had to head to high ground to deliver the message.

I loaded my plazer with a freshly charged power supply and put a spare in my backpack. New Athenia was the only known city with electricity on the other side of the tunnel, and I couldn't go back there. When the power ran dry I'd have to find another way to defend myself.

Flora said, "On my allegiance to the Overseer, I won't tell anyone I found you if you let me go."

"I would've believed you more if you swore allegiance to the stars. Do you still go to the observatory to contemplate?"

"How can you know that?" she quietly asked.

"Not answering that one. You wouldn't believe me if I—wait, why not? No reason to censor myself anymore." I pulled my desk chair in front of her and sat. "We were close in my first incarnation." Smiling, I leaned forward. "*Very* close. We met in PC1332, at Kai's emergence party. You created quite a ruckus by slapping a maroon sleeve and not addressing him by his title. Kai then slapped you for your insubordination. I felt sorry for you and offered to take you home, as it was clear to me you didn't want to be alone. We ended up at the observatory where we gazed at the stars and—" I crossed my arms and grinned at Flora, who seemed to anticipate the closing of my narrative. "If we had more time, we'd finish this discussion over a plate of spaghetti. I grow fresh tomatoes which would've been perfect for your marinara—"

Flora thrust herself forward. "Let me go!"

"What do I get in return?"

"I won't tell anyone about this cabin."

"They've known about it for years." I glanced out the window, thinking how much I was going to miss this view. "You never would have found me if Kai didn't tell you where I was. The only remaining question is what made him and Unity Forces take interest in this cabin again. All the electronics in here are imperceptible to Unitian scanners." I looked at her. "Even your locator signal is blocked in here."

Flora seemed to be waiting for an explanation, which told me I'd made some progress since my last incarnation. She was listening.

"Every Unitian is monitored from the moment they're removed from the tanks."

Flora twisted and shifted around to try and free herself. "You'll say anything to confuse me."

"I don't need to say anything. You're already confused."

"You can have your life back if you return to Unity with me."

"Give it to someone else. I like my new life better."

"Wouldn't you like to be with those who love you?"

"Love is smothered by coercion in Unity," I said.

"You only say that because you forgot what it is."

I stopped and gazed at her. "Love isn't something you forget; it's part of who you are. You don't have the slightest understanding of love because you forgot who you are."

"When we're connected in Unity, love is the feeling of union we experience. Each of us is one small part of the totality that is Unity. Come back with me, and you'll reconnect."

"What connects you to Unity?"

"Love."

I laughed. "You'll never see what's outside your circle if you believe that." I looked into Flora's eyes, searching for anything familiar, but found nothing. "You used to be independent. How did you end up like this?" The question was directed more to myself. If Flora could regress, what was to stop it from happening to me? Before today, I had no knowledge of my past incarnations, and my ignorance of them terrified me. I was powerless to change what was happening and since I left Unity, ceding control had become anathema to me. With freedom exposed as an illusion, I had to accept my eternal bondage. It was a life sentence of the most horrific, unimaginable kind. *What if it never ends?*

"Independence confuses the mind," Flora said. "As long as you think you're separate from us, you'll never be able to find your way back home. You'll be alone and scared until the scourge kills you."

I glanced at the picture of Wade and me, recalling our encounter with the boar hunter. The memory helped lighten my mood. "An Outsider once told me being scared and curious is a hell of a lot more fun."

"Was he right?"

"More often than he was wrong." I untied Flora. "Kai will soon be here, and I'm not his only—"

Flora punched my face and ran to the door. I caught up with her and pinned her against the wall. "I've been reliving the same life, and my memory returns when I see you. I know how nonsensical it sounds, but there's not enough time to ease you into this. You must trust me, or you'll die again."

"And you must trust me," she said. "I can help you through this. Detached from Unity, your mind can't make sense of what's happening around you."

"I'd rather be shot by Kai's plazer than return to Dome Dungeon."

Flora appeared startled.

"Do you remember?" I asked her.

"Remember what?"

The cuckoo clock chimed and I glanced at it. *Kai came after ten chimes, but how long after? Three minutes? Thirty minutes? I can't remember, and I'm still not completely convinced all this is happening. Am I here, reliving my life, or am I being reintegrated?*

"Only reintegration can give you the calm pulse of reality," Flora said as though reading my mind.

Her expression brought me back to the night she took her life. "We can't stay here. Kai arrived here shortly after the ten chimes."

"How can you be so sure?"

"Because he killed you in my last two incarnations."

The creases on Flora's forehead told me she still gave no credence to my story. It was understandable, but I didn't have time to convince her.

I let go of her. "I believe you when you tell me you want to help me. I'm asking you to do the same. If you believe me, you'll be okay. If you don't, your life will end today." I walked over and opened the door. "The decision is yours to make." I went to the desk, watched Flora's reflection in the window, and was relieved that she hadn't gone. I picked up her plazer and removed the power supply. "I'm leaving now, and I advise you to come with me." I handed her the plazer.

"I'm going back to Unity," she said.

"Then you must kill Kai when you meet up with him on the way." I secured my backpack. "If you don't, he'll kill you. You're an unessential to him."

"How am I supposed to fire this?"

A critical choice was forced upon me. Did I want to head to the old tunnel and let Flora and Kai fight it out amongst themselves, or find out why Kai had taken a sudden interest in me? As I was mulling over my decision, another question arose that needed an answer.

"I'll leave the power supply behind the big rock on the eastern side of the waterfall."

I hid behind a thick cluster of bushes. When Kai came into view, I forced him to the ground and struck his head with my plazer.

"Who killed the Overseer?"

"You did," he said.

"Tell me now, or this will be the last hike you ever go on."

"You killed the Overseer, Damon. There were witnesses."

"How is that possible? I haven't been to Unity in four years."

"The scourge has confused your memory."

"My memory is more complete than you can imagine. Why did you follow Flora here?"

"She's my best guard. I wanted to make sure she was okay. Did you hurt her?"

"No, but I know you want her dead, and I want to know why."

I placed my free hand around Kai's neck and started to choke him. "I won't let you kill her again."

"Cease your action, 1300-333-1M!" Flora approached with her plazer pointed at me, just as I'd expected. She was out of breath. She must have run all the way up the path.

Shisa started for her, growling.

I loosened my grip on Kai, cursed myself for dragging Shisa into my bad decision, and then spoke calmly to her. "I'm okay, girl. Go home."

She quieted down but stayed put.

"Go home now!" I yelled.

Shisa whimpered and walked away.

I looked up at Flora. "He'll kill you if I let him go."

"Lay down your weapon now. He's in no position to harm anyone."

I could've killed Kai, and I wanted to. It took all my effort not to pull the trigger, but I needed the answer to my question. I had to know if Flora was the same woman I fell in love with in my first incarnation. I moved my plazer away from Kai's head but kept my hand on the grip.

Kai smiled at Flora. "You're an exceptional guard. Don't forget your duty. Unity is justice, and you're its deliverer."

"Last warning, Damon," Flora said. Move away from Master Kai.

I didn't move. Nothing else mattered but knowing how far Flora would go for Kai. "You must kill him."

"Now!"

"It's the only way this will—" I heard an explosion followed by a sharp sting on my back. *Question answered.*

Kai rolled me off him. Flora stepped on my arm and grabbed my plazer. I could hear Shisa growling.

"I told you to go home!" I yelled. "Go home now!"

A loud blast rung in my ears. Shisa yelped, and the grievous silence that followed told me her fate.

Flora stepped off me and helped Kai up. "Forgive me, Master Kai, for letting him get so close to you."

Kai took Flora's plazer and aimed it at her. She staggered backwards.

"You should've listened to Damon," Kai said.

"I'm only loyal to you. Didn't I just prove that?"

"You've done nothing but disrespect me since you began your assignment. One action isn't enough to absolve all the reprimands you've acquired through the years."

"When we return to Unity, I'll prove my loyalty to you. I'll give you what you asked of me."

Kai spat in her face. "Had I known all it took to get you to submit was to wave a plazer at you, I would've agreed with Master Avery's decision to assign you as a crailer."

"I know you still want us to be together." Flora's voice softened. "I can see it in your eyes, hear it in your voice."

I couldn't tell if the nausea that overtook me came from the loss of blood or from the lustful way Kai was looking at Flora.

Kai positioned himself behind her and cupped her hand that was holding the plazer. "Kill him—then I'll know you speak the truth." He lifted Flora's hand and aimed the plazer at me.

"Prove to me that you're loyal." Kai kissed the side of her neck, and her eyes swelled with tears.

I got onto my knees. "You're not going to escape this." I looked at Shisa, then back at Flora. "That's justice."

"And I'm its deliverer." Flora squeezed her eyes shut. Kai pushed her arm away as she pulled the trigger. Then he shoved her to the ground. I was angry that he was going to have the pleasure of killing her. I never felt so much hatred towards someone than in that instant.

Flora got to her knees. "I did what you asked. Why did you stop me?"

"If you're willing to kill to save yourself, how can I know you wouldn't do the same to me? I demand complete loyalty from my protégés."

Flora looked at me pleadingly. "I'm sorry, Damon. I had to do it. I had no other choice."

I turned away from her.

"If you knew why you'd under—" She was interrupted by a blast from Kai's plazer.

I turned slowly to face Flora, who was flat on her back with a shot to her forehead. A few tears rolled down her cheeks.

Kai aimed his plazer at me.

"I could've shot you," I said.

"Your psychological engineering skills have perished out here. You had the advantage and failed to recognize it."

"An advantageous position isn't always as advantageous as it appears."

"From the direction my plazer is now aimed, it *appears* that death is your only option. I'd say that gives me the advantage."

"It would appear that way."

"And that doesn't bother you?"

"Why did you come here, Kai?"

"There was a lizard who'd been tracking a mouse for his next meal. When the mouse stopped to feed on some berries, the lizard successfully pinned the mouse to the ground—"

"Just as I did to you," I said.

"The lizard was about to kill the mouse, then a hawk landed nearby and told him a lightning bolt was about to strike. The hawk offered to fly the lizard to safety, but the lizard didn't listen. He thought the hawk wanted his meal. Lightning struck moments later and killed the lizard."

"The hawk would've killed the lizard anyway. Hawks eat lizards," I said.

"You were out here so long, you've become paranoid," Kai said. "Rather than accept help, you invite tragedy. Alone we fall; in Unity we stand."

"You don't believe a word of that."

"Yet I managed to make it all the way to the Chosen. And soon I'll be inducted as the 148th Overseer. Apart from the Chosen, you're the first to hear my good news."

"Did you kill the Overseer?"

"Yes. Yes, I did." He laughed. "I must admit, this is the most fun I've had in a while. I can say whatever I want to you and nothing will happen to me."

"For once we agree. It's liberating to speak freely."

"I like this a lot."

"I imagined you as many things Kai, but never as a murderer."

Kai looked solemnly at Flora. "I wanted her respect, but she saw right through me."

"She had a talent for that." I'd recalled the time she called me a sleeve-worshipper.

"Whenever I was around her my actions weren't that of a rational man. Love is the true scourge. Once it infected me, I did things I never imagined myself capable of doing."

"Is there a cure?" I was hoping for one, but my hatred thawed as I gazed at Flora. After all the betrayals, I still loved her.

"Killing Flora cured me." Kai trained his plazer on me. "But I'll return to Unity feeling very distraught because you murdered my lover who came with me for a weekend hike. I had to stop you before you killed me."

"Enjoy your victory because when I see you again—I'm going to kill you."

"Vengeance only works if you're alive."

"I know." I laughed, and my fourth incarnation concluded with a plazer blast to my head. I didn't feel a thing.

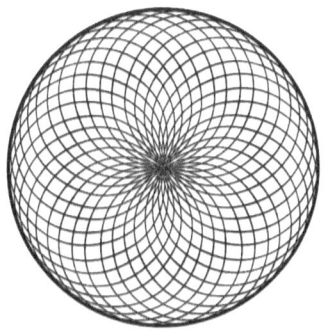

# bandits and good samaritans

### Fifth Incarnation

The karmic backpack I carried with me into the old tunnel had gotten heavier through each passing incarnation. My ignorance of the past hadn't made it any lighter. With each newly added karmic kilo came a new way of dealing with Harmony and Wade's death. On this circuit of my journey, anger followed me into the old tunnel. I was angry at the purple sleeves and Overseer for trying to dominate everyone; I was angry at Wade for allowing his feelings for Nasia to control him, and I was angry at myself for calling Unity Forces because I feared losing control of the perfect life I thought I had. To let go of it would mean to enter a chaotic world where no rules existed. I'd spent my whole life seeped in Unitian dogma that had been pounded into my brain since my emergence. Stepping outside of that structured mindset made me feel like a newborn baby having to learn the rules over again, except there were no rules to learn. I had to make up my own as I went along.

My COR alarm went off when I ran into Sephroy. This time, I decided to investigate my familiarity with him. After a short rest, I knocked on his door.

"Sorry it took so long, Chap. Back's hurting more than usual." He clung to the door frame to keep from falling.

"Don't you have anyone to help you?"

"Used to—until the damned dogs got to her." He looked at Shisa. "Can't stand them."

I had Shisa wait outside and assisted Sephroy back inside where he recounted a graphic explanation of his wife's demise, including a detailed description of her body when he found her.

"What did you want, anyway?" He sat down behind a small stationery desk and searched for something inside a drawer.

"We're leaving."

"That's it?" He took out a folded piece of paper.

"And thanks for your hospitality," I said.

Sephroy handed me the paper. It was a map.

"I already have one."

"Does it have the trade route?"

I examined the map. "How much?"

"No charge."

I searched through my pockets. "Let me at least give you some—"

"Not used to travelers helping me without wanting something in return."

"My former compatriots would laugh at you for saying that."

"They don't see as much as I do. Most people from your end of the tunnel don't say a word to me because they think they're smarter. It's hard to keep myself from telling them they don't know anything—but I got a business to run. Can't be rude to the customers."

"I've done worse." I smiled.

"Show me one human who hasn't done wrong, and I'll show you a flying dog." Sephroy laughed.

"Some of us can do more damage than others."

"That's true." He appeared lost in thought.

"Are you talking from personal experience?" I asked.

"Too personal. It's something I've been trying to forget for what seems like an eternity."

"An eternity is a long time."

"For me, time seems immeasurable," Sephroy said with an anguish that deepened every line in his face.

We talked for a while longer, and I departed with a new map but with no new understanding.

I emerged from out of the tunnel and screened my eyes from the sun's glare with my hand. Shisa ran ahead towards the beach and chased seagulls until she tired herself out. I caught some fish for our dinner and then camped out on the beach for the night.

The next morning we traveled along a forest pathway until we found a small community of stone cottages constructed in a circle formation. The COR alarm sounded, and I turned it off before rapping at the gate.

A woman approached and greeted me speaking alien words.

I gestured to the well inside the grounds. "Water."

She waved over an older portly man who spoke her same language.

I lifted my canteen and looked over at the well. "Water."

The man eye's probed me for several moments and I eyed him back, hoping for some recognition. Nothing about him or the female seemed familiar.

He pointed to my plazer. "You may enter, but no weapons are allowed in here." I slid the weapon through the wooden bars, and he took it.

"How is it that we speak the same language?"

"My grandfather was originally from Unity. Welcome to Littlefield." He unlocked and opened the gate. "I'm Wilfrid."

"I'm Damon, and my furry companion is Shisa."

"No wild animals are permitted inside the gate."

"Shisa isn't wild. She's more civil than most humans I've met."

"That's a referral of the highest measure." He scrutinized Shisa for a moment and then signaled for us to enter.

I followed Wilfrid to the well. "I can offer you something for the water."

"We don't charge for water here," he said. "It belongs to the Earth."

"I like the sound of that."

"My grandfather told me all the world's problems come from us thinking we own pieces of the Earth, but we're pieces of her."

"Your grandfather sounds like a wise man."

"He was, indeed. Where are you headed?"

"New Athenia."

"You have a long journey ahead of you. It'll be getting dark soon. You're welcome to stay in our guest bungalow."

"Thanks for the offer, but I've been stagnant long enough. I'd rather keep moving."

"You'll need weapons. Bandits roam the woodlands once the sun goes down." Wilfrid studied me briefly, then handed me back my plazer.

I expertly flipped it around in my hand. "As long as I have this, I have nothing to worry about."

"Impressive." Wilfrid smiled. "But a weapon can't get you out of every problem."

"Did your grandfather tell you that too?"

"As a matter of fact, he did."

I held out the plazer for him.

"Keep it," he said. "I can see you're no threat to us."

"If I run into a bandit, I hope he won't agree with your appraisal."

After I had drawn some water, I called out to Shisa who was playing with a young boy.

"It seems like Michael made a friend," Wilfrid said.

Shisa and Michael ran over to us.

"Are they staying?" Michael asked Wilfrid.

"You may address Damon directly. He speaks our language, and he'll be leaving soon."

Michael looked up at me, and I reached out to shake his hand.

"You'll probably run into bandits." He looked at Wilfrid. "Did you tell him?"

"I'll be okay," I said. "Shisa will protect me."

Michael bent down to pet Shisa and then looked up at me. "You're either brave or not right in your head."

"Mind your speech, Michael," Wilfrid said.

"I don't *mind* anyone who says what he thinks," I said.

Michael stood up. "I hope you're brave."

"Sometimes I think I'm not right in my head." I winked at him. "Thanks for keeping an eye on Shisa."

Michael petted her. "You be careful, and watch out for the bandits."

I walked along an Ancient road running parallel to a forest. The crickets were loud, but not loud enough to block out Wade's death still fresh in my memory. Lost in my thoughts, I failed to notice the two horses racing up from behind. I'd heard the clacking of hooves against the ground so many times that the sound didn't alert me. It took a few moments to connect Shisa's barks with the riders who came at me, swinging long chains. Before I could seize my plazer, I was thrown to the ground by a chain that lashed my hips and torso. I struggled to my knees, holding my throbbing hip with one hand while firing my plazer blindly with the other. Another chain battered my thighs, and the force threw me on to my back. The two bandits converged over me with their chains. One of them struck my chest, and I lost consciousness.

I awoke to Shisa licking my cheek. I'm still unsure how she escaped the attack, but I was relieved to see that I was not alone. A stabbing pain irradiated from my chest down to my lower extremities. Screaming in agony, I pulled myself onto my forearms. Shisa sat next to me, whimpering.

I was stranded and without supplies. The bandits had taken everything except for my multipurpose knife, which was still strapped to my belt. Unable to get up, I started laughing at my shortsightedness. My failure to think about the consequences of my actions had led to Wade's and Old Woman's deaths. It seemed fitting that I'd probably meet a similar fate. What felt like hours of self-recrimination passed, then a horse and carriage rode past me. The rider had spotted me but continued on his way. This happened several more times. People went by without offering even a sip of water. I wondered whether all Outsiders were this selfish, and I ruminated over my own behavior. My need to advance at the expense of the Unitians's autonomy wasn't any different.

"This is my payback." I petted Shisa. "Question is, who's paying me back?"

Shisa answered in her own way by teaching me the true meaning of compassion. A rabbit scurried past us and she got up and barked, but never left my side. She barked again when an old man on a mule stopped nearby. He approached, peering at me.

"Thanks for stopping," I said.

He answered in words I couldn't understand.

I reached into my pocket and pulled out my last possession—my multipurpose knife. "Take."

The man leaned down and took it.

"You can have it for a ride to the nearest village."

He retracted the various blades and seemed amused by the miniature magnifying glass.

"Do you understand?" I asked. "This is a trade."

He responded in his foreign tongue.

I made a wheel motion with my hands. "Ride. I need a ride."

After a few more unrecognizable words, he walked away. At first I thought he went to get something and would be coming back. *He won't leave me here to die. We made a trade. He'll come back for me.* Under normal circumstances, the old man's thievery would have been obvious. Reality quickly sobered me up when he got onto his mule and rode off.

"Give me back my knife!"

Shisa cried and circled around me.

"I'm slocking dumber than an Outsider, Shisa. You might as well save yourself and go now."

She sat down next to me.

"I said go!" I pushed her away. "I don't want you here anymore!"

Shisa gazed at me and whimpered. It only made me want her to leave more. I didn't want her to die again because of my ignorance. After a few more jabs to her side, she walked over to a nearby tree stump and lay down beside it.

Looking up at the darkening gray sky I felt helpless. *I don't have metallic wings to fly out of here. I'm going to die in the woods without the sacred burning, and my body will become fodder for a pack of wild dogs.*

Night came. I was thankful Shisa hadn't gone. I didn't want to die alone. She nestled beside me, keeping me warm until I fell asleep.

I found no peace in slumber; Wade's death kept replaying in my dreams. After reliving several rounds of him plummeting to his death, I woke up shouting and then wept at the reality of my situation. When I saw Shisa, I was able to relax. I studied the starlit sky until my perception was funneled into the same contained state I experienced while in a coma. I came to accept I'd die alone and no longer felt anchored to my body. Adrift in a stream of calm, my thoughts matched the pace of my slow, almost nonexistent breath. I felt a stirring of soft, pleasant vibrations in different parts of my body, buzzing and producing their own tone, not audible to my ears, but to some other sense I could not readily define. The pulsing originated deep at the base of my abdomen and flowed slowly upward in a slow wavelike motion and stopped at the space between my brows. Behind the shades of my eyelids I beheld a starlit sky, and the brightest star near the center flickered and exploded. A strong electro-magnetic-like sensation poured into me from the top of my head and surged through my entire body. A translucent white spherical torus materialized and deflated into a point of light. The same chord from my vision rang out and was sustained. The light swelled back to a sphere and contained within were countless galaxies, but there was no void in this space. The galaxies were intertwined by an intricate web of light. They gyrated in rhythm to the chord that pulsed rapidly in five-quarter time, stressing the fourth and fifth beat.

Suspended in the center of the sphere was a golden nucleus that glowed brighter than the sun, yet I could stare directly at it with no discomfort. The nucleus projected light particles that streamed in an upward column and dispersed throughout the galactic web. Light appeared to be drawn back in from the southern side of the column, traveling back up to the nucleus where the cycle continued. *Time is relevant to sound,* I heard myself say. I opened my eyes, unsure whether I had died. I turned to my side, relieved to find Shisa fast asleep. After I'd confirmed that my skull was still attached to my head, I closed my eyes. The sphere and I expanded concurrently until we both exploded, merging into one complete awareness. All the knowledge of the universe came to me unspoken but fully understood. Everything within me sparkled, glimmered and communicated in varying colors and vibratory tones. I surrendered to the euphoria that enveloped me. Such pleasure I had never experienced before, and I didn't want it to vanish because I knew my human brain wasn't capable of assimilating so much knowledge.

The ground beneath me started to move, and I opened my eyes. I was now on a horse-drawn cart.

Michael looked down at me. "He's awake, Grandfather."

I passed out again, surrendering to my transcendental odyssey.

# nomad

I lay on a bed weeping, but not from the fountain of light that had illuminated me a few hours earlier. My skin felt as though it were being perpetually stabbed, and I wanted to escape from my damaged body even if it meant my death. Wilfrid and Michael entered with Shisa close behind. She ran up and leaned her head on my forearm, one of the few parts of me that didn't ache.

Michael handed Wilfrid a bottle.

"Go now," Wilfrid said to Michael.

Michael surveyed my pulverized body with barely a trace of emotion, which made me realize the severity of my condition.

"You were right. Something is wrong with my head," I said.

"You're lucky they didn't break that too."

"Michael! Mind your speech!" Wilfrid said.

"No offense taken. I deserved that one." I stroked Shisa's head. "Go with Michael."

Michael waved Shisa over and she followed him out.

Wilfrid came to my bedside. "You're lucky to be alive. If your dog didn't show up here barking for us to follow her, you'd be dead." He gave me the bottle. "Drink."

I took a sip. It burned my throat going down. "What is this?" I coughed.

"Whisky. And you need to drink a lot more of it."

"Why?"

"I have to reset the bones in your legs, and it's going to hurt —a lot."

"Have you ever done that before?"

"Drink," Wilfrid said in a loud voice.

I drank as much as my throat could withstand and handed him back the bottle.

"We're now ready to begin." He gave me a rag. "Prepare yourself."

I needed no further explanation. I bit down on the rag, readying myself for what I was about to endure.

As Wilfrid pulled and twisted my thigh bones, pain streaked through my body like a bolt of electricity. I clenched my teeth so hard I was surprised they didn't shatter. My body stiffened, and tears shot out from my eyes. Focusing on the space between my brows, I hoped for the fountain of light to return and carry me away. I waited until I lost consciousness.

I awoke with both my legs in splints. Michael's mother, Genevieve, entered with a glass of water. She lifted my head and positioned the rim of the cup between my lips. After a few productive swallows, I passed out again.

Sutara returned in a dream. She sat on the stone-carved bench across from my cot.

"Why do you keep coming to me?" I asked.

"You called me." She threw her hands in the air. "You always call me."

"For what?"

"You must remember on your own."

"Then what's the point in my calling you?"

Sutara laughed.

"What's so funny?"

"I ask myself the same question, and the only answer I can come up with is that you choose not to remember. But a part of you, the part that's most awake when you're asleep, wants to hear it. That's why I still come."

"I don't understand."

Sutara grabbed her head. "Why do I still regress to the same foolish faith I had as a child? I keep returning to you, hoping you'll finally acknowledge what's happening."

"How can I acknowledge something that makes so little sense?"

Sutara rolled her eyes. "Go to the cabin, and it will."

"There's nothing there."

"After the passing of four cycles since your departure from Unity, she will be waiting for you. Please, hurry before you miss her again."

"Who is she?"

"When you go back, you'll remember, but you must try to remember sooner next time. I'm tired, and I don't know how much longer I can do this." Sutara got up and walked to the door. "Each time I come to you, I grow weaker. I must go now."

"Don't go. I still don't under—"

I opened my eyes to Wilfrid holding a glass of water towards me. He lifted my head, and I took a sip.

"I heard you moaning. Are you all right?"

"It was just a dream. How long have I been unconscious?"

"For three suns."

I tried to sit up but a wave of pain forced me back down. "I must seem foolish to you."

"We all have our moments."

"I seem to have more of them than most." I laughed, and my ribs ached.

"Finding humor in your own misfortune shows that you're getting better."

"I hope it also shows I'm getting smarter."

Wilfrid nodded his head and smiled. "You must be hungry. I'll have Genevieve bring you food."

Genevieve came daily to feed me, and Michael would sometimes accompany her with Shisa.

Michael reminded me of my son Aaron who also loved animals. Aaron had a hard time at school. He preferred to daydream rather than listen to his teachers. He proclaimed he'd grow up one day to be the world's best astronomer and build a space vessel that would take him to explore new worlds. I could understand his escapist mentality because I had it as well, always wanting to be somewhere other than where I was, especially now. For eight weeks I did nothing but sleep, eat, and talk. When I was alone, I occupied my time composing music. Without paper or a hologue, I pictured the musical staff in my head and mentally drew in the notes and rhythm as I heard the melody. I forgot half the music I wrote, either because the piece didn't interest me enough to remember or I was interrupted.

While I was in the middle of composing a song, Wilfrid entered with warm stew just out of the kettle.

"Where's Genevieve?" I asked.

"She's not feeling well today." Michael came in with freshly baked bread and handed me a piece.

"Is it serious?" I inquired.

"She's fine. It's only the coughing illness that's common to this season," Wilfrid explained.

"Can I go to the river, Grandfather?" Michael asked. "I'm done with all my chores."

"Be back before dark."

"Don't worry. I have Shisa to protect me." Michael hurried out.

"Can I get you anything else, Damon?" Wilfrid asked.

"How about some company?"

He sat on the bench. "Getting restless?"

"Since the attack," I laughed. "Tell me about Littlefield." I tore off a piece of bread, dipped it into the stew, and took a bite.

"My grandfather built this bungalow with his own hands. This was meant to be the only one, but other people came, and he built more."

"What color was he?"

"The same as me." He shook his head. "Strange question."

"I meant his position. All of us are designated a color which identifies what class we're in. Orange is the service class; yellow, the artist—"

"Ah, I understand. My grandfather never spoke of his past."

"Not surprising. Most people who leave Unity prefer not to talk about it."

"How about you?"

"I'd rather meet up with my attackers for another thrashing."

"That's why I told Genevieve and Michael never to ask about your provenance. My grandfather once told me a man keeps silent about where he comes from when he wants to forget." Wilfrid got up. "I must go now. Tranquil time is almost over, and I have some chores to do."

"An elder's job is never done."

"Truer words have never been spoken to me," he said with a smile and walked off.

Alone again, I contemplated every mistake I'd made since leaving Unity. I was rescued by a melody that came to me, and as I pieced together the arrangement, I fell asleep.

Several weeks had passed, and I was able to get around with a cane Wilfrid had carved for me. When I took my first steps outside, curious residents crowded around to gawk at the witless man who tottered about the village all because he had disregarded Wilfrid's warning. Verbal communication was almost impossible; most of the villagers spoke the language of the woman who greeted me at the gate. Some of them demonstrated their friendship and pity by offering me a piece of fruit or bread. Wilfrid extended his hospitality by inviting me to share a meal in his home. He was not only a fine bonesetter but also a well-respected spiritual leader and teacher. Crosses, stars, and constellations were carved into the walls of his bungalow, and one symbol, in particular, intrigued me: a spherical torus.

Wilfrid lifted a silver chalice filled with wine and directed me to do the same with mine.

"Heavenly Sky King, please keep us safe, and may our wheat fields be plentiful through the coming of your gracious spring givings." Wilfrid drank.

I followed along with the ritual and then pointed to the sphere. "What's the significance of that symbol?"

"Why do you ask?"

"I've had visions of it since I was a child."

Wilfrid lifted both brows. "Have you seen anything else?"

I studied his face for a few moments and felt at ease. He viewed life with childlike fascination, yet there was wisdom in his gaze and assuredness to his speech.

"I've had visions since my ninth year," I said. "Some of them are of complex geometric figures and others let me see into future events. But the ones that intrigue me the most are of a woman I never met. She keeps appearing to me, telling me to revisit a cabin in the woods."

"Are you going to go?"

"I haven't decided yet if she's even real. Every time she appears to me, she insists I contacted her, but I didn't—and yet I believe her." I examined the symbols on the wall. "It's the strangest sensation," I said to myself. "I sometimes get the feeling everything I experience has already happened, like this conversation."

Wilfrid walked over to a small table and retrieved a deck of cards. "I knew you came for a reason beyond the observable." He shuffled the cards, drew the top one, and laid it face up. "Ace of diamonds." He smiled. "Such a draw doesn't happen by chance." He set down thirteen more cards and appeared surprised. "Ace of hearts, ten of diamonds." He slowly lifted another card and placed it next to the others. "Seven of diamonds." He looked up at me. "*Damon.*" His eyes were brimming. "Thank the Sky King my grandfather taught me to read and write. Spelled backwards your name is *Nomad.*" He stood and bowed to me. "I'll follow you wherever you go."

It took me a minute to realize he was serious. "I'm...not going anywhere."

"Everything we have is yours."

"You've given me enough."

"The bandits left you with nothing. Surely we can give you more."

"It took my getting beaten and stripped of everything to confirm I don't need much."

"What is your foretelling for Littlefield?" Wilfrid asked as he stacked the cards.

"That's more your talent than mine."

"I only read the cards, whereas you're here to lead us to our future."

"I appreciate your hospitality, but I don't want to lead anyone."

"For the past twenty-eight turns of the winter's longest night, I've seen your name in my dreams. You are the wise seer who is to bring us all together."

"For what?"

"I'm not sure of the purpose, but I have been expecting you." Wilfrid looked down at the cards. "All my life, I foresaw a momentous change originating from beyond this earth. This is an auspicious time to be alive."

"Don't place your hopes on me; I'm not worthy of them. I'm only a traveler who was on the way to New Athenia. The sole reason I'm here with you now is because you saved my life."

"Are you saying you don't believe your visions," he gestured to the sphere on the wall, "even as you witness representations of it with your own eyes?"

"I wish I could give you what you're asking for, Wilfrid. You, Genevieve, and the rest of the villagers have shown me more compassion than I've seen anywhere. After I was attacked, people passed me by, and not one stopped to help. The only person who did stole my last possession. This world was a good idea, but it failed. I wouldn't even lead a horde of rats out of the old tunnel. They're better off living in darkness."

"Perhaps I was mistaken," Wilfrid said. "The person I'm seeking isn't angry or defeatist." He picked up the cards. "I must rest now."

Wilfrid appeared disappointed enough for me to wish I could be what he wanted. "If Nomad exists, I hope you find him."

# phantom worship

My injuries had taken almost twelve weeks to heal. A year passed and I was fully immersed in village life. I sheered sheep, milked the goats, and helped with the planting and harvesting. A rhythmic chant came to me as I picked branches of wheat. *Cut, pull, throw, cut, pull, throw, cut, pull, throw.* It eventually grew into a song I named, "The Whispering Wheat." In the mornings I'd arrive at the field an hour before the crop gathering to watch the sun rise and hear the grass swaying in the wind. My peaceful early morning ritual ended another year later when Michael came running to me, out of breath.

"You have to come now, Damon!"

I followed him to the circle where Wilfrid was leading an injured man to the guest bungalow. His shoulder was wounded and wrapped in a blood-drenched shirt. Although he wasn't in his color, I knew he was Unitian. Unity's limited selection of leisure attire led me to identify him by his tan hiking suit. Clothing aside, he was familiar to me, but I couldn't scan for COR because my hologue had been stolen. I helped Wilfrid walk our guest to the visitor's bungalow, which I'd vacated after I decided to stay.

"I should make more cots—we're turning into a hospital," Wilfrid noted.

"I know you," the Unitian said. He examined me curiously as we laid him down on the cot. "Damon—I can't remember your emergence date, but you're the one who invented Harmony."

"Do you know him?" Wilfrid asked me.

"I'm identifiable by something I'd rather forget."

"They said you were killed," the Unitian remarked.

"I'm sure they said far worse than that."

Wilfrid put his hand on my arm. "Leave us. You can continue this later."

"Should I get the whisky?" I asked.

Wilfrid smiled as Michael entered holding the bottle. The Unitian eyed it nervously.

"They're kind people," I said. "They'll take good care of you." Michael and I went out. When I came back later, the Unitian was in mid-conversation with Wilfrid. He stopped talking when I appeared.

"I've been away from Unity for a long time. You can speak freely."

He skittishly shifted his weight on the cot.

"I don't know how you remember him, but since his arrival, he's done nothing but help us," Wilfrid told him.

I approached the Unitian. "What did they say to you about my disappearance?"

"They said you were murdered by your friend, right after he killed the old lady in the cabin."

"Wade was no murderer."

"They said he had the scourge, and that she—"

"No such illness exists." I pulled up a chair and sat next to him. "It's one of the many lies perpetuated by the Overseer and the purple idiots who follow him."

The Unitian laughed. "Why did you leave?" he asked.

Wilfrid looked at me. "I'll be outside, if you prefer I don't hear."

"Stay," I said. "I never told you why I left because I'm not sure I can explain it."

Wilfrid maneuvered another chair next to mine and sat.

"During my walk through the old tunnel, and throughout the days I spent lying here during my rehabilitation, I had nothing but time to think. I came up with many reasons for my leaving. Every one of them led to one truth that was troubling to admit. Since my emergence, I was shaped and molded into the Unitian ideal as dictated by the Sacred Oath. Wade's death exposed that ideal as a phantom—not real, yet worshipped like a god. I wasted my life believing an illusion."

It didn't get past me that I sounded eerily like Master Franklin, and that I had grown up and agreed with him as he'd predicted. "Wade died over that illusion."

Sensing my torment, Wilfrid placed his hand on my shoulder.

"Once the lie was exposed, I had no idea who I was anymore, but I knew who I wasn't. So I left."

"Thank you," Wilfrid said with tears in his eyes. "For many turns, I never understood the sadness in my grandfather's eyes. Now, I do."

"You speak like a true Striker." The Unitian offered his hand to me. "I'm Roth."

We shook hands.

"Will you tell me what happened?" I asked.

"We were ambushed—"

"We?"

Roth struggled to sit up and I helped him.

"I was transporting a young couple. Halfway into the old tunnel, we stopped at a trainlet to rest. Thieves broke in and beat us—took everything we had and—" He began breathing heavily. "I'm not a fighter."

Wilfrid poured water into a glass and handed it to Roth.

"I must've passed out because when I came to, my passengers were gone. I ran out to search for them and found the man outside. He was lying on the ground with a knife handle sticking out of his chest. Amazingly, he was still alive. Think he hung on to let me know the men who attacked us took the woman. He told me to tell her he loved her—if she was still alive. Then he died." Roth took a sip of water. "I'm lucky this village was close to the tunnel, or I probably would've bled to death."

"How did you plan on returning to Unity without getting reintegrated?"

"The Strikers have a way of manipulating ID markers, but they can't alter the same one more than once because they don't want to raise suspicion. The plan was to alternate conductors until we found a permanent one to replace the Outsider who initially ran freedomline. When I get back to Unity, I'm going to tell my appointer it's too risky to continue moving passengers. Outsiders are better at this than we are. The last two conductors never lost a passenger."

"Beyond the beacons, rules no longer exist," I said. "With freedom comes risk."

"I'm starting to wonder why anyone would want to leave Unity. It's a mess out here."

"What made you question the Sacred Oath?" I asked.

"It's not fair—the way the lower colors are treated in Unity. We're separated into different groups and told we're equal, but the Corporate Hierarchy has more privileges and credits than the rest of us."

Wilfrid nodded his head. "Purple. My grandfather always hated the color purple."

"I can't stand it either." I picked up the bottle of whisky and smelled the contents. "Nearly two years ago, I was where you are right now." Roth gawked at me as I drank. "It's an acquired taste." I handed him the bottle.

He waved dismissively at me. "Maybe later."

I examined the bottle. "Wilfrid first gave me this shortly after I was beaten and left for dead. As unpredictable as things are out here, I'd never go back to Dome Dungeon."

"No one can promise you absolute safety," Wilfrid commented. "A dome can be cracked as easily as your head." He clicked his tongue and knocked on the top of his head.

"Heed this man's words." I patted Wilfrid's shoulder." He speaks only the truth."

Roth said, "Even if I wanted to continue, the Strikers will bring an end to Freedomline if we don't find an Outsider who'll —" He paused and widened his eyes. "Would you consider being our conductor? We can pay you for each transport."

I flashed on having this conversation before, and my answer came instantly. "I finished my last bottle of berry ale three days after I had left Unity. How soon can you get a case over to me?"

"I'll send one over with your first transport," Roth said enthusiastically. "This will help repair your reputation, at least with me."

I looked at him curiously.

"The woman in the cabin was our previous conductor. What was she like?"

I closed my eyes, trying to stay focused on the discussion. Confronting my role in Old Woman's death reawakened all my guilt which I'd managed to put aside for the last two years.

"I understand if you don't want to talk about it," Roth said.

I opened my eyes. "She was opinionated, strong, and one of the wisest Outsiders I've met, next to Wilfrid."

"Why did you report her then?" Roth inquired.

"I had no idea she was helping the Strikers."

"Would it have made a difference?"

"I had my doubts about the Sacred Oath on the day I entered her cabin. Had she told me she was the conductor, I still would've reported her."

"I don't understand."

"Try to stop yourself from admitting to something you don't want to admit to and then you will."

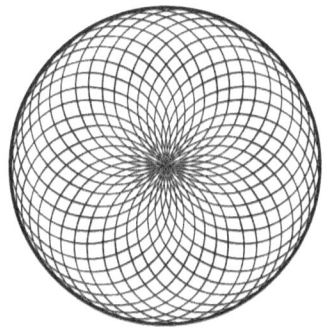

# a souvenir to remember

I traced the etchings of the chalice with my thumbs as I contemplated going back to the cabin. Wilfrid sat down with a deck of cards in his hand and shuffled them.

"Keep my future to yourself, please."

He set the deck on the table.

"I don't want any outside influence this time—I've made my decision."

"You cannot save everyone."

"I'm to blame for what's happening in Unity. I can't turn my back."

"That's a big burden you carry," Wilfrid said. "Are you the only one responsible?"

I had to think about an answer, mostly because I knew where Wilfrid was leading me. "I was well respected for my work and had support."

"Without support, would you have been able to do what you believe you did?"

"No, but that doesn't absolve me."

"You told Roth you left Unity because it doesn't represent who you are."

"I spoke the truth."

"My grandfather told me a man of honor will admit when he's wrong and accept whatever the consequence without making excuses. You, *Nomad*, are a man of honor," he said, emitting a calming energy.

"You're looking for a leader, but Littlefield already has one. Since my first day here, I've never heard you raise your voice. No one speaks against you or even looks at you with hostile intention."

"I never realized you examined me so closely."

"It used to be part of my job—understanding human behavior." I had to laugh. "If only I could understand my own."

Wilfrid picked up the deck of cards and shuffled them. "Old habits cannot be unlearned in one afternoon. If you feel you are needed, go." He laid down a ten of diamonds. "How about that?" He tapped the card. "It would seem the cards agree with your decision." He smiled at me. "You'll find happiness in a new land."

Michael sat by the river fishing with Shisa by his side. He hadn't spoken to me for two days after finding out we were moving on. I thought about leaving Shisa with him, but considering all we had gone through, I couldn't part with her. I sat down beside Michael. He didn't acknowledge my presence. "Catch anything yet?"

He continued to ignore me.

"We'll visit after every other transport."

"It's not fair. While you two are out having your adventures, I'll be stuck here doing the same thing every day."

"What do you think you'd see if you leave here?"

"Something other than Littlefield, and this boring river. It seems like—"

"There's more for you beyond this boring forest?" I smiled at him.

"Yes, but how will I find it if I can't leave this place?"

"You're still young—"

"I'm tired of hearing that. I'm not afraid of facing the bandits. I'm good with a longbow."

"At least wait until you finish your studies before becoming a warrior."

"You don't understand how hard it is to be in one place because you're always moving around."

"That wasn't always the case," I said. "Ever since I was a boy, I wanted to explore the world. I didn't know anything existed beyond Unity, and once I came to this side of the tunnel, Earth became a much bigger place than I ever imagined."

Michael petted Shisa. "It feels like Grandfather and my mother are trying to force me to be a farmer, but I want to decide what to do with my life. Is that wrong?" He gazed at me with the same inquisitive expression I had seen in both my boys.

"I have a proposition for you. If you don't give your mother any trouble, I promise to take you to New Athenia in your sixteenth year."

"Really?"

"As long as your mother approves."

"Thanks, Damon!"

"Will you walk with us?"

He nodded as Wilfrid approached.

Wilfrid and Michael escorted us halfway to the tunnel where we all said our goodbyes.

"Safe travels, Nomad."

"Don't forget your promise," Michael said to me.

"Never." I shook his hand and pulled him towards me for a hug.

Having both your legs broken can bring you good fortune; at least for me it did. For the first time in all my incarnations, I had the closest thing that resembled a family.

Thinking about all the work waiting for me at the cabin made leaving Littlefield difficult. I had gotten used to the interdependence of village life and was uncertain how I'd handle the isolation. Roth detected my unease. He spent the first half of our journey attempting to assuage me by reaffirming that I'd have everything I needed. Our roles reversed when we first spotted the old tunnel. Roth became less talkative and slowed his pace.

"We'll be safe," I said.

Roth eyed Shisa. "No one would dare bother us with your dog around, right?"

"Shisa doesn't take anything from anyone."

"Is that story Michael told me about her true? Did she really go to Littlefield to get help for you?"

"If it weren't for Shisa, I wouldn't be here today."

"How did you train her to obey you?"

"Dogs are naturally loyal creatures. Show them kindness, and they'll stay by your side no matter what."

We soon arrived at the opening of the tunnel. I began to regard my treks through the old tunnel with a hint of romanticism. The trains spoke to me of a world I never knew. To create such wonders meant the Ancients weren't told their inventions went against some god or man-made edict. An Ancient at heart and an Outsider in body, I was born in the wrong age.

The shade was up in the trainlet where the attack on Roth and the passengers took place. We went in to investigate, but nothing seemed amiss.

"Sephroy must have cleaned up." I looked under some of the benches and found a wallet. Inside was a small picture of a couple.

"That's them," Roth said.

I placed the picture in my pocket.

"Why are you saving it?"

"It'll remind me why I'm going back."

Roth didn't want to stay in the trainlet, and I couldn't blame him considering what happened there. After a brief visit with Sephroy, we made our way through the tunnel without resting.

We reached the cabin and found it vacant. Roth gave me a few last-minute details, and he was ready to return to Unity.

"I'll be your only contact with the Strikers," he said. He handed me a crumpled paper with the details of the transport. "When we meet up, I'll bring you a new holologue and wireless signal interface. You'll have to live like a true Outsider for a while."

"Been doing that for the last two years."

"On my way back, I'll run a diagnostic on the transceiver. If there are any problems, I'll replace that as well."

"It's behind the large rock on the western side of the eroded —"

"Already know where it is. The Strikers have been maintaining it for the last conductor. She was good at transporting but knew very little about electronics."

Roth patted my arm, sensing my guilt at the mention of Old Woman. "This is your chance to make things right."

"That's why I'm doing this."

"Anything else you'll need?" Roth asked.

"A set of violin strings and some—"

"Berry ale."

"You're good."

"That's why I got this assignment."

"As a Striker or Unity Guard?"

"Both."

"That takes talent. I only knew one other Unitian who could make the same claim."

"Who?"

"Someone I was very close with." I had no idea to whom I was referring, but it felt as if I did when I said it. After going through a list of people I knew in Unity, not one of them fit the description of the person I mentioned. I surmised COR was active, but without a way to prove it, I turned my attention to the mundane. I cleaned the cabin, restarted the solar trap, and tended to the garden that needed hours of weed pulling, digging and planting to bring back its former glory.

I soon began transporting passengers and visited Littlefield on every other return. In contrast to my previous incarnation, I looked forward to meeting the passengers and engaging them in conversations about their hopes and dreams. Hearing their reasons for leaving Unity strengthened my conviction to continue as the conductor. I liked where I was, and I wanted to remain for a while longer, but fate never agreed with my preferences. Exactly as Sutara predicted, my memory was restored four years after my departure from Unity, when I found Flora unconscious at the bottom of the ridge.

# bones and ruins

I was at my desk when Flora regained consciousness. My incarnations were swarming around in my head out of sequence, and I couldn't decide whether I wanted to smother or make love to her. "I know why you're here, so let's skip over our introductions. Everything you think about me is false, which means everything you're about to say about me will also be false."

"Damon 1300-333-1M, you will submit to the Corporate Hierarchy of Unity and refrain from speech until a confessor is present. All words and actions will be used against you in the court of ideals."

I turned my chair around and saw that she had her plazer aimed at me.

"Not as effective without this." I showed her the power supply.

Flora charged me but stopped when I aimed my plazer at her. I tied her to the chair again, and this time I planned on skipping my reunion with Kai. Executing that decision wasn't as easy as I'd anticipated. While packing my things, I made the mistake of looking at Flora and recalling our first night together in the observatory and noticing the beauty mark just beneath her right ear. Conflicting feelings made me uncertain about what to do next. Music always cleared my thinking, so I got out my violin to reconnect my emotions to the present timeline. I played through "Dreams of New Athenia," a piece I'd written during my stay at the trainlet in my first incarnation. By the song's end, my memories adjusted to their proper chronological order, and my senses told me to leave the cabin before I received another plazer blast to my head.

"I'm not going to waste the little time we have easing you into this." I put my violin in its case. "I didn't kill the Overseer."

"How did you know about the accusation?" Flora asked.

I rolled my eyes at having to go through all of it again. "I relive my life, and my memory returns each time I find you at the bottom of the ridge."

Flora stared at me just as she had the last three times upon hearing my revelation. I'm certain my Outsider appearance made her mistrust me, but I didn't care. I was tired of dying in my thirty-second year. "What I'm saying will shortly be proven. Kai is accusing me of the Overseer's murder because he killed him."

"You can explain all of this to your confessor."

"I don't acknowledge Unitian law—or your interpretation of it." I got out some containers of almonds and dried fruit and threw them into my backpack.

"You have the scourge. Return to Unity with me before you —"

"I'd rather get shot in the back by you again than go back to Dome Dungeon."

For one fleeting moment, Flora looked at me as she had in my first incarnation, but I was too angry to indulge in nostalgia.

"If I thought it would make a difference, I'd ask if you remembered me saying something similar before. But I don't care anymore. You've turned into a sleeve-worshipper and when Kai kills you, it will be too late to rethink your loyalties."

"All these delusions you're experiencing can be stopped," Flora said.

I stormed over to her and pushed the chair onto its back. "The delusion is Unity!" I walked around and stared down at her. "See it for what it is or die again."

"It's you who is living in the delusion. You've been out here so long, the abnormal has become your normal."

"What is your normal?"

"Unity, and the connection we feel when we're a part."

I clenched my fists. "You're drowning and don't even know it." Grabbing my backpack I headed towards the door. "I'm done with trying to save you."

"Aren't you going to free me?"

"Wasn't planning on it." I smiled. "You look comfortable."

"You can't just leave me here."

"Why not?"

"That would be cruel, and you claim you're innocent. No one will believe you if you leave me here."

"If you shot me with my back turned to you, would you consider that cruel?"

"And cowardly."

"Then you're cruel and cowardly by your own definition." I opened the door.

"Please, don't leave me here." Flora's Unity Guard facade cracked, and she began to cry. "Untie me. No one will find me here."

The desperation in her voice pulled me back to her.

I kneeled beside Flora and began untying her. "Understand this, Unity Guard, if you follow me, I won't hesitate to kill you."

"What about my plazer?"

I helped her up.

"You won't be getting it back in this round, so avoid Kai on your way back to that dungeon of yours."

"Please don't go." She lifted her hand to me. "Return with me and reclaim your connection to Unity."

"Unity is just a word used to lump a whole group of people together to control them. I bet you can't even tell the difference between an Outsider and a Unitian." I tugged on my beard. "And please don't state the obvious."

"Unitians don't commit murder."

"The Overseer's death is justice served. I'd proudly admit to killing him if I were responsible."

"The sickness is making you speak these blasphemous words. A visit to the reintegration center will help you."

I tapped my head. "Pillaging my mind of what makes me unique is blasphemous."

"Once you've completed treatment, you'll remember who you are and what you're a part of."

"Which is what?"

We both answered. "Unity."

"You're getting predictable." I crossed my arms.

"Unity is your only salvation."

"No, Flora, it isn't. You're your only salvation. If you don't see that you're—"

I heard the cuckoo clock chime and examined the security holoscreens. Nothing was present but rocks and trees. "Why aren't the motion sensors detecting him?"

"Detecting who?" Flora asked.

"I don't have any more time to debate you." I secured my backpack.

"Where are you going?" Flora asked.

"To a place far away from you and Kai." I headed for the door. "I'm too slocking tired to relive another encounter with you two."

"Come back with me," Flora said. "It's not too late."

I turned to face her. "For me, it won't be." Something about her expression made me wish I'd left her tied to the chair, but there wasn't time to second-guess myself.

I sprinted halfway up the ridge with Shisa. When I had a clear view, I looked through my binoculars and spotted Kai on the middle ridge. He was right on schedule. The physical exertion of my run diffused my anger, and I went back to the cabin hoping Flora was still there. The door was ajar. Shisa ran in ahead of me and straight to Flora, who lay on her back. Blood gently spilled from a long vertical cut on her forearm. I snatched the kitchen knife from her hand and threw it across the room.

"Why did you do this?" I lifted her and gently cradled her in my arms as I'd done in my first incarnation.

"Unity is justice, and I couldn't deliver. I'm no longer a part of Unity. I'm alone," she cried.

I placed my hand against her cheek. "No. That's not true. I'm here."

"You left, and I failed. Kai would've made me go through reintegration." She coughed. "I can't go through that a—"

Flora died in my arms. I hugged her tighter, crying and rocking her in my arms. My anger for Kai had built over five incarnations, and I was eager for him to walk through my front door so I could greet him with it.

Kai entered the cabin. I grabbed him from behind and jabbed my plazer against the small of his back. "Drop it."

He dropped his plazer, and I kicked it across the room.

"What did you do to her?" Kai observed Flora and then Shisa, who was growling at him.

"Save your poorly acted concern for your protégés. I know you came here to kill us, and you already succeeded with Flora."

"It looks as though she got to herself first. She was psychologically unstable. Perhaps if you were still in Unity, your counsel would've saved her."

I forced him to the floor. "You're the one who's unstable, you psychopathic old slock!"

Kai pulled himself up to his knees, and I smacked the side of his head with my plazer.

"Listen to me." He rubbed his head. "This can work in our favor."

"How?"

"I'll tell the confessor that Flora killed the Overseer and implicated you. You can stay here and continue your life—"

"Why should I trust you?" I kicked Kai in the gut. "You came here to kill me."

Clutching his abdomen, he winced in pain. "A female dog plays in a pasture. From out of nowhere, a pack of wild dogs appear. Two of the males approach the female, but only one can mate with her. The bigger male growls, and the smaller dog meekly barks and crawls back to the pack." Kai straightened his posture and glowered at me. "The larger dog believes he's the victor, until the smaller dogs realize they're greater in number and fatally attack their leader."

"Except your little *dogs* aren't around to save you."

"You're surrounded. Everyone knows you killed the Overseer."

"You killed him—so you could take his place."

Kai appeared surprised.

"I'd say congratulations, but I'm not sure you'll be returning to claim your title."

Kai snarled, made another attempt to get up, and I smacked him across the face with my plazer.

"Unity might have been a good idea during its founding, but it's become a prison that you've built around yourselves, and one from which there's no escape. You've become more dangerous than a pack of wild dogs on the hunt, devouring each other over power, prestige and privilege. You'll continue to devour until there's nothing left but bones and ruins." I aimed my plazer at him. "Like the Ancients, you'll soon be forgotten. How does that make you feel?"

"That we can't escape history, any more than we can recapture it."

I looked at Flora's bloody body, recalling my final words to Kai during my last incarnation, *Enjoy your victory while you can because when I see you again, I'm going to kill you.* I intended to keep my promise, but instead I clubbed Kai with my weapon. He passed out, and I made another attempt to shoot him, but my index finger refused to execute my desire for revenge. I dropped to my knees and gave out a yell. In that bleak moment, I believed all was lost, but then fate spoke to me from within the cabin. The pictures of Old Woman and Wade that hung on the wall, a snapshot in my pocket of the murdered couple, and the woman I loved who lay dead on the floor, demanded that I continue fighting Kai and everything he stood for.

I wrapped Flora in a blanket and carried her to the mountain on the eastern side of the cabin. At the clearing before the elevation path, I lay her on the ground and covered her with leaves twigs, grass, and wildflowers. I shot my plazer into the kindling until it caught fire and then I spoke the ceremonial prayer aloud.

"From the ground you arose, and to the ground you shall return. Of this Earth you've been granted life, and from this Earth new life shall arise in your place. Carry on into heaven, where your identity will eternally be stored eternally. Through my memories of you, your presence will be celebrated for all the joy you've brought to our Unity. All together, we were here. All together, we'll be again."

The words seemed truer to me than they ever had. I gazed into the flames until they blurred from my tears. Shisa walked around the pyre, whimpering as she had done with Old Woman. After the fire had gone out and Flora's ashes were reunited with the Earth, I climbed halfway up the ridge where I set up camp. From there, I kept watch over the cabin.

In the late afternoon, Kai staggered outside holding the side of his head. He lost his balance and grabbed hold of the porch rail. After several failed attempts to walk, he went back inside and didn't leave until the next morning.

The fact that he did not call for assistance implied he wanted his presence to remain a secret. To confirm this, I hung around for three extra days to see if Unity Forces would arrive to inspect the cabin. All remained quiet. I contacted Roth and told him what had transpired. Not knowing if Kai would continue to independently monitor my whereabouts, and without any proof he assassinated the Overseer, we agreed I should take a year off before resuming Freedomline. The decision made me recall Wilfrid's declaration about me. Although I disagreed that I was Nomad, I was starting to feel like one.

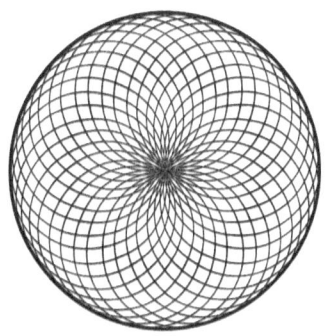

# the well

We caught sight of Littlefield and Shisa sprinted towards the gate. Upon entering, the circle was quiet. A quick look at my hololalogue reminded me it was tranquil time. As I approached the well to fill my canteen, an ominous foreboding came over me. My COR alarm sounded. I shut it off, placed my hand on the well, and closing my eyes, tried to find a connection.

"Damon?"

I turned to see Genevieve.

"I thought you weren't coming for another twelve days."

"So did I. Is the guest bungalow available?"

"For you, always."

Genevieve sensed my unease and tried to console me. Amid our discussion, I thought about the well, wondering why it set off the COR alarm. I politely excused myself and entered the solace of my bungalow. Shisa barked, wanting to be let outside.

"Shhh, they're all asleep." I removed my bow from its case.

She hopped onto the cot and leaned her chin on her paws.

"Rest up. Michael will probably have you running around until the day's end." I finished rosining my bow, got out my violin and played with the intent of retrieving my memory of the well. Long, slow strokes in the lower octaves made my mind more receptive and open. I played "Beneath the Lonely Stars to Nowhere," which I wrote while I lay dying after my attack. At the start of the song, I remembered gazing up at the sky, Shisa lying beside me keeping me warm, and the eternal-light that liberated me from my pain. My thoughts came and went, and I finally disconnected from them by focusing only on my music, until I was no longer aware of my surroundings. The memory I was searching for surfaced, jolting me back into consciousness. During my first incarnation, I followed the map given to me by the Unitian couple I met in the tunnel. I ended up here where I filled my canteen. The whole village was deserted.

A knock on the door broke my concentration. Wilfrid and Michael entered. Shisa hopped off the cot and ran to them.

"Hi Damon. Why are you back so soon?" Michael asked as he leaned down to pet Shisa.

"To give you a surprise test. I want to make sure you're keeping up with your studies."

"It's not a surprise anymore. You just told me about it."

I checked my holologue for the time. "You have until the morning to prepare."

"We'll be by the riverside until then. It's too noisy to study around here." Michael called to Shisa, "Let's go, girl." Shisa followed him outside.

"Are you up for a game of gin rummy?" Wilfrid scanned the room as though looking for something.

"Maybe later. I'd like to rest for a while."

"Rest well. Genevieve is preparing a feast for you tonight. We'll all be waiting for you in the circle."

"I don't want to sound ungrateful, but I'm not in the mood for a celebration tonight." I lay down on my cot.

"I'm sorry for your loss," Wilfrid said.

"Did the cards reveal that to you?"

"I did have an unfavorable reading." He placed his hand over his heart. "But I don't need the cards to tell me the obvious."

"Genevieve told you," I said with a smile.

"It's difficult to trick you, Nomad." Wilfrid's eyes widened when he spotted a hologue I'd left on the table. "How come you never told us about her?"

"I'd rather not talk about this now."

"I understand." He picked up the hologue.

"It's yours."

"Thank you, Nomad." Wilfrid excitedly clasped the hologue around his wrist, looking at it with the most bewildered expression.

"I don't see anything," he said.

"Stare into the delivery optic."

"What's a delivery optic?"

"The small clear circle at the—"

"Ah, I see it…but I still don't *see* anything."

I smiled at his childlike fascination. "Speak your request, and your retinas will receive the image."

"Pictures of Unity." Seconds later, Wilfrid laughed. "Oh my! This is a machine of miracles!" He glanced at me. "How come I never hear you speaking to it?"

"I do, with my implant."

His eyes widened again. "It *knows* what you're thinking?"

I nodded.

"Oh my, my, my." He looked back at the hologue. "It's hard to believe something so beautiful is as horrible as you described. Unity looks like a place I'd like to visit."

"Once inside, you'd be ready to leave."

"I feel the same way about Littlefield. My grandfather told me never to feel settled anywhere because it makes it difficult to leave when trouble comes through the gate."

I sat up. "Are you and the rest of the villagers planning to abandon Littlefield?"

Wilfrid seemed surprised. "No. Why?"

"I was here before."

"Of course, you were here before." He kept glancing at the hololgue. "Almost twenty-five suns set since your last visit. Don't you remember?"

"I was here, in a previous incarnation."

I gestured to Wilfrid as he lowered his arm, his eyes inquiring an explanation.

"This is not about me being your Nomad."

"Oh? What is it about then?"

I told him about my past incarnations, and he became more steadfast in his assertion that I was Nomad.

"If you didn't find us here, that could only mean you led us somewhere else, exactly as it was foretold to me," he said.

"I never met you yet when I first passed by Littlefield."

"But now you have."

"I don't think I led you anywhere." I rubbed my chin and ran through my visual memory of that day. "Maybe I arrived here during tranquil time. I wish there was a way I could be certain."

"Don't worry, Nomad. This is a reason to celebrate, even though you may not think so now." He approached the door. "Rest, and I'm sure you'll agree with me in the morning."

Wilfrid's calm demeanor allowed me to put aside my concerns about Littlefield's fate. The rest of the night I lay restless, thinking about Flora. I'd seen her die in five lifetimes, and every time I closed my eyes I relived her deaths. I needed a distraction. I thought about returning to New Athenia. It wasn't the panacea I dreamed of, but I missed the Alexandrian Repository and playing in the orchestra.

Shisa and I left Littlefield three days later. Wilfrid gave me one of his horses for my trip. When I had a full view of the village, I took out my camcorder and recorded a movie. "PC 1332-156th day, fifth incarnation, on way to New Athenia." The text of my time stamp appeared on the screen along with a recording of my voice. Since I couldn't remember the first time I passed Littlefield, I thought visual images might help me remember more in my next incarnation.

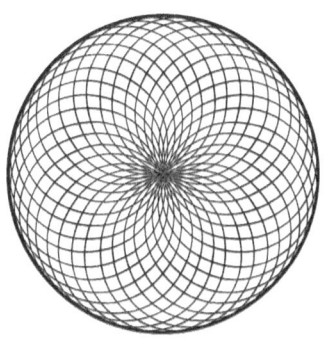

# mirror

I inspected Flora's hollologue. Some of the files had been erased after her vital signs ceased. My attempt to retrieve them failed. I had no way of proving they had anything to do with her being a Striker or that if our never meeting in Unity somehow altered events in her own life. I reread Flora's stories, looking for anything that might help me understand why she went from being a dissenter to a defender of the Corporate Hierarchy. I was surprised to find all of them were unchanged. They still depicted Unity being defeated by the brave unnamed captain.

The uplifting stories cheered me up and made me laugh, particularly when Kai was involved. In one farce, the captain arrived and used a weapon that was given to her by her alien mentor. It slurped off Kai's clothes in the middle of the Overseer's assembly, where he stood naked in front of a laughing audience. The weapon stretched into a long tube and siphoned up Kai along with the Corporate Hierarchy. They were regurgitated onto the deathlands where they were used as fertilizer to help grow flowers and trees. The stories all had the theme of personal empowerment and the liberation of the oppressed. Then I understood...the unnamed captain was Flora. I reread the stories with that awareness. Through her fiction, I got to know her better than I ever had. They proved she was still the same Flora I loved from my first incarnation. What I couldn't fathom was why she fought against me when we desired the same thing...a free Unity.

When I arrived at the gate, the guards were mystified by my fluent Knosian. My penchant for Ancient myths led me to season my history with a hint of mysticism. I told the guard who questioned me that an old female sage traveled to my homeland and taught me the language, art, and music of New Athenia. Wade would've enjoyed my performance, but the guard had no interest in my brand of humor and stuck to procedure. After a few hours of questioning, I vowed to play ignorant in my next incarnation.

I was granted an immediate visitation pass and auditioned for the Orchestra. Manolis was impressed when I played the Mozart violin sonata.

"The sage you studied with taught you well," he said.

"Does that mean I'm in?" I put away my violin while thinking about my favorite Mediterranean restaurant as I hadn't eaten all day.

"Rehearsal is tonight at seven thirty."

"And not one moment past," I said as the phantom smell of chicken smothered in lemon garlic sauce activated my salivary glands.

Manolis elevated both his brows. "I think I'm going to like you, Damon." He smiled. "Continue on like that, and I'll sponsor you for your residence pass."

The cafes weren't to open for another hour, so I took Shisa out for a walk in the central park. I sat on my favorite bench in front of the duck pond with a bag of stale bread I'd brought along. One of the ducks approached me without fear and snatched a piece from my hand. There was an area on his left outer wing where no feathers grew, and judging from his aggressive temperament, I surmised it was from a fight. I tore off another morsel of bread, and the trouble-making duck chased away the other ducks and waddled towards me. I stomped my foot to scare him away so that the rest of the ducks would get a chance to eat, but the feathered hooligan returned when he spied another piece of food in my hand.

"You'd make a great Overseer." I bowed and tossed the remaining bread to him. "But don't expect me to be a feather-worshipper."

I got out my violin and started to play "Rain Dance," a lively song inspired by a memory of Flora from my first incarnation. We had returned from horseback riding and on our way back to the dome, we got caught in the rain. When I arrived at the access, Flora wasn't with me. I glanced back and saw her twirling around and dancing. Recalling her smile saddened me because that was the last time I saw her truly happy.

As I continued to play, a crowd had gathered around to listen. Their appreciation for my music made me eager to perform again until I ran into Lidian at the entrance of the amphitheater.

"Damon!" He shook my hand. "When Manolis couldn't remember your surname because it was a number like mine, I knew it was you. What brings you to New Athenia?"

"Unity was starting to bore me." I smiled as I thought of various ways to escape. "How long have you been here?"

"A little over two years. My wife and I have a large flat. Come over after rehearsal. We'll have more time to talk there. You can also tell me how the slock you picked up Knosian so fast."

I was surprised Lidian got all those sentences out without stuttering. "Learned it in a past life, along with how to play the violin and read cards."

"Card reading…you mean as in fortune telling?" Lidian laughed. "What's my future?"

"You'll find out when it happens."

Lidian laughed again. "Looks as if leaving Unity helped you find your sense of humor."

I got to my chair, and after a few introductions, I tuned my violin. Lidian waved his trumpet at me, and I extended my bow towards him. *This time I'm ready. I won't let you slock up my life again.*

We opened with Mozart's *Symphony No. 40 in G minor*, just the right selection to soothe my tense mood. Hearing all the strings singing along with mine made me forget about Lidian. By the time we got to the fourth movement, I was in a relaxed enough state to deal with another exchange with him. He was the most difficult individual to read as he seemed to change drastically from incarnation to incarnation: a mediocre musician and murderer in one life, a victim of suicide in the next, and now a married trumpet virtuoso. *Expect everything and assume nothing when you're aware you're reliving the same lifetime, Damon.*

At the sight of Holly receiving us at the door, I almost dropped my violin case. Lidian embraced her, and I squeezed the handle of my case until I felt my nails digging into my skin.

"This is my wife, Holly," Lidian said.

"Hi, Damon and welcome to New Athenia." She offered her hand.

"Hello…Holly," I said softly as I shook her hand. I was too stunned to form any other words.

"You're just in time for dinner," she said.

"Excellent," Lidian commented. "In the meantime, we'll continue our discussion on the veranda. We have an excellent view of the central park."

Lidian and I drank wine and played cards while Holly prepared dinner. The smell of cumin, curry, and turmeric told me she still seasoned Athenian dishes with exotic spices from the Far East. My favorite Athenian food was pastitso, a pasta dish with chopped lamb covered in a rich cream sauce. Holly added her own twist using a secret variety of spices, which she wouldn't reveal to me. At my prompting, she opened a cafe. Her business did very well, especially with the Athenian dignitaries and artists who were regulars.

Tonight, Holly made *keftedes*, meatballs made with ground lamb. The aroma traveled up through my nostrils, triggering memories of our life together. After sampling a bite, I recognized the familiar hint of cinnamon.

"Delicious. You should start your own business," I told her.

Lidian kissed her cheek. "I made a similar suggestion. Some of the ingredients she uses are ingenious."

"What kind of ingredients?" I inquired.

"Holly would kill me if I told you."

I squeezed the stem of my glass. Flora's death combined with Lidian's open display of affection for Holly fragmented my entire understanding of justice. Kai and Lidian kept getting away with murder and were seemingly awarded for their crimes. Justice was exposed as another form of idealism that, in reality, failed. Either that or my villainy was worse than Lidian's and Kai's. Everything seemed to lead back to Harmony. As long as I continued to invent it, I'd be guilty of enslaving a whole population.

I guzzled down my wine, intending to get drunk enough to forget past incarnations. "What made you decide to leave?" I asked Lidian.

"I always felt limited in Unity. Tyrus persuaded me to leave with him. He's been a strong influence in my life."

"And mine as well." Holly picked up a carafe and poured more wine into my glass.

"Tyrus is the only one worth remembering from Unity," I said.

"I had a hard time during my early years of study," Lidian said. "I lived through a daily barrage of insults and beatings by the kids in my dorm. The house maroons reprimanded them, but it only made things worse. In my sixteenth year, Tyrus showed up while I was getting beaten up outside the library. He broke up the fight and took me to a satiation center for lunch. We talked for a long time, and I told him I hoped to be selected to play in the Unitian Orchestra for my life assignment. He allowed me to stay at the Academy of Sciences building. There were some spare rooms available for purple sleeves who worked late. Tyrus reserved one for me as payment for keeping the labs clean."

Lidian took a sip of wine and appeared to reflect on something. "Tyrus is different from the rest of the Corporate

Hierarchy. He cares about the Unitians and believes they have the right to make their own decisions. When the Overseer planned to transmit Harmony to the fetuses—"

"When was this decided?"

"Shortly after you had gone. Tyrus couldn't do anything to stop it, so he departed as well." Lidian poured more wine into his glass and topped off mine. "Do you regret inventing Harmony?"

"One of many regrets." Gazing at Holly, I finished my wine in one long swallow.

"Did you use Freedomline?" she asked.

"Did it all on my own. How did you get out?" I asked, hoping she'd mention Flora.

"Tyrus helped Holly and me leave together. That's how we met." Lidian smiled at her.

"Is he still here?"

"He left a little over two weeks ago—said he needed to experience more of the world."

"He almost died," Holly noted.

"How?"

"He suffered from severe headaches. They found a growth in his brain. Doctors here successfully removed it."

"Do you know where he went?"

"The lands of the Ancients' bible," Holly said.

Lidian put his arm around her. "He asked us along, but Holly had just found out she was pregnant."

I looked at Holly and tried to force a smile, but I couldn't. I had to get out of there.

"You're the first person we told." Holly beamed at me.

"I'm honored." I got up, almost stumbling. "It's late. I should get going."

Lidian insisted on accompanying me back to my flat. During our walk, all I could think of was how he had stolen my life. He had my job, my wife, and now he was going to have my children. James and Aaron didn't exist in the last few incarnations, and I couldn't fathom what that meant for them. All the while, Flora's deaths hadn't stopped replaying in my mind. My memories and flashbacks didn't blend well with all the wine I drank. "You're a lucky man," I said to Lidian. "Holly is a treasure. She's going to make a great mother."

"Tyrus knew we'd be good for each other."

With Harmony out of range of the transmission towers, my hatred flowed out violently and unrestrained. "You may have successfully hidden who you really are from Holly and Tyrus, but not from me." I stopped and raised my fist at him. "I see you for what you are—a murderer and a liar."

Lidian gawked at me. "Where is this coming from, Damon? I haven't seen you since—"

"Why did you blame me, you slock!" I yelled. "I was thrown out of New Athenia twice because of you!"

"I think you're confused. Let's get you back to your flat. A good night's sleep will—"

I hauled off and punched him and felt both scared and thrilled by my lack of restraint. I took another swing at him, and he seized my upper arms. "Damon, I will not fight you!"

I pulled back and was ready to strike him again, but something in his gaze gave me pause.

"You're no different from any other Unitian," he said. "Find your own way home." He walked off.

Rattled by my loss of control, I ran and didn't stop until I got to my flat. I passed out on the couch and dreamed about finding Flora dead on the floor. As I held her in my arms, Sutara entered the cabin.

"Why do you keep asking me to come here?" I asked. "I find only death."

She looked down at me. "You still do not want to see."

"I'm trying."

"Do not be afraid to see. The past has already occurred and cannot harm you."

I hugged Flora tighter. "She feels real to me."

"If you don't remember, you'll be here forever."

I continued to hang on to Flora.

"She is going to keep dying if you—"

"I'll save her next time."

"How? You cannot even save yourself."

"I said I'll save her next time!"

"I'm tired of this sparring." Sutara put her hands on her hips. "I finally see what I put my uncle through—always wanting a second serving of carrot halva—"

"I'm tired of all your secrets! If you have nothing else to say, get the slock out of here!"

I woke up then and couldn't get back to sleep, so I visited the observatory and gazed up at the stars. Somewhere from within the Milky Way, inspiration came and helped me decide my next line of action.

What the stars had communicated to me was validated during my morning walk with Shisa on top of the labyrinth. A view of the Parthenon, then at the city below felt more nostalgic than like home. New Athenia's distractions couldn't help me get my mind off Flora, and with Holly married, there was nothing to keep me here. I took the lift down to city level and picked up a fresh loaf of bread and goat's cheese at the market. On my way to Lidian and Holly's flat, I mulled over a variety of excuses, but none seemed persuasive. When Holly opened the door, I handed her the bread and cheese. She crossed her arms and tilted her head to the side.

"I need to speak to Lidian," I said.

"So you can kill him?"

Lidian appeared and took the parcel. "Thanks, Damon." He gave the bag to Holly and stepped outside. "Let's go somewhere else. She's more dangerous than you when she's mad."

I looked at Holly. "I can offer no excuse for my actions. My only hope is that you and Lidian will forgive me someday."

Without saying a word, Holly closed the door.

"She'll be okay," Lidian said.

We walked to the duck pond in the central park. I removed some bread from my pack, and the tyrannical duck from my last visit pushed and pecked himself ahead of his competition. He quacked, and I leaned down to feed him. "Here you go," I pondered over a name. "Gadfly."

Gadfly plucked the bread from between my fingers.

"Gadfly?" Lidian asked.

I pointed at my plumed friend. "At first I thought he was the Overseer of this pond, but now I view him more as a Striker."

"In what way?"

"He opposes the pecking order." I hand-fed Gadfly another piece of bread. "So I gave him a fitting name."

"You're a strange man," Lidian said, shaking his head.

"I just like ducks."

Lidian laughed, breaking the tension between us.

"What I did last night—wish I had a rational explanation, but I don't."

"The wine."

"Wine usually relaxes me." I tossed some more bread into the pond. Several ducks raced towards the morsel, but Gadfly got to it first. I quickly threw crumbs in the opposite direction to feed the others.

"Are you okay, Damon?" Lidian asked.

"I don't think I'll ever be okay."

"What happened last night?"

"I lost sense of time."

"Looked more like you lost sense of your senses."

"That too."

Lidian looked at my backpack. "Where are you going?"

"The lands of the Ancients' bible seems intriguing."

I took a bite of the bread and threw the rest to some pigeons. Shisa chased after them, they flew away and she chomped down on the bread, victorious.

"No one has beat me up since school," Lidian said. "For a brief moment I thought I was back in Unity reliving the worse years of my life."

"I'm not like them."

"I know," Lidian said.

Shisa approached a lanky, dark-skinned man wearing a white kurta. He leaned down to pet her. Then he bowed his head to me and smiled. I returned the gesture, and he walked away.

I faced Lidian. "Does that mean you accept my poorly executed apology?"

He reached out his hand for me to take. "I wish you luck on your travels, and I hope you find what you're looking for."

We shook hands. This time, when I looked at Lidian I recognized him for who he was in this moment, a truly evolved man.

On our way out of the park, we passed by the man with the white kurta, sitting crossed-legged on a small grassy hill, his eyes closed. From his clothing, I knew he came from east of New Athenia. I'd recently heard about their meditative techniques that opened the mind to the highest levels of mystical experiences. The traveler's peaceful expression made me realize the only time I felt similarly was while immersed in the fountain of light. I mused over getting myself beaten up again. *Maybe it would bring back the fountain of light.* The thought made me laugh, and I had to explain to Lidian that I was sometimes prone to hysterical outbursts for no apparent reason.

"And you were a psychological engineer?"

"*Were.*" I smiled and ambled ahead.

Lidian followed me. "I stand by my verdict; you're a strange man. Had your friends known this about you, I don't think I would've appeared as crazy to them."

We exchanged a few more insults, followed by some pointless banter about Manolis's use of dramatic hand gestures to compensate for his lack of masculinity, and I realized I had made another friend.

I reclaimed my horse outside the gate and once I was out far enough for a complete view of New Athenia and the Parthenon, I stopped to capture a still picture. No matter how many times I'd taken this shot, I never saw it the same way. My visual memory, in this particular moment, made me think about what Lidian's successful evolution meant for me, and for all of humanity. If a murderer could evolve, then no absolutes of good and evil existed beyond the realm of time. I needed to know this because it meant I had a chance to stop myself from inventing Harmony. There's an Ancient cliché that says a picture is worth one thousand words; my picture was worth more. Whenever I lost sight of my goal, I only had to look at it to remember. And with that image in my mind, I had no other choice but to continue.

# amulet

After sixty days of travel I entered the lands of the Ancients' bible. When I caught sight of its most sacred city, identified by a dome shrine, I recorded a movie. "PC 1332-281st day, fifth incarnation. Approaching Old Jerusalem." The dome had been destroyed and rebuilt before the Great Cataclysm. The rock on which it sits was so sacred to the Ancients, they fought over it for thousands of years. It's still sacred to the people who live there now, but they no longer fight.

I had acquired some gold coins while in New Athenia and exchanged one for the local currency. I stabled my horse and set up camp, then headed to the open-air market in the middle of the city. The smell of exotic spiced meat filled the air, reminding me I hadn't eaten since the night before. I walked by each stand examining the offerings and decided on curried rice with lentils for myself, and a pork chop for Shisa. She barked as the merchant filled my bowl.

I waved the pork chop over her head. "You'll get this when I find a place to sit."

A female vocalist lured me towards her. She maneuvered smoothly through a complex melodic line, accompanied by a percussionist and guitarist. I'd heard similar songs at the music library, but hearing it live made it sound new to my ears. I found a spot near the band and tossed the pork chop to Shisa. "Don't eat it in one chomp. We'll be here for a while."

In front of the band people danced in a large circle, moving their feet in a similar step-pattern. Observers clapped their hands and stomped their feet in time to the music. A man pulled me by my hand to join their dance. I tried to escape, but a woman seized my other hand and dragged me into the crowd. The music was infectious and I danced along, stepping on feet until I learned the sequence. Spellbound by the atmosphere, I stuck around for several more songs until Shisa grew restless and started barking for us to leave.

We made our way to the dome. The architect must have considered the passing of time as the marble structure appeared to have been recently built. I studied it for several minutes, absorbing the history of another treasure, a gift to us from the Ancients.

Devotees sat quietly praying by the entrance, and as I approached the shrine one of the men rushed over to me, speaking excitedly in the local language.

"No Hebrab," I said and continued towards the entrance.

The man blocked my path to keep me from entering.

"You must kneel to the ground and pray in reverence to their god," another, older man announced in Knosian.

I became fixated on a metallic cylinder hanging from his neck. The amulet glowed in the moonlight, revealing an intricate engraving of curved symbols that seemed very familiar.

"I'm Jall," the man said and shook my hand.

"Damon."

Jall glanced at Shisa. "And who might you be?" He leaned down to pet her.

"That's Shisa."

"Shisa. That's a beautiful name. Is she your protector?"

"Even more so than her name indicates. Are you from New Athenia?" I asked.

"I prefer to say I'm from Earth. Makes it easier to speak with people from all backgrounds when I generalize."

"Do you live here?"

"Full time. They have the best parties here. What's the purpose of your visit?"

"I'll know when I find it."

"You're a seeker."

"Sounds weak hearing it out loud."

"In this part of the world, visitors are either seekers or followers. The contented ones stick to New Athenia, so they can indulge in all the conveniences."

"You don't appreciate modern technology?"

Jall smiled. "Along with generalizing, I find conversations are easier to navigate around when I keep my opinions to myself."

"Is there anything we can discuss?"

"Did you try the local wine?" He held out a bottle. "My lovely lady stood me up this evening, and I have no one to share this with."

We returned to the campground where my tent was pitched. I removed my plazer and fired into a pile of dried sticks and twigs.

"You cheat." Jall warmed his hands in front of the fire I ignited.

"I have nothing against conveniences. Gives me more leisure time."

"Wine is the ideal companion to all things leisure." Jall handed me his bottle.

"Along with a beautiful woman." I envisioned Flora as I took a long swig.

"If they show up."

"And stay with you."

"Very true." Jall laughed. "What's your rating?"

"Rivals the wines from New Athenia. Same goes for the food and people." I gave him back the bottle. "Is everyone always so happy here?"

"Like I said before, they—"

"Have the best parties here."

A group of people camped nearby laughed loudly as they sat and talked around a fire. It made me miss the days when I did the same with my classmates. Master Franklin would have us gather around a campfire while he told a ghost story. He kept embellishing the tale until someone screamed; it was usually Lidian.

Jall looked at me as though he detected my loneliness. "If you help tend my vineyard, I'll teach you Hebrab. You'll feel as though you've belonged here your whole life."

"I accept, but I first want to visit the Great Pyramid. That's where I'm headed tomorrow."

"I'll hold your position until your return."

"Our arrangement will have to be temporary. There are many other places I read about at the repository that I'd like to explore."

"You say that now, but after you live here for a while, you may never want to leave." He drank some wine. "When I first arrived, I wanted to know why this culture lasted while almost every other one died."

"Did you ever find the answer?"

"I stayed." Jall grinned and passed me the bottle.

"I'm not sure I under—"

"The ancestors of these tribes kept their faiths alive because the ideal they created transcended their daily life, and still does. The people here emit an energy that is seemingly infinite. It constantly replenishes itself through each generation. The longer I'm here, the more of it I want to absorb. It's more addicting than what's in that bottle."

I drank some more wine and gave the bottle to Jall. "I thought I belonged in New Athenia. It was similar to my home city—more similar than I wanted to admit. They don't offer much of a second chance to Athenians who break an edict. One mistake and you're banished."

"They accept authority in exchange for their fancy gadgets and ease of life. I prefer to make my own rules."

"Thought you had no opinion." I said.

"For those who don't want their world perspective challenged, I don't offer one."

"My perspective broke a long time ago."

Jall laughed. "Don't make any repairs. You're better off without it."

"Think you're right." I pointed to the amulet. "What is that?"

"The gypsy who sold it to me called it an echoer." He removed it from around his neck and handed it to me. "He claimed it was an Ancient artifact that was found near the pyramids and that it would allow me to see beyond the dimension of time."

"Does it work?" I asked while examining the echoer. It was unusually smooth, and I couldn't feel the etchings on the surface.

"The only thing I see now is that I've been swindled out of a bottle of wine."

"Do you know what language this is?"

"It's not in the linguistic library at the repository, and I'm familiar with many of the Ancient languages. The trickster who made that useless trinket probably has a cart-load of those for sale."

"Are you willing to trade for this?"

"Take it. The damned thing has given me nothing but an ache at the back of my neck."

"Let me give you something for your trouble."

"If you insist on payment, you can work for free at my vineyard for seven days after you get back. Then we'll be even."

"Sounds like a fair trade." I placed the amulet around my neck and examined the engraving. "I've seen these symbols before."

"Where?" Jall observed me as though expecting some great revelation. When none came, he said, "Don't think too hard. It's all nonsense from the mind of an imaginative swindler."

Jall soon left. I stayed up and played my violin. Several of my neighbors arrived and sat around the fire. Although we couldn't communicate, their presence was enough to quell my loneliness, which seemed to grow stronger with each lifetime. The only connection I found with them was Flora. She was the key to understanding why I had knowledge of my incarnations. I'd have to wait to die, be reborn, and grow up to figure out why. Even that didn't guarantee I'd unravel this mystery, or that I'd even remember my current incarnation. The only thing I could rely on now was the present moment, which meant I never knew where I was going to land, or if I ever would again.

We explored the old cities of Bethlehem and Nazareth for three days, arriving finally at an Ancient-built canal. A ferryman crossed us over to what used to be Egypt. Most of the dwellings from the Ancients had been demolished. The locals lived either in tents or small houses made of brick and clay.

By the time we made it to a campground outside of Old Cairo City, Shisa and I were covered in sand. I pitched the tent and secured my horse and we stopped at a public bath to clean up. I exchanged demonstrative hand gestures with the bath-keeper imploring him to allow Shisa inside the baths. Some bathers gathered to arbitrate the situation. I secretly enjoyed the disorder I caused, and Wade would've been equally entertained. I identified my team by the group leader who placed his arm around me. He was on the verge of losing the argument until a young girl came to me with a bucket. Those on my side applauded, laughed, and pointed at the losers. I washed Shisa and paid the girl to watch over her while I cleaned myself up.

In the center of the city was an open air market, twice the size of the one in Jerusalem. I used up the day trading and surveying each stand; examining linens, trinkets, pottery, spices and foods. During our evening meal, I listened to the local music performed on tabla drums, ouds, and flutes. As night fell, I turned down all invitations to dance. The last three days had tired me and I needed sleep. I went back to the campsite, got out my violin and played "Wandering the Labyrinth," which I had composed the night before I left New Athenia. The somber melody attracted a small audience. I played "Rain Dance" next, and people began to dance and clap their hands. I continued for another hour, and at the end of my performance, a group of travelers tossed me some bronze coins. That was the easiest money I'd ever made.

Early the next morning I trekked over to Giza. I shivered as I gazed upon the three pyramids and the Sphinx. They were isolated from everything else in the area, and I felt like a space traveler touching ground on a new world. I looked down at Shisa. "Am I still on Earth?"

She opened her mouth and panted.

"Guess that's a yes."

Placing my hand over the rough surface of the Great Pyramid, I really felt as though I were on an alien world. Then my COR alarm went off and the environment around me changed. I lay in a shallow pool of wine-colored fluid. While I couldn't feel the liquid touching my skin it nonetheless gave off warmth. A spacecraft streaked by overhead, producing a white trail of smoke against a crimson sky. Jumping to my feet I scanned the area. The wine-colored fluid spanned out as far as my eyes could see. An incandescent white spherical torus materialized and floated in front of me. I went to touch it and the ground began to rumble. An incubation tank slowly emerged from the water with a baby floating peacefully inside. I approached and pressed my hands against the tank.

 Someone placed a hand on my shoulder.

I turned to see the alien female who had cast me out of the alien world while I was in a coma. Her gossamer skin was ornamented with green, blue, and pink veins that glistened beneath the sphere's light. When I peered into her large green eyes, I recognized her and was overcome with joy. "Shishandi!"

She smiled and her irises changed to indigo. "Six begin, Six alone, Six unite." Shishandi reached out to me, I took her hand and found myself back at the Great Pyramid with Shisa pacing up and down and whimpering. The amulet felt warm against my chest but cold to the touch. *Did I just see beyond time and space? Who —and what—is Shishandi? Why is she so familiar to me?*

I returned to Jerusalem hoping to learn more about the gypsy who sold Jall the echoer. When I arrived at his vineyard, I discovered he wasn't the owner. I showed a still picture I took of Jall to the locals, but no one recognized him. For now, Shishandi would have to remain another unanswered question. With nowhere else to go, I decided to return to the cabin and continue Freedomline. I'd been gone for almost a year. Kai would have given up the search for me. He'd be indulging in his life as Overseer, not worrying about an eccentric defector who lived in a cabin with a dog, or a dead Unity Guard whom I still loved despite our tragic histories.

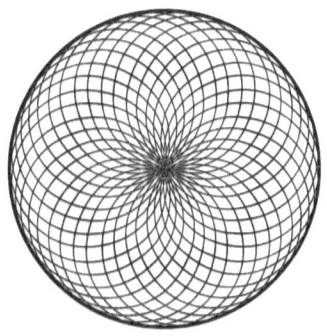

# rats and monsters

Sephroy opened his door and tapped his cane on the floor in quick succession as he said, "Hello, hello, hello. Long time no visit."

"Are you going to invite me in or hit me with that?" I entered his trainlet.

"Welcome back, Chap. You've been away so long, I almost forgot your name."

I handed Sephroy a wood-carved camel I picked up in Egypt.

"What is it?"

"A camel. They ride them like a horse across lands without trees or water."

"Doesn't sound like a place I'd want to—" Sephroy, staring at the echoer, dropped his cane. "Where did you get that?"

"Jerusalem." I picked up the cane, and he tried to snatch the echoer. I stepped back. "What's gotten into you?"

"Give it to me! It doesn't belong to you!"

"You've seen this before?" I gave him the cane. "Can you tell me where it came from?"

"Did Jall give it to you?"

"Yes. How did you—?"

"Why is he starting things up again now? That gluttonous fool has no self-control. He understood the danger he caused and promised never to—" Sephroy squinted his eyes at me. "Did you find out about the Six?"

I didn't answer fast enough, and Sephroy delivered several quick taps on the floor with his cane. "Six begin, Six alone, Six —"

"Unite!"

Sephroy slid onto his chair and rubbed his forehead. "If he gets what he wants, I won't be able to stop it this time."

"Stop what?"

"Evolution. And you're not ready to evolve." He shook his head. "That Jall has never been the patient type."

"What do you...believe we're evolving into?"

Sephroy pointed his cane at me. "Don't act superior around me. You *are* evolving, and you're staring right at your future." He thumped his chest.

I inspected his ragged appearance and laughed. "No offense, Sephroy, but you live in a tunnel, can barely walk, and eat dog. How exactly is that evolving?"

"Don't condescend to me with your microscopic-sized brain!" He reached out to me. "Give me the echoer."

His gaze intensified, radiating a dimension of depth I hadn't seen in him before.

"Trust me when I say you're not ready for this," he said.

"Answer my question first."

"Wouldn't trade anything for the information you seek. Once you're all reunited, you'll understand why."

"Who are the other five?"

"Haven't you been listening to me, Chap? This subject is closed and never to be opened again."

"You can't expect me to forget after everything you just told me."

"I don't, but you should stop now. Forget about the other five, and you'll have a happier life."

I examined the echoer, admiring the engraving. "Since I was a boy, I was plagued by vivid dreams and visions. I spent years researching and experimenting, hoping to understand what was happening to me. Answers never came—only more questions. This is the closest I've ever been to an answer. I can't stop."

"Have you ever lived a satisfying life and when the end came, you thought about everything you did and had no regrets?"

"Once…almost." I thought about Holly, who came closest to that ideal.

Sephroy was pointing at me. "Repeat that life and forget this one. If I was smart enough to follow my own advice, I would've been at home instead of living here like a rat. It's the only thing I deserve now."

"Can't you go back to—where did you say you came from?"

"I didn't, and I can't ever go back because I failed to overlook what I held sacred." He extended his hand, waiting for me to give him the echoer, but I still refused.

"The answer you seek will again lead to more questions." Sephroy opened a desk drawer and removed another echoer. "Thieves broke in here many times and never took this—not that it would've mattered because it only works for the Six."

"Is it true what Jall said?" I held up my echoer. "Can this be used to communicate beyond time?"

Sephroy put his echoer back into the drawer. "Feeling tired. Got a long day tomorrow."

"We'll continue tomorrow then."

"We'll never speak of this again. I want to live out the rest of my years in peace." Sephroy waved his cane towards the door, and I left.

Arriving at my trainlet, I found the door ajar.

Tyrus stepped out. He seemed confused. "How did I get here?"

273

I showed him the echoer. "I think this allows me to communicate with you."

"You're not living in here again, are you?"

"You remember?"

Tyrus shook his head and went back into my 'let.

I followed him in. "Six begin, Six alone, Six—"

"Unite." Tyrus turned to face me and shook his head again. "No. None of this is happening." He started pacing up and down the aisle.

"Then how do you remember I lived here?"

"When I come up with an answer, I'll tell you."

"I thought you went to the lands of the Ancients' bible."

Tyrus froze. "You ran into Lidian and Holly?"

"They told me you were sick."

"In more ways than I thought possible."

"Are you a Six?"

The question spooked him. "The woman with the unbraided hair mentioned something about—"

"Sutara."

"Yes. That's her, but I couldn't recall her name until you mentioned it."

"Three of Six found. Only three more to go."

"Then what?"

"Slock if I know. Sephroy seems to know a lot, but he's not saying anything."

"Sephroy?"

"The man who runs this place."

"That man with the cane who never bathed before in his life knows about the Six?" Tyrus whacked one of the overhead handles and studied his hand. "I'm hallucinating."

"If you're hallucinating then I am as well."

"We can't both be hallucinating the same thing."

"Which means all of this is real," I said.

He slapped the overhead handle again. "I remember now. I'm in reintegration."

"No Tyrus. I'm here with you."

"Maybe," he said, and walked out of the trainlet.

I stepped out behind him, and the Unitian skyline replaced the tunnel walls.

While we sat and waited for a crail, I examined the skyline. I had missed the glass high rises and the way they glistened from the city lights. Their dim reflection on the dome commingled with the stars outside making Unity seem like a self-contained universe.

"Being away for so long makes you appreciate its beauty," said Tyrus.

"Why did you take me here?"

"Unity is firmly entrenched within me because I helped it thrive. I thought I was improving the lives of the Unitians, so it was easy to look past it. When they were scared, I was their protector. When they thought they were alone in their doubts, I stood by them. When they were angry over their oppression, I listened to their grievances until they exhausted themselves back into submission. Those were the most disheartening moments since my memory returned." Tyrus crossed his hands under his chin and closed his eyes as though deep in prayer. "I don't want to live through this again."

"You and I both," I said as a crail stopped in front of us.

"What if it never ends?" Tyrus asked.

"We keep going." I motioned towards the open crail door, and we entered.

Tyrus looked into the navigation lens. "Observatory." The door slid shut, and we were on our way.

"When did you first remember?" I asked him.

"During the meeting with Overseer 147—he announced his intention to chip the fetuses."

"Is this the first incarnation you're aware of?"

"In my last life I had the memories, but I thought they were delusions brought on by my illness. I still haven't discounted that explanation." Tyrus cupped his hand on his forehead. "If there was only some way I could be sure."

We arrived at the observatory. I secured a telescope and viewed the stars that salted the sky in brilliant symmetry and I thought about Flora who found refuge while gazing at them. "Where are you now?" I asked Tyrus.

"Don't come. I'm scheduled to announce my request for death in three days." He stared into the finderscope.

"You're in Unity?"

"I had a frightening vision. Kai sent out an army of Unity Guards to attack the Outsiders. Whole villages along with their inhabitants were incinerated."

My heart pounded, recalling my conversation with Kai when he discussed Overseer 147's dream of a Greater Unity. "It must've happened in one or several of our cycles."

"I wasn't as certain as you, but it scared me enough to come back and help the Chosen unthrone him. With Avery's assistance, I slipped in undetected."

"Avery helped you?"

"With the Chosen's blessing. When I contacted them, they had already been plotting Kai's overthrow and were constructing a case against him."

"What was the charge?"

"Breaking the Sacred Oath. Kai declared that the Prime Wisdom told him he no longer had to consult with the Chosen to issue new edicts. They didn't believe him. Upon my arrival, I helped gather evidence, but Kai found out before we could present it to the Corporate Hierarchy. He threatened to write an edict declaring the Chosen nonessential to the function of Unity. My former colleagues capitulated and made a public apology, retracting their accusation."

Tyrus made a few adjustments to the lens. "I couldn't let things go as easily as them. I snuck into Kai's bed chamber with the intention of talking to him. I found him sleeping peacefully but I knew the man was devoid of a conscience. I strangled him as he slept."

"You killed Kai?"

He looked at me. "I'm no better than him. When my arms were around his neck, I wanted him to die. I placed no value on his life."

"You're a more honorable man than Kai. He never valued anyone's life but his own. You did what you did because you wanted to help free the Unitians."

"The Corporate Hierarchy make a similar claim. Their function is to make life happy for all Unitians, but compassionate acts don't lead to the enslavement of a whole population—or the murder of an individual."

I thought back to the moment that I wanted to kill Kai. Something stopped me from pulling the trigger. *Was it compassion?* "Tell me where you are, Tyrus. I'll come for you," I said.

"Before you went off, did you ever wonder why there was an increase in suicides after reintegration?"

"Hadn't noticed. I was too busy worrying about my next promotion."

"We don't have the resources to sustain those who don't agree with the Sacred Oath. Under direct orders from Overseer 147, a team of engineers made some modifications to reintegration. They can now inject suicidal prompts to Unitians rated nonessential."

"Did they do that to Wade?"

He nodded. "I knew and did nothing—" Tyrus rubbed his chin. "I've contaminated the pureness of Unity. I'm anathema to our peaceful existence." He abruptly cried out, "No, I won't carry all of it!" Opening the door he bolted out of the dome.

I ran outside and chased him across the cold, frosty field. He stopped at the fence that surrounded the ranch. "I can't resist anymore."

"You don't have to listen. In the end, the choice is yours to make."

Tyrus wrung his hands. "I deserve death because I'm a monster I'm—" He looked up and raised his fists defiantly towards the sky. "You're wrong! I'm not the only one responsible! You're all monsters! You value no one's life but your own! Those who choose not to serve you are tossed out! You're monsters because you believe the end exonerates the sacrifice!" Quieting down, he continued, "Those were my last words to Kai, moments before he drew his final breath." He laughed maniacally. "I'd congratulate you for your promotion, Avery, but I never could stand you."

"Avery was elected to Overseer?"

"Yes, and with my help. After I left Unity, many of the Chosen sympathized with me. Avery knew that with my help he could succeed Kai. Simon was his only opposition, but Avery was the biggest sleeve-worshipper of all the Chosen, and also the most callous. He was destined to win." Tyrus laughed again. "I knew all this, but I was angrier with Kai for going against me when the Overseer wanted to transmit the signal to the fetuses. Kai was as horrified as I was at first, but he acquiesced. He thought it could be stopped after I became the next Overseer, which of course never happened because I was gone. I knew that once such a practice was started, it would be impossible to stop. That was proven following Kai's induction. He continued transmitting Harmony. I tried to persuade him to…" His eyes reflected panic. "I didn't kill him! It wasn't me!" Again, he yelled at the sky. "You thought I'd die believing I'm a murderer, but I'm not! I remember! I remember it all!"

"What happened?"

"It had to be Avery. He came in while Kai and I were in a heated discussion over cutting off Harmony's signal. I was close to changing his mind when Avery stormed in with his protégés." Tyrus's eyes filled with tears. "'This is what happens when you resist.' Kai said that to me before they stunned us."

"They probably killed Kai while you were unconscious and then accused you of his murder," I said.

"I denied doing it, up until I was dragged into reintegration. They must've planted false memories, making me think I strangled Kai." Dropping to his knees, he fell forward, mashing his hands and forehead to the ground. "Avery won with my help!" he cried.

"I'm coming for you." I kneeled next to him.

"I'm already a dead man."

"We still have three days to work with. When I get within transmission range, I can contact my appointer and—"

"Don't. I want death to come save me from myself. Maybe I'll be smart enough to stay far away from Unity the next time I leave."

I viewed Tyrus as the strongest amongst the Chosen and watching him give up angered me. "Should I even bother with Freedomline?" I asked. He wouldn't respond. "I could always go back to New Athenia and live out the rest of my life playing music and taking evening strolls around the labyrinth with Shisa." I stood and snapped my fingers. "Can't forget the ducks. I love to feed the ducks, especially Gadfly. He's got the strongest will I've ever witnessed."

Tyrus, now on his knees, stared curiously at me.

"I'll marry a fine woman." I waved my finger in the air. "But she must love ducks because I like to spend time with them at the park." I smiled at the memory of my life with Holly. "We'll eventually have children, who will grow up and have children of their own. Life will be…nice. Unity will be buried deep within my decrepit brain, and I'll die a happy old man."

"Sounds like the plan I should've followed, except for the ducks. I prefer pigeons."

I helped Tyrus up.

"Follow your plan, and forget about Unity," he said. "You can't stop what's happening here."

"I know. But I can try to stop myself. Harmony is too dangerous, and I won't rest until it's erased from this timeline. Until then, I'm going to free as many Unitians as I can. I may not die a happy old man, but I'd rather be aware and scared than ignorant and happy."

Tyrus was smiling now. "Your conviction is still inspiring." He placed his hand on my shoulder. "It's been an honor knowing you, Damon." He brushed some grass off his shirt. "Since you have this all figured out, there's no point in continuing this discussion." Watching the horses grazing nearby, he said, "I'm in the mood for one last ride."

He unhooked the gate latch, and we entered the horse field.

"I can still come for you," I said.

"Go away from here understanding the risk was mine to take, and I must die under the circumstance I've chosen for myself."

I turned away, fearing he would see through my despair at not being able to save him.

"You've grown into a fine man, Damon. Move forward with your life. What's done here is done?"

I looked at him. "You once told me you saw through me, but not in the way I thought. What did you mean?"

"I don't remember saying it, but I know why I would." With a grin, he explained, "Thirty-two reprimands."

"And proud of them all," I said.

"When you spoke in front of the Chosen, you reminded me of Torrin. I haven't heard such passion on display since he left Unity. After you finished your plea for entrance to the University, I couldn't get my mind off what happened to him. I knew the Corporate Hierarchy would eventually destroy you as they destroyed him. That's why I declined your request for entry into University."

Tyrus walked over to one of the horses. "Shooting Star."

"She's beautiful," I said.

"And nonjudgmental." He stroked her mane. "It's easy to confess your sins when you stare into her eyes." He ran his hand gently along her neck.

"My invention is being used to enslave a whole population. Can you beat that one?" I asked.

"I delivered the charge against Torrin. He had enough support to challenge the Overseer, but I was a spineless sleeve-worshipper more interested in my position than...no, I won't look back now." He climbed onto Shooting Star and grabbed the reins. "I prefer to leave with the little dignity I still have. And doing the thing I love most."

"You're more honorable than any purple sleeve I've met, Master Tyrus." I bowed.

"Your sincerity almost makes me believe it." He bowed his head. "Stay strong and live long, Damon."

I held the echoer, closed my eyes, and tried to break off our connection, but nothing happened.

"Guess it didn't come with a manual." Tyrus grinned and rode off.

It took a while but when my mind wandered, thinking about the mundane tasks waiting for me at the cabin, I was returned to the old tunnel. Sephroy was standing in front of me, looking concerned.

"Enjoy your peace," I said. "The Six won't be reuniting in this present timeline."

Without saying a word, he pushed his cart in the opposite direction.

Sephroy's refusal to speak about the echoer made me curious about its structural anatomy. After I'd returned to the cabin, I contacted Roth and requested a portable metallurgical scanner to conduct some tests, and he smuggled one out for me. The results revealed the metal as nonferrous, but no matching data existed in the metallurgical identification table. Three more scans yielded similar results. When I sliced through the metal, each blemish instantly self-repaired.

I couldn't allow Sephroy to remain silent over the echoer's origin. I approached him on my next transport, kept up my questioning and he retreated to his trainlet. No amount of door pounding and shouting could coax him out of hiding. On a second trip, I knocked on his door, and this time he answered with an ancient firearm aimed at me.

"This is called a gun, Chap, and it can do as much damage as your plazer. Our discussion about the Six is finished."

"What material is the echoer made of? Are the walls of New Athenia made with the same—"

Sephroy's gun made a clicking sound and I stepped back.

"Rap on my door over this again, and I might not be as patient with you."

I gave up trying to get answers from him and went to Old Jerusalem to search for Jall. After three weeks of fruitless pursuit, I stopped searching. The meaning of the Six would remain an unanswered question…at least for now.

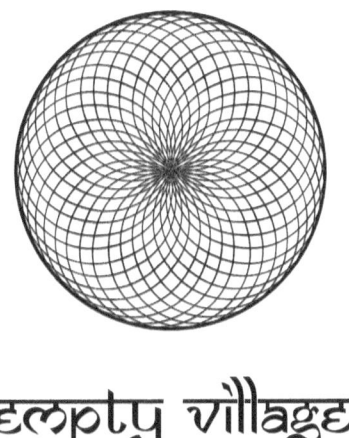

# empty village

I returned to Littlefield and spent most of my days teaching Michael how to speak Knosian. He didn't seem interested in music lessons so I took out my violin hoping to inspire him. I played through "Beneath the Lonely Stars to Nowhere." Out of all my original pieces, this one aroused the deepest emotion in me. Each passing phrase connected me to the night the bandits attacked me and left me for dead. The stroke of my bow carried with it the isolation I felt before I connected with the comforting fountain of light.

Wilfrid and Michael entered my bungalow, but I didn't notice them until I put down my bow.

"Music flows from your heart." Wilfrid said and placed his hand over the left side of his chest.

"I want to learn to play like you," Michael said. "Can you teach me?"

Wilfrid winked at me. "Looks like you found yourself a new student."

I handed Michael the violin. "It's yours, as long as you keep it company every day for at least one hour."

The passion in his eyes made it clear that I was right to give it to him. I showed Michael a few scales and simple melodies to play. I later wrote down some musical lessons and delivered them to him on my next transport.

The following summer, Michael had progressed to where I could teach him some simple concertos and minuets. He was proficient enough to study at the Athenian Conservatory.

Genevieve refused to acknowledge Michael's talent because it would mean she'd have to accept his desire to leave Littlefield. This became apparent when Michael performed for Wilfrid and me. She kept busy with her cooking until I complimented Michael on his technique. She exhibited her displeasure by aggressively chopping up vegetables, hammering the sharp blade on the wood block with such force I was afraid she'd lop one of her fingers. Wilfrid pressed his finger against his pursed lips to silence me.

While Genevieve escaped reality through her cooking, Michael played us a slow rhythmic melody he'd written. His body swayed with each stroke, his eyes shut, raising his eyebrows with each climactic passage. Tears escaped me as I connected to the place he was visiting: the place where creativity flows unrestricted, and where even the most sorrowful emotions are extinguished by the light of creation.

He finished and Wilfrid and I clapped. Genevieve expressed her enthusiasm by slamming the salad bowl on the table.

"I want to go to school in New Athenia," Michael said to me. "My mother won't let me."

Genevieve, mixing the salad, ignored him.

"He'll be safe there," I said.

"Even Grandfather thinks it's a good idea," Michael added.

"Then let *Grandfather* move there." Genevieve glared at Wilfrid, daring him to challenge her.

Wilfrid again looked my way and shook his head for me to remain silent.

"It's a good opportunity for him," I said. "The conservatory is open to anyone who can pass the entrance exam."

Genevieve dropped the spoon in the dish. "He's too young to live on his own."

Michael shoved the bowl off the table and ran out.

Genevieve put her hands on her hips and seemed ready to scold me next. The bond between mother and child taught me something I never learned as a psychological engineer. A mother's attachment can sometimes make her overlook her child's need for independence, either from fear of something bad happening or not wanting to let go of the need to be needed. For Genevieve, it was a little of both. She understood the fragility of life after her husband had died, and Michael was all she had left of him.

I found Michael sitting on a tree stump, drawing a figure-eight pattern in the dirt with a stick.

"Dinner is almost ready…minus a salad." I said.

"I'm not hungry."

"Mind if I eat your portion then?"

He scribbled over the shape. "If I don't leave here, I'll die ordinary—like everyone else in Littlefield."

"When I was your age, I wanted to be the Overseer of Unity."

"Are you disappointed you're not?"

"Not over that."

Michael looked up at me. "What are you disappointed over?"

"I didn't teach you well."

"You're the best teacher—the only teacher I ever had."

"What did I tell you about your mother?"

"I'm lucky to know her." He twirled the stick in his hand. "Sorry. I keep forgetting no one in your village knows their parents."

"Remember what I told you by the river?"

"Wait until I'm sixteen."

"Your mother gave me permission to take you to New Athenia for your birthday."

In frustration, Michael threw the stick away. "I don't want to visit, I want to stay."

"It's a start. If you want to study in New Athenia, you must stop running out of the room whenever you don't get your way. Your mother needs to see you're mature enough to be on your own."

"How? She won't even listen to me."

"She will, if you tell her what you want without yelling or attacking her for disagreeing with you."

"I'll try, but it won't do any good."

"It'll get me to take you seriously and recommend you to the conservatory."

"How are you going to get me in? You don't live there."

"Do what I ask, and I'll make it happen for you."

Michael sprang up from the tree trunk. "I'm finally going to get out of Littlefield!"

"And see that the world is bigger than you imagined."

"This year is going to move so slowly."

"Slower is better. You'll miss what you have here once you're gone."

"I'll never miss this place. Can't wait to leave."

"Lose that attitude before next year. I won't take you if you and your mother can't reach an agreement about your future."

"Why?"

"If anything happens to her while you're gone, you won't have another chance to tell her how you feel. Better to go with nothing more to be said."

The following summer I revisited Littlefield and found the gate wide open. I entered the circle and met a silence that's eternally burned into my memory. Tranquil time had never been this quiet. Shisa ran on ahead and exited through the rear gate, which had been left ajar.

The door of Wilfrid's bungalow was open. Inside, all the tables and chairs were overturned, and his cards were splattered across the floor. The ace of spades—which was face up—symbolizes death when accompanied by a ten and nine. I was relieved that neither of those other cards were visible and shocked at my reaction. I used to tease Wilfrid about his superstitions. There was a ritual for every activity in Littlefield, and he began each Firstday by leading a prayer service. During my stays in Littlefield, I slept late on those days. Wilfrid took no umbrage because he believed I would one day learn *the truth*. By leaving me alone, he surmised I'd feel self-conscious about my lack of faith and join his worship club. I kept silent. I didn't want to tell him the only truth worthy of accepting was one I could discover on my own.

I inspected the rest of the bungalows, which were in similar condition. Shisa's barking pulled me back outside, and the tone of her voice made my heart pound. The last time she barked like that was when I found Flora unconscious at the bottom of the ridge.

I exited the rear gate and found her pacing outside the pig pen, whimpering as she did when I performed the sacred burning for Old Woman. Inside the pen were the remains of the villagers, huddled together as though shielding themselves from an aggressor. I stood paralyzed, my gaze unfixed, my senses clouded. Everything I observed appeared somehow artificial. The decayed bodies more like a display in a museum; a sculpture of death telling the story of an extinct people. Every passerby would have their own interpretation of what happened. I had none—not even a passing thought.

As I journeyed beyond Littlefield and into the nearby forest, the environment seemed equally illusory. Towering trees screened me from the mist of rain that began to fall. The water droplets bouncing off the leaves had a hypnotic effect, and I continued my walk devoid of conscious thought. Besides the splatter of rain, there was an eerie silence. I couldn't hear a bird or even my own heart beating. *Am I as dead as my friends?* Even Shisa seemed bewitched by the scenery. She walked silently, trailing a few meters behind me. I trembled over how easily the senses can be fooled, and I again questioned whether I was dead or in reintegration. To keep from deluding myself, I doubted everything—including my senses. Everything I analyzed was merely a subjective perception of my brain; I used to trust that what it told me was real, but I gave up on trust many incarnations ago. All I knew for certain was that Wilfrid, Genevieve and Michael, who accepted me as part of their family, were now gone. I was alone again.

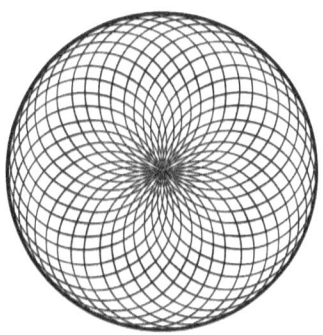

# static sky

The carnage in Littlefield seemed unreal. Either I was in denial or my awareness of previous incarnations desensitized me from my emotions. With no scheduled transport for another four weeks, I decided to lose myself in New Athenia. In the first week, I kept to myself, spending most of my hours at the park feeding the ducks. An elderly woman sat down next to me and I came out of my self-imposed isolation.

"I knew it," she said after Gadfly snatched a piece of bread from my hand. "You're the bird man."

I turned to her and raised a brow.

"There's much talk about you."

"What kind of talk?"

"They say you come here every day and sit on this bench without saying a word to anyone, except to the ducks that flock around you."

"An exaggeration. Only Gadfly comes to me."

"Gadfly?"

I pointed to my feathered pal waddling over to the pond.

"How can you tell him apart from the other ducks?"

"He's the only one that stares directly at me."

"What if another duck starts to do the same thing?"

"Gadfly has an area on his left outer wing where no feathers grow."

The woman laughed. "You almost had me fooled." She looked at Shisa. "Is that your dog?"

"Shisa doesn't belong to anyone." I stared out into the pond. "And I don't belong anywhere."

"Lately I feel as though I don't belong anywhere," she said. "My children are all grown, and the only time they visit is when they want me to watch their kids."

"Don't you like to spend time with your grandchildren?"

"Of course, I do. But I wish they'd invite me over to talk over a cup of coffee. I don't see how that's a lot to ask for." She sighed. "Children are dependent on you when they're young, and when they grow up, you're either an afterthought or a caretaker for the grandchildren. When I'm not needed, I don't even get a call to ask how I'm doing."

She started to cry, and I held her hand. "I suppose I should be grateful for the times I'm needed." We sat together until her grandchildren showed up for a picnic. Her face lit up when she saw them. She invited me along, but I declined the offer. A happy family interaction would have reminded me of what I'd lost, and I preferred to keep my emotions hidden.

On my eighth day in New Athenia, I contacted Lidian. He welcomed me back to his home without bringing up my odious behavior. Holly had given birth to a baby girl named Katerina, now nearly in her second year. Even though some time had passed since my drunken outburst, it took Holly a while to warm up to me. During my first few visits, she'd either lock herself in her room with the baby or be out with friends. Her absence allowed me to distance myself from our previous life together, along with my memories of Aaron and James.

Lidian and I passed the time on the balcony, talking, playing backgammon, and drinking generous quantities of alcohol.

"This is getting to be too easy. Are you sure you're not letting me win?" Lidian asked as he removed his last chip from the board. "That makes three out of three. How about another round?"

"Better quit before my ego cracks beyond repair."

Lidian shook his head. "Your ego, Damon, is one of the most indestructible specimens I've encountered in Unity."

"And it was nearly demolished by three rounds of backgammon."

"You could easily rebuild it with music." He swept the chips off the board. "You should stop by and hear us play before leaving. Maybe it will inspire you to join us."

"I played for Manolis yesterday. I needed to break in my new violin."

"Why don't you make your chair a permanent home? You'll be happier playing with the orchestra than living alone in the woods, helping Unitians cross the old tunnel so they can enjoy the life you deserve." Lidian picked up a carafe and filled my glass with wine.

"I've grown accustomed to being alone." I took a sip of the wine.

"If the situation were reversed, no Unitian would help you."

"I'm not doing this for them."

Holly came out of hiding and sat down beside her husband. "He's had a hard time forgetting Unity."

"I still have dreams," Lidian admitted, "where I wake up in the morning and think I'm still living there."

"Thought I was the only one," I said.

"I put in so much effort to be accepted by the Corporate Hierarchy until I woke up one morning and realized if I succeeded, I'd have to keep bowing to someone until I died. Just thinking about that scared me into stopping. After that, everyone treated me worse than an Outsider, except for Master Tyrus."

Recalling a similar revelation I had while out at sea with Wade, I raised my glass. "To Master Tyrus. If only he'd been around to influence me when I arrived at my own crossroads."

"But you eventually stopped bowing," Lidian said as we toasted.

"A little too late." I drank some wine.

"You'll survive what happened." Holly reached across the table and placed her hand on top of mine. "And you'll be stronger for it."

Her tenderhearted response only added to my pain. I was pleased she had found happiness with Lidian, but a part of me still thought of Holly as my wife. Along with my confused timelines, the massacre at Littlefield and everyone else I had lost surged in my head. I excused myself and went for a walk on the top level of the labyrinth. I stopped at the scenic park to view the Acropolis and my mind finally stopped racing. Gazing upon the Ancient masterpiece that loomed overhead always made my self-pity seem superficial. This night was no different; the spectacular view brought to the surface what had been bothering me for many lifetimes. In Unity, we lost the pride of human vision and ingenuity. We sedated ourselves with conveniences and forgot the meaning of inspiration. I wanted it for myself, so that I could be fulfilled within. I wanted it so badly that I wept as I looked upon the majestic columns of the Parthenon. If the goddess Athena existed, I would've prayed for her to impart her wisdom to me.

Manolis invited me to play with the orchestra until it was time for me to go. The morning after my final performance, I went to the park for some quiet time at the duck pond. As I neared the entrance, a familiar voice shouted out to me. I turned and saw Michael walking up. Whatever emotions I thought had abandoned me were back. We ended up at one of the quieter cafes where he sat twirling a spoon in his coffee cup.

"Glad you taught me how to speak Knosian," he said. "It was easy for me to get in here."

"Did you try out for the conservatory?"

"I'm in—but not until next year."

"That's great news, Michael."

He stopped stirring the coffee and looked up at me. "You're not asking. Why?"

"You'll tell me when you're ready."

"My grandfather and I went fishing. I grew bored and went to find some rocks to finish a mosaic table I was going to give my mother for her birthday. I passed a man feeding his horse—he seemed friendly. He gave me almonds and figs without asking for anything in return, and I thanked him by inviting him to my mother's birthday celebration." Michael nervously made circles in his coffee again. "Next morning, while I was out in the wheat field, I heard horses approaching. I ran to the side of one of the bungalows just as four men on horseback broke through the gate, swinging chains and—"

A large group of people celebrating nearby laughed loudly. Michael pushed back his chair. "It's too noisy here." He got up and walked out.

I paid for our bill, retrieved a bag of bread I had bought for the ducks, and caught up with Michael. We made our way to the park and strolled two laps around the path, ending up on the bench near the duck pond.

Gadfly waddled over to me and I handed him a small piece of bread.

"I miss the river near Littlefield," Michael said as he gazed reflectively at the pond. "I hid as the bandits were pillaging our village, and was missing it already."

"You don't have to tell me anymore tonight." I handed him some scraps of bread.

"They rounded everyone up and led them to the pen." Michael tossed bread crumbs at the ducks. "They let out all the pigs and began to whip everyone with their chains."

I connected the tragedy of the villagers with my own beating and how I would've met the same end if it hadn't been for Shisa.

"My family and friends were huddled together, trying to protect their faces." Michael wiped his eyes with his sleeve. "The man I met the previous day was the last to have his turn at the beatings, and he looked as though he was enjoying himself. He smiled and laughed as he continued with the lashings until one of the bandits had to tell him to stop; everyone was dead." Michael turned to me. "It's all my fault, Damon. If I hadn't told that man about Littlefield—"

"You couldn't have known what would happen. Don't put this all on yourself. Your grandfather and mother wouldn't want that."

"I hated Littlefield and couldn't wait to leave." Michael looked away. "After you'd gone, my mother and I continued fighting. We never agreed about my studying here, and I knew you wouldn't take me with you when you found out. We got into our biggest fight on the day the bandits came. I went down to the river to think. That's why I wasn't around when they showed up." He clutched the side his head. "I can't stop thinking about what went on in her mind before she died."

"She was thankful you weren't in the pen with her and that you'd have a chance to live out your dreams."

"Maybe I wanted this to happen, so I could have my freedom."

I took hold of Michael's arm. "Don't ever believe that. Your desire to travel and see the world had nothing to do with what those murderers did."

"My grandfather always warned me never to tell strangers about Littlefield. If I had obeyed him and kept quiet, my mother and the rest of the villagers would all be alive now, and I'd be on my way here with you."

"Littlefield wasn't exactly a secret. They might have easily stumbled upon it by accident."

"Makes no difference. My mother died believing I hated her, and nothing's going to change that. I'll never forget the look on her face when I left her." Michael began to cry. "Never."

I hugged him, which worked better than words. This was something that only time could heal. I thought about Harmony and realized the damage I'd done with the grieving process. We have to feel the loss of those we love to truly remember them.

Michael's birthday came three days later. He refused to celebrate. I persuaded him to go back to the cabin until his classes began. He went on a few transports with me, and our bond strengthened through each passing of the tunnel and turn of the season. Eventually he started calling me, "Father," and he wasn't any less of a son to me than Aaron and James.

Forty years had passed, and I lived the satisfying life that would've made Sephroy and Tyrus proud. I had relationships with females but nothing long-lasting. I didn't want another unresolved relationship in my next incarnation. My time was spent mostly reading, running Freedomline, and traveling to New Athenia to meet with Michael and his family. He married a nurse and they had three children: two boys and a girl. Michael named his eldest son after me, and the children called me grandfather, a title I honored and treasured. Manolis let me play in the orchestra during every visit. I opted out during my final year, sensing I wouldn't be around for another season.

I filled the remaining time with family and at the duck pond, where I rounded out the last day of my fifth incarnation. As I gazed out at a mother duck leading her younglings across the water, I pondered my actions in my current timeline and what I could change the next time, if there was to be a next time. As things are about to end, there's a sense of closure that relaxes the body and mind into acceptance. In some incarnations, I had time to prepare for my end. In others, I came to it without warning. But ending, in my reality, is a temporary condition. Once my outside life is completed, the only thing left is my inner world which remains static and unchanging like the starlit sky. Of course, that's merely a subjective interpretation; the sky does change, but it's so slow you hardly notice it in your lifetime. This is how I witness my life: unchanging, with outcomes not perceived until many incarnations later.

Moments before my death, Sutara came to me in a vision.

I said to her, "I've done all you asked, and I still don't remember. What else can I do?"

"I don't know anymore," she cried. "This has taken over my whole life. No man will marry me, and everyone in my village is afraid of what secrets I know about them. They think because I can remember my past lives, I can remember every detail of their life."

I felt a jab of pain in my chest and grew short of breath.

Sutara knelt by my side. "Why is it so difficult for you to move past this?"

"I remember too late. I've been studying COR—hoping to find a way to leave myself a message in my next incarnation, but it's impossible. Time is subjective to our reality. I can't tap into something that exists beyond time, which is where COR originates."

"This is not science; it is the Divine manifest in us."

"I don't know what it is. I only know what it isn't—part of time. Wherever it comes from will be where I'll soon be before my return." I massaged my neck. "Slock, I'm not making sense, even to myself."

"You cannot analyze this, Damon."

"I'll eventually figure it out."

"What do you hope to do after the mystery is solved? Put it under a microscope, study it and hope for a cure?"

"I can stop myself from inventing Harmony."

"And then what?"

"I can rest."

"What about the Six? We need to get together. This is too much for me to—"

The pain worsened. I clutched my chest. "My time is almost up. We can discuss this in the next round."

"This is not only about you, Damon. We must find the others —"

"Not until I succeed."

Sutara glared at me. "What if you cannot?"

"I won't stop until I do."

"I will not stay quiet next time. I'm tired of carrying the burden myself."

"You won't for long. I'll succeed next time." I took hold of her hand and neither of us spoke another word. Nothing I said would've wiped away Sutara's doubtful expression or my own uncertainty over being able to live up to my declaration. I'd have to prove it through my actions. I carried that thought out of my fifth incarnation.

# moonlight and wine

### Sixth Incarnation

I stared over the precipice that Wade had just jumped from and I laughed. Laughed harder than I had in previous incarnations, including the time I went mad in the old tunnel. I couldn't rationalize my behavior then, but in this incarnation I could explain my manic reaction to the death of my closest friend. I was struck with the realization that we were more alike than dissimilar. Wade didn't cross the old tunnel with Nasia because he feared losing his assignment. I feared Old Woman's words because had I heard them, I would've been forced to admit that I undervalued my personal desires to be accepted by the Corporate Hierarchy. Wade and I both succumbed to fear. We gave ourselves away willingly and without a fight. Admitting that I had voluntarily enslaved myself, I almost followed Wade off the ridge. I felt foolish for not figuring it out sooner, so I laughed at myself. My laughter persisted during Old Woman's sacred burning. According to her journal, her fear was loneliness. She continued Torrin's work to stay connected to him. I thought about everyone I knew in Unity and how they followed a similar pattern. Out of fear, none of them lived true to themselves. *Real or imagined, fear is epidemic! It infects everyone!* This realization made me miss Wade even more. I knew if I told him what I had just figured out, he'd be guffawing alongside me.

My euphoric mood eased at my first meeting with Shisa, who whimpered as she circled around the pyre. Unafraid, I walked up to her. She growled softly. "It's all right, girl." I kneeled beside her, taken aback by my automatic response and even more so when she stopped growling and came to me, her head held low. I petted her. "Good girl." She whimpered again, and I was reacquainted with my loyal companion. After six incarnations I had not forgotten her name, but could not recall the identity of the woman who named her.

As I headed for the old tunnel, I thought about all the years I'd wasted living in Unity. How much more would I have accomplished if I lived outside the dome? I had no idea what I wanted. In spirit, I was a child again, musing over what I wanted to be when I grew up. Whenever I came up with an idea, I'd either snap my fingers or clap my hands and tell Shisa about my newest revelation. "I could be a painter. I always loved to sketch. What do you think about that, Shisa?" This dialogue continued until I reached the old tunnel. "How about an explorer?" I asked as I turned on my lantern. "I'll travel from place to place and record all my experiences on my holologue. Maybe I'll even publish a book—if publishing exists outside of Unity."

The anticipation of seeing what lay on the other side intensified at my first glimpse of the trainlets. The COR alarm sounded, and I shut it off as Sephroy approached me pushing his cart. He seemed familiar, and scrutinizing his scraggly appearance, I laughed.

"What's so funny, Chap?"

"I know you." I laughed again and gave a welcoming gesture. "I know you."

Sephroy retrieved an oil lantern from his cart. "Let me see you up close to get a better look. I'm real good with faces." He shined the lantern on me. "Nope. Never met you before." He tapped his cane on the ground. "What was that noise all about?"

"I *know* you."

"Heard you the last two times you said it, Chap. I'm asking about that machine of yours."

"It's an alarm. It went off because I know you."

"How is that possible?" Sephroy suddenly appeared worried. "Do you know me?"

"No, no, no. Already told you, no. I never met you before."

"And I don't remember ever meeting you," I said it more to myself while I continued to examine him and perceived something beyond his uncivilized mannerisms. Something that made me feel momentarily small. "Why do you call me, Chap? Who's Chap?"

"You remind me of someone I knew long ago. Sometimes it feels like an eternity has passed since I last saw him." He rested his lantern back on the cart. "When you get older, all the interesting things you've done seem farther away from where you are now." Sephroy reached inside his pocket and handed me a map.

"I already have a—"

"This one includes the trade route."

"How much?" I asked.

"It's yours as long as you keep that alarm away from me." He rubbed his cheek. "I don't do well with noise." He led me to my trainlet and unlocked the door. "Pull up the shades once you're inside, so I can remember this one isn't vacant. My memory's not that great."

His expression contradicted that statement. "Seems yours isn't doing any better." He sniffled loudly.

"Have we met before?"

He shook his head and clutched the handle of his cart. "Enjoy your stay, Chap."

"You're holding something back."

"What are you? Some kind of mind-reader?"

"I was trained to detect deception." I held my lantern near his face. "You know something."

"You're right. I know every crack in this tunnel and how many steps it takes to get from here to your side of the——"

"Stop evading. You know what I meant."

"You sound sure of yourself."

"The more we talk, the more I am."

"Then I'll leave now. I don't want you to go crazy in here. Once had this man working for me. He thought he talked to ghosts." Sephroy chuckled. "He was amusing at first—then he scared me, and I don't get scared easily. Go now before you turn into him."

Sephroy wandered off. I checked into my trainlet and mulled over our conversation. I became convinced that my quest for adventure and knowledge made me idealize my meeting with him. *Sometimes a filthy Outsider with a bad memory is just a filthy Outsider with a bad memory.* Laughing, I went over the map Sephroy gave me, circling Littlefield, my first stop.

At first sight of the stone bungalows, the COR alarm sounded. No one was at the gate or in the circle. I noticed the well in the center and yelled out a greeting. When no one came, I picked up a stick and swept it across the fence. Wilfred emerged from his bungalow.

"What can I do for you?" He stepped back when he saw Shisa.

"She's with me." I raised my canteen and nodded towards the well. "Mind if I fill up?"

"You're welcome to enter, but no wild animals are allowed in here."

"Shisa isn't wild."

Michael approached the gate and kneeled down when he saw Shisa. She walked up to him.

"Keep away, Michael."

"She won't hurt the boy," I said.

Michael cautiously stuck his hand through the gate and stroked Shisa's face. She licked his hand, and he laughed. "She's friendly, Grandfather."

Wilfrid smiled at Michael. "So she is." He opened the gate and let us in.

"Where is everyone?" I asked.

"It's tranquil time. Everyone is at rest," Michael replied.

"Where are you headed?" Wilfrid asked.

"New Athenia."

"It'll be getting dark soon. Bandits roam the woodlands once the sun goes down. You're welcome to stay in our guest bungalow."

I felt as uneasy as I had in my previous incarnation, except this time I listened to Wilfrid and stayed in Littlefield overnight. He echoed a familiarity which I began to trust more through each passing incarnation. Upon reflection, Wilfrid was also more comfortable with me; he never asked me to relinquish my plazer.

Wilfrid shuffled his cards while I finished off my second chalice of wine.

"Slow down, Damon. Our wine is more potent than any you'll find on your way to New Athenia."

"Unitian wine is almost as strong." I poured more into my chalice. "It's impressive. Almost as impressive as your hospitality."

"Would you mind telling that to Michael. Since he was a boy, he's complained about our way of life and dreams of leaving Littlefield to explore the world."

"He has an adventurous spirit. I saw that in him when he approached Shisa; he wasn't afraid."

"That's the problem. The boy takes too many risks. To go beyond Littlefield will get him killed. He doesn't comprehend the danger for someone his age." Wilfrid studied me for a moment. "What are you searching for?"

"New experiences that will hopefully demolish every assumption that was programmed into me."

Wilfrid lifted his hand toward me. "I see Michael's future in you."

"Nothing wrong with wanting to explore the world you live in."

"What do you think you'll find on your adventure?"

"I spent most of my life in one place. I want to be open to every possibility and see as much as I can in my lifetime."

"And you think the only way to fully experience life is to move around like a—" Wilfrid's eyes widened. "Nomad." He reshuffled the deck and set down the top card.

"Ace of diamonds." He smiled. "Occurrences like this don't happen by chance." He laid out thirteen more cards. "Ace of hearts, ten of diamonds..." Closing his eyes, he lifted another card. "Seven of diamonds." He placed it on the table, face up and peered at me. "Damon." He thought for a moment, then slammed his fist on the table. "Nomad!" He looked at me, his eyes brimming. "You are Nomad."

"Spelled backwards, yes." I laughed at Wilfrid making an issue over the spelling of my name. "One of my teachers warned I'd be tossed out of Unity and live the life of a nomad if I didn't learn to focus my attention. I had trouble sitting still in my early years."

Wilfrid tapped the seven of diamonds and then glanced at me. "I've been expecting you, Nomad."

I raised a brow.

"For the past twenty-eight turns of the winter's longest night, I've seen the name, 'Nomad,' before falling asleep. You are to lead us." He stood and bowed.

"Please, sit down," I said, wondering why I had once desired this kind of treatment.

"Wherever you go, we will follow—"

"Whoever you think I am—I'm not him."

"This cannot be a coincidence."

"Life is filled with coincidences. Whenever you search for meaning in something, you'll find it."

"This is more than my imagination. I've had many dreams come and go, but the one with Nomad keeps repeating. Your arrival here today is—" He squinted his eyes. "How old are you?"

"Twenty-eight."

Wilfrid smiled. "No. This is no coincidence."

"I mean you no disrespect. You've been generous with your hospitality and I'm grateful, but your dream has nothing to do with me. I only stopped here to rest before traveling on to New Athenia."

"The cards never deceive me, but go to New Athenia if you must. Perhaps our time has yet to arrive. In the meantime, you're welcome to join us for our feast."

We walked out to the circle, and my stomach almost leapt out and raced ahead of me when I saw the food on the table. Wilfrid recited his prayer to the Sky King, and I proceeded to devour three platefuls of Genevieve's venison stew. By my fourth glass of wine, two men had grabbed their guitars to play samplings of their music. The songs were simple, but they spoke to my hands and I unpacked my violin and bow to accompany the duo. The villagers clapped their hands in rhythm and the women laughed like schoolgirls as the men pulled them up to dance. Between the food, wine, music, and women, I was feeling as carefree as I had during my first two years at University. The comparison was dispiriting because it made me think of Wade, who would by now have been dancing and captivating everyone with his charm. As the celebration continued, my grief dissipated and was replaced by euphoric drunken jollity. I wanted more of it, and imbibed as much atmosphere and wine as I could until the last person left the circle.

"You're going to sleep well tonight." Wilfrid grinned. "I have never seen someone do so much celebrating in such a short span of time."

"I'm trying to make up for all your parties I missed," I said, slurring my words.

"I think you caught up tonight. Do you need help to your bungalow?"

"I need help, but not for that." I laughed and staggered back to my quarters. A few minutes later, Genevieve showed up at my door with a blanket.

"My father says you might be needing this."

"Thanks." I was holding onto the door frame for support and when I let go I almost collapsed.

Genevieve helped me regain my balance and as I looked at her, the moonlight and wine blotted out my inhibitions. I kissed her, and she responded in kind, until I tried to unfasten her dress. She stepped back, and I pulled her towards me. We kissed again but as I made another attempt to pull down her dress, she pushed me away and ran out. Shortly afterwards, Wilfrid barreled into the room, pointing his finger at me. "You were speaking the truth; you're not Nomad. After tomorrow, you're no longer welcome here." He shook his head. "I hope your travels impart some wisdom to your lost soul."

Wilfrid left me alone, and I stayed up most of the night trying to figure out why he was so upset. The relationship between an Outsider woman and her father was a foreign concept to me, but I couldn't identify anything disrespectful about my actions because all that I knew about male and female relations stemmed from Unity. My analysis of the encounter led me nowhere. It didn't seem worth the effort to continue, so I left it alone. Tomorrow, the village would be a memory, and I'd be off to New Athenia.

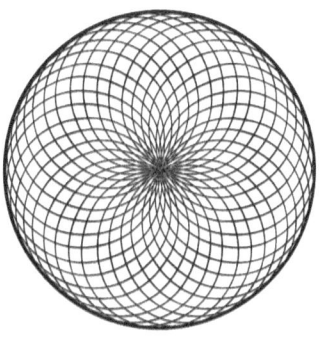

# conductor

Following my first performance with the Orchestra, Lidian invited me to his favorite bar. Several shots of whisky later, he had the patrons laughing at his self-deprecating tales of his Unitian past. He had been infamous for inadvertently insulting women when nervous and one time got his face slapped by a female server at a blue-level satiation center. Whatever he said in response caused her to pick up a plate of spaghetti and empty it over his head. He finished his story and everyone at my table clapped and jeered at him as he bolted up from his seat.

"You think you're all so privileged, but you're nothing but a bunch of slocking sleeve-worshippers," he cried out without his usual stuttering.

"Would you like your server to bring you a bib?" one of my colleagues asked.

Everyone laughed and Lidian barreled over to the table where I was sitting and flipped it on its side. We were all too stunned to react; Lidian was not known for outward displays of aggression.

"You all mock me because you're miserable," he said. "You're too scared to recognize it because you'd then have to admit you've crailered yourselves into bondage!" With that, he stormed out of the satiation center.

While the laughter continued, Lidian's words removed me from the room. Compared to him, everyone else seemed unreal and robotic. My detachment lasted until I took some tranquilizers that delivered me to the Unitian view of reality. It took Wade's death, in my current incarnation, to decipher why Lidian's words haunted me. I had a new respect for him because he was never fooled.

"I told the server she had beautiful eyes," Lidian had said to the crowd. Putting his hands on his hips, he spoke in a high-pitched voice. "'Then why are you staring at my chest?' she asked me. I told her that her bosom brought out the beauty of her eyes."

"Her eyes must've been big!" One of the men shouted.

"They were," Lidian said. "Even her modest uniform couldn't hide them."

"I'll never forget Michelle's mesmerizing mammaries," I said and handed Lidian a shot of whisky. "I got an even closer look at them when I took her back to my loft."

Lidian raised his glass to the crowd. "Ladies and gentlemen, may I present to you the Casanova of this new age. There probably isn't an adult female in Unity whose braids he hasn't unraveled." He swallowed his shot.

The men roared and whistled, and the oldest of them yelled out, "Ladies of New Athenia, beware!"

To uproarious laughter Lidian wrapped his arm around me. "If this man couldn't resist, then you can imagine what it must be like to be facing a pair of very large breasts that could fit a whole—"

"Amphitheater!" someone called out.

"And not an overstatement!" I added. "Which is why Lidian never stood a chance. With such poor visibility of his surroundings, he had no hope for escape," I said.

"A normal person would've stopped and retreated, but Unity never brought out the normal in me," Lidian confessed. "My overactive sweat glands were a constant reminder that I was the resident freak. I could've filled a wine barrel with the amount of sweat I poured out of my body that night."

He held out his glass to the barkeep, who filled it.

"Things got worse after *Michelle* thanked me for my compliment. She smiled at me, and I got nervous and told her she also looked beautiful in her breasts. I meant to say…dress." Lidian drank another round and laughed to himself. "I stuttered on the word, 'breast' a few times. Wish I had a recording to play it back for all of you. Michelle had great rhythm. Her slap landed on my face on the upbeat of three. Bre-bre-breast—slap." Lidian faked a slap on my face, and I almost fell off my barstool. "If she hadn't struck me, I'd still be locked in three-quarter time —unable to see beyond her expressions of female uniqueness."

"I wouldn't have minded!" an old man shouted.

"What brought on the rain of spaghetti?" I asked.

"That happened right after I told her she could learn a lesson from her breasts and soften up."

We all exploded into laughter, but Lidian stopped and looked the same way I did whenever a painful memory of Unity entered my mind.

I raised my glass to him. "Whatever happened to you between Unity and now—keep it."

On our way to the crail stop, Lidian and I sang our own version of the Unitian Hymn.

"Unity, oh Unity. We're slocked up in Unity," Lidian bellowed.

"And we'll fight till there's nothing left of Unity!" I sang.

"To hell we'll cast the Overseer and purple sleeves of Unity!"

"Then we'll finally be free of Unity!" I laughed. "It's liberating to act like drunken heathens in public."

"If we were in Unity they'd throw us into reintegration."

"We'd be reassigned to cleaning septic tanks for daring to mock the hymn." I sat on the bench. "We both sensed something was wrong."

"We did." Lidian sat down beside me.

"Why us?"

"Why not?"

"Don't you ever wonder why so many Unitians never question the Sacred Oath?" I asked.

"Slock the Unitians and everything else that stands for that dome prison. If we figured things out, there's no reason why they can't. If they choose to be enslaved, who are we to tell them otherwise?"

"I'd hope someone would want to help me if I were in their situation."

"Who helped you?" Lidian inquired.

The image of Wade lying dead at the bottom of the ridge came to me. If it wasn't for him, I'd still be living in Unity. I didn't speak his name aloud because I'd have to admit it took his death to expose the Unitian lies.

"The truth is, they don't want to be helped," Lidian said. "They like their little dome world, with their little dome assignments and little dome satiation centers. Their rules and regulations allow them to believe they're above everyone else. Makes no difference it's all based on a lie. As long as they get all their privileges, the deception is disregarded. I've wasted the first half of my life trying to please the purples sleeves so I could be accepted. I never was, and it used to bother me. In the end, my pathetic need for approval freed me. If I had been content, I'd probably still be in Unity, living the lie with them—flaunting my rank to convince the lower colors how privileged I am, so through their worship I could convince myself of my own happiness."

I laughed to myself. "You first have to admit you're suffering to know you're trapped in Unity."

"Why is that so amusing?"

"As you said, most Unitians are convinced they're happy, and happy people never leave the dome. Want to know why?"

"Why?"

I paused, until anticipation showed on Lidian's face. "Because they're already happy! There's no reason to leave!"

We exploded in laughter, and people stared at us as they passed by. A couple cautiously approached to wait for a crail, the woman whispering in her mate's ear.

I winked at Lidian and addressed the couple. "Are you happy?"

"Yes." The woman smiled at her mate who took a little too long to respond. "Aren't you going to answer?" she asked him.

"Of course, I'm happy," the man replied.

"I could tell. You looked really happy staring at every female in the billiard room."

Lidian and I erupted in laughter again. The woman stormed off, and the man followed her.

"They don't look too happy now," Lidian said.

"They probably never were. When I lived in Unity, I thought I was happy, but I was in denial."

"Denial of what?"

"The truth. I knew it but refused to acknowledge it."

"Do you regret leaving?"

"Slock no! I'm happy for real now."

"Too bad we don't have any wine to share a toast."

"Think we had enough for the night."

"Think Holly will agree with you." Lidian burped loudly. "When I stagger into our flat, she's going to think you're a bad influence."

"Better not tell her you were with me. It took years for her to forgive me for the beating I gave you."

Lidian stared at me aghast. "You never lifted a hand towards me, even in Unity."

"I can clearly remember throwing a punch at you."

"Think I'd remember that." Lidian chuckled. "Maybe you *wanted* to hit me. I wasn't easy to like back then."

"I wasn't either."

"You had lots of friends."

"It might've seemed that way, but only one of them was a true friend." A crail stopped in front of us. "Go on ahead," I said. "I'm in the mood for a walk."

"Backgammon tomorrow?" Lidian asked.

"Same time, same balcony. Invite Casanova along to play the winner."

"I would—" Lidian sat down in the crail and poked his head out. "Except he died during the *not-so-forgotten* times." He laughed one more time as the doors closed.

During my walk, I thought about my memory of Lidian. It seemed so real, but perhaps was nothing more than a drunken moment of confusion—not hard to believe considering I had plenty of those with Wade. I recalled a fight we got into over a girl in our biology class. Punches were thrown, blood was shed, followed by an evening of berry ales and vows never to fight over a girl again. I convinced myself that was the memory I recalled, and my self-deception continued.

I showed up at the park the next day for some reflective time at the duck pond. Gadfly reintroduced himself to me. I gave him some bread, and he then spent most of the morning chasing a female duck and terrorizing the competition. During his impassioned courtship, a song came to me. I turned on the recorder of my hololingue and sang the melody. I was at the middle of the chorus and Tyrus showed up. Forgetting I was no longer in Unity, I stood and bowed. "Did you just arrive, Master Tyrus?"

"Don't call me that. I never want to hear 'master' in front of my name again." He sat on the bench. "Heard you playing the other night. You've improved, and I didn't think it was possible for you to get any better." He removed a piece of stale bread from a bag.

Tyrus's familiarity with me made me suspicious. "How did you find out about New Athenia?" I asked.

He stared oddly at me. "Hasn't your memory returned yet?"

"I wasn't aware I lost it."

"Talk about a reversal of roles." Tyrus winced as though he were in pain. "I can't wait for you to remember. We need you to start up the transports again."

"Again? I never transported any—" I stopped and nodded knowingly. "I get what this is about. Kai sent you. He wants me back, so he can get more commendations from my hard work."

"Kai didn't send me. I defected as well." Tyrus tossed some bread at a flock of pigeons. "How familiar are you with the old tunnel?"

"Had to go through it to get here."

"Then you should have no problem going through it again on your way back to the cabin."

"What's my incentive?" I crossed my arms.

"To lead Unitians to their freedom."

I laughed. "You expect me to give up the life I've made for myself to help Unitians make a life for themselves?" I shook my head. "That doesn't sound very enticing to me at all."

"This is something you'll want to do."

"Can't think of any reason why I'd want to live like a hermit."

Tyrus threw more bread at the pigeons. "I like pigeons."

"I prefer ducks."

Tyrus gestured to my feathered companion. "Is that the infamous Gadfly you told me about?"

"I...never told you about Gadfly."

Gadfly chased a female duck after she'd rebuffed him by pecking his head.

"How about that." Tyrus laughed. "He really does have a strong will." Tyrus sat closer and stared directly into my eyes. "Now that I have your attention—the woman who conducted the transports was betrayed by you and is now dead. You must take her place."

"What woman?"

"The old lady in the cabin—the one you reported to Unity."

"I didn't know they'd kill her." I got up and began to pace. "I didn't know Wade was suicidal. I didn't know the scourge was a lie. I didn't know the Overseer is an ordinary man—albeit a psychotic one, if he really believes he channels the Prime Wisdom. It seems I didn't know much at all."

"As hard as this is for you to comprehend, right now I know you better than you know yourself. You want to help. You *need* to help."

I stopped pacing and looked down at him. "We haven't spoken since I ran into you at the Crystal Tower."

Tyrus narrowed his eyes. "We never met at the Crystal Tower."

I sat back down and stroked my chin. "Maybe I'm the psychotic one."

"Your memory must be coming back. Although I'm not familiar with the timeline you're recalling."

"Do you have any idea how crazy this sounds?"

"I do, but it's happening."

I shook my head. "What you're saying is impossible."

"In our last lifetime, on the eve of my death, you told me you wouldn't give up until you stopped yourself from inventing Harmony."

To keep from exposing my feelings, I turned away from him. "If I really said that, I failed."

"You also told me you would keep trying to help free Unitians until you succeeded."

"I won't sacrifice myself like that old woman. I have a chance at a good life here."

"This isn't about sacrifice."

"What is it about then? Forgiveness? Guilt? Shortsightedness?"

"And much more."

"If I can escape on my own, so can they."

"Harmony is now mandatory. They're even transmitting to the fetuses now. That's why I left."

I looked out at the pond, not taking my eyes off the ducks. Right now, they were the only thing in life that brought me peace. "Last night I had a vivid memory of punching Lidian, but it never happened." I turned to Tyrus. "I thought my visions had to do with the future but if what you're telling me is true, they're of events that have already happened. Am I right?"

"I'm reluctant to tell you more. I don't want to risk affecting your timeline in a way that won't work for our benefit. It's better that your memory returns on its own. All you need to know is we can't escape from this." Tyrus touched his forehead. "If my health was better, I would join you. I've played a large enough part in this as well."

I threw the last of my bread into the pond. "I'll play my last performance this Firstday."

The night before I left for the cabin I went for a walk on the top level of the labyrinth, stopping at the small park in front of the Acropolis. No matter how many times I came there, it was as if I saw it for the first time. The Ancients were motivated to build their world out of faith in their gods. Adoration and recognition had guided me throughout most of my life, holding me captive in empty pride. I read about Casanova at the repository. The opening from his memoir could've come from my own journal.

*I was all my life the victim of my senses; I have delighted in going astray, and I have constantly lived in error, with no other consolation than that of knowing I have erred. My follies are the follies of youth. You will see that I laugh at them, and if you are kind you will laugh at them with me.*

The isolation of the cabin seemed the perfect spot for inspiration. Distancing myself from my senses would allow me to connect to the place where it was a constant. I wanted to build my own Acropolis—not for Unity, not for a god, not for the world but only because I desired it. I would build with no expectations of payment or worship. I would build, so that I could say this is why I'm here, and this is my purpose. As I gazed at the Acropolis, the Ancients echoed back the very same words —and I finally heard them.

# gypsy wedding

On the return trip to the cabin, I came across a small community of gypsies celebrating a wedding ceremony. One of the gypsy men saw me watching from a distance and waved me over to join in their celebration. I didn't speak their language, but I recognized the happiness on the bride's face when the groom placed a golden band around her finger. The betrothed couple wore wreaths decorated with a panoply of wildflowers, linked by twine. At the close of the ceremony, they exchanged their wreaths and kissed. A trio played folk music on accordions while the villagers clapped their hands.

The couple sat on chairs and a group of men lifted and paraded them around while everyone continued to clap. When the next song started, the gypsies clasped hands and danced in a circle. The man who invited me to the gathering pulled me over to join in, and I jokingly said, "Maybe I shouldn't. Last time I did this I stepped on a lot of feet and made a complete fool of —" I stopped myself when I realized it was another memory from my alleged past life. Disoriented, I attempted to walk away but was yanked back into the circle. The amiability of the gypsies helped ground me, and the music helped calm my mind. Disregarding my previous confusion, I took out my violin and played alongside the trio.

My unfamiliarity with the language made me more observant of Outsider social behavior, particularly the interaction between the sexes. There were no outward displays of affection, and the women acted like schoolgirls, giggling as they talked to the men. I thought back to the evening feast at Littlefield. The behavior of the females was similar, but I hadn't acknowledged the significance until now. I still had a lot to learn. Genevieve's reaction and Wilfrid's anger were justified. Each Outsider village had its own set of rituals, laws, religion, and art, but they also encompassed social behaviors unique to them. Combined, these qualities make up what is called a *culture*, a concept initially difficult to grasp, and now that I understood, I was eager to discuss my revelation. The opportunity came when a nomadic family that spoke my language invited me to their campsite to share a meal with them. I recounted my lesson for them and felt as ignorant as a child when, after I'd finished, the father guffawed and slapped my back.

"Were you locked in a cage your whole life?" he asked.

"Spent most my life inside a large dome."

"Is that a prison?" A young boy asked as he petted Shisa.

"I see it that way now."

"When did you get out?" the father inquired.

"When I realized it was a prison."

The boy laughed. "You didn't notice that before?"

"No."

"Why not?"

"I couldn't see the bars."

I arrived at Littlefield during tranquil time. Michael was alone in the circle. He spotted me, opened the gate and before I could say a word, he landed his fist against my jaw.

"My grandfather told you to stay away!" He hit me again and shouted an impressive variety of expletives until Wilfrid and some of the other villagers emerged from their bungalows.

"What's all the noise out here?" Wilfrid questioned us.

"The savage returned!"

Wilfrid said, "Michael, please go help your mother prepare dinner."

"It's not for another four hours."

"Don't make me repeat myself."

Michael kicked the dirt with his shoe and stormed off.

Shisa looked at him and then up at me.

"Go," I said.

Shisa followed Michael, who kneeled down to pet her when she caught up to him.

"That dog of yours is smart," Wilfrid said as we walked towards his bungalow.

"And your grandson has a strong right arm."

"You're lucky I didn't come later. I would've had to put you back together."

"I should be thankful of your timing then. One session of bone setting is more than enough for one life—" I gazed at Wilfrid, who in that moment seemed like someone I'd known for years.

"You look as though you just saw a ghost," he remarked as we entered his bungalow.

"What you just said feels like a memory, but it's not connecting to anything I can remember."

Wilfrid helped me to a chair. "Come. I'll get you some water."

I thought about having hit Lidian and the memory of dancing with a large group of people. I never really remembered doing either, but it felt as though I had done both things before. Tyrus's assertion that they were memories of my past life started to sound more credible.

Wilfrid poured me some water. "Why did you come back?" He handed me the cup and I swilled it all down.

"My travels helped me gain some of that wisdom you were talking about."

He seemed unconvinced. "Your words sound sincere, but they must be backed up by action if they're to be believed."

"Words are all I have. What else can I do to prove my sincerity?"

"Why do you care what we think?" He picked up his deck of cards and shuffled them.

"I respect your values, traditions, and customs—they're all so foreign to me. I've lived most my life in a world where people are motivated by what they could acquire, but you—all of you value each other. The concept seemed simplistic to me at first, but now I see that what you have here is richer than anything I've experienced in Unity."

Wilfrid examined the violin case protruding from my backpack. "Your words sound heartfelt, but all the noise you caused during tranquil time angered many of the villagers."

"I'll apologize to them if you wish"

"You can...but playing that stringed instrument of yours would work better." He smiled.

The weather was clear and mild, perfect for an evening concert. I opened with my original compositions and played some of the songs I learned at the gypsy wedding. The villagers clapped and stomped their feet, and Wilfrid got up to dance. Others joined him, and each time I'd end a song, they'd beg me for another with a similar mood and tempo. When everyone was exhausted, I finished with "Quackanova," the song I'd written as Gadfly, to impress his mate, chased away the competition. Lidian came up with the title after I played it for him. He volunteered to write lyrics, but I declined his offer. I have clear diction, but my singing voice is best suited for the shower.

Michael approached me at the close of my performance, and I pointed my bow at him. "You better not be here to throw another fist at me."

"Sorry, Damon," Michael said.

Smiling, I retracted my bow. "Don't be. I deserved it."

Genevieve came over. "Your music is lovely. I haven't danced this much since my husband died."

"Regarding our last meeting, please accept my apology. My behavior was—"

"Apology accepted," she said with a smile. "The way you played tonight tells me you're not who you presented yourself to be that night."

"You can tell that from my playing?"

"Your music let us all see into your soul. Only a man connected to the Sky King has a soul."

"Where can I learn to play like you?" Michael stared in fascination at my violin.

"From me," I said.

"Where did this sudden interest in music come from?" Genevieve asked.

"His music is different. I like it a lot."

I studied Michael's expression for a moment, then handed him my violin and bow.

"I would rather you didn't," Genevieve said to me.

"Why not?" Michael asked.

"I'm sure it's expensive, and he'll expect some form of payment. We cannot afford it."

"Consider it a gift. The only payment I ask for is that you practice every day."

"I will."

"Next time I visit, I'll bring some lessons along."

"Thanks, Damon!"

"That's very kind of you." Genevieve said. "Be safe on your journey tomorrow." She walked off with Michael.

Unbeknownst to me, Wilfrid overheard our discussion.

"You've truly changed," he said.

"Into what?"

He laughed. "That, you'll have to figure out on your own." He showed me his deck of cards. "How about we play a game of gin rummy and drink some wine?"

"As long as you promise not to read my future."

"I promise."

Wilfrid kept true to his word. He even sent me on my way with a cart, two roosters and three hens. When I returned to the cabin, Freedomline started up again. My life became peaceful and predictable. Three years went by and I grew restless and planned a trip to New Athenia. I traded away most of my livestock and contacted Roth to let him know that following my next transport, I wouldn't be back for another year. Freedomline would have to go on hold while I took a much-needed sabbatical.

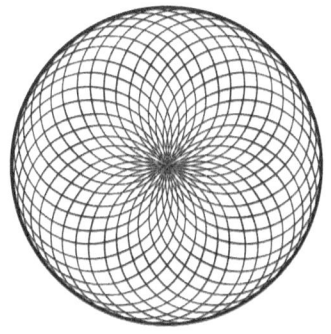

# rainstorm memories

Roth feared his appointer had been compromised, and he delayed my transport for another four weeks. The timing was fortuitous. Three days before our rendezvous, I found Flora at the bottom of the ridge. I would've missed her had I left for my transport when it was originally scheduled. The re-assimilation process was getting more difficult. When I recognized her, vertigo and nausea forced me to the ground. I rolled to my side, wrapped my arms around my calves, and took slow controlled breaths to ease my stomach. Everything I had for breakfast forced its way out from where it entered. My heart rate increased with each memory flowing into consciousness, and I couldn't process the data fast enough.

*Six times the fool, six times defeated*, were the first words that came to me once I was fully reintegrated. All the preparation and planning I'd made in my last incarnation failed to awaken me in time to stop myself from inventing Harmony. Wade still took his life, and my next meeting with Flora would probably end in her death again, regardless of what actions I took. I had no control over anything in my life, no advantage over those without a recollection of their past lives. The human-defined reality I relied upon as a scientist now seemed nonsensical. In Unity, we're taught that chaos exists only outside the dome, but it's the bedrock on which everything is built. My sense of humor from my previous incarnation returned, and I laughed when I realized we all existed in a giant reintegration chamber, constructing and engaging in illusions to force order where there is none. Had someone else told me this, it would have depressed me. Coming up with it on my own had the opposite effect. I needed this shift of perspective to help me endure another round with Flora and Kai.

Shisa cocked her head to the side and stared at me bewildered. "I know what you're thinking," I stopped laughing and sat up. "But we'll make it through together as long as she listens to—"

Flora groaned, and I whispered to Shisa, "The smart thing for us to do would be to leave for New Athenia and avoid the aggravation that's about to follow."

Shisa sat beside me and I petted her. "Don't you worry; I never do the smart thing." I rubbed my long, tangled beard. "Think my Outsider appearance keeps her from trusting me?" I gazed at Flora. "Unfortunately there isn't enough time for a shave." I gently cradled Flora in my arms and carried her to the cabin.

In the middle of my conversation with Roth, I heard groans coming from behind me. "If you don't hear back from me, the next transport is off." I disconnected, swung around on my chair and saw that Flora had regained consciousness. I looked at her for a moment and decided a more playful approach to our conflict might work better—more so for my own benefit. *Nothing*

*else I did worked, so why not? If I have to die again, I'm going to have fun doing it this time.*

I sat facing her, on the verge of laughing at myself over my previous thought. Judging by her expression, I must have appeared very peculiar.

"I know what you're thinking," I said, echoing my earlier remark to Shisa. "But we've been through this many times, and it always leads to either one or both of us dying." I got up from my chair and walked over to her. "This time, we're going to survive together."

Flora seized her plazer and aimed it at me. "Don't come any closer!"

I froze in place and feigned distress by gasping loudly.

"Put your hands up."

Slowly lifting both my hands, I said meekly, "Please don't shoot me."

"Damon 1300-333-1M, you will submit to the Corporate Hierarchy of Unity and refrain from speech until a confessor is present. All words and actions will be used against you in the court of ideals."

Flora stood, and I stomped my foot on the floor and thrust out my hands. She fired her weapon, but nothing happened. Reaching into my shirt pocket, I removed the power supply and showed it to her. "Won't work without this." I grinned and fluttered my brows.

Flora sprinted towards the door. I chased after her and pinned her, face first, against the wall. "I lived many lifetimes—so many I've almost lost count." I flipped her around and held her in place. "As much as I'm starting to enjoy our first encounters, we must stop this. I'd like to see you past today and into tomorrow."

"Let me go, and come back with to Unity," she said calmly. "It's the only way for you to find peace."

Looking into Flora's eyes, I momentarily forgot where I was. "I meant I don't want to tie you up again. I also mean this cabin." I released her and stepped back. "I'd like a change of environment this time a—"

She tried pushing past me, and again I shoved her against the wall.

"Let go of me you slocking Outsider beast!" she screamed. "You're hallucinating!"

"I'm *not* hallucinating! I'm—" I slowed my breathing to regain control. "I'm aware of how absurd I sound."

"Your appearance," Flora turned her head away, "and breath isn't adding to your credibility either."

"My sincerest apologies." I brought my mouth close to her nose. "Had I known a girlfriend from my first incarnation would be visiting my primitive little hovel, I would've cleaned myself up and prepared a romantic dinner for two."

I threw Flora over my shoulder, and carried her out the back door. She flung her arms about and kicked her legs, and this went on until I came to a stop at the pond.

"What are you doing?" she asked.

"Paying you back."

"For what?"

"For everything you did and for everything you're about to do." With that, I tossed her into the water.

She sprang to the surface with clenched fists, her wet clothes clinging to her body in a way that made me forget my anger.

"How you look right now reminds me of a day from my first incarnation that I'll always remember. We finished horseback riding and walking back to the dome got caught in a rainstorm. I can still picture you twirling and dancing around." I smiled at the memory. "When we got to the checkpoint, a Unity Guard lectured us about returning late. That was the first time I wasn't worried about a visit to reintegration."

Flora barreled out of the pond. "You're insane!"

"You said something similar in my past incarnations as well." I crossed my arms. "I'll listen to you go on about the scourge again if you stand there for a few minutes more in silence."

Flora made a move to punch me. I jumped out of the way.

"Maybe if you were a little nicer, I'd listen to you," I said.

"Return with me to Unity." She put her hand on her hip. "*Please.*"

"That is nice—the way you tilt your hip when you do that."

"I'm not leaving without you."

"Then prepare to stay with me forever because I'd rather be mauled by a pack of wild dogs than return to Dome Dungeon."

She stared at me in surprise.

"You don't have authority over me."

"You assassinated the Overseer," she said.

"Unless I have a Doppelganger that would be impossible. I haven't been to Unity since I left four years ago."

"Whatever weapon you used is irrelevant. You were seen."

"By whom?" I tried my hardest not to laugh. "Oh, that's right—only my *confessor* can give me that answer. The problem is Kai doesn't want me to answer to the charges. He'll be here shortly to kill us and call it a murder/suicide."

"What you think you're experiencing isn't real. You must come back with me before you enter the next stage of the disease."

I rolled my eyes. "What will happen to me then?"

"You'll die."

"Is that all?" I laughed and gave a dismissive wave. "How fortunate death isn't a permanent condition for me. But you won't be as lucky. Kai is going to kill you."

"Why would Kai kill me?"

I shook my head. "You forgot to mention his title before his name."

"I can do that when there isn't anyone else around."

"That privilege is about to be terminated. Kai now considers you nonessential."

"Kai values my service. He would never hurt me."

"Does that mean you enjoyed all those slaps across the face he gave you?" Flora was stunned by my remark. "For a while I thought you lost your convictions, but you haven't. I know you agree with me."

"How could you know anything about me? We only just met."

I could have continued my present course and told her the truth, but I would've risked justifying her belief that I was in need of reintegration. I also could've agreed with her assertion that I was crazy, but then she wouldn't consider leaving with me. There was no way to win, so I went back inside. The next move was up to her.

I played my violin, and observed Flora's attentive expression reflected in the window. What my words failed to do, my music accomplished with ease. Music helps the mind enter a contemplative state, so I continued to play while I spoke to her in a soft voice.

"During each of our encounters, I failed to deliver a convincing explanation of our unique situation," I said.

Flora crept closer to me. "Your sickness is going to kill you. That would be a waste for someone with as much talent as you. Please, come with me while there's still time."

"You'd feel sick if you discovered your life keeps repeating, and you can't repair the damage you created in previous lifetimes. You'd feel sick once you realize everything you do is just another drop in an endless well of realities. In my life, everything comes around to the same place and starts all over again. I can't escape from who I am—from what I've done. If hell exists, that's where I am, right now." I stopped playing and put my violin and bow away. "What keeps me going is knowing that if I mess up my life, I'll have another chance to improve myself."

"Do you see yourself as improved?" Flora inquired, sounding almost sincere.

"Not in the least." I gathered up my binoculars, along with the power supply. "Moments before each of my deaths, I focused on one thing I most wanted to change in my life and so far, I've failed. Harmony exists, and I can't stop myself from inventing it because my memory always returns too late. If you believe it sounds more like an excuse than a defense, I deserve your condemnation." I gave her the power supply, walked outside and sat down on the porch steps.

Seconds later, Flora stepped out onto the porch. "You're good, but not that good."

"If I wasn't, you'd have shot me by now."

"Confidence can mask insanity."

"Confidence *is* insanity—and I say this from personal experience."

I looked around at her. She had her plazer aimed at me. I stood, and shrugged my shoulders "Go right ahead. I'm dying of boredom anyway." I started slowly up the stairs. "You can't imagine what it's like when hardly anything scares you." I stopped centimeters from the barrel of Flora's plazer. "I've died so many times that if it happened to me right now, I'd thank you for ending our overplayed exchange."

Lowering her plazer, she looked at me with a hint of sympathy in her eyes. "You don't mean what you're saying. After reintegration, you'll be restored to your previous life."

"If what they're accusing me of is true, they'd never let me keep my sleeves. They'll blame it on my inferior genetic profile and use me as an example for anyone who wants to challenge their own color."

"Reintegration will help return you to what you used to be. Don't let the scourge destroy you and everything you've accomplished."

"You don't know how much I wish your words were true."

"They can be."

"If I could destroy what I've accomplished in Unity, I'd finally be free."

"From what?"

Fixing my gaze on her, the answer filtered into my consciousness. *From your death, from Wade's death, and from every other Unitian who will die because of Harmony.*

"I read through your file," Flora said. "You accomplished so much. Kai told me you were on your way to becoming a Chosen because of Harmony."

"Which I regret inventing."

"It's helping so many Unitians. Why would you want to take that away from them?"

"Did you get the upgrade?"

"I don't discuss my personal life with someone I'm about to apprehend."

"Then we'll pause right here and continue after you answer my question. In the meantime, we should get going; Kai will be here shortly."

"If you're right, we should head back to Unity before he arrives."

She was obviously stalling me, and I was ready to pack up and leave without her until I remembered my conversation with Tyrus in my last incarnation. I grabbed Flora's arms. "You must listen to me. I think your mind has been altered in reintegration."

She pulled away. "I haven't been to reintegration in over a —"

"They take you when you're not aware. At first they only did it to candidates nominated to purple sleeve to test their loyalty. Now they're doing it to dissidents; the only difference is their session doesn't end with a promotion."

"Something like that could never go on undetected."

"Have you ever experienced any missing time?"

Flora's eyes widened, and she averted my gaze.

"You remember something?"

"Three weeks ago—my implant malfunctioned. I felt this intense pain in my head—worse than any stun I ever received. I blacked out and woke up in the hospital three days later."

"What did they tell you was the cause of the malfunction?"

Tears welled in her eyes, and she started to walk away.

I latched onto her arm. "I'm telling you the truth."

"When you were a psychological engineer, what would you have said if someone came to you with your story?"

"I'd say he was suffering from the scourge because back then I didn't know any better. But you're different. You don't believe in the Corporate Hierarchy or anything it stands for. You don't think the Overseer is better than you, and you know you're capable of achieving beyond your color."

Flora's tears now spilled freely. I slowly circled around her.

"You like to spend your free nights at the observatory. When you were a child you dreamed of being an astronomer." I stopped in front of her. "Tyrus used to call you a rare gem, and when you grew up you joined the Strikers."

She jammed her plazer against my stomach. "Who told you that?"

"You did, in your journal."

# gods by design

    Flora gaped at me as I paraphrased an entry from her journal. "Kai reassigned a colleague of yours for failing to catch a Striker. He went against protocol by transferring him without a letter of intent, and you were overheard discussing your disapproval at a satiation center. Kai called you to his office for a reprimand and then tortured you further with one of his stories. Can't remember which one, but after he was finished, he handed you a list of exemptions available only to the Corporate Hierarchy; they can reassign anyone if there's a personnel shortage elsewhere, and there's always a shortage in the sewers. Life as a waste cleaner doesn't equate to a lengthy lifespan." I cleared my throat and did my best impersonation of Kai. "You may think you know all there is to know, Flora, but in the end you really don't know anything. Understand this, and you won't be returning for another reprimand."

Flora stepped back, keeping her plazer leveled at me. "You hacked into my journal."

"Not until you'd died in my first incarnation, and you'll be dead again if you don't go away from here with me."

She looked around nervously. "Am I in reintegration now?"

"I've asked myself the same question throughout all six of my incarnations, and have yet to come up with a convincing answer, but I can at least assure you that you're really here with me, and we must leave if you want to survive."

"Even if I believed you, I wouldn't go with you."

"Why?"

"The Strikers are counting on me."

"They were counting on me as well. I'm the conductor."

Flora lowered her plazer. "Why didn't you tell me?"

"You arrested me, shot me, and killed my dog. That didn't make me comfortable disclosing sensitive information to you."

"I'm not sure what any of that means but with you gone, there's no one else to move the passengers. What will happen to Freedomline?"

"If my appointer can't find a replacement, it will have to be on hold until it's safe for me to return." I glanced at my hololologue. "It's nearly ten. In about forty-five minutes, Kai will be here." I held out my binoculars. "See with your own eyes. He should be making his way down from the middle ridge right about now."

Flora hesitated, and then took the binoculars. She walked to the edge of the porch and stared into the eyepiece. "I don't see any—" Her face flushed, she turned to me. "Kai's on his way down."

"A hand-drawn map is in the top drawer of my desk. I'll meet you at the first clearing, and keep a lookout for dogs and boars."

"Are you going to kill Kai?"

"After all he's done, death would be just payment for him, but I'm not a murderer. There are a few things I need to discuss with him." I clutched my plazer grip. "When I get some answers, I

334

would like nothing better than for Kai to provoke me so that I can kill him in self-defense—again."

I sat calmly on the front porch steps and watched Kai approach with his plazer pointed at me. When he neared the steps, I pulled out my own weapon and took aim. "You should ease up on the berry ale, Kai. Your midsection looks rounder than I last remembered."

"And you look more like an apeman." He took a few more steps forward and stopped. "A wildcat wanders through the woods in search of shelter from a storm. He happens upon two caves, one of which has an exit on the back side of the mountain. The wildcat chooses the one with no other way out but his point of entry. The storm is fierce and unleashes a flood of water from the neighboring sea. He tries to escape the surge, but hits the dead end and is swallowed up by the deluge. Had he taken a moment to look up, he would have seen an overhead ledge he could've climbed on to and saved himself."

"The man who doesn't keep an eye out for all possibilities risks failure," I said.

"You were an attentive student."

"But I was never a good follower."

"Which is why you're an Outsider."

"When current theories aren't routinely tested, they become dogma."

Master Kai smiled ironically. "I said that to you, when we were considering your entry into the Science University. You had such promise back then, but I was wrong about you. You lack the strength to stand by your convictions."

"What convictions are those? To transmit Harmony to the public against their will? To make Unitians worship all those in the Corporate Hierarchy as gods?"

"The founders of Unity understood that the masses need gods to lead them, and we were created to perform that role. We watch over the Unitians' safety and welfare like gods, we exact control over their life and death like gods, and thanks to you, we now control almost all of their emotions. You, Damon

1300-333-1M, acted like a god when you invented Harmony, so don't get all pious with—"

I fired a beam of plasma inches from Kai's head. "I believed what we were doing was for the good of all, until I realized I was deluding myself. Since leaving Unity I found truth, while you, the Overseer, and the rest of the Corporate Hierarchy remain locked in a unified psychosis."

"Aspiring to Unity is born from compassion, and we were given the authority to make it a reality. Only a madman would try to stop us."

"Curious. Do you sound convincing to yourself?"

"Why should I need to convince myself when our destiny is by design? We emerged from the tanks ordained to rule over the inferior colors."

"How does that bring about unity?"

"Once everyone knows their place, they won't desire more than they have. Jealousy, greed, and personal dissatisfaction will be eradicated by default. A septic tank cleaner will be as content as a psychological engi—"

Kai's eyes bulged as a plazer blast pierced his chest. He fell to the ground.

Flora came out from hiding. "Did you get your answers?" She had her plazer directed at the spot where Kai had stood.

"I barely got past my first."

"If our lives were planned since our emergence, all my hopes and dreams have been meaningless." She trained her plazer on me. "Did you know about this?"

"I had my suspicions."

"Is that why you left?" Fresh tears trailed down her cheeks.

"It wasn't for anything that noble. The first time I said goodbye to Unity was because of you."

"I don't know you."

"But I've known you…for many lifetimes. You forced me to answer to my own conscience. Besides my friend Wade, no one else in Unity had that effect on me."

Flora went back into my cabin, after which I dragged Kai's body to the backyard to perform the sacred burning ceremony. He wouldn't be destroying any Outsider villages in this lifetime.

As the fires burned his flesh, I wondered if, at the end, he realized—as I had in my own previous last moments—that he died a slave to an ideal, an ideal that turned him into a murderer.

Flora remained inside, emptily gazing out the window as the flames continued to burn. She seemed as lost as on the day she took her life in my last incarnation. I doubted if she had the strength to pull through this time either. The reintegration programming would be difficult to resist. If Flora was to survive, she had to regain her strength.

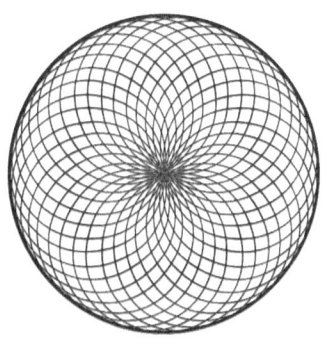

# looking in

I groomed myself back to a civilized appearance and then went to fetch some eggs from the coop. My culinary talent had improved, but as I scrutinized the muck in the pan that was supposed to be a lentil omelet, I was almost embarrassed to serve it to Flora.

"Justice was served, and now so is our dinner." I placed two dishes on the table.

Flora stared unenthusiastically at her food.

"You haven't eaten all day, and you'll need your strength before we leave." I sampled my omelet.

"Killing a man ruined my appetite." She got up and walked to the window.

I picked up the remote control and closed the shutter. "Indifference ruins mine," I said.

Flora turned to me. "Neither of us will be eating then."

I slammed my fist onto my plate, splattering food all over myself. "You're weak-willed and weak-minded. A disgrace to what you used to be." I wiped my face. "Did Kai also take away your ability to think for yourself?"

Flora darted toward the table and shoved it against me.

Pushing back my chair I jumped to my feet. "*That's* what I wanted to see! You must fight hard to—"

She charged again and thrust the heel of her foot against my stomach with such force that I almost fell.

"That's for reading my journal!"

I sat and leaned forward to relieve my aching abdomen. "You were dead."

"My thoughts are private," she cried. "You had no authority to invade my personal life."

"In Unity, nothing is private. The Corporate Hierarchy views you as their property to use in whatever way they desire. Direct your anger at them for what they've done to you and will continue to do to the rest of the Unitians who believe in the Sacred Oath." I placed my hand over my heart. "All hail Unity. Together we unite in Unity. Together we fight to keep alive the flames of Unity. Together we live for our Unity. Together we die for our Unity. We are one in Unity. I am—"

"Shut your slocking mouth!"

Flora tried to kick me again. I grabbed her calf, and she went down.

"Why did you become a Striker?" I asked.

"What do you want me to say?"

"Anything that tells me your mind is your own again."

She sat up. "I thought my actions proved that."

"Killing Kai doesn't prove anything other than you wanted him dead. *Why* did you kill him?" I helped her to her feet.

"I…I just got angry."

"Over what?"

"I don't want to talk about this now. Killing a man also makes me tired."

She headed to the back door, and I let her go. She needed time to think, and I had a mess to clean up on the floor. *Better spilled food than spilled blood, Damon. Let's keep it that way, at least until we make it to New Athenia.*

I washed up, went out back and found Flora sitting and gazing at the mountains.

"Sorry if I pushed too hard." I sat down beside her.

She turned to me. "You almost look human without all that fur on your face."

"In between transports I avoid my mirror."

"And the shower."

"Shisa doesn't care what I look…or smell like."

"If she could speak, I think she'd disagree." Flora said with a smile.

"I forgot how much I miss that."

"Miss what?"

"Your smile."

Hearing that, she turned away.

"Sorry. I sometimes get lost in time."

"How did Kai find us?"

"Are you sure you want to continue? There'll be no turning back," I said.

"That was obvious when I fired my plazer."

I paused for a moment to think of what to say. In my past incarnations I had no trouble revealing everything to Flora, but now that she wanted to know so much, I was reluctant to speak.

Anticipating an explanation, she raised her brows.

"The scourge is a lie. It's used to make people afraid to leave Unity and accept the implant."

"I've seen people die from it."

"Whatever is killing them has nothing to do with the so-called scourge. I've traveled beyond the other side of the old tunnel and haven't seen even one case."

"What is its purpose then?"

"To track you."

"That can't be. There are purple sleeves who are Strikers. They would've informed us if that was true."

"I met up with Tyrus. They know."

"He's alive?" Flora's face brightened and tears streamed from her eyes. "Kai told me he died."

"He's in New Athenia."

"Why did he leave?"

"They're now transmitting Harmony to fetuses, and Tyrus couldn't stop—"

"It's too late," Flora cried. "The Strikers failed. The Corporate Hierarchy will never be defeated." She squeezed my arm. "Was everything I did in my life monitored since I was removed from the tank?"

"Why don't we break for a—"

"I have to know now—before I lose the last few pieces of myself that are still mine."

"It only feels that way now. You can reclaim yourself. I did, and you can—"

Flora got up and ran into the cabin, and I chased her to the kitchen counter where she grabbed her plazer. Seizing her arm, I got it away from her.

"Give it to me! Things have gone too far!" she cried, "They can't be stopped!"

I recalled her saying something similar to me in my first incarnation, and I started to wonder if it had anything to do with her last reintegration session. "That's true only in Uni—"

Flora punched me in the stomach. Rage overtook me and I aimed the plazer at her.

"What are you waiting for?" she asked. "Do it!"

I slammed the plazer against the cabinet. "This isn't you speaking! You have to see through this if you want to survive! Don't give any more of yourself to the Corporate Hierarchy. They've taken enough."

"I can't live like this—knowing I've been monitored like some germ under a microscope."

Flora's defeatism was overpowering her, and I needed some of my old psychological engineering tricks to challenge the programming done to her. "I'll return your plazer on one condition—" At first it seemed to make good sense. *Are you slocking serious Damon? Remember the patients you couldn't help? The ones that filled out a request for death? Maybe you do have the scourge or worse...*

*maybe you're being reintegrated.* In frustration, I pounded the cabinet, and then, calming down, I said, "Sorry. Wasn't talking to you."

She crinkled her brow. "Who were you talking to?"

I removed the power supply from Flora's plazer. "Psychoanalyzing myself would take too long, and we have to get out of here soon."

"I never said I was going with you."

I handed her the plazer. "In my last incarnation, I knocked Kai out with my weapon. I set up camp nearby and kept watch over the cabin. He didn't come out until the next day. I hung around for three more days, waiting to see if Unity Forces would show up. They never did. I'm assuming Kai kept quiet because he couldn't frame me for assassinating the Overseer. Since he won't be making any calls this time around either, we should be okay for a while, but I'm not counting on that. Kai died and his implant stored all his final vital signs along with his last tracked position."

"If Kai really did all of this on his own, no search party will be sent out until they discover him missing. That won't be for another five days."

"Why five days?"

"Assuming he told the Chosen he was going on holiday, he would've requested his usual five days off. He's been doing that ever since I became his protégé, and he'd continue the same trend if he wanted to avoid suspicion."

"As much as I appreciate your professional assessment, I'm sticking to my three-day schedule. You're welcome to join me."

"What if I don't?"

I held out the power supply. "I'll give this back to you."

Flora eyed the power supply. "Three days," she said with a backward glance as she walked away.

I had no intention to follow through with my offer, and I had no idea what I'd say if Flora decided to take her life again. She had three days to persuade herself to fight, and I had three days to come up with a good response in case she opted for a loaded plazer.

Flora quietly stared out at the pond. Under the moonlight, the beauty mark below her ear brought me back to the night we first met.

"Can we stay in this spot forever?" she asked.

Shisa came over and squeezed in between us. Flora gently stroked her coat.

"The longer you're away, the more at peace you'll be." I traced a circle in the dirt and drew three smaller circles inside. "Think of this moment as the start of your true life—one you'll have more control over. You'll be surprised how much better you'll function once you're completely removed from Unity."

"But I don't belong anywhere else."

"Do you really want to belong anywhere?"

"I'm not sure how to answer that."

"The time I spent alone taught me that invention and creativity flow freely when I don't need to censor myself. They were easier to find once I let go of Unity, in mind and spirit. My only purpose now is to satisfy my own curiosity. No one tells me what to read, how to dress, what to invent, how to think, or what to believe or not believe in. I don't keep quiet when I see an injustice, and I won't compromise my values to belong anywhere. That's what belonging does—you must compromise your values to fit someone else's agenda. To me, belonging to something means being owned by something." I drew an "x" outside of the circle. "I choose un-belonging. I choose freedom."

"What about the Outsiders? What are they like?"

"Most tribes live without electricity. Some live in small villages while others migrate each spring in search of food. The only exception is New Athenia. It's filled with culture and art. I had a great life there for a few of my incarnations."

"Why did you leave?"

"To help the Strikers. My restitution for the damage I caused with Harmony. Each transport I conducted brought me closer to reclaiming my humanity." I reached down to pet Shisa. "Someday I'll feel whole again."

"You won't be able to return here because of what I did."

"Seeing New Athenia through your eyes will make this all worthwhile."

"Wish I could say I'm looking forward to all of this, but all I feel now is emptiness."

"I felt that way too, the time I first left. I wasn't accustomed to being alone. All that talk of being together in Unity was programmed into my mind, and I had to work hard to remove myself from that trap. Eventually, I found solitude comforting." I took Flora's hand in mine. "It's in the silence that you hear your voice the clearest."

# motherhood

For most of the following day, Flora stayed in my bedroom and refused to come out for dinner. I knocked on the door and when she didn't answer, I entered.

She lay on her side with her back to me, not budging from her position, even when my steps made the floorboards creak.

"Since you didn't get a chance to try out my lentil omelet last night, I made another one just for you."

Flora remained silent and eerily still. Fearing she'd changed her mind about waiting three days, I rushed over to her. I was relieved to see her staring out the window.

"I'll keep it warm for you on the burner," I said and left the room.

Shisa came up to me, and I motioned through the open door to Flora. "Keep watch on her. You're better at this than me."

She entered the bedroom, jumped on the bed and lay beside Flora. I stood watching until Flora began to pet her. I completed some chores, then went back to the bedroom with a piece of chicken breast and dangled it in the air.

Shisa lifted her head.

"You earned this. Your technique is more effective than a curate."

She jumped off the bed and snatched the chicken breast from my hand.

"Thanks for your help."

Flora still lay on her side facing the window. She probably needed more time alone, but I had to get her ready to run.

"I have something I'd like to show you." I turned on the light and sat beside her. "When we get to New Athenia, the first place you'll want to visit is the Alexandrian Repository. It features books from around the world. You can't check them out, but most of them are scanned into the digital library. The knowledge contained within those walls overwhelmed me. I wanted to set up a cot and move in, but the librarian turned down my request."

I placed my hologue in front of Flora. She picked it up and peered into the optic. On screen was an image of a man standing beside a woman holding a baby in her arms.

"What do you think?"

"I'm…not sure." She studied the image, her eyes filling with tears.

"You may not be thinking, but you're definitely feeling something."

"It's a beautiful picture." Flora sat up and leaned her back against the wall. "I never cried upon seeing something beautiful." She handed me the hologue. "Hope you're right about the scourge not being real because confused emotions is one of the symptoms."

"You're not ill, or confused; I had many moments such as the one you're experiencing. There isn't anything in Unity that evokes that kind of emotion." I examined the image. "No words are required once you recognize a truth. It speaks by pulling itself out of you where you can see it, and when you do, it's as though you're seeing for the first time."

348

"What truth is this?"

"The man and woman are the baby's *parents*. The woman is referred to as 'mother' and the man, 'father.' The baby is *born* from the woman and remains with her parents until adulthood."

"Born…like an *animal*?" Flora grimaced and turned her head away.

I showed her an image of a pregnant woman. "Not all babies are grown in tanks. Outside of Unity they're brought into the world by its mother."

"Impossible. We're not animals. Only animals grow their young inside them."

"We're not that much different. The fetus grows in the mother's *womb*, just like it does in all mammals. Three quarters of a year later, the baby is born. All the Outsider women have children this way. When we get to the other side of the tunnel, you'll see for yourself."

"I don't believe it. Something this big could never be kept secret."

"Several women who've ventured past the beacons have mentioned Outsider women having babies like wild dogs. They were immediately reintegrated and told they were suffering from the scourge. Even if they spoke out, whatever the Overseer deems as truth is accepted—regardless of whether it's true. It's an easy sell. All the Corporate Hierarchy has to do is agree with each other in public, making anyone who doubts their wisdom think they're alone. You must be very secure in your own thinking to break free from the Unitian herd."

"Why can't Unitian women make babies?"

"A signal sent to the implant prevents conception. When you passed the range of the towers, you became fertile."

I felt uncomfortable discussing the mechanics of what that meant and found a page in the hololigue that explained female reproduction. Flora read through it and winced.

"Seems barbaric, and disgusting." She contorted her face like a child who's been served dark green vegetables without any seasoning.

I couldn't help but smile at her reaction. "Only because you haven't known anything else besides the incubation tanks."

Flora lifted both her brows. "Our way seems more efficient and civilized."

"Most mothers don't seem to mind and even look forward to the experience."

I thought about Aaron and James. The day of their birth was traumatic. After five incarnations, I could still hear Holly's screams. Even as she yelled out in pain, she refused anesthesia.

"I want to be lucid when they come into the world," Holly said.

"You will, in comfort. It makes no sense to suffer when they have medicine to take away the pain."

"I had enough of the safe and artificial environment of Unity. I want to feel everything, even pain because it's real."

Holly wasn't the only one in pain that day. As she screamed, she squeezed my hand so hard that she nearly broke it. I took it without complaint. If Holly could endure the torture, so could I, and the reward was worth every agonizing moment. Her screams were replaced with the cries of my sons, echoing against the tiled walls. I was euphoric when I laid eyes on them. *Where are they now?* I had never stopped asking. Holly and Lidian were together again and would have a child of their own soon. I accepted that's how things were meant to be, but I was also torn. While I loved Holly, Flora existed beyond the physical definition of love. The admission troubled me because that meant I was willing to not have my sons.

I climbed the ridge to examine the motion sensors and cameras. Both were functional. How Kai managed to get past them without being detected was a mystery. It was almost as though he knew where the sensors were located.

Coming back to the cabin, I was relieved to find that Flora had migrated from my bed to the sofa. She was reading one of the history books in my hololoogue.

"The Ancients chose their own life assignments," she said.

"The Athenians still do."

"Do they have astronomers?"

"They do, and the Science University has an observatory on top of the labyrinth. It's open to the public on weekends."

Flora mused, "When I was a child, space fascinated me. I wanted, more than anything, to be an astronomer."

I sat down next to her. "The Ancients traveled all around the planet in flying machines called airplanes. Large ships glided through space, and they came close to developing travel beyond the speed of light. There was even an Earth colony on Mars. The Great Cataclysm brought an end to the space age."

Flora's eyes gleamed as mine did whenever I discussed this topic.

"I used to write about adventures in space," she said. "I wrote almost every day—before doing my homework. One of my schoolmasters threatened to erase all my stories from my holologue if I didn't improve my grades, but I couldn't help it. Whenever I wrote, it made me feel as though I was somewhere far away from Unity." Tears rolled down Flora's cheeks. She wiped them with the back of her hand. "In each session I made myself the captain of a spaceship, and I led my crew to other worlds. As ridiculous as it sounds, it made me feel better."

"Not ridiculous at all. I could see a woman piloting her own spaceship *and* conquering Unity with alien allies she met in space."

Flora's eyes held an innocent gaze. "I wrote a story very similar to that." Then, with a smirk she said, "You had access to my files."

"And what you wrote is not beyond the realm of possibility—including Kai being stripped of his clothing in the middle of the Overseer's assembly." I crossed my arms. "Oh, the creative things I would do if such a device existed."

Snickering, she said, "I'd have it strip the Overseer and Chosen and broadcast it on every city screen."

"Your imagination and determination is inspiring. Had you been born before the Great Cataclysm, you would've stood a good chance of commanding your own ship. Growing up I had similar dreams."

"Like what?"

"I had visions of flying through space and landing on a world inhabited by felineoid aliens. By a strange coincidence, the mythology about the founding of New Athenia mentions a race of felineoid demons. As they descended upon the city to destroy it"—I stretched my hands above my head—"a magical shield descended from the heavens and saved the day."

Flora rolled her eyes and grinned. "If only my imagination was that vivid."

"Wrap your imagination around this possibility: New Athenian scholars believe humans still live in the Mars colony, and that some of them may have colonized other worlds by now." I smiled to myself. "I hope that's true."

"Why?"

"Think about all the things they would have discovered. They'd have a lot to teach us."

"They could also tell us about what we lost."

"Time holds many secrets. I left Unity, naively believing I'd learn the truth about the Great Cataclysm. When I first saw the Ancient ruins on the other side of the old tunnel, the mystery became even more elusive."

Flora angrily handed me my holologue. "No one elected the Corporate Hierarchy as the guardians of truth. They twist it and shape it to advance themselves." She began to cry. "But even worse than that, they steal our dreams by keeping us from living them."

I took hold of her hand. I knew this was difficult for her, openly displaying so much emotion in one day.

"I never believed in the Sacred Oath," Flora said, "or that the Overseer was worthy of worship. When Kai asked me to track his assassin, I wanted to meet and congratulate the Outsider who assassinated him."

"Why did you give me such a hard time?" I asked.

"I couldn't trust you. Your strange behavior made me think you had the scourge."

"Strange? I thought I was rather charming." I beamed my best smile, but she wasn't impressed.

"Your arrest would've earned me a position in the next Overseer's private security team. I would've been able to give valuable information to the Strikers. I couldn't give up my cover for an opportunity like that—even if it meant turning you in."

*Or killing me.* I thought back to my fourth incarnation. I couldn't imagine the inner-conflict Flora must have endured to pull the trigger. "That sounded like an ambitious *and* dangerous plan."

"One I can't take part in anymore," Flora said. "You need to contact the Strikers and tell them you've been compromised."

"I already sent a message to my appointer."

"You're handling this a lot better than me."

"What they did to you can be beaten."

"How? I don't even know what thoughts are my own anymore."

"None of them are. They all came from what you learned in Unity. Think of it that way, and it will be a lot easier. All the knowledge you acquire—from this day forward—will be yours to assimilate, however you see fit." I picked up the Ganesha and with my index finger, traced the fracture on the trunk. "Wish I'd figured all this out sooner."

"You look sad when you say that."

I fixated on the picture of Old Woman and Torrin. "When I first showed up here I refused to listen to Old Woman. She tried to free me, but back then I considered only my own aspirations. I was so caught up in reaching my goal of becoming a Chosen, I had no time to think about the consequences of Harmony until it was too late."

"What did you expect the Overseer to do with such technology?"

"I used to believe in the Sacred Oath and never even considered such a question"—I looked at Flora—"until you interrupted my induction and asked if I could promise Harmony wouldn't be misused."

"Are you sure you lived before? That wasn't me."

"You confessed to doing it."

"I wanted to. My friend asked me to go with her to protest Harmony, but I never showed up. She's the one who interrupted you, and she got away with it. I regretted not going with her."

"Why didn't you?"

"I was scared of getting caught. Strikers don't keep anyone who draws attention to themselves. It's too risky."

"Who was your friend?"

"Danielle."

I was acquainted with many women in Unity and had only met one Danielle. "1314-203?"

"2F. You know her?" Flora asked.

"She was one of my mystery dates."

"Danielle played a lot. She liked the easy credits she could earn there."

I leaned back against the couch and took a moment to process this new information.

"The way you look, you almost seem disappointed it wasn't me," Flora said.

"Why would you have confessed to something you've never done? What would you have hoped to gain?"

"If you got me mad, that would've been motivation enough. I have a bad temper."

"I've known you many lifetimes, and there's so much I either overlooked or misinterpreted."

"Not that I believe you, or your *strange* story, but you should listen to me more this time around, or you'll see my temper flare again."

Flora smiled, bringing me back to our first incarnation. I desperately wanted to take her in my arms and kiss her, and it took all my will to restrain myself. A brisk walk with Shisa helped reconnect me with my present incarnation.

When I got back, Flora was asleep on the couch. I carried her to my room and stayed up the rest of the night thinking about everything I was about to leave behind. The cabin had become more than a home to me. It tied me to Torrin and Old Woman. Their influence kept me fighting, and in many ways I felt as though I had continued where they left off. Ruminating over the legacy I was about to lose reawakened my resentment towards Flora. After arguing between my feelings of love and hatred for her, I decided to start clean. It wasn't fair to judge Flora on her past. If I did that with her, I'd have to judge myself —and I had done far worse things.

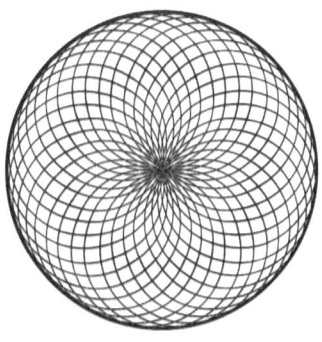

# hero

I woke up with that feeling you get right before something disastrous is about to happen. A vigorous run outside followed by a cup of tea failed to banish my anxiety, so I made my way to the ridge to perform some maintenance work on the motion sensors. In the middle of inspecting my first one, Shisa ran to me, barking. A quick scan of the upper tier with my binoculars revealed Unity Forces on their way down. "Go home, Shisa." She scurried off, and I ran down the path at full speed.

I got to the cabin, rushed out to the backyard, opened the coop and freed the hens and roosters.

Flora came outside. "What's going on?"

"We leave now. Unity Forces will be here soon."

"They shouldn't be here so soon. Are you sure Kai did this all on his own?"

"Since I left Unity, I learned I could be sure of nothing, which is why I always have an alternative plan." I hurried into the cabin and collected my backpack. "Hope you packed ahead as I asked."

Flora retrieved her pack from the bedroom and we raced for the cover of the woods. After we'd gained some distance, we slowed our pace and walked for most of the day. I kept my hand on my plazer. Every sound I heard made me tighten my grip. Arriving at the old tunnel, I eased up but Flora became more apprehensive.

"Is there another way?"

"We'll be safe. Outsiders are nomadic and mostly peaceful, and for those who aren't—" I removed my plazer from its holster and twirled it around.

"Not bad for a maroon."

"You taught me that."

"Hope I taught you to shoot as well."

"That I learned before my first trip out of the dome." I looked at Flora's plazer. "Yours set for a grab and shoot?"

"I'm a…was a Unity Guard. What do you think?"

I nodded and turned on my lantern. "I know this tunnel well. We'll be okay."

We entered into the darkness, the echoes of our footsteps, with their varied strides, producing a jazz-style melody. As it played in my head, I pictured the arrangement printed on manuscript paper. The violin played *rubato* in the opening lyric and the standup bass, drums, and piano came in *a tempo* at the start of the chorus. I hummed the melody aloud and recorded it on to my holol32gue.

"Sounds beautiful. Is it one of—?"

"Shhh!" My agitation at being cut off almost made me lose the chorus and I had to start over. Once I'd successfully captured the melody, I returned to the land of the uninspired. "What did you want to say?" I asked.

"Is it safe for me to speak?"

"Sorry. You kept quiet for most of the walk, and I forgot you were beside me."

"Don't know how I should take that."

"It's not only you. I shut off the whole world during the creative process. I've been that way since I was a child. It used to get me into a lot of trouble."

"What kind of trouble?"

"In my first year at the master's apprentice school, I failed to show up at formation during the monthly fire drill. I was practicing my violin when the alarm went off. It was loud, but it sounded more like background noise. I couldn't shut myself off and kept playing, even when Master Franklin entered my room. I didn't notice him until he pulled the bow from my hand and struck my mattress with it. *That* I noticed." I shook my head in amusement, recalling the frustrated look on my mentor's face.

"Did you get a reprimand?"

"No, but Master Franklin instructed me never to do any creative work on days when a fire drill was scheduled. Can't say I blame him. Had it been a real fire, I would've died in the middle of playing *Mozart's Violin Sonata No. 22 in A Major* without ever knowing that's what I was playing."

"What did you think you were playing?"

"One of my own compositions. I auditioned for the New Athenian Orchestra, and discovered I had stolen it from one of the Ancients' greatest composers. I put that one on my list of most humbling experiences."

"How many are on your list?"

"Too many for the memory of my hologue to store." I laughed.

"Can you play me one of your songs?"

"When we stop to rest."

"How long will it take to get to the other side?"

I held my hologue near the lantern. "About seven hours more. We've already walked three."

"I need to rest."

"We should make it to the trainlets in another hour."

Flora stopped walking. "I don't want to stay in here."

"I won't let anything happen to you."

Flora shined her lantern in my face and looked up at me. "You really mean that."

"I do, and soon you'll know that as a fact."

"I know now." She lowered the lantern. "Before today, the only other Unitian I trusted was Master Tyrus. Now I see he's not the only brave man I know."

"What I've done is hardly brave. It's something I had to do."

"No." Flora took my hand. "You could've left, but you chose to live all alone in your cabin just so you could help free Unitians." She smiled, inspired. "I could write you into one of my stories. You have all the characteristics of a hero."

Normally, such a remark disturbed me. Being alone gave me an independence that I couldn't fathom when I lived in Unity. The higher I advanced in color, the more bound I became by everyone's perception of my celebrity. Living up to a myth was impossible, and my constant failure to attain the greatness attached to my color kept me reaching for a level impossible to attain, impossible for anyone to attain. I preferred not to live through that delusion again, but if it helped Flora overcome the destructive programming that still lurked in her mind, I was willing to play the hero for her.

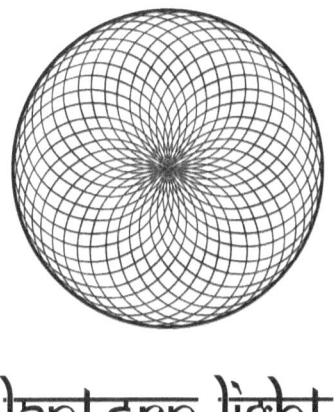

# lantern light

The trainlets were all vacant, which pleased me as I had always preferred the last car. I felt around in my pocket for payment. As in all my other incarnations, the only thing I was willing to give up was my multipurpose knife. "Do you have anything you don't mind parting with?" I asked Flora.

"I didn't pack anything of value."

"This is going to be hard to replace." I opened the payment box. "I never learn."

"Wait." Flora removed a ring with as small ruby from her finger. The lantern's reflection on her face betrayed her reluctance.

"I don't want you to give away something that's important to you."

She dropped the ring in the payment box. "I'm sure Master Tyrus won't mind."

I was about to ask what she meant, but stopped myself and we entered our 'let. Flora grew worried when I drew the shades.

"Relax, you're safe. This is only to inform travelers this 'let is taken." I set my lantern on the bench, removed my pack, and collapsed onto one of the sleeping bags.

Flora sat down next to me. "He got it for me when I graduated from the academy."

"Got what?" I asked.

"The ring."

"It's not my business."

"I know. But the look on your face made me think you wanted an explanation."

"What look on my face?"

"The kind that tells me you wanted an explanation."

"Unity Guards." I laughed.

"We don't miss much." Flora sighed and lay on her side, facing me.

The reflection from the lantern on the windows and walls produced a soft glow that carried me into an altered state of awareness. I studied Flora for a moment, and the recognition of our joint survival struck me. *We finally made it together.* "I love this place."

She gave me a curious look. "Think you've been out here too long. I miss my warm shower."

"You'll have one of those in New Athenia. But you'll never have an experience like this anywhere else."

Flora surveyed the room. "Can't see why anyone would want to experience anything in here."

"Every time I enter this Ancient mode of transit, I'm transported back in time." I turned onto my back and rested my head on my hands. "I'm here with the passengers, engaged in conversations about how their day went as we cross the tunnel."

"Where do you end up?"

"Back here, but unbeknownst to the other passengers, they're trapped in a perpetual existence, riding back and forth on a train that never stops. Their ghosts are unaware that in this present timeline, we inhabit the same exact space." My eyelids grew heavy, and I almost drifted off.

Flora waved her hand in front of my face. "Are you in here with me?"

"Sorry. Got lost in time."

"Looked more like you disappeared into it."

I sat up. "Thanks for pulling me back out." I removed an apple from my pack and waved my knife in the air. "Your ring wouldn't have been as useful." I shaved off the peel in one long strand. "The tunnel took fifteen years to build. It's one of the greatest architectural masterpieces of the forgotten times. This train transported people between two lands that were once only accessible by air or boat." I handed her an apple slice. "It's unfortunate the Ancients didn't last long enough to expand their engineering feats." I smiled to myself as I often did when I marveled over the Ancients. "I can't even imagine how much further along we'd be if the Great Cataclysm never happened." I cut another slice of apple and gave it to Shisa.

"Where you see history and mystique, I see only a dark and dreary room that smells as though it hasn't been cleaned since the forgotten times."

"You must stop seeing everything out here through Unitian eyes. The founders of Unity put a stop to progress because they believed they could conquer our flaws by minimizing the use of technology. All they did was deaden progress."

"Everything in Unity is dead," Flora said. "The purple sleeves and Overseer drained the life out of all of us."

"Fortunately their control is limited to the dome. Out here, you're free to make your own life and have full authority over it." I handed Flora another slice of apple. "Did you make your decision?"

"Can I study astronomy in New Athenia?"

"You can study whatever you'd like."

"Guess I should start learning Knosian." Flora smiled and finished off the apple.

My body and bow swayed in unison as I played the melody that came to me a few hours earlier. The slow and even strides of the verse allowed the energy to build until I reached the chorus where the speed doubled. My heart beat along as though keeping the tempo. My shirt was drenched with sweat. I slowed back down at the coda. As it ended, I opened my eyes and saw tears on Flora's cheeks.

"That was the most beautiful music I ever heard."

"I call it 'Beyond Today.'" I set down my bow.

Flora's crying intensified.

"I don't think anyone has ever reacted that strongly to my music."

"It's not only that. All the great things you can do make me realize how much I've missed in my life."

"Once we get to New Athenia, you'll have no more excuses."

"You have lifetimes of advantages."

"You believe me now?"

"Not completely. But after I saw Kai walking down that ridge, you didn't sound as crazy to me anymore."

"One step closer to credibility. Now *that's* progress."

"Why do you think you can remember your past lives?"

"I have my theories, but I can't prove them. It's frustrating at times because I'm mostly alone, and I sometimes wonder if I'm deluding myself."

"Tell me, and I'll let you know."

"I'm certain you will. You've never held your opinions back before." I tuned my E-string which sounded a little sharp. "I find it refreshing that I can talk about this with someone less gloomy than Tyrus."

"Master Tyrus believed you?"

"Yes. He had started remembering his own past lives."

Flora stared at me in amazement.

"I'm serious—and I probably looked as you just did when I first found out."

"Can you take me to him?"

"I'm not sure where he is, but I know our lives will intersect again."

"How can you be so certain?"

"Whenever I walk alone in the woods, I sense this surrounding calm that ties together everything I perceive in the physical world. I couldn't comprehend the significance until I lay near death in my last incarnation—after being attacked by bandits. Although my eyes were closed, I saw the brightest light I had ever seen. When it exploded, I dispersed along with it and plugged into something so immense and powerful that it seemed as if it could fuel everything in existence. 'Time is relative to sound,' my own voice said back to me."

"I did pretty well in physics at school, but nothing you just said made sense to me."

"It didn't to me either, until I related it to music." I plucked the E-string on my violin. "All atoms vibrate and produce a sound. Without this constant action and reaction, nothing would exist."

"Not sure I like the idea of being played by a hand I can't see."

"Technically, we're plucking ourselves." I picked up my bow and played "Beyond Today."

"We're all music performed by a timeless orchestra. We each have our own constant frequency, which is always in existence within what I call the Progenitor. Our strings independently vibrate, and the tone resonates in unison to our constant, which exists within the Progenitor. All that we do in this life is uploaded and stored in our constant through something I've come to know as COR. It's our personal conduit between us and our constant frequency. When we're reborn, our prerecorded data is downloaded back to us, and all our newly formed experiences are uploaded to our constant and recorded. This cycle can go on infinitely." I stopped playing. "Of course this is only a theory."

"Hope you're wrong. Participating in events most of us aren't even aware we've participated in before makes life sound predetermined. I like to think I'm in charge of my own actions."

"You are." I put my violin back in the case. "Every calamitous decision I made in my previous incarnations is my constant reminder."

Flora grinned. "How do you do it?"

"What?"

"Hang on to your sense of humor?"

"One thing I've learned throughout my lifetimes is not to take anything seriously. I prefer to laugh at all the nonsensical, inconceivable, impractical, preposterous developments in my life than worry over having to relive through my most difficult memories."

Eyeing me with pity, she said, "I just realized what you must be going through. Maybe I'm better off not remembering."

"What keeps me going is that with each passing lifetime, I realize how little I know—how little anyone knows. The quest for understanding the implications of that truth is both maddening and thrilling."

"Why?"

"I always had an insatiable appetite for puzzles, especially unanswerable ones. I know I'll never solve this one, but I won't give up because of the quest itself. It's a constant reminder to me of what it means to be free. I can pursue what's in here"—I tapped my head—"and speak out about what I'm thinking, without the fear of breaking a law or being condemned for merely asking questions, disagreeing or expressing doubts. I kept myself enslaved in Unity—and not by the Overseer. Out of fear of getting demoted and Kai taking over my project, I said nothing to challenge him. He's now in control of Harmony, and it's being used on the most innocent among us."

Tears welled in Flora's eyes.

"That admission is enough to keep me going, and I won't stop until everyone in Unity has the opportunity to feel what I feel. Freedom is too powerful a force for the Corporate Hierarchy to contain."

Tears were still running down Flora's face as she moved closer to me. "Even though I can't remember you, there's something familiar about you."

"You said that to me when we first met in Unity."

"What else did I tell you?"

"You really want to know?"

She merely shrugged her shoulders.

"We went to the observatory, and you told me you went there whenever you needed to relax. I asked why you found it so calming, and you said you pictured yourself as one of the stars—distant, unnoticed, and beyond capture."

"You speak the truth." She placed her hand on my cheek.

I covered her hand with mine. "When you spoke those words, I found them disturbing, but now, I find them comforting."

"Why?"

"I understand their meaning, and I feel the same way."

Flora leaned back, took hold of one of her braids and started to slowly unravel it. "I don't ever want to be bound again."

I held Flora's other braid and slowly unwound each strand. This maneuver still aroused me even though I'd been out of Unity for a while. The smell of sandalwood filled the room as her hair cascaded down past her elbows and on to the floor. There, under the lantern light, Flora became the embodiment of Venus as visualized by Ancient artists.

She leaned towards me and we kissed. When she wrapped her arms around me, a surge of energy shot through my body. Since I'd seen the internal light, all my senses intensified, but I didn't want to rush things. We had the rest of our lives to look forward to.

"I love you," I said. "I've always loved you." I held her in my arms. "I'm starting to think that's why my memory is revived only when I see you."

"Kai always told me I'm hard to forget."

"Sometimes I wish you were, especially the you from my first incarnation." I held Flora's hand. "Now that we're together again, I want to be honest with the present you."

"You can tell me anything."

"I've had visions since I was a boy. In my first incarnation, I had one of you lying dead on the floor from a plazer blast. I didn't tell you about it because I believed it was I who killed you. I also wanted events to play out naturally so I could prove my theory about COR. Then we got into an argument, and you confessed to interrupting my induction. You shot yourself after I almost choked you to death, and I had the audacity to think you were the one who needed reintegration. The only thing I managed to prove to myself that day was that I had no conscience."

"But you didn't kill me."

"I pushed you to it. I saw the look in your eyes when I mentioned reintegration. The life from you drained before you fired your plazer. It took your death to make me realize what I did to you, along with how much I loved you. I carried that feeling through every encounter we had since then, and it was difficult because I carried it alone. Each time my memory came back, I was a stranger to you—and I still am."

Flora cupped my face and kissed my forehead. "Thanks for being honest with me. It must've been difficult."

"Feels good to get it all out. I lost track of how many nights that day replayed in my mind." I kissed her hand. "Forgive me for placing my ambition above you."

"There's nothing for me to forgive. I don't remember anything, so there's no reason to feel bad anymore." She gazed lovingly at me. "And I *insist* you don't."

"No point in arguing with you. Once you've made up your mind, there's no changing it."

"You need to tell me more about yourself. It's not fair you know more about me than I know about you."

After answering several questions about my past histories, Flora and I fell asleep in each other's arms. It was the soundest sleep I had had in years, until the motion detector alarm woke me. Shisa ran out the door that had been left ajar, and Flora was gone.

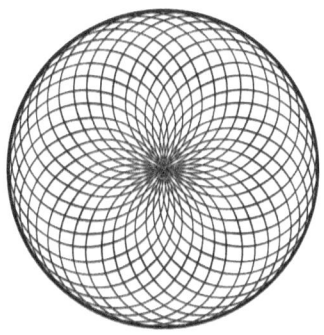

# world without justice

I approached a small group of travelers awakened by my alarm. They spoke in a language I wasn't familiar with, and I gestured with my hands to depict long flowing hair. A young woman turned to her mate and spoke excitedly. He pointed to the western side of the tunnel.

"Did he get away?" Sephroy walked up, holding out his lantern.

"False alarm," I said. "My travel companion tripped the alarm."

"That was no false alarm. Someone just tried to break into my 'let. I met him with this." He held up his gun. "Scared him away."

I thought about Roth's encounter with the bandits and worried that Flora met a similar fate. However, the alarm woke me up and I would've seen something, and Shisa would've caught them as she ran out of our 'let. Instead, I'd found her outside, waiting for me.

The man who saw something at the western side of the tunnel was talking to Sephroy.

"What is he saying?" I asked.

"He came out to smoke a little over an hour ago. Said he saw a woman who was crying. When he went to check on her, she yelled at him and ran towards your side of the tunnel."

"That has to be my friend," I said, relieved. "I'm going to look for her."

"Bring that firearm of yours, Chap. The tunnel is crawling with men who would love to have that lovely lady of yours for themselves."

I whistled for Shisa.

"If you need any help, knock on my door. It'll be a while until I fall back asleep." He slapped his chest. "Heart's racing faster than the last time I chased a bandit out of here."

I hurried back to my trainlet to retrieve my plazer. Before I could get to it, someone grabbed me from behind and shoved a knife under my chin.

Shisa snarled and lowered her head. My attacker grazed the blade against my skin and said something in a language I didn't recognize.

"Sit, Shisa," I said calmly. Any slight movement and that knife would've damaged me beyond repair.

Shisa continued growling and then stopped when Flora appeared, gripping her plazer and taking aim. "Let go of him, or I'll shoot!"

"Get away," I told her. "They never work alone."

"Let him go!" she yelled.

The attacker's accomplice snuck up from behind and wrapped his arm around Flora's neck. Her eyes filled with tears and she fell to the ground. A large knife protruded from her back.

I squeezed my attacker's arm and he writhed and screamed as if in grave pain. He dropped the knife, and I flipped him onto the floor.

The accomplice who stabbed Flora came at me, then backed off when Shisa snarled at him. He ran out of the trainlet with Shisa in pursuit. Screams, growls, and the clanking of trainlet doors reverberated against the walls of the tunnel.

The man who'd attacked me got to his knees. I was about to stab him with his own knife, then froze when he lifted up his arms and I saw my hand prints burned into his skin.

Sephroy showed up and halted at the door. He directed a deadly stare at my attacker, who was now trying to get up. The man gagged and gasped, grabbed his throat, and fell back down. He was finished.

"Now you only have one thing to worry about," Sephroy said.

"I'll ask how the slock you did that later."

I got my med kit and ran to Flora, who had lost a lot of blood. There was nothing I could do but keep her comfortable. I held her in my arms, as Shisa came inside whimpering. She sat next to Flora and licked her hand.

"Guess that wasn't you that set off the alarm," I said.

"Slipped right past it," Flora answered in a weak voice. "It was an amateur job." She petted Shisa.

"You should've stayed away."

"Then we both would've died."

"You're not going to die."

"Don't humor me." She coughed. "I hate that."

"You were always too smart for your own good."

"I recorded a visual message on my hologue and left it in your pack. It'll explain everything." She coughed again. "After you play it, I want you to know I changed my mind. That's why I came back."

I looked at Sephroy. "Can you do anything for her?"

He shook his head.

"You killed a man by looking at him. If you can take life so easily, you must be able to give it back."

"I'm the careman, not a god."

I looked at Flora and forced a smile. I wanted her last moments in this lifetime to be as peaceful as I could make them for her.

"Tell me what we're going to do when we get to New Athenia," she said.

"Who's humoring whom now?" I kissed her cheek.

"I don't want you to see me as something that's about to end because that's not how I see myself. I left here and ran until I passed out. I dreamed that Kai slapped me, and I escaped to the observatory to look at the stars. A woman with dark skin and long unbraided hair came to me and said, 'Like the stars, you're not the only one. There are others who shine like you. Each star shines separately but together they light up the night sky.' Something inside me turned on. All my life I did things for others, and now I thought about everything I wanted to do for myself." Tears streaked down Flora's face. "I saw so many possibilities and woke up feeling as if I was reborn, and that a whole new life lay ahead of me."

I first suspected Flora was a Six when she recalled my remarks about not wanting to return to Dome Dungeon, and now I was certain of it. The confirmation made no difference to me. My connection to Flora existed beyond biology and label.

I continued to cradle her in my arms. "Our first stop will be the space exhibit at the Alexandrian Repository because I'm sure that's what you'll want to see first. You'll hear all about the Ancients' space exploits. They have a model of the Mars colony and the original fighter craft flown by Callias Zane, one of the biggest heroes of the Ancient world. We'll then go to the music library where it will take a lifetime to get through all the music that starts with the letter A."

"Lifetime? When will we have time to eat?" She coughed.

"The cafes open at noon. We'll head over to my favorite bistro. They specialize in authentic Ancient Greek cuisine. There's this cheese—smells like the inside of someone's shoes after many days of hiking—but when you mix it into a salad or with pasta, you'll become as addicted to it as I am."

"Can't wait—" She gasped for air. "Not for the cheese."

Holding her close, I spoke gently "Afterwards, we'll go to the central park to feed the ducks. When the sun sets we'll take the lift to the top of the labyrinth and gaze up at the Parthenon. We'll end the night with a visit to the observatory."

"Thanks."

I kissed her hand.

"Don't be sad when you think of me." Flora smiled. "I chose to live." She blinked her eyes for the last time, and then she left me, taking my heart with her.

Flora's message was ready for playback. I sat on the bench and stared at the still picture of her, kneeling next to the lantern. I stared at her face for a moment and then pressed play.

"When you open this I'll be gone, and you'll want to know why," she said softly. "You fell asleep and my mind wouldn't stop racing between two destinations. I can't go back to Unity after everything I learned, and I can't stay here because I'm not like you. I can't start over. Too much of me was taken away. Too much that I don't think I can ever feel whole again. This isn't reintegration speaking; it's me, fully aware of the action I'm about to take. The voices of Unity live in my mind and never give me peace. All I see is darkness in a world without justice, which seems impossible to deliver. I can't bear that." She wiped her eyes. "When you told me you wouldn't stop until every Unitian was as free as you, I believed it, and I believe you'll help free them one day. And if you're right—that we live the same lifetime and can improve ourselves—maybe we'll all eventually be born free. Only then will I have the strength to live and know you as well as you know me. Don't give up, Damon. You're our best hope for a free Unity. Love, Flora."

I lay her body in Sephroy's cart, and he covered her with a blanket.

He placed his cane in a lower compartment. "I'm pushing."

"You're coming with me?"

"Could use some fresh air."

"Who's going to watch the trainlets?"

Sephroy touched a spot between his brows. "Look here."

"Why?"

"Look here," he said louder, and I obliged.

"Now look there." He gestured to where the trainlets used to be and were now gone.

"How did you—?"

"I never believed in miracles until I witnessed something I thought was impossible. But when I thought about it longer, it wasn't. On the outside, I'm like you. On the inside, we're very different. But that doesn't make me beyond explanation." He walked on ahead.

"Why do you stay here?"

He stopped and glanced back at me. "We're always where we deserve to be. This is where I deserve to be."

We got outside and I performed the sacred burning on the beach. Shisa whimpered and walked around the pyre, while Sephroy stared into the blaze. "Imagine living within these flames and all that exists out here is invisible to your eyes. But everyone of us on the outside sees the flames, what's inside the flames, and the whole of this universe, all at once." He nodded faintly. "We all see the same thing, and yet...we all have our own interpretation about its meaning."

"Is that where you're from? Outside the flames?"

"*Was* from."

"Why leave such a place?"

Sephroy moved his hand near the flame. "If I could go back, I would." He retracted his hand. "That would truly be a miracle."

"The man who attacked me—I burned his skin with my hands. How did I do that?"

"If you don't know, then you're not ready to know."

By now, I had gotten used to Sephroy's evasiveness and I took the conversation no further. As we headed back to the old tunnel, I had trouble associating his feebleness with the great powers he possessed.

"Why can't you heal yourself?" I asked.

"For the same reason you can't."

"I don't have your powers."

"But you do have the power to move forward—yet you don't."

"This is the farthest I ever went."

"Further towards…or farther away?" He smiled. "Ponder that one on your way to New Athenia."

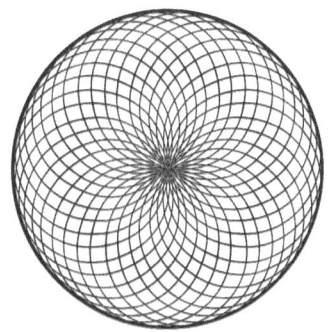

# colors within the pale illusion

Wilfrid handed me his favorite chalice and poured me some wine. "It's yours."

"What's the occasion?"

"Michael listens to his mother and does all his chores without question." He passed me the bottle. "It's because of you. He sees you as his father."

"And I see him as a son, which is why you have to stop letting him go to the river alone."

"I always watch out for him." Wilfrid sat down and shuffled his cards. He laid out a three of diamonds, two of spades, queen of hearts, eight of diamonds and then slowly lifted up the last card. "Ace of diamonds." He looked at me. "You bring news."

"And I have a gift for you." I handed him a hologue.

"Thank you, Nomad." He excitedly clasped it around his wrist and waved his forearm in front of his face. "How does it work?"

"I'll show you later. Do you keep arms here?"

Wilfrid walked over to a trunk and removed a wooden spear with elaborate etchings carved into the handle. "My father taught me how to make these. There is no greater weapon to hunt boar—or to scare the occasional bandit that dares to block my path."

"Not a fan of the longbow?"

"Too easy."

"How long will it take to make enough for the whole village?"

He put the spear back in the trunk. "Why the sudden worry? Bandits have always been around, and they're not known to strike villages."

"That's about to change."

Wilfrid leered at me. "How do you know?" He sat and picked up the cards. "I never got such a reading."

"I can remember what happened in my previous lives."

He slammed the deck of cards on the table. "I knew you were different!"

"I'm not your Nomad."

"I've heard your name in my dreams for twenty-eight turns of winter's longest night." Leaning forward he narrowed his eyes. "And you're twenty-eight. I don't believe in coincidences."

I raised my chalice. "And I still don't *believe* in anything that requires belief," I said without my usual conviction.

"Perhaps you will one day."

"Belief got me into trouble. I don't think I'll attempt it again anytime soon. Whatever I take under consideration, I'll have to see with my own eyes."

"What you see can also have more than one meaning. How will you know your interpretation is the correct one and worthy of belief?"

I answered by taking a sip of wine.

"You've been through a lot. Take some time to rest. I'll make sure no one disturbs you, including myself." He glanced at his hololouge. "Michael can show me how to use this."

I spent two days in my bungalow contemplating, drinking, crying, and cursing myself. The next seven days I slept. I only got up to quench my thirst and empty my bladder. On the tenth day, I had a vision. I was walking in an unlit tunnel, pushing a cart with squeaky wheels that sounded like the beating of a heart. *Squeak squeak, squeak squeak, squeak squeak.* As I neared the opening, I stayed focused on the light. My breath grew louder until I stepped outside. The light was blinding and hurt my eyes. Once I'd adjusted to the brightness, I recognized where I was: the paradise I created when I was in a coma. I looked in the cart and saw Flora. She opened her eyes and gasped. Frightened, she vaulted out of the cart, but then appeared mesmerized as she examined the surrounding wilderness. She walked over to a fern, ran her hands against the leaves and continued to touch everything around her.

"What do you see?" I asked her.

She looked at me and started to cry. "I don't know…but it's beautiful." She stretched out her arms and danced as she had done in the middle of the rainstorm.

I awoke to the happiness on her face and sprang out of bed, waking Shisa. "She saw colors!" Unable to contain my euphoria, I ran outside. "She saw colors!" I repeated the phrase as Michael ran up to me.

"I thought you'd never come out again." He suddenly winced. "What's that smell?"

I put my hands on his shoulders. "She saw colors. *That's* why she changed her mind."

He stepped back. "Think you'll make more sense after you bathe."

The few villagers who were outside stared at me as though I were a lunatic. I was used to that by now, so I raised a dismissive palm at Michael. "Appearances are only a scrape on the surface."

"But smells aren't." He pinched his nostrils. "I'll talk to you, but clean up first."

I laughed as he walked off. I didn't know if what I experienced was a vision or dream, but whatever it was, it allowed me to see beyond Flora's death. She had moved farther than ever and that was reason to celebrate.

Thirty days passed. I grew restless and decided to venture to New Athenia and visit Holly and Lidian. Wilfrid lent me one of his horses and midway through my journey, the elation from my vision vanished. I had to rescue an infant who lay crying beside his murdered parents. I took him to the next village along the trade route and handed him over to a kind woman. The boy smiled in the way only a baby can; with no awareness of the evil that claimed the life of his parents, and the woman I loved. I departed the scene without mentioning the circumstances in which I found him.

During the rest of my journey, I cogitated over Flora's remark about living in a world without justice. The baby lived in that world, the same world I inhabited. Justice was uncovered as another illusion—inspiring to believe in—but not a required feature of humanity. Notwithstanding all that, Flora saw colors, and that shone a light over the possibility that we'd move forward together.

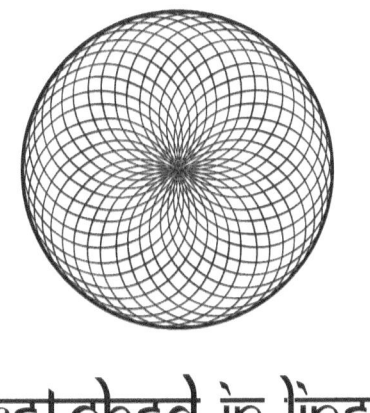

# sketched in linen

Seeing Holly and Lidian inspired me to remain in New Athenia. The wine, late-night card games on the balcony, and trips to the jazz club cleared away the darkness that surrounded me during my journey. I continued my position with the orchestra and resurrected my Mozart versus Chopin feud with Manolis—only this time, I didn't take my fame seriously. I didn't take *anything* seriously. Towards the end of the year, everything felt worn and old and my restlessness returned. I needed a deeper connection to something, but I couldn't fathom what that something was. Every person I met here reminded me of what I used to be, which made it difficult to build relationships. When I spoke, I said nothing meaningful; when I worked, I kept mostly to myself, and when I joined, I never committed. I refused to place myself in a position where I'd have to censor myself again.

Around Lidian and Holly, I was more relaxed, but I still couldn't reveal the true nature of my existence. All that made me an Outsider in the truest meaning of the term. Keeping the real part of myself hidden was exhausting and apart from playing with the orchestra, the only other place where I found solace was the duck pond. It was there that I decided to give up my residence pass.

While feeding Gadfly and going over an internal recitation of my departure speech to Manolis, a tall man with light brown skin and long slender limbs made an appearance. His white kurta caught my attention, and I tried to remember where I'd seen him before.

"You are a compassionate soul," he said and slithered away without waiting for a response.

Later, as I approached the edge of the park, I noticed him sitting in a lotus position on the grass. His eyes were closed, and his hands rested, palms up, on his thighs. His peaceful expression never changed, even when some children chased past him. I still found no connection and surmised it was his exotic features and clothing that resonated with me. I came back to the duck pond the next day. I was playing my violin and the man appeared again.

"You are a compassionate soul," he repeated himself.

"What have I done to deserve such a virtuous title?"

"Your music of veneration flows from the highest sphere."

"Who am I venerating?"

"No one," he laughed. "It is nothing but superstitious nonsense. I just like how it sounds."

"I play mostly for myself anyway."

"That is more virtuous than you make it sound." He laughed again.

I threw a piece of bread to Gadfly, and the last of the crumbs into the pond. A legion of ducks raced over to stake their claim.

"I see self-interest as necessary," the stranger said. "It shed all the layers of nonsense my mind accumulated since birth."

"I have too many layers to shed in this lifetime." I tossed some more bread to Gadfly. "Where are you from?"

"Middle Crest."

"Where is that?"

"Deep within the Himalayas."

"You're far from home."

"I like long travel. It accelerates the shedding process." He offered his hand. "I am Vivek."

Vivek and I spent the rest of the afternoon talking and we continued our discussion at a nearby cafe. He was well traveled and spoke quietly, yet he gestured spiritedly with his hands, arms and eyes as he answered my questions about the places he'd visited. I was disappointed to learn this was his last week in New Athenia.

"I visit here every three years to exercise my Knosian and explore the new exhibits in the repository," Vivek said.

"I'm leaving soon as well." I poured some sugar into my cup. "There are still many mountains I've yet to climb."

"Which one do you plan to climb next?"

"The Himalayas sound challenging."

"If you'd like to join me, you are more than welcome, but life in the mountains is difficult. We have no electricity, no running water, and we grow our own food."

"Had my own farm before I came here."

Vivek squinted at me. "You have an appealing life here. Why would you want to exchange it for yak manure, treacherous weather, and isolation?"

"Sounds exciting. When do we leave?" I sipped some tea.

"I find there is always a reason behind every action I take, even when I am not consciously aware of one."

"How can you know that if you're not conscious of it?"

"It eventually presents itself, and I raise my finger in the air and say, 'Ah, now I see.'" He sipped his tea. "Which is it for you then?"

"You ask a lot of questions."

"I do not normally extend an invitation to Middle Crest without knowing my guest."

I'd decided to leave New Athenia because I no longer wanted to censor myself, and I refused to do so during my hike to the Himalayas. If I were to go with Vivek, I had to know I could be open with him. "I want to learn about the keeper of past, present, and future."

"You think you will find this *keeper* within the Himalayas?"

"I hope to."

"Why?"

"So I can discover why I remember."

He eyed me curiously. "Remember what?"

"My previous incarnations."

All the lines on Vivek's face crinkled.

"I thought your people had special insight about reincarnation," I said.

He waved his hand forward. "Pah! Everyone thinks they hold the key to some divinely inspired knowledge, and I have yet to see any proof of their assertions."

"I thought you were a mystic."

"I am more of a scientist than sage. I do not seek out supernatural explanations to define the natural world. Mysticism is nothing but balderdash."

"If you're right, I'm either insane or lying in a reintegration chamber believing I'm reliving the same life."

Vivek widened his eyes and said softly, "She was right."

I stared at him, puzzled.

"Forgive my deception, but I had to be sure. My approaching you is not a coincidence." Vivek reached into his pocket, removed a piece of worn linen and handed it to me. Sketched into the fabric was a face that looked very similar to mine.

"My niece, Suti, is highly revered in Middle Crest. She sent me here to bring you to her."

"Suti?"

"Do you know about her?"

"Sutara?"

Vivek's eyes grew enormous in a way I thought not humanly possible.

"She comes to me in my dreams! Why didn't you tell me this sooner?"

"I did not believe any of this," he said more to himself. "Even after I found you where she told me I would, I still thought there was a more rational explanation."

I showed him the sketch of me. "Did you come up with one?"

"Not as yet. However, that does not negate a logical explanation." He nervously poured sugar into his cup. "There are other abilities that could explain her visions of you. The human brain is not fully understood." He picked up a spoon and stirred his tea. "Perhaps there is something in our biology that allows us to see things at great distances. That would make more sense than—"

"Did she tell you about the Six?"

Vivek dropped the spoon.

Holly gave birth to Katerina during my last night in New Athenia. It was the perfect going-away gift—to witness new life brought into this world as nature had willed. I held Katerina in my arms. "Bye, little one. Be sure to take good care of your mother." I handed her back to Holly.

"Why are you leaving, Damon?" Holly asked. "You've made a great life for yourself here."

"I'm looking for something beyond great, and I hope to find it."

"Maybe you need companionship. I can introduce you to my friend. She's—"

"A woman is the last thing I want right now."

Holly reached out with her free hand and placed it over mine. Gazing at her face, I was again reminded that Aaron and James would never exist in this lifetime, but being here for Katerina's birth, I felt only happiness.

"What do you want then?" Lidian stood by the door holding two cups of coffee.

"Caffeine. I'm not going to get any sleep tonight."

I finished my coffee, exchanged farewells, and did one last lap around the labyrinth with Shisa. As the sun rose, I gazed at the Parthenon and thought about how some of my most joyous moments were spent alone. This was one of those moments. I sat in silence and took in the beauty of the environment without analyzing it. I planned to carry this with me on the road to Middle Crest.

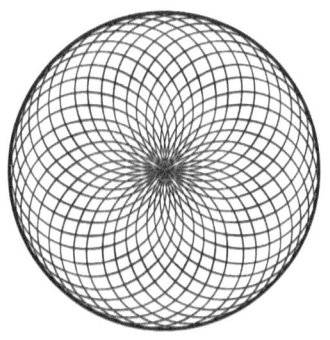

# ancient chant

We caught our first glimpse of the Black Sea after one-hundred and fifty kilometers of travel. No borders survived the Great Cataclysm, but I longed to experience the landmarks through the eyes of an Ancient. I persuaded Vivek to follow an antiquated map I scanned into my hololoque. On the periphery of Old Istanbul, we stopped to feed Shisa and the horses. Vivek and I needed to eat as well, so we went to the open-air market in town. The crowds overwhelmed the stands where merchants sold everything from pottery and exotic spices to rugs and furniture. "My nose just told me what I'm having," I said as I smelled lamb spiced with cardamom and cinnamon.

We ate our meal on stairs that led to an old collapsed cement building. Most of the city is littered with these old structures. For those who live here, it's a constant reminder of what the Great

Cataclysm stole from them. Small shrines with candles lined the streets as though paying reverence to the once thriving land that bridged two continents.

I closed my eyes, smelled the smells and listened to the voices. Yes, I was really here, connecting to a world long forgotten.

Vivek tapped his fork on my plate, pulling me out of my exaltation of the Ancients. "Enjoy your meals along the way because everyone in the Crossings is a vegetarian."

"Including yourself?"

He lifted his plate of chickpeas and rice. "My housemaid, Tanzin, is an excellent cook. I promise your taste-buds will be satisfied."

With full bellies, we strolled over to the Hagia Sophia, one of the few buildings from the Ancients' world still standing. If it were possible for a building to be alive, the Hagia Sophia would be the apotheosis of a beating heart. All the pictures I'd seen of this sacred edifice failed to communicate the faith it drew and emitted for its worshippers, several of whom were out in front praying, alongside a few beggars with hands outstretched to each new visitor entering the building.

"Why are we following an Ancient map?" Vivek asked. "It is generations out of date."

I stared out at the sea and imagined what the Ancient devotees thought about when they stood on this hallowed ground. "I know exactly where I am." I got out my camcorder and captured some images for my journal.

"The Ancients do not deserve your admiration. They almost destroyed our world."

"That's still debatable. There's no consensus over what caused the Great Cataclysm. It very well could've been a natural event."

"In any case, your romanticism is misguided. Conflicting religions and ideologies is why humanity still exists in a dark age. All the Ancient readings at the repository prove our inability to recognize the good life while we're living it."

"You would get along with my friend Tyrus." I removed my shoes and walked to the center archway. A man dressed in a white robe stood near the entrance chanting a haunting melody.

His voice echoed throughout the interior, and his almost perfect pitch made the hair on my arms stand on end.

Vivek reached into his pocket and tossed some coins into a collection dish, which sat in front of a row of candles. "Why? Because I dare speak the truth? They did not believe the words of their own gods."

"I found my truth crossing the old tunnel for the first time." I looked up at the support columns of the arches and slowly turned to assimilate the full grandeur of the dome. Some of the tesserae were faded and cracked, but the windows around the dome had been maintained through the centuries. The beams of light entering though them produced an otherworldly glow and made the mosaic tiles reflect like tiny lights. "No matter what trials we force ourselves through, the soul of man refuses to be obliterated. We find ways to survive." I walked around the main room and touched the wall. "Religion may have separated the Ancients, but it also saved them and gave them the strength to endure the Great Cataclysm."

"Pah! If there was no religion, they would not have placed themselves in a position where they needed to be saved."

I smiled and said nothing. Vivek was as right as he was wrong. I couldn't be as fatalistic as he and Tyrus, yet neither could I exercise absolute faith. The best position for me fell somewhere in the middle, though I wasn't sure what that meant, or it if meant anything at all.

As we continued our travels through Ancient Iran and Afghanistan, Vivek began teaching me Tibindi, the language of Middle Crest. We crossed over into Pakistan and stopped for a rest in the Kashmir Valley. A thriving community of Outsiders lived in huts made of stone and mud, and a large outdoor market stood in the center. We set up our tents nearby and traded our horses for mules, which would fare better during the climb.

We began our ascent of the Himalayas following an Ancient traveling route. Arriving in Middle Crest Valley, we came across a monastery built into the cliff, overlooking the Indus River. The monks invited us inside, and we joined them for a meal that we ate in silence. To our relief, we were offered a room for the night. Vivek and I were not in the mood to pitch tents in weather that was unusually cold for the season. The next morning, we continued our journey, riding on stone-carved paths along the Indus River. After half a day of travel, Shisa and the mules needed water. We stopped for a break.

"Merchants still travel these roads," Vivek said. "This route has been used for the same purpose, long before the borders on that map of yours existed."

"How did they manage to maintain all of this?"

"The surrounding mountains on the east, west and north protect local communities from the outside world. During the winter, most of the paths are obstructed due to heavy snowfall. The only way out is to hike along a mostly frozen river to the Indus Valley, and the journey is hazardous. One slip could land the hapless traveler under a sheet of ice."

I raised both brows. "I never died by drowning before."

"You may get your chance this time if you are not careful." Vivek laughed.

I got out my camcorder and set it to take still pictures.

"Wait until you cast your eyes on the Crossings," Vivek said. "The foundation sits in front of the Indus River."

We continued on our trek, and I told Vivek about Unity and how I lost Flora through each of my incarnations.

"Even Suti knows that to move forward, you must learn from your errors," Vivek said.

"It's not that easy."

"No more effort than a snap!" He snapped his fingers. "Just like that! Then once you reflect back on everything, you will realize you wasted your time on balderdash."

I snapped my finger. "Strange. I don't feel any different."

"Pah! You are a very funny man. They will love you at the Crossings."

We approached one of the first villages in the valley, and three children ran up to us. A girl handed me a flower and invited us to dine in her home. We did so, and following our meal we got back onto our mules. As we rode off I watched a boy and his father plowing a small field assisted by a few yaks.

"The children work hard here," I said.

"All the tribes along the Himalayas have to be self-reliant. Men push handheld plows to till the land while the women gather the crops to prepare them for trade. The boys shear sheep and plow with their fathers, and the girls tend to the yaks and make cheeses from their milk."

At first I was galled that a young child would be assigned such difficult work, but it seemed to bother me more than Vivek. The boy working the land with his father was laughing and looked genuinely happy. While I had happy moments in my own childhood, they never endured. I hoped to have a father in a future incarnation, so I could laugh like that boy.

# middle crest

We passed a meadow filled with wildflowers, trekked up another stretch of the Indus River and finally arrived at Middle Crest. The main complex was carved into the cliff like the monastery we'd visited. Beneath was a stable that housed yaks and sheep, and off to the side a small stretch of farmland irrigated by the annual melting glaciers.

"What is your impression?" Vivek asked me.

"The view alone is worth the sixteen weeks of travel." I got off my mule and aimed my camcorder at Vivek.

He raised his hand towards home. "May I present to you the Crossings, the largest enclave in all of Middle Crest. It was founded shortly after the Great Cataclysm by two friends of opposing faiths. They were tired of the fighting and decided to form their own community. As the population grew, the male residents helped build homes for each family that chose to stay here. We continue the practice to this day."

Vivek led me to his living quarters, and Tanzin greeted us at the door. She placed her palms together and bowed to me. "I brewed some tea a while ago. It's still warm," she said to Vivek.

"Thank you, Tanzin. We'll take it in the sitting room."

I followed Vivek inside.

"We have a guest," Tanzin called out. "I'll bring him to you."

Vivek led me to an almost barren living room with large yak skin pillows scattered around a small rug. A small unlit candle sat in the middle.

"I imagined you as a minimalist," I said.

"I prefer to keep things simple."

Tanzin entered the room holding a tea tray. Vivek and I took our cups, and I almost spilled my tea when Tyrus appeared. He seemed equally startled by my presence.

"How did you find this place?" I asked.

"I was going to ask you the same question."

"I met Vivek in New Athenia. He made Middle Crest sound interesting, so I came."

Tyrus shook Vivek's hand and spoke to him in Knosian. "Your chambermaid has been very kind to me—and patient with my inability to communicate." He took a cup of tea from the tray and bowed to Tanzin.

"Tanzin understands the language of kindness," Vivek said.

"That she does." Tyrus looked at me. "Do you speak Tibindi?"

"Not fluently, but enough to get by."

"I've never done so much nodding and head-shaking in this lifetime. Suti has been attempting to teach me the language, but I'm a slow learner."

"What is she like?"

Tyrus smiled. "You'll meet her soon. She's napping now." He sat on one of the pillows. "I had recurring dreams about her and the Himalayas. They were so vivid, and my compulsion to visit was too strong to resist. I traveled alone until I got to the outer valley, and from there I recruited a stable hand to take me up here. I spotted the Crossings and immediately recognized it from my dreams." Tyrus stroked his forehead as though in pain.

"Are you still sick?"

"Never mind me. How did your meeting with Flora turn out?"

He only had to look at my expression to know the answer. After filling him in on what happened, I told him I never wanted to discuss it again. The final expression on Flora's face was with me each time I thought about that dreadful night; I had managed to put it out of my mind, until now.

Everyone devoured the lentils and barley stew Tanzin had made, but I was too stunned to eat. Sutara sat in front of me. She had the same eyes, same hair, same dark skin as the Sutara from my visions, but there was one difference: she was in her ninth year of life. She peered at me as though she knew what I was thinking.

I pointed to a dish in the center of the table. "Carrot halva?"

Sutara nodded and took a bite of her food.

"Why didn't you tell me she was a child?" I asked Vivek in Knosian.

"I told Uncle Vivek not to tell you," Sutara responded in flawless Knosian. Unlike Vivek, there wasn't even a hint of an accent.

"Why not?" I leaned my elbows on the table and crossed my hands.

"I didn't think you'd come if you knew."

"And I wanted to see the look on your face when you found out." Tyrus laughed.

I smiled at him. "The next move is mine, and you'll never see it until after it happens."

Sutara laughed. I took a bite of food. Vivek was right about Tanzin's cooking. If every meal was like this one, I could easily do without meat.

"You eat fast, like Master Tyrus," Sutara said. "Does all your tribe eat that way?"

"When we're taken by surprise," I answered in Tibindi.

"How did you learn our language so fast?"

"Vivek taught me."

Sutara glanced at Vivek.

"You were correct," Vivek said. "You and Master Damon have a lot in common."

"Like what?" Sutara cupped her ear in his direction.

Vivek shook his head. "I concede. He has a good memory, just like yours."

Sutara crossed her arms and smiled victoriously.

"However, one truth uncovered does not make every claim you make valid. If you ponder the meaning behind your foreknowledge, you can come up with a variety of explanations," Vivek said. "We should question everything before believing in it."

Sutara looked at me. "My uncle always has to speak the last words." She leaned her elbows on the table and cradled her chin between her hands. "How much do you remember, Master Damon?"

"I can recall five previous incarnations."

Tanzin, who'd been bored with most of the discussion, looked at me. "You are a prophet like Suti!" She bowed.

"I'm not a prophet."

"You said you have a timeless memory—like Sutara."

"Tanzin thinks what we do is a miracle. I say no way." Sutara sat up. "What do you think?"

"I haven't decided yet," I said.

She smiled at Tanzin. "See, even he doesn't believe such nonsense."

"I never said—"

"Uncertainty means you don't believe. Right Uncle Vivek?"

Vivek tossed a roll at her and she giggled.

I took Shisa out to explore the valley, and Sutara came along. We walked over a small bridge and paused to admire the river below.

"Why did you come, Master Damon?" Sutara asked.

A cool wind brushed against us, and Sutara pulled down her cap to cover her ears.

"Damon. Call me, Damon."

"Uncle Vivek will be mad."

"Tell him to see me if he has any problems with my request."

"Okay, Damon. Answer my question."

"I want to find out about the keeper of past, present, and future."

"Who is that?"

"I'll let you know when I find out."

"What makes you think he's here?"

"How do you know *he* isn't a she?"

"I don't." Sutara crouched down to pet Shisa. "It's about time you made it here. I was almost ready to give up."

"What do you expect from me?"

"I can't tell you. I wasn't even supposed to ask you here."

"Why not?"

She stood and gestured to a cloud in the sky. "See that cloud?"

I looked up to where she was pointing.

"What does it look like to you?"

"A cloud." I smiled at her.

Sutara crossed her arms. "I say it's not just a cloud. Stare at it longer—until it reminds you of something."

I observed the cloud until a distinct form came to mind. "An elephant."

"Uncle Vivek told me about them," she laughed. "He promised to take me for a ride on one someday." She pointed to another cloud. "That's a hawk."

"Looks like a lobster to me."

"What's a lobster?"

"A small animal that lives in the ocean. It has a skeleton on the outside and walks on ten legs—two of which have large claws." I simulated the snapping motion of a lobster's claws with my hands. "They can cut off your toes if you walk in their way."

"I'm glad I don't live near the ocean," she laughed. "It's funny how we both see different things."

"We each have our own unique way of interpreting what we see."

Sutara gazed at me. "That feeling you got when it looked like a lobster. You have to have that about why you're here, or it won't work."

"What won't work?"

"If I tell you, it's not the same thing as seeing. You can only see what's ahead of you with your own eyes."

"Who's giving you your information?"

"Me, from the future, who doesn't want me to talk to you because I'm too young to understand—which is silly. My memory returns and I grow up very fast."

I rubbed my chin. "So, your future self is contacting me in this current timeline?"

Sutara nodded.

"What does the future version of yourself expect me to do?"

"See the lobster soon."

"Does this have to do with the Six?"

She nodded her head again.

"Do you know who they are?"

"I only know about you and Tyrus. The future me knows all but one."

"Did your future self tell you the identity of the other two?"

"I asked and was told I have to see the eagle for myself."

Smiling, I said, "Like I have to see the lobster for myself."

"And we have to do it soon. Whatever is going to happen to me will make me very tired, and I won't even have enough energy to get up in the morning."

"You, or rather your future self, said something similar to me."

Sutara cried, "I'm scared. I don't want that to happen to me."

I held her hand. "I'll make sure it doesn't."

"How?"

"Find the others, but it won't happen in this incarnation." Seeing Sutara before me made me realize I had to put my own interests on hold. "Including Tyrus, I identified another Six, but she keeps dying and no matter what action I take, I can't save her."

"She's closed to me. You have to help her understand what she is."

"Do you know what we are? Why we're being drawn together?"

Sutara gazed up at the clouds. "I see two yaks walking."

I looked up and saw a camel. This wasn't going to be easy.

Sutara went home to help Tanzin, and I explored the riverside until it got dark. When I returned to the Crossings, Vivek found me a vacant corner room with a view of the river below.

"Suti must like you. She helped Tanzin clean up your room."

"What happened to her parents?"

"Shortly after her birth, my brother abandoned her and her mother. People here do not respect women who bear children before marriage, and most refused to even speak to her. I looked after both mother and child, hoping my brother would succumb to guilt and return home. He never did."

Tanzin stepped inside the room and set a folded blanket at the foot of my bed. "Does Master Damon have all he requires?"

"Even more so," I answered. "You've all been very kind."

Tanzin smiled and left.

"Did you ever hear from your brother?" I asked.

"I have not seen him since he left. Thirty days following his departure, I heard a rap at my door. Suti was left at the bottom of the stairs, and her mother was never seen again. I still do not know what happened to her, or my brother."

"What do you tell Sutara?"

"Whenever Suti asks me if I think her mother will ever return, she always answers the question before any words leave my mouth. She tells me, 'Have faith, Uncle Vivek. I do.'" He laughed softly. "She sounds so certain that I almost believe her."

"Maybe she knows something you don't."

"I thought about that as well, but until I see Suti's parents with both my eyes, I will have to assume they are gone forever."

"Forever," I said softly.

"What about it?" Vivek asked.

"The magnitude of that word scares me."

"And me as well. It's one of the reasons I abandoned my belief in an afterlife. The idea of living eternally seems more like a prison sentence."

"With no way out, it is a prison sentence."

Vivek left and I surveyed the river below, pondering the uncertainty of why I came to be here. The Crossings seemed more than a building. The name reflected my present circumstance. My old way of thinking conflicted with most of my new endeavors and assimilating the two took constant effort. I wondered if my incarnations would ever flow as effortlessly as the river below. And I wondered if I'd ever be free of them.

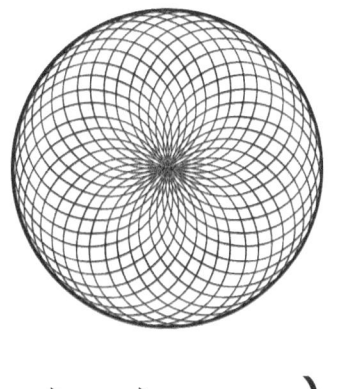

# reluctant prophets

Silence had taken on a whole new meaning for me in Middle Crest. At first, hearing the sound of my breath made it difficult to sleep as my mind constantly raced through six incarnations of experiences. By my second night, the isolation within the walls of the Crossings became my cocoon, sheltering me from places that reminded me of events I preferred to forget. I needed this security because I had none while I was asleep. Flora, Wade, and Kai continued to invade my dreams, refusing to let me forget what happened. To get my mind off my past, I immersed myself in Middle Crest life by helping with the harvesting. As long as I kept busy during the day, it was easy to forget my dreams. Coming back from a walk, I found Vivek gathering straw and volunteered for another chore.

"Slow down," he said as I started filling another basket with straw. "You have not stopped working since your arrival."

"I don't know the meaning of slow." I inspected my hands, recalling Sephroy's comment about them. "These were built for manual labor."

"Pah hah hah!" Vivek's eyes grew wide and he laughed. "If I did not see you working as you are now, I would have assumed you spent your whole life in New Athenia."

"I've done this for many lifetimes—and without the aid of yaks. Although I wouldn't call my existence primitive. I had electricity to help keep my cabin warm at night."

"Shall I have Tanzin bring you another blanket? They do not allow modern technology here."

"A wise decision. Our inventions have evolved beyond our ability to reason. I never stopped to realize technology has the potential to harm, and my shortsightedness condemned a whole population to servitude. Better to be free by candlelight than enslaved by conveniences."

"So what is your solution? Should we live with candles and the smell of yak manure for the rest of eternity? Would that not make us all defeatists—surrendering ourselves to the dark side of human nature?"

We emptied the baskets in the stable.

"Doesn't sound so bad to me." I walked away. "There are some parts of me I would rather avoid."

Vivek followed behind me. "You choose to surrender?"

"Knowing when to stop is different from surrendering." I set the basket near the pile of straw. "How long can I stay here?"

"For as long as you want. I shall be leaving after the melting. I can only tolerate limitations for one season."

"Find a place that has none and come get me. I'll live there for *all* seasons."

Vivek laughed. "Do not expect a visit from me any time soon. No such city, town, or village exists—which is why I travel a lot. There is always some pointless ritual, custom, or law I must conform to, and I can only comply for so long before it feels like a rope tightening around me." He wrapped his long fingers around his neck.

"Don't you think you're being a little over-dramatic?"

"Not at all. If not for Suti, I would say good riddance to this place."

"The only way out is to live alone."

"If I had that cabin of yours, I would never want to leave."

"Isolation can be lonely without a companion."

"Pah! Not for me. I do not want a woman to keep me chained to my home. I prefer to glide with the wind. Swoosh!" Vivek stretched his arms out to the side like a bird.

"Why do you believe in Sutara?" I asked.

"You may think me rigid, but I want to be proven wrong. I *want* to believe I am more than a pile of useless flesh."

"You think she'll ever prove you wrong?"

"When Suti talks to me, she sometimes seems beyond my years."

"She's far older than her nine years."

Vivek looked up at the mountains. "She can be very convincing. If my presumptions are incorrect, Suti will be my proof."

Sutara and I, without speaking a word, walked along a snowy path beside the river. I didn't mind the silence; it allowed me to fully absorb the stunning scenery. The clouds and mountains reflected on the surface of the icy river that seemed to stretch out infinitely.

"Very soon, you will not even see the river," Sutara said. "It will be covered in snow."

I picked up a small rock, and Shisa started barking. I raised my hand to throw it.

"Don't you dare hit her!" Sutara shouted.

"You misunderstand. Watch." I tossed the rock and Shisa ran off. She came back with the rock and dropped it at my feet.

"She's very smart!" Sutara picked up the rock and threw it. She giggled as she watched Shisa chase after it.

I touched Sutara's nose. It was cold. "Would you like to try again?" I handed her another rock.

"Stop treating me like a child!"

"You *are* a child."

"Then why do I feel older than everyone else here?"

"How many incarnations can you recall?"

"Twelve—since I began counting."

I arched my brows. "That technically makes you older than me."

"Uncle Vivek says the same thing, but he still treats me like a child. I hate that, but I wouldn't care if everyone else here treated me that way."

"Why?

"It's hard to make friends when everyone believes you're a prophet." Sutara walked over to a large rock and sat down. "I only had one friend—Ajeet. He didn't fear me."

"You have to introduce me to him. He sounds wise for his years."

"He died three winters ago." Sutara wiped her eyes with her coat sleeve. "When he got sick, Vivek would not let me see him. He was afraid I would get sick too. Three nights later I woke up at the sound of purring. I opened my eyes and saw a snow leopard sitting at the foot of my cot. He sat quietly and stared at me. I wasn't afraid, so I petted him. 'Remember,' he said. He then jumped off my bed and ran off." Sutara looked at me. "What do you think that meant?"

"You were obviously very sad because you missed Ajeet. The mind finds ways to help us cope with—"

"It was not a dream!" Sutara glared at me. "I woke up and found everyone awake. It was too early in the morning to plow the field. That's when I knew Ajeet died. He came to me as the snow leopard in my dream. From that morning on, I remembered, like he told me I would." She jumped off the rock, and we headed back down the path. "When did you first remember?"

"It always happens the same way. I find Flora lying unconscious at the bottom of the ridge by my cabin."

"Where is she now?"

"She died."

Sutara stopped and looked at me with eyes that seemed to belong to an old soul. "She's the other Six?"

"She is," I said.

Sutara took my hand and peered at me as she had in my visions. "Do not give up, Damon. With each life comes a new way of seeing things."

Shisa barked. Sutara picked up a rock and tossed it. Shisa ran after it and Sutara giggled, reminding me that she was a child. It was heartening to know her twelve incarnations had failed to steal her innocence.

Vivek taught me to meditate to help alleviate my anxiety. During each meditation my focus improved. As he had promised, I was more at peace, but my nights were still plagued by dreams, most of them now focused around Kai, in both familiar and unfamiliar situations.

"You may be experiencing a bardo," Vivek said during our morning tea. "You must suspend the needless jabbering in your head and observe, so that you may understand the meaning behind your visions. In the *Adhyatma Upanishad*, it is written, 'Of detachment the fruit is knowledge, of knowledge the fruit is withdrawal. Experience of Self as bliss leads to peace; peace is the fruit of withdrawal.'"

"I thought a bardo only happened after death," I said.

"From our experience, does death even exist?" Tyrus asked as he entered the room.

"That's why reality makes no sense to this objective observer." Vivek laughed loudly. "Everyone has a counter opinion, which further proves no one has the answer to anything."

"What's your opinion?" I asked.

"As one of the objective observers, I am smart enough to know an opinion is a myth in disguise, so I do not invest much energy in forming one."

"Then why are you trying to sell me your bardo?"

"I am not *selling* anything. I view the concept of a bardo as a clever method to induce clarity in thinking. If you are truly experiencing memories of past incarnations, it would be beneficial to take a step back and watch events as they unfold.

You would then have a clearer perspective in your next incarnation." Vivek paused to sip his tea. "You would make far fewer mistakes."

"That would make all my actions predetermined, and I've never seen any evidence of that," I said.

"Perhaps you are a slow learner." Vivek smiled.

"I'm a slow learner as well." Tyrus poured hot water into his cup. "I think it's because I can't make sense of this reality, which seems to get more confusing with each lifetime."

"You sound like Wade." I added some sugar to my tea and stirred. "With six incarnations worth of data to ponder, I'm convinced this reality is a fabrication we all planned and agreed upon. No supernatural intelligence would create something as flawed as us."

"It would also explain why we are in the midst of a collective psychotic breakdown," Vivek said.

"I'd say we already had one and are now locked up in an asylum." Tyrus took a sip of tea.

"I knew you two would get along." I laughed aloud. "I better give up now because neither of you will hear me any—"

"Every place I visited, the craziest ideas are presented as normal, and all who dare disagree are looked upon as the insane ones," Vivek said to Tyrus.

"Exactly," Tyrus replied. "Which is why I stay far away from any group that discusses politics or religion." He rubbed his scalp. "I really will go insane if this pain in my head doesn't cease."

I instinctively stood and placed my hands over his head as I had done for Master Franklin. My palms heated up along with the rest of my body.

Vivek's eyes widened. "I…see your aura. It's whiter than the snow outside."

The sensation I felt was similar to what I had experienced during my childhood vision when I touched the incubation tank. I had an awareness that I was the conduit for this energy surging through me, and I had to stay connected to Tyrus to heal him.

My body temperature soon dropped and I collapsed onto the chair.

Tyrus stared incredulously at me. "What did you do to me? My headache—it's gone."

Vivek poured some water into a cup and handed it to me. His hand was shaking.

"I haven't felt this good since before I got sick," Tyrus said.

"He healed you." Sutara came into the room, smiling. She turned to Vivek. "Are you a believer now?"

"How many times must I tell you, Suti, belief is the death of learning. No matter what wonders you see, there will always be more than one interpretation."

"Like what?" Sutara crossed her arms.

Tyrus and Vivek looked at me, awaiting an answer. I had none, and I refused to be viewed as a sage.

"The weather is nice today," I said. "Think I'll go out for a walk." I got Shisa and went outside. It was starting to snow. "What do you think? Should we go back inside?"

Shisa ran ahead, and I eagerly followed her, preferring the blistering cold to being looked upon as a prophet.

# shaky foundations

Eager to observe my dreams as Vivek had instructed, I turned in early. It took a while to relax. I couldn't get my mind off how I healed Tyrus, or if I had healed him at all. I finally fell asleep and was transported to the cabin, moments after Kai had shot Flora.

Kai aimed his plazer towards me. "You're a nonessential," he said.

"I agree."

He shot me. The blast dissipated a few centimeters in front of my face.

"I said you're a nonessential." Kai fired again, and the same thing happened.

"I agree."

"Then why won't you die?"

"I'm always here."

"Where?"

"A place where you have no power over me."

"You're wrong. You're as useless as the Unitians you tested Harmony on. Remember what you told me about the lower colors?"

"They don't understand how to put our complex theories into practice, and we must steer them towards our desired goal of Unity."

"That still sounds brilliant." Kai smiled. "We're so alike we might as well be one Unitian."

"I'm more than a Unitian, and I'm nothing like you. I left when I realized you wanted to use Harmony to enslave everyone."

"You may have escaped from Unity, but you can't escape from actions you've already taken. You think I'm evil? If you truly believe that, you must reassess your opinion of yourself." Kai gestured at me. "*You* invented Harmony. *You* believed you could harness the power of God inside an implant and fix everything."

I shoved Kai back against the wall and choked him. He laughed. The harder I squeezed my hands around his neck, the louder he laughed.

"You should be dead, not her!"

"Stop yelling!"

I opened my eyes, and the moonlight revealed Sutara's face.

"You were dreaming," she said.

I sat up. "I'm sorry if I woke you."

Sutara smiled. "I was right. Ajeet really did come to me in my dreams."

"What makes you say that?"

"If you can call me, that means everything I figured out in my last few lifetimes is right."

"I...called you?"

"We're going home soon," Sutara said, excited.

"You *are* home, Sutara."

"Not this home. Our next home."

"Which is where?"

"I don't know where, but it's beautiful. The sky is golden, and we live there always. You are going to take us there."

I placed my hand under her chin. "You're mistaken. I never called you, and I'm not here to lead you anywhere."

Sutara cried. "I don't believe you, and neither does Vivek." She stepped back and crossed her arms. "He brought you here this time because he agrees with me."

"This time?"

"I told him to find you—in your last lifetime, but he came back alone. He said you were a very strange man because you spent all day talking to ducks, fighting, and yelling at people."

"No wonder he doesn't take me seriously."

"Stop trying, and maybe he will." Sutara went to the door. "Come with me. I have something to show you."

I followed her outside and we faced the Crossings.

"The day the ground shook, almost everyone inside died," she said.

Sutara took my hand. "See through my eyes."

I looked at the Crossings again and saw that it had been crushed by a rock slide.

"Did this happen?" I asked.

"Many times."

"How did you all survive such devastation?"

"In my first lifetime, I died." She rubbed her eyes. "In my second lifetime, my memory returned before it happened, and I tried to warn everyone. I woke them as the yaks, sheep, and mules cried out, but it was a snow leopard killing one of the sheep. No one took me seriously after that. They thought I was still depressed over Ajeet's death—which I was." Sutara broke down and cried. "But I was also scared about losing everyone here and being left all alone."

"How did you convince them?"

"How do you know I did?"

"You're here to tell me what happened, and the people of the Crossings are still alive." I caressed the back of her hand with my thumb.

"After a few more nights of standing outside in the cold, no one believed me. They thought I made up the memories of my past life. They all thought I was crazy—except Vivek."

We walked to the river's edge, Sutara staring out at the water. "I told them I wouldn't warn them again. I was so mad, I didn't care anymore. Vivek wanted me to keep waking him. Each time the animals cried at night, we would come outside together."

She was shivering. I put my arm around her. "The more I talk about my memories with others, the more problems I seem to create. I've lost two people close to me, and I can't save them. How did you do it?"

"In my sixth lifetime, Vivek and I stood outside on the night the ground shook. This time, I kept quiet and listened to the animals. Their cries sounded slightly higher in pitch. I never noticed that before. The air was very still, and I had a funny feeling here." Sutara placed her hand over her chest. "Then it happened a few minutes later." She sobbed quietly. "I had to watch my friends die again."

"I know." I hugged her. "My sadness doesn't lessen with the passage of each incarnation either."

"In my lifetime that followed, I didn't say anything until I heard the same high-pitched cries of the animals. I yelled for everyone to go outside, and they listened. The ground shook and half the Crossings crumbled, but everyone survived and rebuilt."

I thought for a moment. "Do nothing?"

Sutara peered at me as the older version of herself had done in my visions. "Listen and do nothing until the time is right, and you will save your friends." She looked back at the water. "Then we will all be together soon."

Tyrus got stronger every day, and news of my healing abilities spread throughout Middle Crest. Most of the conditions I healed originated in the nervous system. Whatever properties I emitted during the process didn't work with bacterial infections. I had no idea why, and a COR scan failed to reveal anything new. I was forced to continue on faith alone, something I'd never done before.

Many of the locals identified me as another prophet, but I thought my ability to heal was part of the natural stage of evolution. I tried to explain I was an ordinary man, but no one believed me. They brought me gifts, cooked my meals, sewed clothing for me, and started construction on my own room. My pleas for them to stop failed. I gave up and let them believe what they wanted. As long as I was able to help people, what did it matter what they believed?

In the early spring, during a morning walk with Shisa, I passed some builders who were adding an addition to their home. When they recognized me, they ran over. Among them was a young boy who bowed.

"We build this shrine in your honor. What do you think, Master Damon?" he asked.

I recalled the gypsy woman who read my palm during my third incarnation. I hadn't thought about her reading until this moment. *You're going to travel the world, find riches, and rule over a tribe who will worship you like a god.*

The admiring faces gazing back at me demonstrated how even a remote location couldn't improve my character. I once again allowed myself to be imprinted by a collective ideal. My indifference was as destructive as my playing along in my first incarnation. I placed my hand on the boy's shoulder. "You would honor me if you devote this shrine to all the people of Middle Crest."

The boy nodded his head and smiled, freeing me from my role as a prophet.

Tyrus entered my room while I was in the middle of packing.

"I used to believe we weren't worthy of rescue or salvation," he said.

"Salvation is nothing more than an ancient myth."

"Maybe. But after you healed me, I saw new possibilities where I never had before. Whatever is happening to us is an improvement."

"Whoever you are, bring Tyrus back."

"I never left—and thanks to what you showed me, I'm better."

"I didn't show you anything. My healing ability isn't unique to me. It's part of something that would show up on my brain scan and probably on yours and Sutara's as well."

"You ran several already. What did they tell you?"

When I didn't answer fast enough, Tyrus smirked and shrugged his shoulders. "Science will never explain what's happening to us. Accept you can't scrutinize everything with a diagnostic tool, and life will flow easier."

"Okay Master Tyrus, impart the knowledge you received from your channeling of the Prime Wisdom." I crossed my arms and smiled.

"I'm healed. What slocking difference does it make how you did or didn't do it?"

"I'm a scientist. It's my job to understand, to hypothesize and to seek answers for life's unsolved mysteries. It's what motivated me since I awoke from my coma."

"You may uncover some truths, but in the end, you'll only find yourself with more questions. I found that harder to deal with than my illness."

I thought about Socrates and how he demonstrated we could question our way out of any commonly held opinion. "The more I ask, the less I understand; the less I understand, the least likely I am to judge others." I zipped up my backpack and looked at Tyrus.

"And yourself," Tyrus said.

"You don't miss much."

"Are you returning to the cabin?"

"The hermetic life is what I need right now."

"You're not going to heal again?"

"You and I both know I'm not a prophet."

"How do you know you're not?"

"You and Sutara are like me."

At that moment Sutara walked in. "No, we're not, and you'll eventually believe me." She hugged me.

"I wish I could be what you want, Sutara."

"Stop and listen to the animals like me, and you'll know what to do."

Sutara seemed as certain of her conviction as Wilfrid was of his, but I knew I wasn't a prophet. I had to depart from Middle Crest to avoid starting another religion. The world had enough of them already.

Vivek rode with me for several kilometers, and we stopped near the path that led out of the valley. I got off my mule and removed my camcorder from my pack.

"You took a picture here when we arrived, why take another one leaving?"

"A lot has happened since then." I took a picture of Vivek.

"I thought I would be leaving before you." He jumped off his mule.

"Why not come with me?"

"I promised Suti I would stay until mid-summer."

"You could always take her with you."

"She won't go. She wants to be here for her mother when she returns."

"You have to appreciate her faith," I said.

"It both inspires and saddens me."

"She's strong."

"I know." Vivek smiled at Shisa and leaned down to pet her. "Take good care of your master."

"I'm no one's master." I looked at Vivek for a few seconds and then touched his arm. "Now I remember where I saw you. In my last incarnation I was at the central park in New Athenia. You came by and petted Shisa."

"I will have to take your word for that as I do not remember." He smiled. "Normally, that would not be enough for me, but after what I saw you do for Tyrus and the other villagers, I am willing to accept the possibility that we might have met before."

"Sutara told me you didn't think too highly of me back then."

"Do not feel so bad, I do not think highly of anyone—including myself." He looked at Shisa. "There are exceptions.

Suti said I told her only your dog was worthy of an invitation to Middle Crest."

"I would've agreed with you. Shisa is hard to compete with."

"You are catching up."

"I'll be satisfied with a tie."

I bid Vivek farewell and rode off with Shisa following close behind.

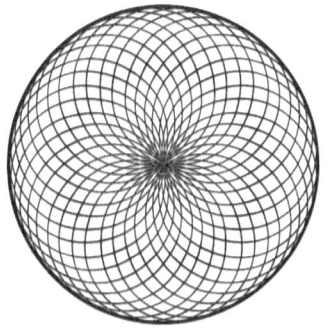

# last night, starlight

On my way back to the cabin, I stopped at Littlefield. It was tranquil time, so I headed to the coop to visit the hens. Since raising my own, I had gained an appreciation for these social birds that now rivaled my affection for ducks—except for Gadfly. He was my favorite until he stopped showing up at the pond three years ago.

I opened the gate and the hens scurried towards me, quickly joggling their heads forward and back. I smiled in recollection of the woman who referred to me as Bird Man.

"You have a way with the hens, Nomad."

I turned to face Wilfrid who had just appeared. "They know I like them more than people."

"Your sarcasm fails to hide your compassion."

"It also fails to hide my hunger." I patted my stomach. "Is there any food left over from last night's feast?"

"Even better than that. Genevieve has some venison stew on the pot, but I have something to show you first."

I winced at the mention of venison.

"Is there something wrong with your face?" Wilfrid asked. "You always have at least three bowls of stew before anyone else has their first serving."

Wilfrid led me to the supply bungalow, and I explained my involuntary transition to a vegetarian diet and how I'd gotten used to it. Since my return, I hadn't regained the taste for meat.

Inside the bungalow, he opened a door to a tall cabinet containing a row of hand-carved spears.

"When you told me about the bandits, I became very concerned over our security."

"I warned Michael not to talk to strangers about Littlefield."

"In case his mouth refuses to obey, we'll be ready." He handed me a spear with *Nomad* carved on the handle. It was the most heartfelt gift I'd ever received.

"Carry this with you in remembrance of your loyal friends here," Wilfrid said.

"I'll come visit after each transport, and be back in time to fight by your side."

"You're a true friend, Nomad."

Wilfrid smiled, and in that instant, I recognized him beyond his tangible identity. "You're a Six."

"Me? No." He held up his hand, his palm towards me. "It's all in the cards. I'm just the interpreter."

"Apart from your dreams about Nomad, have you ever experienced any visions that feel like memories?"

"Some nights I have these strange dreams. They feel as though they've already happened, but—"

"Tell me about them."

"I recently had one where you almost died from being attacked by two bandits on horseback. It seemed so real to me, but I knew it couldn't be true. You're not foolish enough to leave on a long journey after the shadow's first cast."

"I used to be."

"It happened?" He laughed and pointed at me. "You *are* the Nomad I've been dreaming about."

"That makes four."

"Four what?"

"Four who remember." Speaking those words, I felt a connection to something greater. Whatever we were a part of, I sensed it would make all my incarnations seem insignificant in comparison.

Michael avoided the man with the horse, and Littlefield was spared from the invasion. Shisa died seven years after I came back from Middle Crest, and I never got another dog. I read about an Ancient Yogi who spoke of an amulet that materialized in his mother's hands while she was meditating. She passed it down to him, and he was told that once the amulet had fulfilled his destiny, it would disappear. I interpreted Shisa's parting similarly. I gave up my material possessions and my need to be admired. Whatever part of me remained was all I required.

Michael graduated from the Athenian Music Conservatory with the highest honors. He composed an opera that was performed for three seasons. It became part of the New Athenian repertoire and was one of the featured operas during the summer festival. In the remaining span of my life, Michael went on to write six more operas and built up a large catalog of orchestral pieces. For every performance where I was present, I couldn't help but announce to whomever was seated nearby, "That's my son."

I ventured to New Athenia annually to visit Michael and his family, and I spent the rest of my time back at the cabin. As the years moved forward, I lived quietly, tending to my hens and garden and taking long walks. I was still fit enough for transports until the day I died. In my eighty-first year, Sutara came to me in my dreams and held my hand.

"Remember," she said.

"What?"

"The earthquake—how I made things change when I was still only a child."

"You stopped to listen to the sound of the animals."

Sutara smiled. "Listen, and you too will hear."

I shut my eyes after taking my last breath and merged with the fountain of light. Together we exploded into an infinite brilliance, bringing a close to my sixth incarnation.

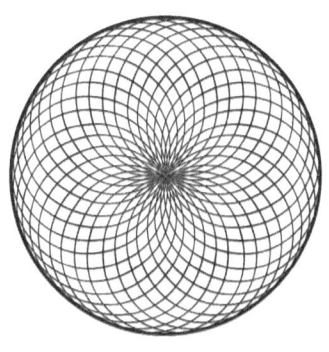

# natural man

### Seventh Incarnation

Wade marched around the edge of the ridge, and I crept towards him as I had in my past six incarnations. "This is about Nasia?" I asked, vividly recalling having said it before.

"It's always about Nasia," he answered. "No, that's not true. It's about me being a coward."

"What happened to her was her own—" I grew dizzy, overpowered by a rush of vertigo. Memories of all my past lives swarmed into my consciousness. "I remember," I said to myself. Fully reacquainted with my former selves, I jumped as high as I could. "I remember everything!" I laughed harder than I ever laughed before.

Wade cocked his head to the side. "What do you find so amusing about all of this?"

"I find *everything* amusing. Want to know why?"

Wade crossed his arms. "Harmony scrambled your brain and is preventing you from acting appropriately in situations that aren't meant to be funny."

"Wrong!" I laughed again. "Try again."

"If this isn't Harmony then you're crazier than you're always accusing me of being."

"Would've agreed with you back in my third incarnation. I spent some time in the old tunnel talking to your ghost. You wouldn't have wanted to know me back then—let alone smell me." I gazed at him reflectively. He was really here...alive for longer than he'd ever been. "Thanks for being a good friend and helping me see beyond the dome."

"Is this some new technique you're working on again?"

"And one that actually works. I'll tell you all about it on the way to the old tunnel."

"How foolish do you think I am?"

"If you jump off that ridge, you're a bigger fool than I've ever been. You're right about Harmony. I didn't want to believe it could be used for anything other than for the reasons I—" My hologue beeped and I glanced at the screen. "Unity Forces are on their way. We have to get out of here now."

"And go where?"

"New Athenia."

Wade laughed. "What happened to your concern about the scourge?"

"It doesn't exist. It more than likely never did." I walked up to the ledge, off to the side from where Wade stood, and tilted my head down. "That's a far drop."

"I'm not falling for it this time. Go ahead and jump." Wade put his hands on his hips. "I dare you."

"My visions of you dying don't come from the future. They're memories of events that have already happened. You can't escape from the past, Wade. I tried and failed at each attempt."

He stared at me open-mouthed. "My god…you *believe* what you're saying."

"For six lifetimes I heard you tell me how Nasia crossed the old tunnel, and you didn't go with her because you feared risking your assignment placement."

Wade shook his head. "Nasia must have talked when Unity Forces questioned her."

"Even if she had, how would I know about it?"

He shook his head again. "What you're saying is impossible."

"Her last words to you were, 'sleeve-worshipper.' You were so angry, you never said goodbye to her before she left. Shortly after you told me that, you jumped off this ridge."

He covered his face with his hands. "She's dead because of me."

"She's dead because of the Corporate Hierarchy, and their relentless need to control everyone." I held out my hand to him.

"Get out!" he yelled. "I don't want your pity!"

I kept my hand extended. "I'm not going to let you do this again."

"My life isn't yours to save."

"Don't do this. Don't end your life over what the Overseer and purple sleeves have done to you. They think they own you and every Unitian. They think the only time you're worthy of existing is when you serve them. And if you're not subservient enough, they think they have the right to prescribe a suicide order, and serve it to you in reintegration."

I gave Wade a moment to take everything in and then said, "If you jump, *they* win!"

His competitive nature triumphed, and he ran back towards the woods.

I chased after him. "Where are you going?"

"Back to the cabin."

I got hold of his arm. "It's too late."

He swung around to face me. "It will be if we don't warn Ingrid."

My mouth opened and froze at learning Old Woman's name. *Ingrid. Her name is Ingrid.*

Wade shook his head and walked away.

"Unity Forces killed her," I said.

Wade stopped but wouldn't look back at me. He clenched his fists and ran off. I caught up with him by the ridge that overlooked the cabin. Unity Forces were searching the perimeter.

"Maybe next time your memory will return sooner," Wade said without taking his eyes off the cabin.

Wade berated and blamed me for the tragedy that befell Ingrid, and as we set up camp the verbal condemnation didn't stop. There were many moments where I wanted to challenge him, but I listened, keeping my promise to Sutara to listen and do nothing. It was one of the most difficult evenings I'd ever endured. All the good I had done in my past lifetimes was overshadowed by the contempt on my friend's face. Wade hated me, but I was okay with it. At least he was alive.

We arrived at the cabin the next morning and performed the sacred burning for Ingrid. Shisa reappeared, and I called out to her in my calm voice. She slowly approached with her head held low. Wade, who witnessed the exchange, appeared astonished.

"Shisa accompanied me on almost every trek across the old tunnel." I kneeled down to pet her. "She's been there for me, always by my side—even through most of my deaths. Her actions showed me traits I'm in dire need of."

"I'll be leaving in the morning," Wade said indifferently.

"I can take you to New Athenia, but I'll be coming back."

"I don't need an escort. I have a map."

I stared into the simmering pyre and felt a cool breeze brush against my back. It was too soon. While I was inwardly celebrating the early return of my memory and Wade's survival, he still saw me as the sleeve-worshipper responsible for the crackling flames that were devouring Ingrid's flesh. In the passing of one day, Wade and I had moved lifetimes apart.

After a few laps around the pyre, Shisa whimpered and sat beside me.

Wade glanced at her and then back at me. "I look at you, and I see Damon, but you're nothing like him."

There were many things I wanted to say in response. I'd waited lifetimes for Wade to see how much I changed since my first incarnation and how his influence helped me accomplish it. I stopped myself, realizing the futility of trying to explain what I was becoming. He would have to witness my transformation for himself, and I had to accept that it might not happen in this lifetime. What he said was enough to produce the first sincere smile I'd experienced since my memory returned, and I wanted to hold on to it for as long as I could.

The next morning, Wade left for New Athenia. It would be dishonest to say I didn't envy him. I missed the civilized life and longed for my friends and to reclaim my chair with the orchestra. But I missed Flora even more. I surmised the only way I could save her was if I stayed away from all the things that got me into trouble in the past. I thought about my promise to Sutara to listen and do nothing. The more I listened, the more I aspired to be an authentic man, a truly natural man, fueled by inner-purpose, irrespective of opinion or ideal. The following four years were serene, and my hermetic life inspired a peace I had never possessed. I wasn't sure I had the strength to maintain this mood when Flora materialized, but I learned to stop looking ahead and to accept things as they come.

Tyrus's memory had been restored and he showed up at the cabin to be cured. My healing skills advanced. Like a medical scanner, I imaged the cancerous growth at the base of his skull and knew exactly where to direct the energy. My hands heated up as I placed them a few inches away from his tumor. As my hands cooled back down, I stopped the treatment.

"Thanks." Tyrus massaged his forehead. "Haven't felt this good in years."

I poured myself a glass of water to cool down. "What happened after I left Middle Crest?"

"I stayed there, got married and had three children—two girls and a boy. My youngest succumbed to a fever at age three. I don't want to go through that again."

"In my first incarnation, I married as well. I had two sons, Aaron and James. I keep wondering what the changes in my life means for them. Will they exist again in some other reality? Not knowing is difficult." I drank all the water and poured another cup.

"Why don't you return to that life?"

"All the great sages I've read about seem to agree that we can't ever go back. I found their words to be true. I tried to go back, but things didn't work out the same way. The mother of my children married Lidian."

"Holly was your wife? Forgive me, Damon. Why didn't you tell me? Had I known, I never would've introduced them in this lifetime."

"That's why I never told you. Your act of kindness turned Lidian's life around. You saved him—and by saving him, you saved his victims."

"It's not enough. The scale between my good and evil actions is still unbalanced. The Corporate Hierarchy subjugated the Unitians with my help—and yours. Perhaps if I had your training as a psychological engineer, I'd handle all of this as well as you."

"Training has nothing to do with it. I listened to your advice and helped with Freedomline. I'd ask you to stay and help me continue, but my iniquity can only be paid by my service alone."

"I understand." He gazed out the window. "That mountain reminds me of the home I made with Payma. She was good to me—the perfect counter to my morose personality. I'd wake up in the middle of the night from a nightmare and she'd sit in silence and listen to my jabbering and self-blame until I calmed down." He touched the window with the palm of his hand. "I found salvation in her silence." He turned to face me. "What if it never ends?"

I didn't answer him in this incarnation, but Tyrus picked up on my irresolution, identified by my thumb and pointer cradling my chin.

"What a slocking mess we're in," Tyrus said.

One certainty I started to rely on throughout my incarnations: I could never hide anything from Tyrus. I was counting on Flora being equally readable. I met her on the ridge, and struck her with my plazer. I would've rather let her walk down with me, but I didn't want to risk her recognizing me.

I looked down at Shisa. "Think she'll thank me for preventing her nasty fall?"

Shisa panted and whimpered.

"You're probably right." I scooped Flora into my arms and for the fifth time carried her to my cabin. She seemed to get heavier with each haul.

# damon's dungeon

Flora awoke bound to the chair. Seeing her reignited my memory of the night she was taken from me. As painful as it was to be forgotten, I was grateful she had no memory of the savagery that had befallen her.

"Sorry I had to knock you out." I picked up the remote controller and lowered the shades. "I didn't want you to see me."

The only light now came from two lanterns on a table I positioned behind Flora.

"I wasn't alone," she said. "There are other guards on their way."

I grabbed an apple from the table, flipped it in the air and caught it. "Then we'll start now." I stood behind her and spoke softly. "Every time we meet I'm reminded of the *Allegory of the Cave*. It was written during the forgotten times, and I'm going to present to you my version. Before we begin, I'd like to ask if you're comfortable?"

Flora thrust her body forward. "Untie me now!"

"Whatever you're feeling—hold on to it. Comfort equals surrender, and I don't want you to surrender."

"Why am I tied up then?"

"Imagine that you lived your whole life strapped to that chair, facing only the shadow in front of you." I swayed side to side with my arms extended outward.

"Are you Damon 1300-333-1M?" Flora turned her head to identify the possessor of the shadow.

I stepped out of the light beam's path. "Imagine you can't move your head and can only observe what's in front of you."

"Why should I do anything you ask?"

"Imagine, and you'll answer your own question. After I'm finished, you'll be free to leave…if that's your decision."

"I've already decided." She swiveled her head back to the shadow. "Let's get this over with so I can go."

I reentered the light. "You see the illumination in front of you, but you're unaware that the lanterns are producing the glow because you can't see what's behind you. You accept the light as a naturally occurring part of your reality." I rested the apple on the palm of my hand and placed it beneath Flora's nose. "The shadow brings you sustenance, but you can't detect the actual hand that feeds you. Your head can't move, and neither can your eyes. You only recognize your food by smell and—"

"This is an impossible *and* ridiculous scenario. What are you trying to prove? That I'm your prisoner, and you're in control? I already get that. What do you want from—"

I clutched Flora's shoulder and she gasped.

"Just imagine." Leaning down, I whispered in her ear. "And then you'll realize you can never comprehend the apple's shape and color." Maintaining focus was difficult. The scent of sandalwood on Flora's hair reminded me of the night we spent in the trainlet when I unraveled one of her braids. "You can only know it by its taste"—I bit the apple—"and smell." Another waft of sandalwood blew up my nostrils and scrambled all the incarnations in my brain.

Flora turned her head to the side. "I'm not hungry."

I took another bite of the apple and chewed slowly, allowing myself time to reconnect to my current timeline.

"If you let me go, I won't tell anyone about this cabin."

"My secret is safe with you. It's impossible to know where you are because you have no comprehension that anything exists beyond this space, and you have no desire to even consider the possibility of leaving. The shadow shows you interesting visual displays, accompanied by entertaining stories that don't contradict your reality." I made flapping motions with my arms. "You live for these moments. It's the only time you're happy." I stroked Flora's cheek. "The shadow also gives you sensations of pleasure. These times are your favorite because they take away your loneliness, and you can't understand why you feel this way. You have everything you desire…but something is missing, and you don't know what it is."

Warm tears trickled down her face. The impulse to take her in my arms was strong, and I had to remind myself I was a stranger to her.

"And you're so lonely." I retracted my hand. "So lonely. What are you missing?"

"Freedom. I can't go anywhere."

"If you never experienced motion, how would you know you could leave?"

"There must be a somewhere else."

"Why?"

"There must be more than what's here."

"Would you believe anything else existed if all you've ever understood was the shadow in front of you?"

She started to speak, hesitated, then began to cry softly. "No."

"Would you think you had everything you needed because it was brought to you—before you even asked for it?"

Flora looked down at the floor. "I would."

"If you have all you need, why would you think there's something missing?"

"I'm…not sure. I just know that there is." Her words were choppy as she tried to stop herself from crying. "There has to be something more than this, something more than being forced to do the same thing every day."

I stepped back and said no more.

"Is that it?" She sniffled loudly. "I'll be tied up forever?"

"Until you free yourself—yes."

I walked to the table and picked up a knife.

"Are you Damon 1300-333-1M?"

"Shadows remain unnamed…until you're willing to see who casts them."

Exiting the back of the cabin, I shielded my eyes from the sun and turned to face Flora. I knew this day was coming, and I'd groomed myself so she'd take me seriously. As her eyes adjusted to the brightness, she looked at me as though I wasn't what she had expected. I liked that—her not seeing me as some wild, uncivilized apeman.

"When I first stepped outside, the sunlight was unbearable and painful." I led Flora past the vegetable garden and towards the pond. "After the blinding effect of the sun wore off, I started to distinguish other colors and shapes." I stopped to gaze at the mountain. "Seduced by the sights and sounds of the outside world, I wanted to learn more."

We continued walking towards the mountain. "I was moved by the amazing things I'd seen here and on the other side of the old tunnel. World philosophies, cultures, and art flooded my brain, which became part of my new understanding. I tried to tell a woman about my experiences, but she failed to understand me because she was still bound by chains. To her, nothing existed beyond the shadows."

"You could help free her."

"The previous owner of this cabin showed me the truth, but I refused to acknowledge it because all I recognized were the shadows. It wasn't until I left Unity that I realized how much I was missing." I recalled the vision I had of Flora in my last incarnation, when I pushed her in Sephroy's cart. "No one else sees through your eyes but you. Only you can decide whether you want to limit your vision to the shadows or step outside and see what's real."

"Did you kill the Overseer?"

"What do you think would be my motivation?"

"You want to be Overseer."

"Who would induct me to such a high honor? I haven't been to Unity in years."

"Kai discovered your loyalists inside the dome."

"I have no *loyalists,* and I'll leave you to ponder what I've said. It's up to you whether you want to free yourself from your chains. These are my final words on the subject. Time is a luxury I can't afford now, and I have a few tasks to take care of before I leave."

Without saying a word, Flora followed me back into the cabin. She explored the various items on the shelf and picked up the Ganesha.

"The eight lives of Ganesha: jealousy, arrogance, confusion, greed, anger, lust, possessiveness, and pride. I've managed to experience all of them—in each of my incarnations."

"You can be helped. This confusion is caused by the scourge."

I couldn't help but smile at her. "You know I'm not sick."

"Your answer confirms you are."

"Nothing you say can ruin my mood because I know you understand."

"I'm here to help you, not ruin you."

"I know that now. Your intentions were always transparent." I tossed my hands in the air. "I'm not the great psychological engineer I once believed myself to be because I couldn't see it."

"So you'll go with me?"

"No."

"You said you agreed with me."

"I understand your motivation now. You act out from compassion, which you view as a burden. It's not, Flora. What you have is a gift. Tyrus agrees, and that's why he calls you a rare gem."

"How did you know about that?"

"I know many things about you."

"Like what?" she asked.

"You like to hear the truth."

"Then start speaking it."

I gestured to my eyes. "This time, you must observe for yourself."

# happy journey

I sat on the front porch chair pondering what my confrontation with Kai would bring, what story he'd tell me, and what insult he'd throw my way to get a reaction.

Flora stood near the edge of the porch, gazing at the waterfall. She hadn't spoken since we came outside.

"He'll be here soon," I said. "There's a listening device in the cabin. It's on the table. Go get it, and leave from the path behind the vegetable garden. I'll begin transmitting when Kai arrives. You'll be able to hear everything he says, and you'll be angry. Resist your desire for vengeance; it never turns out well."

Shisa came running from the base of the ridge. I got up and located Kai with my binoculars. I handed them to Flora.

She examined the middle ridge and turned to me, surprised. "It's Kai."

I checked my hologue for the time. It was 9:57. "It'll take him a little under thirty minutes to get here, and he's not only after me."

"Kai would never do anything to hurt me."

Resisting the urge to elucidate further, I crossed my hands on my lap and said nothing.

"Is this some kind of reintegration test?" Flora marched towards the stairs, and I pulled her back.

"He'll see you," I said.

"He knows I'm here."

"If you want the truth, you must do as I ask."

"Why don't you run?"

"Everything I've done yielded a similar outcome. I want to see what happens when I do nothing."

"He'll arrest you for the assassination of the Overseer."

"He'll do far worse if you don't follow my instructions." I unclasped my hologue and gave it to Flora. "The map to New Athenia is in here, along with my journal of what to expect. My passcode is A5673. Did you get that?"

Flora reached for my hologue, but I didn't let go. "Repeat it," I said.

"A5673."

"Again."

"I said I got it!" She snatched the hologue from me.

"A5673—keep repeating the code until you remember."

"You may have left Unity a maroon sleeve, but you act like a typical paranoid purple sleeve."

"Paranoid, yes. Typical—not me." I smiled.

"I'm leaving now." She started down the stairs.

"Happy journey, Unity Guard."

She whirled around and appeared to have remembered something. I saluted and probably would have been able to knock her over with my breath had she been standing closer.

"Isn't it peculiar how a moment in your life can leave you feeling as though it happened before?" I asked.

"Why are you doing this? Kai will never let you go, and if you really have something on him, he'll—"

"Kill me?"

434

Flora studied me as intently, as she had done on the crail the night we first met.

"I'm glad to see you're finally concerned about my well-being," I said.

"Not concerned." She cooled and placed her hands on her hips. "I'm just stating a fact. Kai will never let you get in his way of being the next Overseer."

"You know him well."

"So are you coming with me?"

I responded with a closed smile.

"It's your slocking life." She turned to go.

"It stopped feeling like it was mine lifetimes ago."

Flora halted and swiftly swung around to face me. "Are you *sure* you don't have the scourge?"

I smiled again. Flora creased her forehead. "Kai accused you of many things, but he never mentioned you were this annoying."

I held onto my silence.

"I'll do what you say," she said, "but if you're wrong—"

"I won't be alive to see you gloat."

Flora opened her mouth and when I saluted her again, she turned and walked away.

Kai approached with his plazer aimed in my direction. I reached for mine, then remembered I'd left it inside in response to a dream I had the previous night of Flora emerging from the other side of the tunnel. I wasn't with her, but she looked happy. I heard Sutara say, "Listen and do nothing until the time is right, and you will save your friends." Admittedly, I had my doubts regarding my interpretation of the dream, but my plazer failed to get me out of trouble in my last six incarnations. I was so desperate for a favorable result that I would've even confessed to killing the Overseer if it meant Flora's survival.

Kai stopped a few meters in front of me. "After a snake had discovered a mouse's home, the mouse searched for a vacant hole to live in. He found one near the base of a large tree trunk. The mouse moved in, confident he wouldn't be discovered. But he didn't take into account that his own footprints led back to his home."

"Clean up your prints or lose your strategic advantage—but how are you so sure you're not the mouse?"

"I'm the one with the plazer."

"I had a perfect view of you on the ridge. You wouldn't be standing here had I wanted you dead."

Kai looked around nervously. "Where's the guard?"

"On her way to a new life. You'll need to find someone else to blame for the murder of the Overseer."

"I already have." Kai leveled his plazer at me. "I'm looking at him."

Shisa came running up out of nowhere and jumped on Kai, who reactively fired his plazer. The beam nailed me in the abdomen. Kai went down on all fours, losing his weapon. He tried to reach for it, and Shisa nipped his arm.

"Shisa fetch!" I placed my hand over my wound, cursing myself for leaving my plazer in the cabin because of a dream.

Shisa backed off Kai, clamped the plazer between her teeth, ran over to me, and dropped it on my lap.

"Leave now, Kai." I aimed the plazer at him. "Before she really gets mad."

Kai got up and started to run, but was shot in the leg and collapsed.

Flora stood at the door of the cabin, her plazer still aimed at him. She rushed over to me and lifted my hand. "That looks pretty bad. I'll get the med kit."

I held onto her. "There's no time."

"If I don't get this bleeding to stop you'll—"

"You have to hear the truth now." I glared at Kai. "All of it."

Flora retrained her plazer on Kai. "What are you doing here?"

"Unity is justice, and you're its deliverer. Have you forgotten your promise?" Kai asked.

I looked from Kai to Flora. Both had used a similar phrase. It couldn't be a coincidence.

Flora shook her head and seemed confused.

"Don't listen to him. That phrase is a post-hypnotic suggestion."

She looked at me with a blank expression, similar to what I saw before she killed herself in my first incarnation.

"Unity is justice," she repeated.

"That's right Flora. Unity is justice," Kai said. "Don't let an Outsider corrupt your mind and stop you from delivering it."

Flora turned her plazer towards me.

"You don't have to listen," I said. "This was programmed into you during reintegration."

"I wasn't reintegrated."

"They can do it without you knowing, as Kai already admitted to me once before."

"He's lying," Kai said. "I never spoke to Damon about you."

"Did you ever experience any missing time?" I asked Flora.

She redirected her plazer at Kai. "What happened to me after our dinner out?"

"You know what happened. Your implant malfunctioned and you passed out."

Flora looked back at me. "I woke up the next day with no memory of what happened."

"You know how much I care for you, Flora," Kai said. "I would never do anything to hurt you. It's Damon who's the enemy. He wants to destroy Unity."

Flora walked up to Kai, her plazer still pointed at him.

"Unity is justice, and you're its deliverer," Kai said.

"And I will. I'll contact Unity Forces to come get you—after you answer all my questions."

Kai got to his knees. "How can I trust you'll keep your word?"

"I never back down on a promise. You said that was my best attribute after I passed the loyalty test to become your personal guard."

Kai nodded.

"Did my implant really malfunction?"

"No."

"Why did you follow me?"

"Damon can be influential to an impressionable mind like yours."

"But he does it out in the open, unlike you. Did you reprogram my mind in reintegration?"

"I had to ensure you'd complete your mission. You destroyed the tower, so I knew you couldn't be trusted."

"How did you know it was me?"

"You really did that?" I asked, both surprised and impressed.

"It was part of my initiation into the Strikers."

I looked at Kai. "Answer her question."

"Are any of the Strikers with you?" Flora asked Kai.

"*All* the architects are with us, as are most of the appointers."

"Why would you put some Unitians in reintegration for staying outside too long and then help others escape?" Flora asked.

"Most Unitians are easy to control. Make their life appear comfortable, and they'll go along with everything we tell them. But a small percentage of you who insist on living by your own rules need to be diffused, so we give you the illusion of fighting back." Kai faced me. "The only reason Ingrid was killed was because you reported her. Had we known you wouldn't be coming back, we would've allowed her to continue the transports. Your disappearance slowed us down for a while."

"The Unitians will find out about this," Flora said. "I'll make sure of that."

"Even if you record our conversation and play it back on all the city screens, no one will believe me. They'll say I was infected with the scourge."

Flora slapped Kai's face. "Do you like how that feels?"

Kai frowned at her. "You see me as something evil, but I used to think like you and lord of the wilderness over there. As a boy, I questioned everything—including my own mentor, Master Torrin." He looked at me. "I would've followed Torrin anywhere, but when the rest of the Chosen turned on him, I realized all his talk about independence and autonomy was impossible in Unity. After Torrin was humiliated and stripped of his color, he destroyed the towers and disappeared. I had one choice to make:

continue Torrin's teachings and meet his end or join the ranks of those whom I despised, where I could enjoy an influential and successful life. My choice should be obvious."

"You're worse than all of them," Flora said.

"Yes, and I have no problem admitting it because I made the conscious decision to play along. I no longer recognize the weak, pathetic, idealistic protégé I used to be. People need to be led and controlled. Without us around to tell you lower colors how to think, you'd be running around like wild dogs, slaughtering each other."

"While you're looking out for us, who's watching out for you? What makes you better than us?" Flora asked.

"Nothing." Kai laughed. "All I had to do was give the illusion of surrendering my individuality to the right purple sleeve, and now I'm on my way to being the 148th Overseer." He laughed again. "It's slocked up, I know it is, but that's how everything works—how it always worked, and how it'll continue to work, whether we like it or not." Kai stared at his holologue for a moment, then unclasped it. "There's no way out of what we've allowed ourselves to become." He gazed deeply at Flora and handed her the holologue. "See for yourself."

"Bring it to me," I said.

"What you want is impossible," Kai said. "Admit that and you'll live easier."

Flora was crying. "Do you?"

Kai looked at her but said nothing.

Flora brought me the holologue. I turned off the camera and called Kai's recent contact. Roth's face appeared on screen. His locator signal revealed he was in Unity.

"Your visual isn't coming through, Master Kai. Do you need assistance?"

"Who do you see?" Flora asked.

I closed the connection. "When Kai said most of the appointers were with them, I suspected Roth was as well. I had to find out for sure."

"He may not be with them. I wasn't."

"Each time Kai made his way down this face of the ridge, the motion sensors never picked him up. Roth must have told him about their location." Shisa came up and laid her head on my lap and I petted her. "And in my last incarnation, I was going to head out to New Athenia for a year. Roth delayed my last transport because his appointer was supposedly compromised. If all went according to schedule, I wouldn't have met up with you." My breathing became more labored, and I couldn't produce much volume with my voice. "He wanted me here because that's what Kai wanted."

Flora kneeled next to me

"When Unity Forces showed up earlier than I anticipated, it should've been obvious. Typical of me." I laughed and started coughing. "Too late to learn and too late to undo what's been done."

"So my appointer—the one who asked me to fry the tower —"

"He set you up," Kai said.

Flora turned to Kai, now kneeling at the base of the steps. "Why?"

"To test your loyalty," Kai said. "Once we established whose side you were on, we used you to service our mission, and once we didn't need you anymore, you were retired."

"That's how you became Kai's nonessential," I said.

Kai gazed at Flora. "It was another Chosen who viewed you as nonessential and brought it up for a vote. All nine concurred; I had no choice. Even if I abstained from the vote, the outcome would've been the same."

Flora, tears streaking down her face, glared at Kai. "Why is the Corporate Hierarchy so brutal? Why can't they honor the Sacred Oath and live up to their promise of Unity for all of us?"

"Unity is as much a fantasy as the Sacred Oath."

"As much as I hate to admit it, I agree with him," I said. "What we both want, what we've fought so hard for, is unattainable. I used to think it was the Overseer that was the problem, but it's everyone who supports him that keeps the Unitian myth alive. Without his supporters, the Overseer would have no power over anyone. Unitians continue to follow him because they've confused their privileges for freedom. It's easy to see why; compared to Unity, life as an Outsider isn't glamorous.

There's no one to give you credits for your servitude or places like the pleasure room to help erase the emptiness you feel. Out here, you won't find Unity Guards protecting you from bandits who exist in large numbers because there's no reintegration. You only have yourself to rely on, and yourself to blame if you don't plan wisely. But even with all that, I'd never go back to Unity."

Flora aimed the barrel of her plazer at her head. "That doesn't sound appealing to me. A world without justice isn't a world worth living in."

All my remaining strength released in one final burst, and I grabbed hold of Flora's arm. "When you stop expecting everyone to follow your standards, you'll see you're about to pay a high price for an illusion. You can only live the kind of life you want for yourself. Want a better one, Flora. You deserve it."

A few tense moments passed and she relaxed her plazer. I was surprised when Kai sighed in relief.

I released Flora's arm and fell back onto the chair. Closing my eyes, I took what I thought would be my last breath. The whole of my essence coalesced and swirled within my abdomen. It then ascended to the top of my head, and my entire body began to vibrate. The fountain of light appeared, beckoning me with its beatific siren song. I resisted, and it grew louder. *Not yet*! I forced open my eyes.

"I'll get the med kit," Flora said.

"I don't have much longer. Please, let me finish what I have to say."

She nodded.

"I used to believe the Sacred Oath was the only path to a civilized society. When I encountered individuals who didn't live by my code, I was in conflict with them before I even said a word. In all my travels, I realized unity comes from shared beliefs. No matter where you end up, if you think differently or set off to do your own thing, you're challenged by all those who want to keep things as they are. After seven incarnations, I'm tired of conforming. I'd rather stay here alone than compromise who I am just so I can get promotions and be worshipped by people who want to be like me—because they believe I'm happy." I smiled as I recalled Lidian saying something similar.

"Were you ever happy?"

"Not so much."

"I've been lonely most of my life because I find it hard to trust people," Flora said. "Master Tyrus was the only one. And then he was gone."

"To trust, you must believe in the individual whom you're trusting. Humans are not religion. We're all flawed—some of us more so than others."

Kai looked at me as though he thought I was referring to him.

"The only thing worthy of trust is what's in here." I placed my hand on my chest. "I don't know what it is, but it's always here—this presence. It never betrays me, it's always honest, and it isn't afraid to throw me a few punches any time I refuse to listen. When I'm quiet long enough to hear, it guides me to where I must be, not in words, not in thoughts, but in mutual agreement."

Shisa cried and leaned her head on my lap. "How many times must I tell you, Shisa—all of this is more comedy than tragedy. The tragedy only arises because most people don't understand the humor that lurks underneath all the self-imposed drama."

Flora petted Shisa. "You're not alone, Shisa." She peered at me with tears in her eyes. "I don't see any of this as humorous."

"I don't get the humor either," Kai said. "And I don't see how our misery can be self-imposed. No matter who you are in Unity, you must capitulate to someone, and everything I've heard about the Outside is no different. You're forced to be an actor in this drama, and that's what makes it a tragedy to me. There's always an understudy around to take your place."

"Like Avery?" I inquired.

"Everywhere I turn, he's there, challenging me, searching for ways to make me look weak in front of the Chosen."

"Was he the one who brought up the charge of me being a nonessential?" Flora asked.

Kai nodded. "The thing about capitulation is that if you do it once, you find that's all you're doing. Eventually, your own dreams and desires are obliterated, replaced by an insatiable need to hold on to what you have at any cost. Sometimes I get tired, and I try to remember the way I used to be. I wonder how my life would've turned out had I left with Torrin."

"You may yet leave—either now or in another lifetime," I said. "And you'll realize, as I did, that the tragedy is capitulation." I turned to Flora. "Roth probably contacted Unity Forces when he got no response to my call. You must go now, and take Shisa with you. She'll protect you. In the tunnel, watch out for bandits. You were killed by one in my last incarnation when you tried to save my life."

Everything around me started shimmering, and the ethereal music was now too loud to ignore. A white aura surrounded Flora, and I was gratified to see one around Kai as well. Tyrus helped Lidian move forward, and I supposed Flora helped Kai, even after all he'd done to her.

"Is there anything I can do to make you more comfortable?" Flora asked, sobbing softly.

"Hold my hand."

She took my hand and cupped it between hers.

"Thanks for not listening to me." I brushed her cheek with my free hand. "Once you get to the other side of the tunnel, you won't want to stop. Go to the Alexandrian Repository, and learn all you can—but believe nothing. Continue picturing yourself as one of the stars…distant, unnoticed, and beyond capture." I took my last breath. "Happy journey, Unity Guard. I have a feeling you'll have many."

"I will," Flora smiled, "because I'd rather be killed again than return to Dome Dungeon." She gently pressed her lips against mine.

*Better late and remembered than early and forgotten*, I said to myself as my seventh incarnation concluded.

# PART THREE

*"To be yourself requires extraordinary intelligence. You are blessed with that intelligence; nobody need give it to you; nobody can take it away from you. He who lets that express itself in its own way is a Natural Man."*
U.G. Krishnamurti

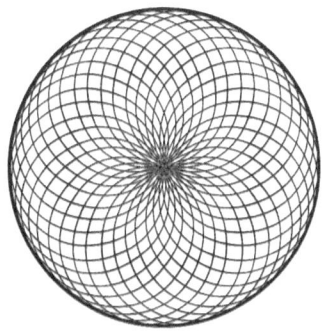

# third one from the left

### Eighth Incarnation

I walked alone in the dark until I witnessed the incubation tank filled with white light. I examined the baby floating peacefully within. It was a female. I knew her—but not by name. She drifted towards me and pressed her tiny hands against the glass. I did the same and felt a warm vibration. My body glowed white as rays of light from each color of the rainbow flowed out of me and into the baby. Her skin was illuminated as the color rays swirled around her and rebounded back to me. While this was going on, I vibrated like a tuning fork with the tank. I kept my hands pressed against the glass until my palms cooled. My own voice echoed back to me, "Six begin, Six alone, Six unite."

The light within the tank grew brighter as a strong sense of recognition swept through me.

"Remember," my voice echoed as a baby's cries woke me. I glanced up at one of the holomonitors as a baby was being removed from its incubation tank. The action seemed so familiar; I had the strongest urge to investigate. I sat up with great effort and when I got off the bed, I collapsed. An Overmaiden ran to my room and assisted me back into bed and called for a doctor. I kept my eyes on all the holomonitors as a young Overmaiden carried the infant away. She entered the emergence room and placed the baby inside one of the bassinets. *Third one from the left.* I stored it into memory and drifted off to sleep.

I awoke a few hours later and made another attempt to get out of bed. I took my first step and fell again. Grasping the mattress, I pulled myself up and staggered out to the hallway. The Overmaiden, whom I had seen with the baby, spotted me.

"Where do you think you're going, child?"

"For a walk."

"You can't be here unattended." She took my hand and walked me back to my room.

"Can you take me to the emergence room?"

The Overmaiden gave me a peculiar stare.

"Please take me. I need to see one of the babies."

"Why?"

"I like babies."

She scratched her chin and glanced towards the monitoring station, where a technician was focused on his holologue.

The Overmaiden looked at me and raised her pointer finger to her mouth. "It'll be just between you and me." Smiling, she led me to the emergence room.

We entered and I headed to the third bassinet from the left. My body began to feel the same vibratory sensations I'd experienced in my vision. They intensified after I read the name tag: Flora: *1309-119-24F*. She was the baby from my vision!

Flashes of the cabin and New Athenia streamed into my consciousness. The awakening memories frightened me, but Flora's beautiful heart-shaped face soon eased my fears. Her expression communicated lifetimes of experiences, even as she lay sleeping. I touched her tiny feet, and she fanned her toes outward. I took hold of her little hand and she opened her eyes and smiled at me.

"Hi Flora." I held her hand while COR downloaded eight incarnations worth of data into my nine-year-old brain.

The Overmaiden held me by the forearm. "Time to go now. The Overseer doesn't appreciate wandering children." She walked me back to my room, where I watched Flora on the holomonitor until I drifted off to sleep. Key moments that shaped me into who I had become presented themselves all night.

I awoke the next morning, glanced at the emergence room holomonitor and saw that Flora was missing from her bassinet. Jumping out of bed I ran out into to the hall, nearly plowing over an Overmaiden.

"You can't leave your room without permission!" She seized my wrist.

I pulled free and raced to the emergence room. Flora's bassinet was neatly made up as though no baby had slept inside. The kind Overmaiden from the day before approached me.

"Where's Flora?" I asked.

"She had some trouble breathing through the night."

"Is she okay?"

"She's under observation in a special care unit."

"Can you take me to her?"

"I'm sorry. I can't."

"Why not?"

"Those are the rules."

I started crying, and the Overmaiden who had yelled at me arrived. She left the room when she saw I was being watched after.

"This is why it's better you don't see Flora again." The kindly Overmaiden took hold of my hand. "Look how bad you're feeling. It's not right for a boy your age to suffer. You should be out playing with your friends in the schoolyard." She smiled. "Do you like to do that?"

I nodded my head.

"Then let's get you back to your room so you can rest and get better soon."

"Will you tell me when she's okay?"

"I will."

"Do you promise?"

"I promise."

The Overmaiden nodded and took me back to my room. Up to the day I left, I asked repeatedly about Flora but received no updates.

After my release from the hospital I couldn't get my mind off her. I called the hospital every day to ask about her condition, and no one would tell me how she was doing. Master Franklin was informed about my calls. He summoned me to his office to tell me Flora was okay and to stop pestering the hospital staff; they had lives to save. There was nothing more I could do. I gave up my inquiries and attempted to live life as I'd been doing.

Having my memories return at such a young age and with so little experience behind me in my present incarnation made it hard to trust what I was seeing. I began to test and verify my visions starting with the day of the camping expedition. Everything happened exactly as I remembered. Master Franklin had requested I go to the dorm. I went first to the essential shop with the violin in the display window. Upon seeing it, I was stricken by a visual history of my performances in front of the purple sleeves and on the concert stage of New Athenia. It took me less than a day to regain my proficiency on the violin. The first piece I played through was "Beneath the Lonely Stars to Nowhere." As my bow gently skimmed over the strings, I envisioned myself lying on the ground and staring up at the starry sky. The memory was so vivid I felt the pain from the beating, the warmth of Shisa's fur as I petted her, and the fountain of light that kept me safe until Wilfrid came for me. By now I knew there was something more to my visions. With seven lifetimes of experience behind me, life in the dome suddenly felt very small.

On my first day back at school, we visited the Unity Museum of Overseers. I was bored with the exhibits until I glanced at a picture of the 146th Overseer. Standing beside him was Torrin. I recalled the picture of him with Ingrid and dreamed about them that night.

The next day, during Master Franklin's drawn-out lecture about the writing of the Sacred Oath, I had a vision of the cabin. As I stared out of the panoramic window, Sutara materialized next to me as a child. She tugged at my arm.

"Come with me," she said.

"Where are we going?"

"Home."

I followed her to the door. She opened it and we stepped out into Middle Crest and walked along the path in front of the Crossings.

"You must find a way to leave your village," Sutara said.

"I'm not allowed out of the dome."

"You must, if you want your nightmares to end."

"If I get caught, they'll put me in reintegration."

Sutara stopped and crossed her arms. "I cannot believe you said that."

"What?"

"When I met you, you did whatever you wanted."

"I was older, and remembering was easier."

Sutara climbed onto the large rock and sat. "I cannot blame you for being scared. It's difficult to capture all the memories when your memory returns at such a young age."

"I'm *not* scared." I put my hands on my hips in protest.

"Prove it."

I thought for a moment and then snapped my fingers. "Next summer I'm going on a camping trip. I can leave then, but I still don't know where to go." I thought about Torrin and Ingrid. They were living in the cabin now and helping Unitians escape.

Sutara spoke my thoughts aloud. "You can go to the cabin."

I crossed my arms. "That's what I was thinking."

"But I said it first," she giggled.

"Technically I did, because you're not born yet." I narrowed my eyes. "How can I see you if you're not born yet?"

Her demeanor turned grave. "Beyond time, beyond space, we are always. But not here. I cannot go on much longer. You must make it this time."

Sutara began to fade and as I took her hand, she vanished.

Master Franklin forced me out of my vision by slamming his pointer on my desk. "Is my lecture *boring* you?"

All my classmates stared at me in anticipation of a typically incendiary response, but I didn't feel typical anymore. "I don't feel well."

Master Franklin looked at his hololusing. "You're excused for the rest of the day. Report to the hospital for a—"

"I'm not sick. I had a bad dream last night, and I couldn't get back to sleep." I looked around the room again, wishing everyone would get back to their own business.

"What was it about?" Master Franklin asked in a way that implied he didn't believe me.

"I fell off Emerald Mountain and died."

His expression softened. "After all that you went through, that's understandable. Dreams sometimes bring out what we fear most. Don't allow your accident to control you. You must confront your fear, or it'll control—" He held the side of his head and winced.

"Are you okay, Master Franklin?" I asked.

A black aura surrounded him. "I haven't been getting enough sleep either."

I quickly climbed up onto my chair and placed my hands over his head. My body temperature rose as a rush of energy surged within me. Then my hands cooled. I withdrew them and hopped off the chair.

Master Franklin stared at me aghast. He grasped my arms and examined them. "What did you just do to me? I feel rejuvenated, as though I just got a few hours sleep."

His aura expanded about a half meter all around him. Terrified, I ran out of the classroom and bumped into an approaching purple sleeve. Without looking back to see who it was, I kept going.

I put my hand over Wade's mouth and he opened his eyes. "Keep quiet. It's me." I released my hand.

"Damon? How did you get in here?"

Wade's roommate moaned.

"Let's talk somewhere else." Wade got out of bed. "I know a safe place."

We kept quiet until we entered the dining hall.

"Where did you go after you ran out of class?" Wade asked. "No one would tell me what happened to you."

"Don't have time to explain." I threw my pack on the table.

"How did you get in here?"

"I tapped into the main database and got the override code to unlock the door. My implant ID marker wasn't even scanned when I entered."

Wade gawked at me, and I smiled at him in a way that communicated it was worth waiting eight lifetimes to see him on the receiving end of one of our escapades.

He stared at my pack. "Where are you going?"

"I'm leaving."

"For how long?"

"Forever."

"Why?"

"Can't tell you now, but I'll come back for you soon as I find a place to live."

"I don't want to leave Unity."

"It's better outside than here."

"You think living with the Outsiders is better?" Wade stepped back. He seemed afraid of me. "You have the scourge."

The fear in his eyes made me think it was a mistake coming here. "There's no such thing as the scourge."

"How would you know that if you never even left the dome?"

"When I come back, you'll see that I'm okay. Then you'll—"

I heard the door creak open. "I thought you said it was safe in here."

"It is." Wade looked towards the door. "Slock. I forgot it was ice cream night. Master Simon always comes down to finish up the leftovers."

I picked up my pack and ran to the window. "That's why his belly is fatter than Ganesha's." I lifted up the pane, trying to figure out who Ganesha was.

"Who?"

"Never mind." I looked at Wade.

"You're starting to act as weird as Lidian," he said. "I told you that would happen if you hang out with him."

"I can't wait till you go back to hating it here. You were a lot more fun." I climbed out the window, headed to the access and hid myself in a delivery crail to wait for the unpacker to leave with his first carry. I then ran for the protective cover of the forest.

# family

As I ascended Emerald Mountain, I was surprised that I'd remembered what path to take. I even recalled the location on the high ridge where I could get the best view of the dome now gleaming under the moonlight. Everything was exactly as I remembered, right down to the transceiver hidden behind the large rock. I recalled my final days with Wade in my previous incarnations. Such despair I had never known in my young life. I wanted to run back to the safety of Unity, but images of Torrin and Ingrid were scorched into my mind.

Climbing up the eastern side of the eroded ridge and gazing upon the large mountain resurrected my enthusiasm. Several hours later I found the waterfall, glanced down at the valley and spotted the cabin. Excited, I ran down the path, until I tired. I arrived to find Torrin sitting on a chair on the porch.

He spotted me and stood. "Did you come alone?" He nervously looked around.

"Are you Torrin 1250-032-3M?" I asked.

"How do you know my name?"

Ingrid opened the door—only she wasn't old. She appeared as she had in the picture that hung on the wall inside the cabin. "Where did he come from?" she asked Torrin.

"I'm a passenger," I said.

She walked over to me. "You're one of the youngest I've met."

"Not as young as you think."

"And one of the most precocious ones."

Ingrid took my hand and led me inside where I would be staying. She couldn't have children of her own and believed my visit was part of some divine path to motherhood. The early return of my memory was equally fortuitous. After eight incarnations, I finally had a mother and a father. Torrin was initially against my remaining in the cabin, but we soon bonded over long hikes in the woods. It filled me with sadness whenever I thought of Wade being raised by strict and emotionally distant Overmaidens. During one of our return trips across the old tunnel, I begged Father to rescue Wade from Unity.

"When you told him you'd go back for him, what did he say?" he asked.

"No. But that's only because he was never out this far before. I know he'll change his mind once he sees this place."

"If he doesn't want to leave now, nothing you tell him will make him want to come with you."

"I know he's not happy there."

"Maybe. But we can't risk taking a boy out of Unity against his will. It will draw attention to us and risk Freedomline."

"How about Lidian? I know he wants out."

"We can't risk it."

To avoid showing my disappointment, I looked away from him.

"Don't give up on a reunion. Perhaps in a few years, your friends will be ready to leave on their own."

I had only to think about my initial reaction to Wade and Ingrid to agree with him, but Lidian was different. He never liked living in Unity, though I wasn't too concerned; I knew Tyrus would look after him.

I spent the next year learning from Father, and my remaining levels were completed in New Athenia. My audition on violin impressed the music schoolmaster, who personally sponsored me for residence. He invited me to live with his family; he had two sons close to my age. It was an invitation I eagerly accepted because dorm life reminded me too much of Unity. I came home every summer to help Father with the transports and even brought him to Littlefield. While Mother believed I lived before, he never took the claim seriously until Wilfrid recognized me as Nomad. During every transport, we'd visit him on our return. In my eighteenth year, Father and I began building a new cabin for me. It took us a little more than ninety days to complete. I was pleased with the design: one spacious room and a loft for my bedroom, with a window facing the mountain. Since I was only home during the summer, the rest of the time Father used my cabin as an inn for passengers who wanted to rest before leaving for the old tunnel.

The two summers that followed passed quickly. On my final transport before returning to New Athenia, I was surprised to find Nasia among the passengers. In my previous incarnations, she left Unity the following year. I planned a rescue operation, but Nasia no longer needed rescuing. She was in a relationship with a man she met at University who was also part of the transport. After we had emerged from the eastern side of the tunnel, Father gave his usual harrowing lecture about what happens to Unitians who dare to return to Unity. At the end of his discourse, Nasia hugged her mate tightly. I was relieved she wouldn't be filling out a request for death in this lifetime but disappointed Wade would never meet her. Without her influence, would he rebel against the Corporate Hierarchy? That question would haunt me for the next few years.

When Father turned seventy-eight, I pleaded with him to stop the transports as this was the year he died in the old tunnel. He acquiesced, only because Mother wouldn't let up until he did. Four days after he had agreed to stop the transports, Mother frantically knocked on my cabin door.

"He's gone! I knew he wouldn't listen! He's such a stubborn old slock," she cried. "We have to find him, Damon. I don't want to lose him."

Mother and I caught up with Father about three kilometers past the mouth of the tunnel. He had three passengers with him.

"Damon will continue the transport," Mother said. "Come back with me now."

"I'm okay." He continued to walk.

"Stop with all the heroics!" Mother said. "No one can save this slocking world."

"I'm no one's hero. This is something I must do."

"What is driving you to do this?" Mother pleaded. "Why do you hold on to your secret? It's worse than poison. It's slowly killing you inside."

"Can we discuss our private business on the way back? I have passengers to transport." Father walked off, and we followed. By the time we made it to the trainlets, he was weak. I helped the passengers get settled in their trainlet and then proceeded to ours where Mother was setting the motion sensor alarm.

I assisted Father onto a sleeping bag. His complexion was pale.

"Why didn't you listen?" I asked.

"I'll be fine after a rest."

"You're coming home with me," Mother said.

"No." He lay on his back. "I'm not stopping."

"This is a crusade you know you can't win." Mother kneeled beside him. "Now you're going to leave us alone because you're too filled with pride to concede defeat." She began to cry.

"Our son is strong. He'll take over for me."

"I don't want him to take over. I want him to be freed from everything that ties him to Unity."

"If you really believe he's lived before, you know he's already tied." Father looked at me. "Continue Freedomline. Be there to lead the passengers."

"I won't have to be." I sat beside him and placed my hands over his head. "You'll be there for them." I closed my eyes and waited for the energy to heat up my hands but nothing happened. "Why isn't it working?" I stared at my hands. "It worked for Tyrus and Master Franklin."

"Maybe I don't have any life left in me," Father said.

"You did," Mother said, "but you gave it all away and kept none for yourself."

"I've lived long enough. Before I left Unity, I never thought I'd make it past my fiftieth year."

"I can't do this without you, Father," I said.

"You can't…or you won't?"

As I was about to speak, Mother gave a scolding look for me to keep my remark to myself. "I will, Father." I held his hand.

"There's something I must tell you, and I hope you won't hate me." His eyes filled with tears.

"I can never hate you," I said. "You gave me a life I never would've—"

"I helped create the scourge."

"How?" Mother was surprised.

"The scourge isn't real," I said.

"It's very real. The curative signal sent to the implant causes tumors to grow in the brain. When I found out, I shut off the transmission, but the Overseer overrode my decision and used the scourge to explain it away. It was then that I discovered the disease was originally a fabrication—a clever way to keep Unitians from wanting to leave."

"Why did the Chosen continue using the liberation pulse?" I asked.

"For any nonessential who failed to succumb to the curative signal. The Overseer liked to be thorough."

"Oh, Torrin." Mother ran her hand through his hair. "All these years—the guilt you carried all alone." She started sobbing again. "I'm so sorry I couldn't help comfort you."

"It's not your fault. I was naive. As a scientist, I believed my work would serve humanity, but I soon realized very few purple sleeves were loyal to the Sacred Oath. And a few dead Unitians were acceptable to the Overseer if it meant his vision of Unity could be achieved."

That last sentence triggered a buried memory from my first incarnation, along with the strongest vertigo I'd ever experienced.

"That's why you can't give up." Father took my hand. "Please, don't give up on the Unitians."

I rolled onto my side and curled into a tight ball. My stomach felt like a bomb ready to detonate.

Mother came over to me and held my arm. "What's wrong, Damon?"

I took slow, deep breaths, trying to keep from vomiting. "Water."

Mother got me my canteen, and I slowly sat up and drank.

"Did a new memory just awaken?" she asked.

I gazed at my parents who loved me, doubting whether they still would after I revealed to them what I'd just remembered, what I kept hidden from myself for eight incarnations, until now. I would've preferred to keep silent, but the words escaped from my mouth. "In my first incarnation—I was the Overseer."

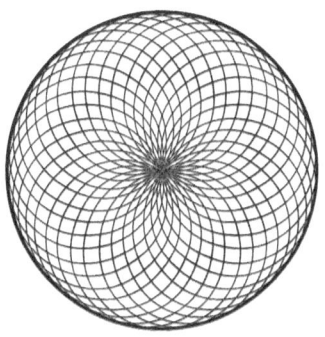

# OVERSEER

## First Incarnation

After I'd shot Kai, my escape from Unity was interrupted when Danielle surprised me in the lobby.

"Master Damon." She bowed. "I wanted to make sure you were okay."

"A good night's sleep was all I needed."

"You had me worried last night. I would've stayed till morning, but I had to work early." She noticed my backpack. "Are you going on vacation?"

"Camping. I always relax better under a starry sky."

We walked to the crail stop in front of my building.

"You surprised me last night," she said.

"In what way?"

"I don't think I've ever heard anyone nominated to purple sleeve speak as openly as you. That takes a lot of courage. I was starting to lose faith in the Corporate Hierarchy, but you made me believe in the Sacred Oath again."

"That's very kind of you."

"It's the truth. All of Unity would be better off with you as a Chosen. I'd even elect you for Overseer if I had a voting privilege."

A crail pulled up and the door opened. I hesitated, stuck somewhere between my grief over Flora and a moment of inspiration. One conversation with Danielle is all it took for me to believe I could make things better for the Unitians. If I succeeded, I'd be absolved of Wade's and Flora's deaths.

I kissed Danielle's forehead. "Thanks."

"For what?"

"We'll continue this later." I motioned to the open door of the crail. "You can have this one. I forgot something in my loft."

"Enjoy your vacation." She smiled and went off.

Before contacting Unity Forces, I wiped my finger prints off the plazer I'd stolen and placed it in Kai's carryall. I then connected his holologue to the transmission towers feed. Two Unity Guards arrived to question me while a search and retrieval team gathered evidence.

Garrison, the leader of the unit, kept his gaze fixed on the optic of his motion camera as he talked to me. "For audio/visual identification, please state your full name."

I stared directly at the lens and answered without hesitation. "Master Elect Damon 1300-333-1M."

Garrison bowed to me in a way that seemed forced. "Congratulations on your nomination," he said with a trace of disinterest and looked back into the lens. "Why do you believe Master Kai 1277-103-4M, a man of the highest honor, came here with the pretext to kill you?"

"I don't make this accusation without merit."

"Upon close inspection of your loft, there are no signs of struggle, and you've suffered no injury. Is this statement correct?"

The younger guard leered at Garrison and then shook my hand. "I'm Steven. My partner and I are here to help you get through this ordeal. All these questions are routine, and if you'd prefer to do this a little later, we can accommodate you."

"I appreciate your consideration. This has been the most traumatic and saddest day of my life. I'd rather finish this up today, so I can take some time off to heal."

"We understand." Steven glared at Garrison. "Don't we?"

"Of course, we do. I only wish to resolve this in a manner that works best for you, Master Elect Damon. Can you please tell us the purpose of Master Kai's visit?" He went back to peering into the optic.

"He wanted to destroy Harmony."

"Destroy? Why?" Steven asked.

"Kai was delusional. He thought Harmony's real purpose was for mind control, and he came here to force a confession from me. When he didn't get the answer he wanted, he threatened to destroy the towers to free the Unitians from my alleged control."

Steven eyed Garrison as though he were concealing something.

"The towers were fried a little over an hour ago," Garrison said.

One of the guards searching my loft overheard our discussion and handed Kai's hololouge to Garrison. After he'd examined it, he shouted to the guards in the room, "Return to headquarters! We found what we're looking for!"

Steven bowed to me. "My sincerest apologies for any inconvenience our questioning may have caused you."

"If you can think of anything you might have forgotten, please call us," Garrison said. "You will no doubt be rewarded for the heroics you've displayed here today."

"We can take you to a curate if you'd like," Steven said.

"I'd rather be alone."

They left, and the evidence I'd planted on Kai was accepted without any further investigation. For my treachery, I became purple sleeve and was awarded a seat among the Chosen. Five years later I became Overseer for my campaign promise of identifying the COR frequency and turning off the stun on the implant. Shortly after I'd won, I ran tests on volunteers and learned that the frequency was only present in my brain. I kept it a secret and later told the Chosen that COR couldn't be harnessed by technology. By then, I was well-respected and no one cared, even though the stun remained. All I had to do was promise each Unitian a few more extra credits a week; that was enough to satisfy them.

I entered the immediate-care wing of Unity Hospital and approached the desk.

The receptionist stood and bowed. "Honor to meet you, my Lord."

"What room?" I asked.

"I'll take you there." She led me down a hall to Danielle's room. She had been diagnosed with the scourge four weeks after I'd been inducted the 148th Overseer.

"Will she awaken?" I asked the nurse who was tending to her.

"I'm sorry, my Lord. We've done all we can. The disease has progressed too far."

"Forward all her medical files to my secretary."

"I'll do that now."

"I'd like to be alone."

The receptionist and nurse bowed and left the room. I looked at Danielle who was my first Overmaiden. Unlike Flora, she never questioned my devotion to the Corporate Hierarchy or the Unitian Oath.

As I took Danielle's limp hand in mine, I was overcome by ambivalence. I liked the respect and honor that came with being Overseer, but underneath I felt unchanged. Unitians were kind to me because of my title. Danielle stayed with me because she caught a glimpse of who I truly was during our mystery date. She believed I'd help save Unity, and I believed I had. I never had the chance to ask her if I had lived up to her expectations; in three weeks she was dead.

I read through Danielle's autopsy report and discovered what Torrin uncovered many years earlier: The signal sent to the implant was responsible for Danielle's death, and it created tumors in forty percent of Unitians. My Harmony upgrade seemed to accelerate the onset of the disease. The report went out to my Chosen, and I called a meeting to discuss the issue.

"What is your decision, my Lord?" asked one of my Chosen.

Although I still grieved over Danielle's death, Unity wasn't only about me. I had to consider what effects the truth of the implant would have on Unitians. "We continue as we are."

Steven, whom I promoted for being kind to me, lifted a wand that lit when he touched it.

"Let's all acknowledge Steven, who'll deliver his testimony to the Chosen," I said.

Everyone lifted their light wands and set them back down.

"You may proceed," I said.

"My Lord, I don't see how we can continue transmitting if it's causing fatalities."

"Did you ask yourself what would happen once we cut off the signal?" I asked.

"No, my Lord, I—"

"I've considered this from every possible angle, and each outcome is equally unsettling to me."

"But Unitians are dying."

"Do you have a plan to calm the riots that will most certainly break out as a result of this coming out?"

Steven was unresponsive as the rest of the Chosen stared at him.

"How about us?" Avery asked. "We're also susceptible to the side effects."

"As of this morning, your implants have stopped receiving both the Harmony and curative signals," I said.

"Have you considered that this may work well alongside the liberation pulse?" Avery asked.

"I haven't even considered it. We're not murderers. The liberation pulse comes only after a Unitian has served his purpose. To take someone at the prime of their lifespan is barbaric."

All the Chosen leered at Avery.

"Please forgive my blasphemous assertion, my Lord."

"You're forgiven. But should I ever hear you say something so inhumane again, your membership with the Chosen may have to be reconsidered."

I turned to Steven. "As you can see, I'm not heartless. I have a team of scientists searching for a way to transmit the signals without the side effects. In the meantime, our discussion is finished." I looked directly into the eyes of all my Chosen to show them I meant my words. "If we lose control, we lose everything Unitians have worked for over the last few centuries, and you'll all lose the privileges you've earned through your faithful service. Do you find that acceptable?"

Not one of my Chosen said a word.

I turned to Steven again. "Do you?"

"No, my Lord."

"Then you may take the vote."

"For the official record: all those in favor of keeping the signals operational please make your vote known," Steven said.

Nine of the Chosen raised their light wands. I glanced at Steven and he reluctantly lifted his light wand.

The night after Danielle's sacred burning, I dreamt that I lay dying on a hospital bed. An Overmaiden with large expressive eyes tended to me. It took me a few moments to recognize it was Sutara.

"Who am I?" I asked.

"You're what cannot be defined."

"I must be something."

She smiled and wiped my face with a cool towel.

"Do you remember?" She removed the cloth and placed it into a dish of ice water.

"Remember what?"

"Who you're not." Sutara unbuttoned my shirt. "You're not a scientist."

"I'm not?"

"You're not the Overseer, who believes it's his decision to preside over life and death."

"Who am I then?"

She took the cloth out of the water dish, wrung it, and placed it on my chest. The coldness bled through to my bones. "I cannot answer that," she said.

"Why?"

"The knowledge is only yours to unlock. You must internalize this, or it will not carry over."

"Carry over? To where? Yes, I remember now," I said more to myself and then looked at her. "Why is this so hard for me? Why do I keep forgetting?"

"Because you don't trust yourself yet."

"What I've done is unforgivable." I covered my face with my hands. "I became more concerned with the ideal of Unity than the lives of the Unitians. My desire to fix things made everything worse. How can wanting to help turn out so wrong? It makes no sense." I grabbed Sutara's hand. "Promise you'll keep coming. Only you can remind me what happened here."

She removed her hand from mine. "I'm tired." She stood. "We seem to keep moving in circles, and my life has been on hold because of your refusal to see."

"Maybe we have this all wrong. Maybe I'm supposed to be where I am right now, doing what I'm doing."

"Where else can you be other than where you are now?" Sutara raised her arms in the air and laughed. "Listen to me, I sound like my Uncle Vivek."

"Who's Vivek?"

Sutara smiled. "A wise old man who never gave up on me." She sat beside me. "I cannot be angry with you, no matter how much I want to." She put her hand on my arm. "Call me anytime."

"I still don't know how I did."

"You will figure it out, if you're serious about what you want to do."

"I am."

She stared at me with a doubtful expression.

"I'll do what I must do, hear what I must hear, and see whatever I must see in my next incarnation."

"If you cannot turn away from this now, how do you expect to turn away next time?"

The scenery around us changed; we were now in my study. I surveyed all the work that sat waiting for me on my desk. "I have responsibilities here. The Unitians need me." Pointing to my commendations, I said, "I worked hard for what I have. What will remain if I leave this all behind?"

Sutara leaned against the wall and crossed her arms.

"It's easy for you to sit here and judge me. You don't know how difficult it is to be responsible for a whole civilization."

"I cannot see you anymore. Your ego spans higher than the Himalayas."

"And you can't comprehend what it's like when everyone looks to you for the answers, and you're the only one who realizes you don't know anything more than the people you're giving them to. But you know you have to try because if you don't, someone will come into power like my predecessor, who had aspirations of a greater Unity. Had he lived longer, I have no doubt in my mind that he would've killed every Outsider to accomplish it."

"You cannot control everyone's fate, Damon. You must choose to liberate yourself. And you must allow others the freedom to do the same."

Sutara walked towards the door, and I noticed my thirty-two reprimands that hung on the wall, which awoke something in me that I'd long forgotten.

"I'll resign!" I shouted.

Sutara turned and faced me. "Why now?"

Still looking at my thirty-two reprimands, I said, "I want to find something I lost."

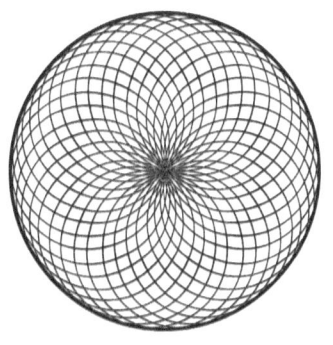

# defeating the dragon

## Eighth Incarnation

"Sutara helped me alter my destiny. After my vision, I instructed my Chosen to disable the towers and appointed Steven to succeed me."

Mother hugged me. "I'm so proud of you, Damon. To turn away from such power is near impossible, but you did it."

"And it made no difference. Avery called a meeting declaring he'd connected to the Prime Wisdom and was told that Harmony wasn't malfunctioning; its signal had been divinely sanctioned to rule over life and death. I thought for certain my Chosen would view him as insane. Only the Overseer has access to the ordained dose of escape that permits direct communication with the Prime Wisdom."

"And for anyone else who took the drug, they were merely hallucinating," Father said, shaking his head. "I still laugh at myself for believing in such nonsense."

"The Chosen didn't believe in it enough and rejected Steve," I said. "They didn't want Unity for all. They wanted slaves, and looking back at my own motives for keeping the signals active— so did I. At least Avery had the nerve to admit it openly."

"Did he become Overseer?" Mother asked.

I nodded. "And I ran away defeated, humiliated, and a coward. I ended up back here, hoping to find you. That's when I first discovered they killed you."

"You must continue," Father said. "If you can change, we all can. It means goodness conquers evil on a far greater scale than we've ever anticipated."

"If I'm your example of goodness, humanity is in trouble."

"It's not only your burden," he said. "To survive, we must all act according to our mutual interests, as individuals, not while under the threat of reintegration or some other ideological form of control. That's why I'll die happy. Unity will soon fall because it goes against this natural order."

Father's comment reminded me of his journal entry—how there existed a self-destructive mechanism in the Ancients that led to their downfall and how we weren't any different. When I'd first read it, I was elated. After all I'd been through, I wasn't sure I agreed with Father's current assessment, but I kept silent.

"Never doubt your ability to lead," Father continued. "I see a greatness that's been longing to break out since you first showed up at the cabin."

"Thanks Father. I'll do my best." I didn't believe those words, but I didn't want our last night together to end with a debate.

Mother wept and laid her head upon Father's chest. "I wish you'd told me. You wouldn't have been alone."

Father caressed her hair. "I wasn't."

I placed my hand on Father's shoulder and kept it there until he fell asleep. It was the last memory I have of him alive. He died in his sleep that night.

We came back to the cabin and Mother and I performed the sacred burning. She recited the ceremonial prayer.

"From the ground you arose, and to the ground you shall return. Of this Earth you've been granted life, and from this Earth new life shall arise in your place. Carry on into heaven, where your identity will eternally be stored as sacred. Through our memories of you, your presence will be celebrated for all the joy you've brought to our Unity." Mother cried as she spoke the final words. "All together, we were here. All together…we'll be again."

Mother stared at me as though some new realization came upon her. "Eight lifetimes of pain are looking out at me right now, which means I'll be adding still more to your suffering." New tears streamed from her eyes. "Stay away from us next time. Go to New Athenia, and don't look back."

I hugged her. "Don't say that, Mother. I wanted a family, and I was given that with you and Father. I couldn't improve upon the life you both gave me."

She pushed me away. "I don't want to come back again, even if I can't remember. I'll only have to look at your face, and I'll know your pain…just as I know now." She ran into the cabin.

My attempt to console her failed. It would take time for both of us to heal, and all I could do was be an available presence for her when she was ready to talk.

The following night, Sutara came to me in a vision as an infant. I looked down at her lying in a crib. I attempted to rouse her but she wouldn't move, and her skin was cold. Picking her up, I embraced her limp body. "Forgive me for being too weak to remember on time." I put my hand over her head. "I can't do anything else but give back what I've taken." My hand heated up, and Sutara's skin warmed. I could feel her blood pulsing through her veins. "You're alive!" I kissed her cheek and gazed upon her smiling face.

Vivek entered the room and approached me with his eyes beaming. "I cannot believe the miracle I see before me!"

"Sutara is the miracle." I handed her to him and woke up.

Unsure how to interpret my vision, I considered a trip to Middle Crest. But it would have to wait. Mother's state of mind deteriorated since Father died, and I had to take care of her. Over ten days had passed since our return to the cabin, and she seemed to be getting worse. She only emerged from the cabin to tend to the garden. I would come back from my daily hike and find her on the back porch, sitting on father's chair and staring emptily into the mountains. I'd cook dinner and we'd eat together in silence. Nothing I said cheered her up. This ritual continued for another five days. On the sixth day, I was on my way back to the cabin when mother ran to greet me along the path. Trailing behind her was a canine pup with golden hair that I recognized immediately.

"Shisa!" I leaned down to pet her.

"I was sitting on the porch, and I heard crying," Mother said. "She was eating a tomato when I found her." She laughed. "I always believed dogs were strictly meat-eaters."

"Shisa was never picky about food," I said as she licked my hand.

"She looked up at me and I knew she was your Shisa."

"Shisa belongs to no one." I said.

Mother picked her up and stroked the top of her head. "She was all alone. Her mother must have abandoned her."

I scratched her behind her ear. "It's hard to believe how big she's going to get in one year's time."

Mother smiled at me and then narrowed her eyes. "Think you need a shave. You look like a bear."

I pulled at my beard. "Shisa has seen me with a beard down to my chest."

"Go."

"I'll shave after dinner."

"I meant to Unity. They can't be allowed to win."

"I can't leave you like this."

"Like what?"

"You haven't left the cabin since we got back here."

"Things are different now. Torrin came to me in a dream last night."

Shisa wiggled about and Mother let her back down.

"I was walking in the woods alone. As I approached the old tunnel, Sephroy waved his walking stick and led me inside. I entered one of the trainlets where Torrin lay on the ground as he had done right before he died. 'Keep Freedomline moving,' he told me. 'You and Damon are the only ones that can help the Unitians now. Don't forget them.'" Mother looked from Shisa to me. "There is a reason Shisa came to us on this day of all days. Are you aware of the legend behind Shisa?"

"A dragon terrorized a small village in Ancient China, and the king held up a figurine of a Shisa Dog. It roared loudly and brought down a large boulder from the heavens that landed on the dragon. The town folk erected a statue of Shisa, believing it protected them from evil."

"Shisa is your protector."

"She's yours as well. You named her," I said.

"I know. It's the name I would've picked. Shisa dropped into my life and saved me from my own dragon: self-defeat. When your father died, I felt lost. For so many years, it was just the two of us. I couldn't imagine a life without him."

Mother watched Shisa running around in a circle. "Look at her…barely a few weeks old. The whole world is new to her and ready to be explored. Her curiosity inspires me to start over."

"I'm glad to hear that."

"And so can you."

"I don't need to start over. I did what I set out to do; I uninvented Harmony. I don't owe anyone anything."

Mother shook her head. "You're as selfish as your father. That man only lived to satisfy his own personal sense of justice, and it killed him in the end. I don't want to see the same thing happen to you."

"If I were selfish, I'd be the Overseer again."

I headed back to the cabin with Mother and Shisa following me. "He should've listened to you," I said. "This world is beyond repair, and it didn't take me eight lifetimes to learn that truth."

"That's no excuse for you to give up," Mother said.

"Why was it acceptable to you for Father to give up Freedomline, but not me?"

"You're different."

"Different, but not better."

"What else do you have to do besides grow your beard?"

"Rest. I earned it."

"You sound older than me—and you're starting to look that way too."

"In some ways I am."

"How can you think only of yourself after what your father told you about the curative signal?"

"I won't be believed. The Chosen will tell everyone I'm suffering from the scourge."

"Just be there for them. That's all your father wanted."

"I've done enough."

"I'm not going to pretend to understand what you've gone through. However, I do know one thing for certain: The brave little boy who showed up at our door has grown into a man. Sitting around here gardening and talking to an old woman isn't enough for you. It won't help you forget, and it won't lessen your pain. You have to find a way to release it."

"I tried eight times, and eight times I failed."

"You can help save them, and yourself."

"I don't want to be the basis of a new religion."

"This isn't about religion. You're real—not someone's idea to be followed and misinterpreted. There must be a reason why you're endowed with the gift of remembering all your lifetimes."

"My brain perceives a yet to be identified frequency. It's more than likely a natural part of evolution."

"If you're evolved, could that mean you're here to help us do so as well?" She held onto my forearm. "I'm okay, Damon. You must do what's right for you. Don't wait until moments before your death to see the light again. That would be tragic."

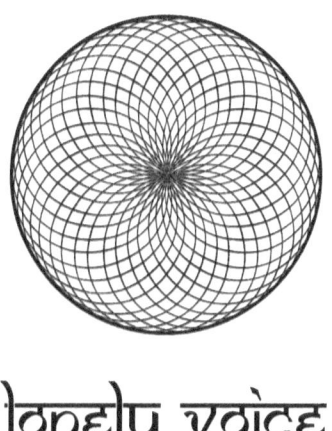

# lonely voice

    The hypnotic lights of Unity Hall switched on, and the Unitians stood and applauded. Like Zeus on Mount Olympus, Overseer 147 stood behind the podium, his white gown flowing loosely around his thin frame. While he gave his speech I snuck into his loft with an implant I programmed using his ID marker. When I took my first step onto the marble floor, I recalled the oil paintings lining one wall, and the large gold-framed mirror that hung on the opposite side. However, I wasn't there to admire the decor. I headed straight to the Overseer's desk, rummaged through a stack of papers and stopped when I found the object of my quest: an acquisition order with a list of books, music, and technology on the way over from New Athenia. The Overseer had an exclusive trade agreement with them. No one in Unity knew, apart from the Chosen who enjoyed similar luxurious surroundings.

With the evidence in my hand, I barged into the Overseer's assembly and fired a shot into the air with my plazer. Everyone turned to look at me.

"You're all being deceived! While you beg for privileges, the Overseer lives like a god!" I waved the papers in the air. "Here is the proof!"

Two Unity Guards slowly approached, and I pointed my plazer at them.

"He's willing to kill you all to stay in pow—" A sharp sting on my back brought me to my knees.

A woman screamed as the evidence and my plazer was ripped from my hands. Blurry, formless smudges of color circled above me.

"Bring him to the stage, so he can be heard," the Overseer said. "We're all free to speak here."

The guards dragged me to the podium. I could feel every eye in the room probing me.

"There's no reason to be so rough," the Overseer said. "Let him go."

My vision cleared enough to see things within close proximity. The Overseer smiled with such sincerity, I almost forgot why I had come here. He stepped aside as I made my way to the podium. Sweat trickled down my face. I glanced at the Chosen on the balcony, then at the purple sleeves in the front tier.

One of them stood and shouted, "What are you waiting for?"

"He's silent because he knows he's lying!" a maroon sleeve hollered and almost every Unitian in the assembly applauded.

The passionate response against me was unexpected. As I stared at the angry faces, the urge to leave was strong, but my feet wouldn't move. I slammed my fist on the podium and yelled into the microphone. "You're all primitives! No amount of promotions or privileges will elevate you! Intoxicated on self-praise, you believe your own lies! While the Outsiders move forward, you continue to devolve!"

"It's you who's devolved!" a yellow sleeve shouted.

"He even looks like an apeman!" another voice called out.

Everybody laughed, and I looked on, hating them all. "You'll eventually be outmaneuvered and defeated because you stand for nothing!" I barely heard my own voice over the deafening jeers from the crowd. "You're automatons! Every last slocking one of you are automatons! Brainless and unable to think for yourselves!" I wanted to strike out and hurt them as much as I was hurting in that instant. My desire to free the Unitians kept me fighting lifetime after lifetime, and it now seemed like my efforts had been wasted.

The Overseer stepped in, and everyone fell silent. "If we don't allow this man to speak freely, we can't honestly call ourselves a free people." He gestured for me to continue.

I squeezed the sides of the podium, trying to empty myself of the anger that made me want to resume my diatribe. It took all my strength to tone down my voice, but by then I had lost all credibility. I continued anyway. "The Overseer tells you you're all free, but you don't even understand the meaning of freedom. Most of you never traveled beyond the dome. You don't know anything other than Unity. When I began to explore the other side of the tunnel, I realized freedom has nothing to do with privileges or the ability to rise up within the Corporate Hierarchy."

Some of the purple sleeves started talking amongst themselves.

"You're told the purpose of the implant is to heal you from the scourge, but it's a lie. I lived as an Outsider for many years, and I can tell you with certainty, no such illness exists. The implant only monitors your whereabouts and notifies Unity Forces if you've strayed too far. Most of you die prematurely from tumors in your brain—a side effect of the curative signal sent to the implant. The Chosen and Overseer guard this secret because they're exempted from the curative signal as well as from being monitored." Directing my gaze at the purple sleeves, "It appears not all of you are as privileged as you believed."

I pointed to the lower colors in the back. "For those of you who manage to survive, a *liberation pulse* is sent to your implant. It's a lethal shock that kills you instantly, after you've served your purpose. It's a very effective way to keep the population at a sustainable level." I pointed at the purple sleeves. "And you're not exempt from that either."

"More lies!" A purple sleeve yelled out.

Pounding my fist on the rostrum, I shouted, "Everything I said here can be verified! Torrin 1250-032-3M, one of the highest regarded members of the Chosen, made the discovery. The Corporate Hierarchy turned against him when he threatened to reveal the truth. They believed the ends exonerated the sacrifice, and you're paying for their pseudo-definition of Unity with your lives."

A volley of dismissive cries were thrown in my direction.

"Most of you don't live past fifty. Outside of Unity, people live much longer. My father lived to be seventy-eight, and he was active until the day of his death."

More purple sleeves were shouting. One stood up to be heard over the din. It was Kai.

"I knew Torrin!" he roared.

Everyone stopped talking. The Overseer motioned for him to continue.

"I was his First," Kai said. "Torrin was the most honorable purple sleeve until he succumbed to the scourge. The man worked hard to find a cure, and he became so obsessed he wouldn't sleep for days. Shortly before he disappeared, I walked in on him after he injected something into his arm. He said it was a counteragent that would destroy the implant. Torrin believed it produced voices and images in his head that instructed him to do terrible things. The next day he blew up the towers. When he asked me to leave with him, I told him proudly that Unity is my home, and that I would die loyal to the Corporate Hierarchy."

All the colors applauded, and Kai sat down.

A maroon sleeve pointed his finger at me. "You can't turn us against the Overseer. He protects us from savages like you!" They all cheered.

An orange sleeve, the least respected of all ranks, stood and thrust his fist in the air. "We are one in Unity, we are one in Unity!"

Everyone got up and cycled through the phrase. Through each pass, the words cut through me, defeated me. I had believed the lower ranks would scream for freedom once they had heard the truth, but they heard nothing. Their minds had been successfully conquered by the Unitian Oath, as mine had once been.

"You win!" I shouted. "I thought I could erase my mistakes by freeing you, but I can't." By making that admission, all the pressure I'd put on myself lightened.

The room quieted down, and I took a moment to catch my breath. "I don't want to force my truth on you. If I do that, it becomes a lie because it doesn't belong to you. That's why the words I spoke here today are as arrogant as the Overseer's. Truth isn't given to you by someone speaking behind a pulpit. Mine emerged from my experiences and my understanding of them. I cannot release your truth, nor would I want to. You all deserve the circumstances you accept, as I deserve mine."

The crowd hurled obscenities at me, reigniting my anger. "Enjoy your servitude," I said and pushed the microphone away.

The guards escorted me out of Unity Hall. I expected to be taken to reintegration. Instead, they led me out of the dome and even handed me my plazer. Something didn't seem right. I suspected they might be following me, so I hiked a longer route back to the cabin taking frequent breaks to make sure I was alone.

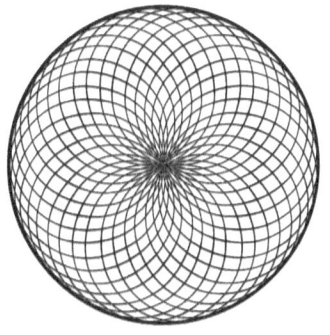

# loosen your sleeves

I climbed Emerald Mountain and stopped at the high ridge to take a final look at Unity. Under the peaceful night sky lifetimes of regrets were amplified in my head, and I wanted them silenced. I got out my plazer, aimed it towards my head, and vowed to keep on the opposite side of the old tunnel in my next incarnation.

"Damon."

Beside me stood Sutara, who appeared closer in age to my mother. She gently unclasped my fingers and took my plazer.

"I got what I wanted, and it was all for nothing. For seven incarnations I made it my mission to stop myself from inventing Harmony, but the Unitians don't want to be saved."

Sutara tossed my plazer over the cliff.

"How will I protect myself if I run into a pack of wild dogs?" I asked her.

"Run the other way."

"I can't run that fast," I said.

"Then *stop*."

"We're not really talking about wild dogs, are we?"

"What are we talking about then?"

"Why do you think we remember our incarnations?"

"To humble ourselves—and become less foolish." Sutara smiled. "Uncle Vivek said something similar. The older I get, the more like him I sound."

"There are worse people to sound like." I patted my chest. "How is your uncle? I'm thinking about visiting within the next year."

"He died two years ago, shortly after he broke his hip," Sutara said. "I believe he welcomed his death. He could no longer travel, and you know Uncle Vivek. Traveling was his life."

"Stagnation was probably more deadly to him than his injury."

"You knew him well."

"Did he suffer?"

"If he did, he never told me. Uncle Vivek was his usual self to the end. On his last night the priest came in to offer prayer, and he shooed him away." Sutara continued in a low, exaggerated pitch. "'Now I can die in peace, Suti, without all the metaphysical balderdash.'"

"That was a good impression of your uncle." I glanced at the dome.

"Do you know where you are now?" Sutara asked.

"On the high ridge, overlooking what used to be my—" *Something isn't right. If I were really here I wouldn't be talking to Sutara. And the Overseer—why did he allow me to speak? No Unitian ever got away with challenging him.* My whole body trembled when recognition struck. "I'm in reintegration."

"They captured you after you fired your weapon in Unity Hall."

"How do you know all this?"

"It happened all before," she said. "I contacted Tyrus. He's going to ask Wade to help free you. You can then return to the cabin."

"How do I know you're not part of reintegration?"

When Sutara wouldn't answer, I waved my finger at her. "If you're not real that means everything I experienced up to this moment was a delusion. Am I right?" I couldn't read her expression. "Tell me now!" Still no answer. I positioned myself at the very edge of the cliff and flapped my arms wildly. "I'm getting ready to fly!" I yelled and squawked.

"Damon, please"—she cried—"I cannot bear to see you do this again."

"Don't worry. I can't be harmed! Anything is possible in reintegration! When I hit the ground and die, I'll be reanimated for another round." I laughed, but it wasn't amusing. I felt as delusional as the time I talked to ghosts in the trainlets.

Sutara glared at me. "I have done all I can for you. My conscience is clear." She walked away.

I fell to my knees and screamed until I ran out of breath. Collapsing on my back, I recalled the time I lay dying in my fifth incarnation and how the sky looked the same as now. Like Shisa, Sutara never left. She sat nearby and listened as I continued to scream, cry, and admonish myself over my lifetimes of mistakes. Finally exhausting myself into silence, I sat up and probed her. "How can I be sure you're here?"

"You cannot."

"Is that why you refused to talk to me?"

"Each time I come to you, I feel weaker. I'm not sure I can visit you again."

I got to my feet. "How many times were we here together?"

"I can recall three."

"Three? I don't even remember one," I said, reflecting on my first incarnation. I had memories of killing Kai in my office after he'd told me about the Overseer's genocidal plans to spread Unity; however, I still couldn't remember actually doing it. It seemed as though my omni-consciousness was awakened in stages throughout each incarnation, and Sutara was somehow ahead of me.

"What happened?" I asked Sutara.

"You couldn't trust your memories. I tried to help, but I only made you more confused and angry." She got up and walked towards the cliff edge. "You jumped. Right from where I'm standing."

Sutara wept and I rushed over to hug her.

"I could not find you in this incarnation again."

"I probably died," I said. "Jumping from this height in reintegration can be as lethal as doing it for real." I held both of Sutara's hands. "Forgive me. You're the last person in this damaged world I'd want to hurt."

"After I saw you take your life, I dreamed about it for many nights. I thought we would never escape."

"This time, we will."

"Do you believe that?" she asked.

"No. But I'd rather *believe* I'm free than surrender my life to the Overseer." I took out my holologue, momentarily forgetting I was in reintegration. "I'm not sure if I exposed the location of the cabin."

"You didn't."

"Are you sure?"

"Your mother lived for several years after you died. Wilfrid and Michael watched after her."

I hurled my holologue and backpack off the cliff. "Might as well lighten my load."

"Will you try to deliver your message to your people again?"

"If I'm ever seen in Unity again, they'll throw me back into reintegration."

"If you want to free yourself from all of this, you will find another way."

"Considering there are infinite *another ways*, I'll eventually get it right."

Sutara took my hand and held it. We gazed up at the night sky and talked about Vivek's final years, laughing over how he died still viewing metaphysical explanations as nothing but balderdash.

Wade helped me up from the reintegration chamber. Tyrus was standing beside him.

"Did you find Flora?" I asked Tyrus.

"She passed out during the assembly and was taken to the hospital."

"When?"

"Right after you were dragged out."

I recalled a female screaming before one of the Unity Guards stunned me. "Do they know what's wrong with her?"

Tyrus placed his hand on my arm. "Don't worry. I was told she'll be okay. We'll come back for her later."

I nodded in agreement and looked at Wade. "Good to see you." I shook his hand.

"Now I know." He smiled.

"Know what?"

"There's no such thing as the scourge."

"Thanks for helping us."

"I'd help anyone who challenges the Overseer," Wade said. "Your brazen stand against him was inspiring—and enviable. Wish it had been me holding the plazer."

"Looks like I'm the one leading you into trouble for a change." I laughed.

"If firing a plazer into the air is the best you can do, you'll be easy to surpass."

I raised a brow. "Don't be so quick to assess your competition. You'll find I'm a much more formidable opponent."

"Can you engage in this tired show of masculinity at a later time?" Tyrus said. "The next night patrol will be around shortly."

"Stop taking the fun out of my rescue, Tyrus." I slapped his back. "Worse that could happen is we get killed."

Tyrus rolled his eyes. "You get more slocking obnoxious with each lifetime," he said and walked away.

Wade laughed. "What fun we would've had if we were in University together." He eyed me seriously when I didn't laugh along with him.

I smiled devilishly and followed Tyrus out.

"You were joking...right?" Wade followed. "Because I'm too young to die."

"Loosen your sleeves," I said. "Once we're out of Unity, we'll all live longer," I said.

We rendezvoused with a Striker at the rear access. Wearing a mask to avoid being recognized, he let us out without saying a word. We climbed up into the surrounding foothills, and I stopped for a final look at Unity. As much as I hated everything it stood for, a part of me would always exist within the dome. Many of my memories, dreams and desires were ghosts forever drifting within its utopian illusion.

"They say don't look back, but I never agreed with it either," Tyrus said. "If you don't look back, you don't learn."

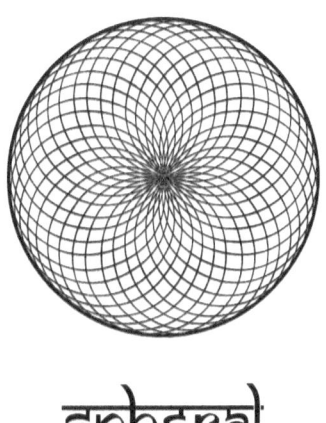

# spheral

The myriad of incarnations I had lived through placed me in every conceivable mode of existence. I was a murderer, a victim, a man of honor, a liar, a tyrant, and a savior. These discordant roles defined my experiences, but I had no idea who or what I was. I needed answers, and Sephroy was the only one who could give them to me.

"What's the hurry, Chap?" he asked as I pushed my way inside his trainlet.

"I want to know what the Six are, and you're going to tell me now." I removed the echoer from the desk drawer and thrust it in Sephroy's face. "And where did this technology come from? According to my metallurgical scanner, this metal doesn't exist."

Sephroy angrily tapped his cane on the floor. "Your level of understanding hasn't advanced enough for you to demand answers from me!"

"I'll go find Jall." I headed towards the door. "I'm sure he'll be willing to tell me about Sutara, and why she's contacting me."

"Sutara is contacting you?"

I smiled victoriously and turned to face Sephroy. "From the future."

"Jall made them. I managed to get all of them except for the one you had."

"Where did we arrive from?"

"That I can't tell you because no one knows. Spherals are born into the Outersphere, the realm of which I'm originally from. I was fortunate to witness the birth of this spheral." Sephroy smiled reflectively. "Its spore materialized in front of me, sang its song of creation and expanded into a spheral."

"Time...is relevant to sound," I said. "I spoke those words to myself as I lay dying after being attacked by bandits. I didn't understand what it meant—until now. Without sound, there would be no vibration, no movement...no expansion. Everything would be at a standstill. Time wouldn't exist."

Sephroy smiled and peered at me like Master Franklin when he heard me play the violin for the first time.

"Is Earth within a spheral?"

Sephroy pointed to the echoer. "Give it to me, and I'll show you."

I reluctantly handed the echoer to Sephroy. He pressed it against his chest and closed his eyes. Moments later, a beam of light shot out of the echoer and projected a hologram that looked exactly like the spherical torus I witnessed in so many of my visions. Contained in the center was the nucleus emitting specks of light that poured out like a fountain and connected to all the galaxies. Now that I had a chance to examine it longer, it somewhat reminded me of one of the plasma globes in the Nikola Tesla exhibit at the Alexandrian Repository.

Sephroy amplified one section of the spheral and pointed to a flashing red light. "Earth."

"I saw this in a vision I had while I was playing a difficult passage on my violin. It produced the most radiant chord I ever heard."

"It's the most beautiful music to our awareness. We've never been able to duplicate it," Sephroy said.

"The music of veneration flows from the highest sphere."

"A wise observation."

"My friend made it. He said it was superstitious nonsense. I have the urge to hike to the Himalayas and show him this projection to prove him wrong." I laughed.

Sephroy gestured towards the spheral. "How do you think he'd react if he knew this is the size of a spheral as seen through our vantage point in the Outersphere?"

I studied Sephroy for confirmation of what he said and he snickered.

I walked around the projection to grasp the magnitude of what I'd just learned. "He'd handle it better than I am."

Through my incarnations, I was able to comprehend the nature of man and why civilizations rise and fall, but this stretched beyond that limited perception. It took some time to grasp we were nothing but a small blip within a sea of light, contained, finite and observable by a race of beings outside our level of understanding and size.

"How do the Six fit into all of this?" I asked.

"Six collectors of experiences inhabit each spheral and coexist on worlds with sentient life forms. The knowledge they accumulate gets stored in the spheral membrane. As evolution nears, the Six are born geographically closer together, improving the chances of Union. When they join, they ring in Unison, and it can be heard from outside. Once every sample enters this stage, the spheral membrane vibrates. All the knowledge since the beginning of this evolutionary cycle is released in one pulse that feeds our main consciousness."

"You…eat us?"

"Not *you*!" Sephroy winced. "Your knowledge. And as we're eating, the spheral membrane absorbs the instructions for your next stage of evolution. Once the process is completed, the spheral swirls in two opposing directions, expanding until it separates, producing an exact duplicate of itself."

"It's like cell division!"

"It is cell division. The first spheral dies, and the energy it releases powers our worlds for a time that's incalculable by your present level of mathematical cognition."

"How is that possible? If I'm here, how can I exist on other worlds?"

Sephroy shook his head. "You're still thinking in subjective time. Beyond time exists a vein that ties you to your proto-awareness."

"COR!"

Sephroy covered his ears. "No need to shout, Chap. I'm in the room with you."

"You're talking about COR! If I can connect to the vein, can I identify all the Six?"

"You can, and Sutara already knows how. That's why I took her away long before you all had the chance to meet."

"Why?"

"Earth is the only world in this spheral that has yet to ring in Unison. For this reason, the unenlightened of my world wish to force you all together because they can't get your knowledge fast enough. The sages I followed taught me that evolution must occur naturally and without interference. The effect of progression for sentients who aren't ready is dangerous to both your universe and a large portion of the Outersphere."

"How dangerous?"

"If there is a defect in the specimen, it dies. It's not as if spherals grow on trees, Chap. They're rare in the Outersphere. If they cease to exist, so will we. I had to stop Jall and the rest of our gluttonous leaders from setting a dangerous precedent. My intervention saved this spheral, which may have already been destroyed if I hadn't stopped them. For my insubordination I was rebuked for going against my orders, and an inquisition was scheduled. I was so angry I refused to attend. By the time my senses returned, it was too late. When we're within this spheral, we can only stay inside for the equivalent of one-hundred Earth years before our individual pattern becomes indistinguishable from the rest of the matter in the universe."

"You can never go back?"

"Only a miracle can help me get back, and I don't believe in miracles." Sephroy narrowed his eyes. "Did Sutara really contact you from the future?"

"Yes."

"In how many of your rotations?"

"In all of them I can recall."

"Did you ever meet her—in person?"

"In my last incarnation."

"She's doing it to me again."

"Doing what?"

"Trying to get me to believe in miracles." Sephroy sat on the chair behind his desk. "Sutara is the most powerful of the Six within this spheral because she lived the most varied personalities."

"How can we be varied when we repeat the same life?"

"There you go with your linear sense of time again. After death, your present organism duplicates itself and recycles, which is why you can recall your past rotations. The newly created organism then divides in two, and a new individual is born to interpret the world. The data of your combined experiences is stored within your proto-awareness. The more varied your lifecycle, the higher the grade of wisdom you acquire."

I cupped my hands around the spheral. "But that's all dependent on your willingness to let us continue." I slapped my hands together. "All it would take for our annihilation is one strike from a hand in your world. We're at your mercy."

Sephroy shut down the hologram and handed me the echoer. "You're only aware of your size if you have something to compare yourself with. Size is nothing more than another subjective perception."

"Why did Jall give this to me?" I asked.

"He invented it to speed up Union between the Six. Think of it as a COR to COR communication device."

"Sutara can already do that without the echoer."

"The miracle I spoke of in your last rotation happened a very long time ago. Two Sixes, from different species, had a child who was born in the exact moment another Six passed away. This child gained knowledge from both species. We've never witnessed such a joining before, and when I first laid eyes on her, she was the closest thing to a miracle I'd ever witnessed. Such a sweet little wonder—the girl with two worlds in her mind. I used to sing that to her before she went to sleep." Sephroy pointed his cane at me. "She was your daughter, Chap."

"Shishandi?"

Sephroy's eyes widened.

"I've seen her in a vision—after Jall gave me the echoer. Is Sutara a future incarnation of Shishandi?"

"She is."

"What happens when the Six meet?"

"Union is a rare event. Spherals take long to erupt, which is why many on my world want to speed up your meeting."

"What do we get in return?"

"Everlasting life in our realm, where you'll still be gaining knowledge from your extensions who'll continue to exist in this reality. When the next evolutionary age begins, a new band will materialize, and your upgraded physical existences will continue to acquire knowledge until the next stage of evolution."

I asked Sephroy all the questions I had about the Ancients. I inquired how long ago the events occurred and he couldn't answer as he'd lost track of time long before the Great Cataclysm, which he refused to discuss. "They even had their calendars all wrong back then," he told me. "I was so confused, I stopped trying to remember the age of this spheral. There's no reason to remember." He opened a drawer and removed a gold ring and examined it. "Not knowing how much time has passed makes my sentence easier to serve."

"Why should I look forward to joining your world? Your people don't seem any better than us. What they're doing to you is cruel."

"Given the choice again, I wouldn't have gone against my orders. I witnessed the birth of this spheral and got too attached. It's a hazard in my vocation. I could've backed down from this assignment, but the opportunity to witness your development was too difficult to resist." He sighed. "At least I stopped them from destroying you."

"If your people are anything like us, they'll try again."

"That is possible."

"Do you know who the last Six is?"

"Yes, but I won't reveal her to you."

"Her?"

"That's all I'm giving you. Enjoy the happy life you've created for yourself. It will remain that way as long as the Six don't rush to Union."

Although the answers Sephroy had given me led to more questions, I left his 'let with a new understanding of time. My sons would continue to exist. Somewhere beyond this incarnation, I was still teaching Aaron how to play violin and attending James's soccer matches. Holly was still making me a tray of pastitso on Firstday nights, and I was still clashing with Maestro Manolis over repertoire selections. I laughed to myself as I recalled the Mozart versus Chopin duels with Manolis and appreciated how the universe never failed to shine its light over my darkest moments.

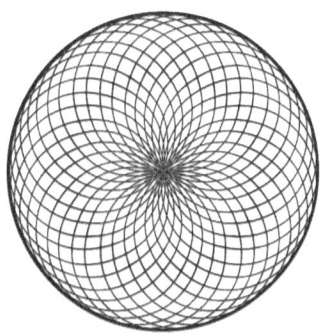

# the sixth

While working on my message to deliver to Unity, I was interrupted by a knock at the door. I opened it and was stunned to see Mother holding a female infant. Standing beside her was a friend whom I hadn't seen since my sixth incarnation.

"Vivek!" I excitedly hugged him.

Mother gazed wide-eyed at Vivek and then at the infant in her arms. "Is this Sutara?"

Vivek stepped back, bewildered.

"Yes, but this one is the youngest version I've met in person." I slapped the side of Vivek's arm. "What brings you to my side of the tunnel?" I asked in Tibindi.

"Your emissary guided me here. He told me this is where I would find you."

"I don't have an emissary. Did he tell you his name?"

"Sephroy. He told me you were the man I seek."

"Is he here with you?" I stepped outside and had a look around.

"We parted company at the top of the mountain. He said he did not appreciate crowds."

"What made you come looking for me?"

"Suti was dying. No one knew what was wrong. She became very weak and had difficulty breathing. I believed she was going to die. One night I fell asleep with her in my arms and in a dream witnessed you save her life. You placed your hands over her head, and a white aura surrounded the both of you."

"I had a similar dream a little over thirty days ago. How did you get here so fast?"

"Our journey took far longer than that."

Sutara offered her hand to me and I picked her up. She felt slightly heavier than in my dream.

"Damon," she said with perfect diction.

"I must have traveled back in time during my vision." I brushed a few delicate strands of hair away from Sutara's eyes. "Just as you traveled back in time to save me."

Vivek's eyes sprung open.

"How did you find Sephroy?" I asked.

"I had another dream. Suti came to me as a grown woman and told me I must find you if I want to save her. She said your healing was only temporary and that she was still dying. She showed me where to find the man with the walking stick who would lead us to you and that her father would also be here. Is he?"

"Technically, he is."

Vivek creased his forehead.

"This is going to take some explaining," I said.

"And the only person who could make sense of this conveniently ran off," Mother added.

"Sephroy can't run."

"I thought he was against Union?"

"He is, but Vivek just told me that Sutara is dying." I laid my hand over her head. "Maybe that's why he brought her here." My body heated up as it always did when I healed.

"She looks perfectly healthy to me."

A black aura surrounded Sutara, and I quickly handed her to Mother.

"I have to find Sephroy," I said. "He couldn't have gotten that far."

"What's wrong?" Mother hugged Sutara, cupping the back of her head. "You look scared."

"Don't take your eyes off her until I get back."

"I won't." Mother kissed Sutara's cheek.

I turned to Vivek. "We'll continue this later."

I caught up with Sephroy halfway up the ridge. "You fought this from happening, and now you bring her to me?"

Sephroy halted. "Jall was right to give you the echoer when he did." He stopped walking and jabbed his cane into the ground to prevent himself from falling. "He's attempting to save the spheral."

"I thought he wanted to speed up evolution?"

Sephroy quickly tapped the ground with his cane. "He did and still does! I make no promises you'll still be here once Union takes place."

"Then why now?"

"Seeing Sutara again helped remind me of something Jall and I overlooked when we studied the spheral: Balance. Not just in the evolutionary process as a whole, but between the Six as well. As Sutara progresses forward in her rotations, the five of you lag behind her. The burden of knowledge drawn from her is wearing her down, and she's close to dying—permanently." Sephroy held his lower back and grunted. "I'll never make it back to the old tunnel."

I helped him to a nearby tree trunk.

"I didn't think I was doing any harm." Sephroy planted his cane and sat. "The worse I thought would happen was this spheral would weaken, sending out less energy. While we would be denied a little extra sustenance, you would all be permitted to evolve naturally. I was arrogant enough to believe I could rejoin you when the time came for Union, but the process is irreversible, so I thought." He pointed to the sky. "The divine will is stronger than mortal interference."

My sense of familiarity was renewed as I examined Sephroy's face. "Did you ever say that to me before?"

"Not in this rotation, Chap." He paused to smile as though recalling a fond memory. "But none of that matters now. You must all join in Unison before Sutara dies. She doesn't have time to wait for the rest of you to catch up."

"What will happen if we don't join?"

"When her life force can't absorb the energy any longer, the spheral will stop evolving and die. And a dying spheral is messy. It will swell until—" He clutched the side of his head. "The explosion will be so vast, the aftershock will destroy everything, including the portion of the Outersphere from where I originated." Sephroy stared at me, his eyes filling with tears. "I'll be responsible for an incalculable amount of deaths."

"How much time do we have?" I asked.

"I don't believe Sutara can endure beyond this incarnation."

"Who's the Sixth?"

Sephroy handed me the echoer. "Ask your question, and you'll get your answer."

I closed my eyes and placed the echoer against my chest as he had done when he produced the spheral. *Who is the Sixth?* I asked silently, but nothing came.

"You must have enough faith to know the answer is already within you," Sephroy said.

I opened my eyes. "Faith isn't my strength."

"Union must be now—if you're to succeed."

"Every time I believed in something, I ended up destroying all those who were closest to me." I tried to hand him the echoer. "Who's the Sixth? Tell me."

"Your carnal interpretation of faith and belief is what holds you back. For a successful Union, doubts, fears, and worries must cease so you can connect with the primordial reality within you. Without faith in yourself—Union will surely fail."

Sephroy leered at me. He dug his cane into the ground and hoisted himself to his feet. "Wretched specimen!" He seized the echoer. "Your meager supply of wisdom wouldn't feed my people through one millisecond of your time! Go home! Everything will soon be obliterated, along with your memory of the destruction that will follow as the result of your dereliction!"

I snatched the echoer back, placed it against my chest and closed my eyes, focusing internally on my question. Words kept materializing and I finally connected to my simple desire to make everything okay for myself and everyone. That desire expanded into a pure awareness, unbound by the physical boundaries of mind. An electromagnetic sensation pulsed and swirled at the top of my head.

"The Sixth!" Sephroy yelled.

I opened my eyes to a projection of a familiar face. "Signy?" I stared at her image, surprised I had forgotten her. "I haven't seen her since my first incarnation. She should be easy to find. Her village is on this side of the old tunnel." I went to hand him the echoer.

He held up his palm. "Got no use for it."

I placed it in my pocket. "Come back with me. If Union happens, you should be there."

"I'll be the first of my kind to see a spheral's birth and rebirth." He sighed. "But my name won't be recorded for this momentous occasion. I've long been forgotten."

"I'll make sure you're remembered."

Sephroy peered at me. "Jall didn't think you had the strength, but I told him otherwise."

"What did you tell him?"

"That you'd be the one to move things forward…at the right time." He dug the tip of his cane into the dirt to balance himself. "However, I'm still not certain that time is now."

I crossed my arms. "Lucky for you I'm not a *wretched specimen*."

"We'll have to wait for Union to determine whether that's true."

# old mentor

I traveled to Signy's village and approached a group of children playing hide and seek near the corn field. A boy ran out to me from the cover of the stalks.

"Sorry. I didn't see you," he said.

"I'm looking for Signy. Can you take me to her?"

"Does she know you?"

"I'm an old friend."

The boy led me to Signy's hut, and I was stunned when she opened the door. She was barely past her sixteenth year. I had forgotten the last time we met was almost twenty years into the future.

"Hi Signy," I said.

"Have we met?"

"Name's Damon." I forced my way in and pulled out the echoer. "We must speak privately."

Signy ran to the table, grabbed a knife and thrust the blade at me. "My parents will be back shortly! If you don't leave here now, I'll—" Speechless as she cast her eyes upon the spheral I had just projected, she slowly lifted her arm in its direction. "I've seen this before—in a dream." She approached and waved her hand through the spheral.

The boy who'd been standing outside the door, came inside, his mouth wide open. "How did you get a whole planet in here?"

"It's a light projection."

"It's beautiful." Signy looked at me. "Do you know what it is?"

"Our home." I expanded the portion of space that housed Earth and pointed to the red flickering light.

The boy snickered. "We're so tiny."

"You said you came here to show this to me. Why?" Signy asked.

"Your presence is needed."

"For what?"

I nodded at the spheral. "To keep the lights within shining."

Signy gawked at me. "Why me? I don't know anything about this."

"You're one of six beings who helps this all continue."

"He's only joking with you," the boy said, not taking his eyes off the spheral. "Girls can't be heroes."

"This one is." I turned to Signy. "You once told me you dreamed of exploring the world. Those weren't dreams, Signy—they're your memories."

"How could I tell you anything if I never met you?"

"I understand how this all sounds, but the Six must reunite soon. If we don't"—I gestured to the spheral—"all this will be gone."

"I never even left this village. How do you expect me to help?"

Signy's parents hurried into the room. They froze when they saw the hologram.

"What is that?" Signy's father asked.

502

"It's all right," Signy told him.

I shut off the projection and handed Signy the echoer.

"Don't touch that!" Signy's father got in between us. "It might hurt you."

"It won't hurt her," I said.

"Father, please. I've been seeing this in my dreams ever since I can remember, and I want to know what it means."

"They're just dreams," he said.

"No. They're not." Signy took the echoer.

"Only we can operate it," I said. "I'll leave you alone while you ask your questions. I'll be outside when you're ready."

"Ready for what?" Signy's mother rushed over and put her arm around her daughter.

Signy examined the echoer. "Do I talk to it?"

"Not with words."

"With what?"

"Desire."

I took the boy outside and told him about the spheral and Sephroy. After I'd finished he crossed his arms and said, "I wouldn't have believed him."

"I didn't either, but I learned everything is not always as it appears."

Signy ran outside her hut, and both her parents followed, wearing the same expressions as when they first witnessed the projection.

"I remember." Signy hugged me. "It's so good to see you again." She handed me the echoer. "How about the others? Am I the last?"

The boy gazed open-mouthed at Signy.

"Five remember." I patted the boy's head. "We're still waiting for one."

During our walk back to the cabin I got to know Signy's father and was able to put his mind at ease. I explained to him the importance of us being together and his fatherly pride emerged.

"I always knew there was something special about Signy. Ever since she was a child, she talked ahead of her years. Were you like that?"

"Yes, except my talents weren't appreciated. Only my two mentors realized my potential."

"You're lucky to have had them."

Signy smiled at me. "Do you agree with me now?"

"About what?"

"The Sacred Oath is our enemy. It rules us through our complacency and blind loyalty—"

"It never gives up until we surrender to it, and most of us do." I stopped walking. "Master Franklin said that to me when I was a boy. How did you know?"

Signy pointed to herself and smiled.

"You're...Master Franklin?" I asked.

"Were." She giggled, and her parents stared at her in shock.

"Why did you have a black aura around you? I tried to heal you, but it didn't work."

"You couldn't add more life to me because that would have affected my present cycle."

"How much do you remember?" I asked.

"Only the few memories the echoer showed me. I remember you yelling at me after I disappointed you about a camping trip. And then you played a song for me on your—"

"Violin."

"I was very moved by your performance." Signy's expression reminded me of the way Master Franklin looked at me after the competition.

"That night I had a dream of you playing on a crowded stage. The theater got all dark, and this bright light shined on you. You looked at me and told me to help you or you'd die again. I then saw you take your life by jumping off a tall building."

"You saved me." I took Signy's hand and recalled the time I tried to kill myself after Headmaster had refused my entrance to the master's apprentice school. "But one thing I don't understand. How did you find me in your new incarnation? The chance of our meeting seems almost impossible."

"I had a dream the night before we met. I got up from my bed, grabbed my longbow and headed for the woods. I passed a thicket and came across a glade and a large dog charged me. It leapt into the air and I shot it through the heart. There was a bright glow of light, it cleared, and a woman who called herself Sutara appeared and told me that once I awoke to go to the glade. I asked her why, and she said I was to meet someone and help them on their journey, but I wasn't to mention I knew about our meeting ahead of time. It wasn't hard to do. When I realized you were from Dome Dungeon, it was easy to keep my distance."

I bowed. "Thank you, Wise Mentor."

"You don't have to thank me. I owed you."

"For what?"

"Reminding me of what I had given up because I thought winning was impossible." She held my hand. "We won."

"We won't know that until all of us are together."

"We won where it counts."

When we returned to the cabins, I continued working on my message. Vivek joked about telepathically delivering it through COR, which gave me the idea of using the implants as receivers. I only had one chance at transmitting to them before Unity Forces changed all the security codes, so I had to get it right on my first try.

On the day of the broadcast, I nervously rehearsed my message in front of Tyrus and Wade. They hurried outside as I started my fourth pass, I assumed it was their way of telling me I was ready. Looking into the optic of my hologue I began transmission.

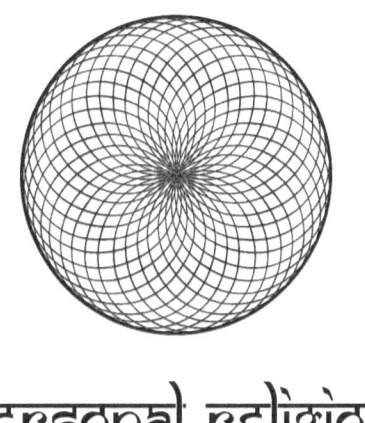

# personal religion

## PC 1327-130th day
## Message to Unitians

*Don't be alarmed by my voice in your head. This message is transmitting through your implant, so a trip to a curate isn't necessary; this isn't a malfunction. While performing a system upgrade, one of the purple sleeves forgot to log out. I used his clearance and created an access gate that permits me to speak with you. Miraculously, the codes never changed through eight incarnations of which I'm aware. You'll no longer hear my voice after today as Unity Forces are now aware of my invasion. They won't find me because I'm a deleted file in the Unitian database, long forgotten but not silenced. By the time they stop my broadcast, my message will be delivered.*

*During my past seven incarnations, I attempted to stop myself from inventing technology used by the Corporate Hierarchy to enslave you. I succeeded, but if that were my only objective, I wouldn't be here, talking to you. Who I am requires a new definition. Since destruction inevitably follows definitions, I prefer to remain unlabeled and undefined. I have no expectations you'll believe one word of my message. The Unitian quagmire spread from the virus of belief, so I encourage your mistrust. Go to your window and look outside. Each visible face will prove you're not alone in your doubts. Verify what you hear is real. If I'm a worthy messenger, you'll distinguish yourself from a system run by a small group of men who've placed themselves as gods above you. To tune me out, simply keep your faith and trust in the Corporate Hierarchy. My voice will eventually fade, and your life will continue on as it always has. The choice is yours.*

*I spent all my lifetimes attempting to understand my experiences, and the answers I got only led to more questions. I've been called a prophet and a savior, but I'm neither. I'm only a messenger sent by something I can't define, wouldn't want to define, and couldn't define even if I so desired. Whatever it is that guides me, I trust it with my life. This is my personal religion, which is natural to all of us but presents itself in a way that we can understand only as individuals. By religion, I refer to connecting to the undefined that presents itself as an internal light, so bright, and so powerful that it opened all my senses to the true reality that is nature, of which we're a part. The only place worthy of trust and reverence is here. When we detach from this sanctum, we relinquish our trust to rulers and tyrants, distancing ourselves from what we truly are...beings filled with this vast, immeasurable consciousness of eternal light. From within this light, our knowledge flows out like a fountain throughout our universe and never dies. You don't need to live eight lifetimes to connect to this truth. The purple sleeves and the Overseer use your fears to keep you trapped inside the dome, which has become your dungeon. Once you loosen the chains that keep you shackled in fear, they can no longer bind you.*

*If you're still listening, you're ready to leave. As an individual, you must decide what kind of life you want to live. Being taken care of within the walls of Unity may keep you secure, but you've given up too much as a consequence. Safety is an illusion. It isn't any more real than the Overseer's claims at godhood. Life is hard, filled with challenges, heartaches, death, and failures, and I lived through them all. The rewards make it all worthwhile. The first cry from a baby born from the womb of its mother, the look on the face of a Unitian who tastes freedom for the first time, and a friend who sacrificed his life to save mine—these are only a few examples that made me listen and trust my intuition.*

*I won't tell you to leave Unity. That will have to be up to you to decide. I can only tell you—from my personal experience—I'm lucky to have a family that would've been denied to me had I grown up in Unity. You all have the right to be born from your parents, get married, and raise your own children. This is your natural right, should you want to exercise it. The sound of nature is within all of you, and it's the true harbinger of Unity. Listen, and you will hear it for yourselves. Leave your personal dungeon, and contemplate the world with your own eyes. Only then will you understand the true meaning of Unity. And Flora, if you're listening, I'm waiting for you. If you remember, you'll know where to find me.*

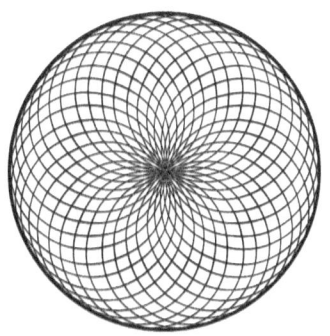

# reunion

Mother pounded on my cabin door. "You must come now! Tyrus collapsed!"

I ran outside as Sephroy was helping Tyrus up.

"He's okay…for now," Sephroy said.

"What happened?" I asked.

"I'm not sure," Tyrus said. "I was overcome by an intense pain in my head. I must've blacked out."

"Were you sick this early in your previous incarnations?"

"I did have symptoms…but not this debilitating."

I turned to Sephroy. "Did you heal him?"

Sephroy dug his cane into the ground and sighed. "I did."

"Why couldn't you help Flora?"

"I don't have a limitless supply of life, and Tyrus wasn't as far gone as Flora." Sephroy winced in pain. "My body is broken because I gave too much of myself to my wife, and she died anyway. Seeing what those savage dogs did to her, I couldn't stop myself. I couldn't bear seeing her torn to pieces." He tapped his cane in succession as he said, "I kept giving and giving and giving."

Sephroy lost his balance. Tyrus and I held on to him and led him to the cabin.

"I gave until my body withered into this useless pile of matter. I had to stop healing for years to regain some of my strength."

"I hope I didn't take too much from you," Tyrus said.

"It'll take years for me to recover, providing we have enough of them left. No Six has ever been healed before a Union. What I did was trickery. I've never seen nature successfully tricked, but I had to try because I started all this."

"When will we know if it worked?" Tyrus asked.

"When Union happens…or doesn't."

Twelve days following the delivery of my message, I returned to the cabins with Wilfrid, Genevieve and Michael. Flora still hadn't shown up, and Sephroy doubted she'd arrive on her own. I shared his concern and had Tyrus contact one of his protégés still loyal to him. He received no response, and I decided to go after Flora myself. Three days before I was to leave for Unity, I was monitoring the security holoscreens as I normally had when Flora appeared near the top of the waterfall. I sprang from my chair and ran outside yelling like a madman. "She remembers! She remembers!"

Mother rushed out of the cabin. I picked her up, swung her around, and put her back down. "Gather the others. Flora's here." I ran all the way up the path. I got to the ridge near the waterfall and Flora cupped her mouth and cried.

"You remember!" I said.

She ran to me, and we embraced. "All these years I thought I had an overactive imagination until I saw you in Unity Hall." Flora stepped back. "The guards took you away before you could speak, and I started to think I was crazy—until I heard your message through my implant." She laughed. "When I heard the sound of your voice I wasn't afraid anymore. I didn't stop until I got here."

Flora and I walked to the ridge and she paused to gaze at the cabins.

"I still can't believe I'm here," she said.

"Took me a couple of incarnations to get used to it."

"After you died, Kai and I performed your sacred burning together. He decided not to return to Unity and came to New Athenia with me. I found a record-keeping job at the repository, and I traveled to many of the places you mentioned in your journal. I didn't see too much of Kai. He kept to himself and spent most of his time volunteering at the hospital. He died ten years later of a brain tumor."

"You read my journal?" I asked.

"You gave me the code—A5673."

"Good memory."

"You had me repeat it over twenty times."

"Let's not exaggerate now."

"Hope you're less paranoid in this cycle."

I smiled. "I read through your journal as well...twice through." I placed my arm around her, and Flora leaned her head against my shoulder.

"Guess we don't have any more secrets," she said.

"No more secrets."

We lingered in silence for a while. All we'd been through finally brought us here, to a place where words were no longer necessary. I looked at Flora, sensing she felt something similar. At least I hoped she did.

We approached the cabins and everyone came out to greet Flora. Understanding the significance of this day, they formed a circle around us. I was uncertain if this Union would move us forward, but it no longer mattered. The Six were together. Wilfrid, Signy, and Tyrus joined us in the center of the circle, and Mother handed Sutara to me.

"Torrin and I knew great things would follow you." Mother kissed my cheek, and went to stand near Sephroy.

Sutara reached up and put her hand over my head. I felt a warm vibration as I lay my hand over Flora's head. She repeated the gesture with Tyrus who touched Signy, who then touched Wilfrid. As Wilfrid rested his hand on Sutara's head, a loud hum echoed all around, then a stream of light shot out from us and rained back down to form a surrounding translucent veil of light.

"It's beautiful." Mother cried.

"I see with my own eyes, and I still cannot believe," Vivek said.

"I know what you mean," Wade said.

"What is that?" Mother motioned to the sky where a massive golden helix had just materialized.

"Six begin, Six alone, Six united," I said.

Tyrus fell to the ground. "I can't hold on!"

"You must!" Sephroy yelled. "If you stop it now, everything ends now!"

"I can't breathe! The air is too heavy!" Tyrus was panting heavily.

I handed Sutara to Flora, got down on my knees and placed my hand over his head. "Don't give up on us. We've come too far to give up now."

Tyrus pushed me away. "It's too much information! I can't contain it!"

"Slow down your breathing. Just let it all through without fighting."

Tyrus screamed in pain, I called for the others to join me and we all placed our hands on top of his head.

"Everything is moving," Tyrus said. "I can't make it stop!"

Sutara waved her arm and Flora moved her closer to Tyrus. She rested her small hand on his face, and his breathing slowed. He smiled at Sutara and said, "Maybe you can show the others how it's done."

"Looks as though you have competition, Nomad," Wilfrid said.

I helped Tyrus up as the helix descended and merged with the light around us, bathing us in its brilliant golden light of knowledge that we echoed back. Six remember; this is our always from which we're a part. We are *Potential*, made available to all sentient life. We're always here, open to all possibilities, without judgment, and without fear of what's to come. We're also the expression of that potential and the guardians of experience. From every conceivable and inconceivable direction, we're with you, always present, always ready to transmit and receive. We resonate eternal in Unison. One light, one mind, one sound…so it is recorded for all to see.

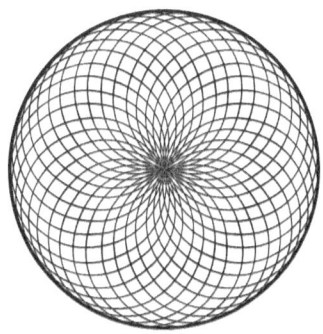

# STORY BEHIND UNISON
## THE SPHERAL - BOOK ONE

This is the second version of *Unison* that you've either finished reading or skipped to this page before doing so. Either which way, thanks for buying my book. I had originally written *Unison* as a screenplay. Little did I know it would evolve into an entire series. Luckily for me, I went in ignorant. I have a short attention span and finishing projects had always been difficult for me. I was pushed out of my comfort zone from the first draft until the publication date. The challenges continued even after that, and there were many times I had to remind myself why I was doing this. My answer was always the same:

*It's about the story…*

I had to take my ego out of the equation to make *Unison* the best it could be.

Before I started writing novels, I was primarily a screenwriter. To kick start my career, I went to LA for a screenwriting class and left disheartened when I learned most screenplays get rewritten. Not wanting to put all my energy into a project that would more than likely get changed, I decided to write a novel and then try to sell the story to a producer. At least I'd get the story out my way first! However, something shifted during the process. Writing the book became more important than the idea of selling it as a screenplay. I wasn't writing for the purpose of selling a story; I was writing with the pure intention of telling one. I was hooked!

### EVOLUTION OF A WRITER

*Unison* was originally entitled, *The Cabin*. It was about a man named Damon, who relived his life, and his lover from a previous lifetime, who arrived to arrest him for assassinating their leader. There was only one setting: a cabin in the woods. As I began to plot the story, I realized I needed something more to fill the pages. Novels are a lot longer than screenplays! I started to build what I at first thought were sub-plots. When I introduced the echoer, a talisman from another screenplay, the story changed direction. I was forced to ask more questions, and as the plotting continued, the story expanded to where the screenplay I'd taken the echoer from led me to develop the story into a series! The main plot points of *The Cabin* shifted as Damon's journey expanded, and the cast increased from four to over twenty! After I had developed the mythology and constructed the story world, I changed the title to *Unison*. I also included some of my own visions in the story. While it's fiction, the spheral is something that I see as highly possible and likely. Explaining it was one of the most challenging aspects of writing the book.

## MIRRORING DAMON

Damon is the most complex character I'd ever written as he does things I could never even imagine myself doing. To make him real I had to tap into the darkest parts of my mind. At first, I didn't think anyone would sympathize with him because of the selfish choices he makes. How could he possibly redeem himself in my eyes? As I continued to write Damon's story, I noticed I was growing alongside him as he suffered the consequences of every bad decision he made. If I had a difficult day, I felt dishonest writing about his personal growth and would take a break. I'd journal, introspect, and go on long walks. After I had cleared up whatever issue was bothering me, I'd return to the story and know exactly where I had to go. Writing developed into another form of meditation, and by the time I finished writing *Unison*, Damon had surpassed me. I see him as the potential of what I could become. As I wrote *The Sixth*, the second book in the series, Damon continued to grow from his experiences, demonstrating that evolution is an ongoing process. Through this understanding, I was deeply humbled.

## VISIONARY FICTION

When I was almost ready to publish, I discovered there was a genre that dealt with my style of writing: visionary fiction. It was like finding my home. I soon met other writers of the genre, and together we formed the Visionary Fiction Alliance.

After over twenty years of writing, I'm finally committing to calling myself an author. I hope I live long enough to hit my goal of writing one-hundred books!

Love and light,
Eleni

# UNITIAN LEXICON

**Adjudicator** - judge

**Chosen** - the Overseer's ten advisors.

**Confessor** - lawyer

**COR** (consciously obtained reflections) - extra brainwave Damon detected in his head. He postulates that it enables him to recall his incarnations.

**Corporate Hierarchy** - ruling class made up of the Overseer, Chosen and purple sleeves.

**Crail** - vehicles that traverse Unity on single tracks.

**Crailers** - prostitutes who service men in crails.

**Curate** - operators who run reintegration sessions.

**Curative implant** - In addition to receiving the curative signal, it's also used to track and identify Unitians.

**Curative signal** - signal transmitted to the implant that keeps Unitians from succumbing to the scourge.

**Emergence day** - Unitian's birth date:
Damon 1300-333-1M
- ◆ 1300 - calendar year
- ◆ 333 - day of the year
- ◆ 1M - sex and order in which the baby was born.

**Escape** - hallucinatory drug used for religious ceremonies, recreation and suicide requests.

**Essential shop** - all purpose stores in Unity.

**Exploiters** - reporters

**First** - favored protégé of a purple sleeve or the Overseer.

**Harmony** - signal transmitted to the curative implant that dissipates negatively stored emotions.

**Holologue** - wrist computer with a delivery optic.

**Holoscreen** - public display

**Liberation Pulse** - A suicide signal sent to the curative implant when a Unitian is deemed nonessential.

**Nonessential** - A status that's given to Unitians who have either fulfilled their purpose or are a threat to the Corporate Hierarchy.

**Overmaidens** - The Overseer's wives. They also work in the nursery and tend to sick children in the hospital.

**PC** - Post Cataclysm

**Pleasure room** - gambling facility

**Prime Wisdom** - supreme godhead made up of all deceased Overseers and is said to be channeled by the currently reigning Overseer.

**Progenitor** - parent frequency of COR.

**Protégé** - purple sleeve's apprentice. (see rank)

**Quiescent neurogenic encoder** - transmits the Harmony signal to the curative implants upon detecting negative emotions and eliminates them.

**Rank**
- ◆**Overseer** - supreme ruler of Unity
- ◆**Purple sleeve** - master class
- ◆**Maroon sleeve** - professional class (only those nominated by the Chosen make it to this level).
- ◆**Blue sleeve** - first tier professional class
- ◆**Yellow sleeve** - artist class
- ◆**Green sleeve** - security class
- ◆**Orange sleev**e - service class

**Reintegration** - sophisticated virtual reality mind control programming used to keep Unitians in line.

**Request for Death** - for Unitians who wish to end their lives. If approved, they are given a lethal injection of escape.

**Sacred burning ceremony** - Unitian funeral rites.

**Satiation center** - dining and recreation facilities organized by rank.

**Scourge** - a sickness that infects Outsiders and makes them go insane. It's believed to be a residual effect left over from the Great Cataclysm.

**Sleeve worshipper** - Unitians who slavishly follow their mentors.

**Slock** - Unitian all-purpose swear word.

**Strikers** - rebel group seeking to free Unity.
- ◆Architects - those who orchestrate rebel strikes
- ◆Appointers - tap the undertakers
- ◆Undertakers - those who execute the strikes

**Undermaiden** - women in the sexual service industry. They work in nightclubs and restaurants and are considered a step up from a crailer.

**Unity** - dome city with a theocratic/corporate governance. Citizens are genetically engineered and organized by color rank to perform specific tasks. (see rank)

.

**Unity Hall** - formal meeting place for assemblies.

**Unitian Oath**
Together we Unite in Unity. Together we fight to keep alive the flames of Unity. Together we live for our Unity. Together we die for our Unity. We are one in Unity. I am Unity.

# OUTSIDE THE DOME

**Ancients** - all humans who lived before the Great Cataclysm.

**Callias Zane** - founder of New Athenia.

**Deathlands** - all territory beyond the beacons believed to be contaminated by poison left after the Great Cataclysm.

**Echoer** - a talisman believed to allow communication beyond time.

**Dome Dungeon** - what Unity is referred to by the Outsiders.

**Forgotten times** - all aspects of human civilization pre-dating the Great Cataclysm.

**Great Cataclysm** - A catastrophic event that destroyed most of Earth's civilizations. No one agrees as to how it happened.

**Hebrab** - language of the lands of the Ancient bible.

**Knosian** - language of New Athenia.

**Lands of the Ancients bible** - All countries mentioned in the bible.

**Littlefield** - Wilfrid's village founded by his grandfather.

**Middle Crest** - community hidden deep within the Himalayas.

**New Athenia** - utopian labyrinth city on the eastern side of the old tunnel that was constructed with an indestructible material.

**Old tunnel** - tunnel built by the Ancients.

**Outsiders** - all the tribes that live on the outside.

**Tibindi** - language spoken by tribes in the Himalayan regions.

**Trainlets** - subway cars in the old tunnel used as inns for travelers.

# UNISON CAST SHEET

## Unitians

**Damon 1300-333-1M**
A charismatic psychological engineer who learns he's reliving his life.

**Flora 1309-119-24F**
The rebellious Unity Guard Damon loves.

**Holly 1306-111-3F**
A woman who escapes Unity after she's selected to be an Overmaiden.

**Lidian 1299-201-11M**
Socially awkward maroon sleeve and a growing embarrassment to his mentor, Master Tyrus.

**Master Franklin 1273-014-8F**
Damon's childhood mentor.

**Master Kai 1277-103-4M**
Member of the Chosen and Damon's mentor.

**Master Theodore 1264-02-8M**
Damon's violin instructor.

**Master Tyrus 1268-23-3M**
Member of the Chosen and favored to be the next Overseer.

**Wade 1300-099-33M**
Damon's rebellious friend who dreams of life outside of Unity.

# Outsiders

**Genevieve**
A widow from Littlefield who does her best to raise her restless son, Michael.

**Jall**
A mysterious drifter who gives Damon the echoer, a talisman believed to allow communication beyond time.

**Michael**
A boy from Littlefield who dreams of growing up and traveling the world.

**Old Woman**
A Unitian defector who lives in a remote mountain cabin.

**Sephroy**
A grungy man who runs the trainlets in the old tunnel.

**Shisa**
Old Woman's golden-haired dog.

**Sutara**
A woman who enters Damon's dreams throughout his incarnations. She wants him to remember a memory he's been suppressing, but Damon is unsure if she's real or an illusion.

**Signy**
A huntress who is an expert with a longbow.

**Torrin**
Old Woman's husband, and a Unitian defector who was a member of the Chosen when he left Unity.

**Vivek**

Enigmatic mystic and skeptic caught between his desire for the modernity in New Athenia and his home in Middle Crest, a small enclave in the Himalayas.

**Wilfrid**

Elder of Littlefield and a mystic who reads cards.

# UNISON FACTS

◆ The opening line, "Time is relative to sound," came to me while meditating.

◆ Damon's eight incarnations were inspired by Shri Ganesha, who spent eight lifetimes overcoming his eight weaknesses: envy, conceit, illusion, greed, anger, lust, attachment and arrogance.

◆ Damon was modeled after Nikola Tesla for his imagination and method of invention.

◆ The underlying theme of the book was inspired by Plato's Cave.

◆ Damon's nickname, Nomad, happened completely by chance.

◆ Damon's fountain of light experience happened to me in real life while meditating.

◆ Sephroy was intended to be a minor character. He forced himself into a bigger role, and I literally jumped out of my chair when it happened!

- I used Google Maps to track all of Damon's journeys.

- The character of Vivek was inspired by U.G. Krishnamurti.

# ACKNOWLEDGEMENTS

Thanks to my husband, Russ, for reading all my stories and giving me the critical advice I needed to take this book to the next level.

Thanks Mom, for offering your input and inspiring me.

Thanks and hugs to my daughters, Daphne and Tiggy. Your support encouraged me from the start to finish of this book. And thanks Tiggy, for spending your whole summer reading it. I still can't believe you finished it all!

Thanks David Trottier, author of *The Screenwriter's Bible*. Your brutal and honest comments about my one page synopsis prompted me to re-examine my structure and rewrite the first act. It led to a major breakthrough and helped deepen the characterization.

I would also like to extend my thanks to Margaret Duarte. I deeply appreciate your assistance and support.

Thanks Mary Kenner, Ron Kenner and Tom Puckett from RK Edit. You really did help make *Unison* a smooth read.

Thanks to Erica Orloff and Dr. George for proofreading my manuscript.

The first incarnation of *Unison* was brought to life at:

Home: from Oahu to Maui
Starbucks - Oahu
Hawaii Technology Academy - Oahu
Fisher House - Palo Alto, California
Kapolei Public Library - Oahu
Kihei Public Library
Luana Kai Resort - Maui
Waianae Public Library - Oahu
Waipahu Public Library - Oahu
Hickam Air Force Base Library - Oahu
Hickam Air Force Base Gym - Oahu
YMCA Gym - Waipahu - Oahu

Music that inspired me most during the writing of this book:

Assemblage 23
Wolfgang Amadeus Mozart
Steve Roach
Robert Rich
Lustmord

# ABOUT THE AUTHOR

Eleni Papanou wrote her first poem when she was an outcast at school. Honored with the name, "Greek Freak," she started to feel like one and believed life was plagued with torment and endless suffering. A spontaneous kundalini awakening thrust Eleni on a spiritual path and constantly tested her to the breaking point by challenging her world-view and everything else she held sacred. Through visions and personal insights, Eleni eventually discovered the universe has a sense of humor. She started laughing more—mostly at herself—whenever she caught herself taking things too seriously. After many years on the path of self-rediscovery, along with the addition of a husband, two daughters and a bout with cancer; Eleni had a lot to say. Having already written several screenplays, she decided to describe her experiences in a novel. The book you now hold in your hands is a product of that desire.

# MORE BY THIS AUTHOR

*Jessie's Song* - A man must make the greatest sacrifice to save his daughter from a kidnapper. It's a story of love, and how far a father would go to save his daughter.

Readers' Favorite International Book Award Winner - Bronze Medal (2013)

## Titles from
## Philophrosyne Publishing

*Between Now and Forever*
**By Margaret Duarte**
A rookie teacher challenges school tradition and authority to help seven troubled students with psychic abilities fight for their spiritual and emotional freedom.
*Now available on Kindle.*

**December 2013**
*Beyond Omega's Sunrise*
**By Eleni Papanou**
A character study that follows seven people on the eve before Earth's destruction. Linking them together is a shuttle crash that happened ten years prior and ties into their fate that will become apparent by the next Sunrise.

www.ingramcontent.com/pod-product-compliance
Lightning Source LLC
Chambersburg PA
CBHW030236030726
47493CB00022B/57